AFFILIATE

Also by K.A. Linde

The AFFILIATE

THE ASCENSION SERIES
book one

K.A. LINDE

To Brittany and Shea,
who have been this book's champion since the beginning.

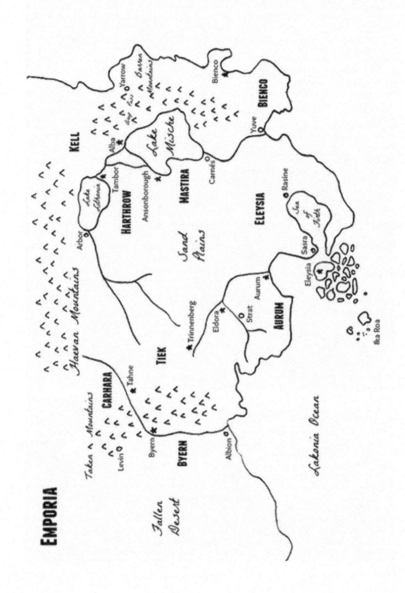

PRONUNCIATION GUIDE

AHLVIE GUNN: AL-VEE GUN

ARALYN STROHM: AIR-UH-LIN STRAHM

BASILLE SELBY: BAH-SEAL SEL-BEE

BRAJ: BRAHJ

BYERN: BY-URN

CARO BARCA: CAR-O BARS-UH

CYRENE STROHM: SAH-REEN STRAHM

DAUFINA BIRKET (CONSORT): DAW-FEEN-UH BUR-KET

EDRIC DREMYLON (KING): EDGE-RICK DREM-LIN

ELEA STROHM: EL-YA STRAHM

ELEYSIA: EL-A-SEE-UH

EMPORIA: EM-POR-EE-UH

EREN: AIR-EN

HAILLE MARDAS: HAYL MAR-DUS

INDRES: IN-DRESS

JARDANA: JAR-DON-UH

JESTRE FARRANAY: JEST-RAY FAIR-UH-NAY

KAEL DREMYLON (PRINCE): KAYL DREM-LIN

KALIANA DREMYLON (QUEEN): KAL-EE-AH-NUH DREM-LIN

KEYLANI RIVER: KEY-LAHN-EE

KRISANA (ALBION CASTLE): KRIS-ON-UH

LEIF: LEEF

MAELIA DALLMER: MAY-LEE-UH DAL-MER

NIT DECUS (BYERN CASTLE): NIT DAKE-US

REEVE STROHM: REEV STRAHM

RHEA GRAMM: RAY GRAM

SERAFINA (DOMINA): SER-UH-FEEN-UH

VIKTOR DREMYLON: VICK-TER DREM-LIN

PROLOGUE

"LET THEM IN." KING MALTRIER PULLED IN A SHUDDERING breath and then coughed raggedly for a minute.

"Your Majesty, are you sure?" his longtime servant asked. He had the same relentless attitude that he always had, but he sounded more earnest than ever, as if he could will the King not to die.

"Get them, Solmis. Now."

Solmis walked wearily across the darkened room. He heaved open the weathered door to the King's bedchamber and spoke to the pair of guards standing watch, "Get the boys. The King wishes to speak with them."

One guard punched his right fist to the left side of his chest in a formal Byern salute and then walked into the outer chamber. A moment later, he returned with two young boys with the same dark hair and blue-gray eyes that marked them as Dremylon heirs.

"This way, boys," Solmis said. He was one of the few people who could get away with calling the Princes boys.

"Thank you, Solmis," Edric, the crown prince, said with a smile and the confidence of someone who never wanted for anything.

The second son, Kael, pushed past them both, mimicking his brother's stride. His face was set in a scowl. Some of his youthful exuberance had already drained out of him, and in its place was cynicism from losing a mother too young and from having a sick father, but mostly, it was from being second.

"Father," he called out.

"Come here, Kael," the King said. He patted the side of the bed. "You, too, Edric."

Edric walked to his side and settled into a chair while Kael hoisted himself up onto the bed.

With Edric being fifteen and Kael at thirteen, both were much too young for this kind of loss.

The King had seen his youngest, Jesalyn, earlier that day. She had cried the entire time, understanding what was coming and knowing she could do nothing to stop it. In tears, she had run out of the room and straight into Consort Shamira's arms. She had all but raised the child after his wife, Queen Adelaida's unceremonious death.

But he couldn't waste thoughts on that now. He was tiring with every passing moment. The boys...they had to know.

"Solmis," the King said, regaining a shred of strength.

His servant, his old friend, left the room, giving them the privacy they needed.

"Father," Kael repeated impatiently.

"I'm dying," King Maltrier said.

Silence followed the declaration. Kael looked aghast. Edric tried to hide the shock of what he knew would be coming next.

"Edric will succeed me."

"I'm too young to be king," Edric whispered.

"Fifteen is not too young." The King thought that was questionable, but he would not dispute it with his son. Edric had to be strong. He had to rule. "You have the Consort and my High Order to help and guide you."

Edric swallowed and nodded. "Yes, Father."

"Trust in yourself, and all will go as planned. I have formed an alliance with Aurum for Jesalyn to be queen and another with Tiek, who has offered you their young Princess Kaliana. Honor these matches to keep our people safe. A strong king is one with an heir."

The King leaned over and coughed into a handkerchief for several minutes. His throat was raw, and his lungs ached. He didn't know how much more he could take, but he had to pass on their legacy.

But could he put that burden on them?

He had to decide now.

No. He would tell only one. He would pass it on to the boy most like himself—the one who could handle the knowledge, the one destined to rule.

The King turned to one of his sons and said, "I need to speak with your brother alone for a moment."

His eyebrows knit together as hurt and confusion clouded his features. "But, Father—"

"Go," King Maltrier commanded.

He clenched his jaw, stood, and left without another word.

It was the last time the King would ever see his son.

The door closed roughly behind him.

King Maltrier turned to his other son. "You know the story of our ancestor Viktor Dremylon."

He nodded, but the King continued anyway.

"Viktor struck down the evil Doma court that subjugated our people. Then he claimed the throne for himself with the sole purpose of ruling in a fair and just system."

"Yes, Father."

"History is told by the winners."

"What do you mean?" He tilted his head and looked concerned.

Perhaps he thought the King had already lost his mind.

"Viktor did destroy the Doma court, and he ushered in a new era of Dremylon rule that has persisted two thousand years up until you today. But what is not in the stories is that the Doma court had ruled because they had powerful...abilities."

His son laughed like his father was telling a fairy tale.

"Listen!" the King snapped. That sent him into another fit, and his son helped him sit up, so he could cough into his handkerchief.

When King Maltrier leaned back again, the King saw blood had coated the white silk.

"Father, you should rest."

"I need to tell you—" He was interrupted by another cough. "—the truth. Viktor beat the Doma court and the most powerful leader they had ever known, Domina Serafina, by stealing magic— dark magic, a magic that cursed Viktor and all his ancestors. It cursed me...and you...the entire Dremylon line."

His son remained silent and still. The King had gained his attention.

"Now, I must leave you with this, Son." The King retrieved a heavy gold key from around his neck and placed it in his son's hands. "A lockbox in the wall in my closet contains Viktor Dremylon's writings. Collect it, and tell no one. You must continue our legacy. Anyone who has Doma blood and discovers their magic must be eliminated. They threaten our power, your power. They threaten the very world we live in."

1

The
LETTER

"A STORM IS BREWING." CYRENE PUSHED OPEN THE textured glass windowpane to better assess the ever-darkening sky.

"It looks dreadful out there," her sister, Elea said.

Cyrene could smell the dankness of the damp air and feel the pressing humidity against her pores. She brushed her long dark brown hair off her shoulders and stepped away from the window.

"Of course it would rain on the day of my Presenting. It hasn't rained in a month."

"It will hold off."

"I hope so." Today was her Presenting ceremony, and it would be the biggest day of her entire life. She swallowed hard, but her mouth felt as if she had gone without water for days in the middle of the Fallen Desert.

"Oh, Cyrene, you'll do fine today." Elea grabbed Cyrene's hand, lacing their fingers. "Aralyn was selected as an Affiliate, and I'm sure you will be, too."

Cyrene refocused her thoughts, channeling the self-assurance that so often came to her, and she put on a brave face for Elea. "Of course I will. I hope Rhea is feeling as confident."

"Don't worry about Rhea. She will be fine." Elea retrieved a neat ribbon of pearls from the dresser and strung them around Cyrene's neck. "There. All done."

"Thank you, Elea," Cyrene said. She pulled her sister into a fierce hug. "I'll miss you when I become an Affiliate."

"I'll miss you, too," Elea said, laughing. "You don't even know if you'll be selected into the First Class, but you practically believe you will be the next consort by nightfall."

"I will be, right?" Cyrene asked sarcastically.

One of the most revered positions in all of Byern, the consort was personally chosen by the king and acted as his right hand in all matters of the state.

Elea snorted. "Don't count your chickens before they have hatched."

"Now, you sound like Mother!"

"Someone has to," Elea said, shaking her head at Cyrene. "Come on. We can't keep everyone waiting." She ushered Cyrene out of the bedchamber.

Cyrene and Elea descended the spiral staircase to the large open foyer where their mother, Herlana, awaited them. Her daughters were mirror images of her, but Herlana had poise and grace that could only have been acquired through age and from serving as the previous queen's Affiliate.

"Girls, you both look stunning. Though, I do say, Elea, I'm glad you still have another year. You need to get over that gawky awkwardness you still possess to have a chance at the First Class. Luckily, Cyrene never underwent that, or else I would have been more nervous for her," Herlana muttered unabashedly.

Elea's cheeks colored in embarrassment. She had grown to a surprising height in the past couple of years and was having trouble adjusting to the changes that had accompanied such a growth spurt.

"Thank you, Mother," Cyrene said, redirecting the full weight of their mother's attention.

"Well, you're not out of it yet." She eyed her daughter up and down. "Why your father ever approved of that harlot-red color on you, I have no idea. You'll be the only one wearing something so tawdry."

"I'll stand out then."

"As if you wouldn't already at your own Presenting," Herlana huffed.

"I think she is a vision in red," Elea said, defending her sister.

"Thank you, Elea."

"Yes, well…she would do better in your green," Herlana said. "Do you remember everything required?"

Cyrene gulped back her moment of fear. "Yes, Mother. The very words I must speak have been etched into my brain since infancy."

"You'll need to watch that mouth of yours. The King doesn't take kindly to insolent subjects. Now, where is that husband of mine?"

"I'm right here, Herlana," Hamidon called. Entering the foyer, he thumbed through a small stack of letters in his hand.

He was a bulky man of medium height with a stern, self-important air about him. Despite his aristocratic appearance, he dearly loved his four children and doted on them even when his wife would scold him about it.

"Good morning, my beautiful children." Hamidon kissed Elea and then Cyrene. "The Royal Guard have arrived," he said, turning to his wife. "Are the Gramms here yet?"

"Yes. They've arrived just now," Herlana said. She gestured out the door where a pair of carriages pulled into the circle drive.

"Perfect," he said, wearing a pompous smile. "Shall we depart?"

Cyrene's mother and father paraded out of their house, and as she was about to follow them, Elea threw her arms around her older sister.

"Who is going to tend the garden?" Elea croaked.

"What?" Cyrene asked. She attempted to pry herself out of Elea's grip.

"I'm certain to kill everything without you here."

"Just remember to water, and the garden will be fine." She couldn't help her disbelieving giggle. "Really, Elea, you're only going to miss me because of the garden?"

Elea looked back at her sister and shook her head.

"Ladies," Herlana snapped as they stalled in the foyer.

The girls jumped at their mother's voice and hurried out of the house. Royal Guard ushered them toward three magnificent horse-drawn carriages attached to black stallions. Her family sat in one with a pattern of interchanging blue and silver diamonds, the colors of Cyrene's family house. The Gramms' two carriages were striped in orange, brown, and gold.

Rhea was demurely seated in the Gramms' second carriage. She waved at Cyrene as she approached.

Cyrene and Rhea had been born on the same day, and thus, they were a rare exception for a First Class Presenting.

Members of the First Class would have their children individually presented on their seventeenth birthday. Every member of the Second and Third Classes who had a child turning seventeen in that year would celebrate their Presenting on the same day as the Eos holiday. In honor of Byern's emancipation, an enormous party would be thrown in the capital city each year, and all would be invited to attend the festivities.

Cyrene clambered into the carriage seat beside Rhea. "Rhea, can you believe it's finally here?" She reached out and grasped Rhea's hand.

"No." The wavy wisps of Rhea's dark red hair brushed against her back as she shook her head. Her forest-green gown was simple and light with flowing long sleeves and lace edging. It really brought out the green in her eyes.

"Me either," Cyrene whispered. Her gaze shifted out to their surroundings.

The carriage pulled them forward through the inner city. Towering stone mansions lined the streets as they navigated the First Class quarters and headed for the immense Nit Decus castle carved into the side of the Taken Mountains.

Second and Third Class families lived nearest their occupational crafts. Seconds were prone to martial involvement as well as careers related to and assisting with guard services. Thirds were a mix of craftsmen, merchants, and farmers who performed essential functions to support the kingdom. Both Seconds and Thirds lived along the second tier of the city walls, farther down the rocky foothills of the capital city. Additionally, Seconds assisted with border protection, and many Thirds traversed the land for mercantile purposes or lived in remote villages, assisting in the daily functions of life.

The roads through the inner city were cobbled, and the two girls jostled lightly as they rolled higher and higher toward the castle looming on the horizon. It was a nearly impenetrable fortress forged from gray-and-black limestone carved out of the mountain. More than half of the colossal structure was hidden within the heart of the Taken Mountains. What remained visible was a glorious edifice with high peaked towers, arching railed bridges, and intricate stone masonry that had withstood thousands of years of wear.

The sight of the sky-high towers had been a fixture throughout Cyrene's entire life, yet the grandiose structure always managed to elicit gasps of awe from her. As they approached, the girls gazed up at the impossibly tall barred doors.

"Do you think we'll make the First Class?" Rhea whispered.

Cyrene looked at Rhea whose ever-present pallid complexion had only turned more ashen with fear. The touch of rouge on her cheeks couldn't hide her waxen appearance. In the faint carriage light, her hands visibly trembled, a problem she'd had since childhood.

"How could we not?" Cyrene asked with a false sense of confidence.

"What if we don't?"

"Don't even think about it, Rhea. We've been together this long…"

She couldn't imagine life without Rhea. Cyrene knew that the First Class children were rarely placed into a lower Class, but it had happened. Only last year, a girl from Cyrene's own neighborhood had been selected into the Third Class.

Cyrene shuddered at the thought. She had worked and studied too hard to spend the rest of her life reaching for a place where she already belonged.

The three carriages swiftly passed through the gates, entering the lush garden paradise. As far as the eye could see, the royal grounds were covered with flourishing trees, brightly colored flowers, acres of fresh green grass, and even a slowly trickling creek with a stone bridge. Birds chirped overhead as the carriages rattled forward through the sprawling garden. In such a natural habitat, the drone of city life was all but obscured.

A footman descended the castle stairs and opened the carriage door. Cyrene dropped Rhea's hand and exited first. She regally tilted her head up as she placed her expensive Biencan gold slippers onto royal land. The corners of her lips turned up, and years of etiquette training took over.

A gentleman directed her inside, and Rhea followed behind on the arm of another escort. Their families had already entered the castle and were being ushered into the Grand Hall.

Allowing her escort to lead her away from Rhea, Cyrene silently wished she had told her friend good luck. Each Affiliate was given his or her own Presenting chamber, so Cyrene wouldn't see Rhea until this was all over.

Cyrene's escort walked her through several winding hallways to a broad stone door. With anticipation, her heart thudded wildly in her chest. This was the entrance to her Presenting chamber.

Richly colored curtains and tapestries hung on the walls. The cost of the thick Aurumian carpet could provide a year's worth of meals from the Laelish Market. An ornate silver pitcher and several crystal glasses sat atop an artfully constructed mahogany table against the back wall.

Cyrene poured herself a glass of water and brought the cup to her lips.

The room reminded her about the ancient history of the reign of the Doma court under the dreaded Domina Serafina. Nearly two thousand years ago, Byern had been ruled by an aristocracy that took everything for themselves, laid waste to the land, and starved the populace they deemed to be lesser. Then Viktor Dremylon had risen up against the court, seized Byern for the people, and freed the realm from oppressive rule. All the Doma's horrible practices had been reversed, and the prosperity of the past two millennia had validated the Dremylon victory. Now, only rare artifacts, history lessons, and folktales were left of that time period.

A rustling of the carpet drew her out of her thoughts, and she turned quickly.

Shrieking in surprise, she nearly dropped the glass. She rushed across the room and threw her arms around her older sister. "Aralyn!"

Aralyn held her tightly.

"It's so good to see you," Cyrene gasped out.

"I've missed you." Aralyn examined Cyrene at arm's length. "Why, you are positively gorgeous! And in red! Did Father approve this color?"

"Of course."

"It's not a court color."

Cyrene ignored her sister's slight. "Forget about the color, Aralyn. I haven't seen you in a year. What is it like in Kell as an Affiliate Ambassador? Tell me everything!"

"I didn't come to discuss my travels with you. I came to make sure you were prepared. I have your Presenting letter."

Aralyn extracted a letter from the sash on her gown. Cyrene reverently took the letter in her hand.

"You don't have much time before they call. I came to be your Advisor." A small smile played on her features. "I couldn't miss my little sister's Presenting."

Questions bubbled inside of Cyrene, but she held her tongue.

"What you read inside that envelope may not be spoken of to anyone, save other citizens in kind as well as King Edric, Queen Kaliana, and Consort Daufina, but know that they might not hold any answers, or they might even lead you astray. Do you understand?"

No. How could I possibly understand until I read the letter? She prayed to the Creator that she'd become an Affiliate, so she could ask Aralyn all these pressing questions.

"Cyrene, do you understand?" Aralyn repeated more sternly.

"Yes," she whispered.

"Very well. After you read your letter, proceed to the far door, and wait for an official to open it for you. When you are given the signal for dismissal, return to this room to await your Selecting."

"Will you be here?" Cyrene blurted out.

"No. You must await your Selecting alone."

Cyrene glanced down at the letter within her hands and back up at Aralyn. "Do you think I'll make First Class?"

Aralyn produced her first real smile. "I've no doubt you will be selected to your proper place," she said, pulling Cyrene into a hug. "You'll do fine. Now, I must go. I'll see you on the other side."

Aralyn placed a peck on each side of Cyrene's cheeks and departed the room.

A weight formed in the pit of Cyrene's stomach. It was judgment day. The small piece of paper in her hands felt like a heavy load.

After turning the cream envelope over, she tore the royal seal back from the parchment and pulled out the letter. The royal crest, a green Dremylon D wrapped in gold flames, was stamped on the front of the card.

She flipped the card open.

WHAT YOU SEEK LIES WHERE YOU CANNOT SEEK IT.

WHAT YOU FIND CANNOT BE FOUND.

THE THING YOU DESIRE ABOVE ALL ELSE RISKS ALL ELSE.

THE THING YOU FIGHT FOR CANNOT BE WON.

WHEN ALL SEEMS LOST, WHAT WAS LOST CAN BE FOUND.

WHEN ALL BEND, YOU CANNOT BE AS YOU WERE.

It's gibberish! Just a series of riddles!
What am I seeking? A position as an Affiliate, next to my sister? Yet that makes no sense because that position is available to me. Is it the same thing I need to find? If it is, how can I find something that I can't pursue and that can't be found?
The second part was slightly more straightforward. *But what do I desire?* She didn't know how becoming an Affiliate would risk everything else in her life. Plus, she wasn't fighting anyone. Byern hadn't been at war for two hundred years!
The next line made even less sense. She felt pretty lost right now, but she hardly thought that was what the line was referring to. *Am I to lose something…everything?* She reread the final line once more and tried to puzzle out the hidden meaning. *Who is bending? If people were bending in some way, how would I lose myself?* That seemed to be the most troubling part to her. She didn't know how she could possibly be something she was not.
She didn't have time to figure it out now. She had to complete her Presenting. She stuffed the card back into the envelope, placed it on the table, and walked to the far wall. As soon as she reached the entrance, the doors began to creak open.
Standing before her was the Royal Court of Byern.

The
PRESENTING

THE BYERN COURT ROSE FROM THEIR ELEGANTLY CRAFTED chairs, turned to the corner of the ballroom, and stared at Cyrene in the open doorway.

Cyrene held in her gasp. The ballroom was exquisite with interchanging cerulean, jade, and mother-of-pearl columns and gold-outlined ornamental moldings. Her eyes tilted upward to the hand-painted ceiling with a grand clock designed into the artwork. Through a dozen floor-to-ceiling windows, the ever-darkening clouds outside shed a murky glow on the room.

Soft music came to life from the strings of a musician's harpsichord.

That was her cue.

Pushing her shoulders back, Cyrene stepped one gold slipper and then another onto the marble ballroom floor. All traces of her previous anxiety vanished from her powdered face, and she produced an easy smile for the awaiting crowd. She walked gracefully down the back of the room to a long center aisle. At the end of the path sat King Edric on a high-backed gold throne. With her fair hair tied up into a tight bun, Queen Kaliana was on his left, and the dark-haired Consort Daufina was to his right.

Cyrene's heartbeat pulsed through her fingertips and thumped against her neck. Her stomach seemed to drop out of her body as she made eye contact with the King. The intensity of his gaze made her cheeks flush. She hoped her rouge hid her nervousness.

With her chin held high, Cyrene proceeded. She passed her parents seated in the front row alongside Aralyn, Elea, and her older brother, Reeve. On the other side of the aisle sat the Gramm family. Cyrene wondered if Rhea had been presented first. Cyrene couldn't judge from the Gramms' expressions.

After walking the remaining few feet to the front of the dais, she climbed the stairs to stand before her King, and then she dropped into the lowest curtsy possible.

She held her position for what felt like an eternity before King Edric's voice boomed throughout the ballroom. "You may rise."

Her knees shook as she lifted herself off the ground.

King Edric had changed since she last saw him at Aralyn's Presenting. His father, King Maltrier, had died from unknown causes when Edric was only fifteen years old. Edric had shouldered the responsibility of the kingdom as well as the welfare of his younger sister, Jesalyn—now Queen of Aurum—and his younger brother, Prince Kael. Five years later, King Edric was now twenty and had rightfully come into his own. His very presence exuded a confidence no one but a king could manage.

Slowly, King Edric rose from his throne to his full height. In her thoughts, Cyrene couldn't even capture the full extent of his intrigue. He was incredibly tall with a strong jawline covered in stubble and piercing blue-gray eyes that surveyed the crowd behind her.

"Welcome. We are here today for the Presenting of a daughter of the Strohm family, who nobly served my father, King Maltrier— son of King Herold, son of King Viktor of the royal line of Dremylon. Creator rest their souls."

The crowd softly murmured their own blessings to the former kings.

"Come today to stand before the throne to be presented is one of our own," he said. "She was raised in our land, educated in our land, and will forever be part of our land. Her Presenting today signals acceptance of the traditions and values of Byern. Such a step represents her desire to be part of the everyday improvement of our land. Acceptance of her Selecting requires responsibility and adherence to the foundation of Byern principles."

Cyrene's head swam. She was agreeing to be presented and selected, no matter the consequences. No matter if she was placed in the Third Class. This would decide her entire future, and her heart constricted painfully as possibilities flooded her conscious.

"Today, I Present Cyrene Sera Strohm, daughter of Hamidon and Herlana; sister to our own devoted member of the High Order, Reeve; and our trusted Affiliate, Aralyn. We shall begin the Presenting now."

King Edric took a step toward her, and her blue eyes met his. An electric shock shot through her at his nearness. For a moment, while locked in the King's gaze, all she saw was the here and now. There was neither time nor distance between them. It was just a pull as if they would be tethered together from this point on.

King Edric jerked back a step and shook his head, pulling her out of the trance that had come over her. *What just happened?*

His Adam's apple bobbed as he pulled himself back together. Then, he spoke softly for her ears only, "Cyrene."

She silently cursed and dropped her gaze to the polished floor. *What am I doing?* She wasn't even supposed to directly look at him yet.

"You may look at me."

Surprised, Cyrene did as commanded. She didn't understand what had passed between them, but looking at him made something within her fall into place.

"Miss Strohm, I stand here as your King, willing to select you into a proper position within the Byern community. Are you prepared to do your duty?"

Her lips quirked up into a haughty smirk. "Yes, My King."

King Edric paused, eyeing her mouth. "Do you always wear that smirk?"

She tried to tamp down the expression on her face, but she didn't seem to be able to. "Yes, My King."

His blue-gray eyes narrowed, and her heart thumped. *Why can't I keep a lid on my attitude today of all days?*

"Every Class performs fundamental tasks for the improvement of Byern. Are you aware of the three Class tasks?" He returned to the Presenting dialogue.

"The Guardians, Auxiliaries, and Essentials," she said, giving the formal names for the three Classes, "perform vital tasks to improve Byern. Guardians keep the system functional. Auxiliaries offer protection. The Essentials see to the daily needs of the many."

"And why are the Classes necessary?"

Cyrene responded as if she were reading straight from a script but with more conviction than she had ever felt before, "To maintain peace and prosperity. After Viktor Dremylon freed our people from the Doma overlord, he founded the Class system to utilize the benefits of all his citizens."

"Have you any skills necessary for acceptance into one of these three Classes?"

Cyrene knew she was supposed to admit that the skills she had learned would be sufficient for any Class, that no talents dominated one Class over another, yet the words were stuck on her tongue like a lie. She did have talents that would be more useful for the First Class, and she couldn't stand before her own King and tell him that she did not, no matter how much training she had been given to say otherwise. Staring up into his face, she felt compelled to offer him the truth even if she knew that she should not.

"Yes, My King."

King Edric cocked his head to the side. The silence between them stretched and felt weighted with her indiscretion. She bit her lip, and the stress of the afternoon pressed in on her. *Did I just ruin my chance at the First Class?*

"Well, what are your skills?" King Edric demanded.

"My sister says I can predict the weather."

"As can most witches."

Cyrene looked up at him under her full black lashes. "I don't believe I like your accusation," she murmured in a near whisper, "My King."

"My apologies."

The King of Byern had just apologized to her.

Her breathing was heavy as she forced herself to keep going. "Of course, it's not possible to predict the weather, but I believe I have more determination and will than you might find in a hundred people. I will fight for my kingdom until my last breath." Her voice was hoarse with emotion.

"A loyal subject."

"Byern's *most* loyal subject."

"And as Byern's most loyal subject, you would use this determination and will as instructed?"

"Yes, of course, My King."

"Do you always wear this shade of red? Few wear such a daring color in my court."

Much of her family had said as much. Soft colors were always in fashion, but Cyrene was not soft. She had never cared about how it would look if she wore red until the moment she was standing before the King.

"Do you like it?" she couldn't help asking.

After a moment, he nodded. "Yes, my lady. It seems it is not just your clothing that is daring." He did not seem displeased. "Once you are selected, you will be announced to your Receiver and placed in his or her charge for proper training. Do you accept the circumstances of your Selecting?"

"However I am fit and however I am able," she breathed. She had never meant the words more than when she was speaking them to King Edric. She felt an electric tug when she delivered the words.

He quickly stepped away, and she wondered if he'd felt it, too.

"You may proceed, Miss Strohm."

Cyrene faced her audience with a million thoughts running through her mind. *How did that conversation go so far off course? And why would I give anything to speak to the King one more time?*

She pushed her thoughts away from King Edric and continued with her Presenting ceremony.

"The Royal Court of Byern, I have taken the Oath of Acceptance, tying myself to my Selecting, to my Receiver, and to the land. I trust in the decision of the court to utilize my services to the best of their abilities for the people of Byern. I, Cyrene Sera Strohm, daughter of Hamidon and Herlana, fully present myself on the day of my seventeenth birthday to shirk the immaturity of my youth and take on the responsibility of my adulthood."

Cyrene dipped into another low curtsy.

"Miss Strohm, you may return to your anteroom until you are received for Selecting," King Edric announced.

"Thank you," she said before walking back the way she had come.

Soft murmurs sounded all around her, but she couldn't hear anything that was said. Her head was abuzz with her conversation with the King and the pull that made her want to turn around and go back.

A member of the Royal Guard opened the door to her waiting room. She ducked inside and breathed out a huge sigh of relief. She had successfully been presented to the Royal Court.

It was over, yet it had just begun.

3

The SELECTING

CYRENE STUMBLED TOWARD A DIVAN COVERED IN A mountain of throw pillows and collapsed on top of the heap. Her body sank into the padded plush seat as she crumpled from exhaustion. For so long, she had been anticipating her Presenting. She could hardly believe it was over. Her fate was out of her hands now.

She buried her face into the pillows. Her body was shaking from shock. *I just spoke to the King of Byern as if he were a common suitor!* She didn't care how handsome he was. *And he was very handsome.* It was not proper to flirt with the King, and it was certainly not proper to reprimand him for his tone, yet she hadn't been able to stop herself.

She felt drawn to him in some inexplicable way. And she was almost positive it had affected him, too. *Why else would he have responded to me in such a manner?* It hardly fit with her vision of the King of Byern.

Just as her frustration about the Presenting ceremony was about to become unbearable, the far door pried open. Cyrene rushed to the door, expecting to be ushered out of the room by a castle official. Instead, a tall figure walked inside.

"Reeve," she said aghast, "what are you doing here? Aralyn said I'm not supposed to have any visitors."

"I know, Cyrene." Her brother crossed his arms over his chest.

"Then, what are you doing here?" She stomach knotted.

"I came at the request of King Edric to inform you that he needs a longer period of deliberation before your Selecting."

"What?" she nearly shrieked. "Why would he need more time?"

"Your tone, Cyrene."

"It's just you. It's not like he can hear me," she grumbled.

"If King Edric wants more time, then he is perfectly entitled to it even if it is slightly unconventional."

"Slightly unconventional? Have you ever heard of this happening?"

Reeve sighed and dropped his arms to his sides. "No, I haven't. I don't know what the King could possibly be considering. Do you?"

"No." She shifted on the balls of her feet.

"What did you and King Edric talk about when you were standing before him?" He narrowed his eyes as if he already knew she had done something wrong.

"Nothing. We went through the questions and the Oath of Acceptance. That's all," she lied, defiantly crossing her arms.

"It took longer than it should have."

"What are you still doing here, Reeve?" She turned away from him and strolled over to the mahogany table. "You've delivered your message."

Reeve cursed under his breath. "What have you done, Cyrene? Don't you know how serious this is?" He strode toward her. "Your life hangs in the balance."

She whirled around. "I am not going to die for bantering with the King."

He hissed through his teeth. "You bantered with him in the middle of your Presenting?"

She rolled her eyes to the ceiling. "Yes. He went off script, and I followed his lead."

"Off script? You think it was right to go off script for something you have been preparing for your entire life? A script every single person of age recites?"

The last thing Cyrene wanted to do was give in to this line of reasoning. Otherwise, she might legitimately have a breakdown right then and there.

"Yes," she finally answered him.

"And you think this has nothing to do with his extended deliberation?"

"It...could."

Reeve paced the room once before looking back at her. "What did you two discuss?"

Cyrene shrugged. "I told him I was a loyal Byern subject, and he commented that he liked my dress, but no one wore red in his court."

"He commented on your dress?" He raised his eyebrows.

"Yes."

He rubbed his chin. "And that was all?"

She nodded.

"That doesn't sound too damaging," he admitted.

"Are you finished?"

"Cyrene," he said soothingly, "you know I'm just worried about you."

"Well, don't. You have as much control over what happens as I do." As much as she wanted her brother to comfort her, she couldn't let herself show weakness. She still had to get through her Selecting in one piece.

"High Order Strohm," a royal official called into the room, "you are needed at your seat."

Reeve moved to give Cyrene a hug, but she backed away from him. Reeve's face hardened before he exited the room, leaving her all alone once more. Her body heaved. She hated acting like that to Reeve, but she did not want him to know how terrified she was.

After another thirty minutes, the door finally opened once more.

"Miss Strohm, the King has come to a decision. He is ready for you."

Cyrene briskly exited the room and walked across the marble floors. The King had made her wait nearly three times as long as any other presented individual, and she was ready to get this over with. She stalked up the front steps to the platform and nearly forgot to bob her curtsy. At the last second, she politely dipped down.

King Edric gestured for her to stand. "Cyrene Sera Strohm, you have been presented before the Royal Court of Byern and have taken the Oath of Acceptance to fulfill your duties to your land. Under deliberation with Queen Kaliana and Consort Daufina, I have come to a decision regarding your Selection."

Cyrene gulped, nervously wringing her hands in front of her. She glanced left into the pale blue eyes of Queen Kaliana, who looked none too pleased, and then right into the hooded eyes of Consort Daufina, who was practically glowing. Cyrene did not understand either response.

"It has been decided that you will be selected into the Guardian First Class."

Cyrene's heart leaped with joy. *First Class!*

The King rose from his throne and walked to Cyrene. "Your Receiver will be Queen Kaliana."

Cyrene's mouth dropped open in utter shock.

"And from this day forth, you shall be known as the Queen's Affiliate."

The applause from the court was deafening as people stood and cheered for their newest Affiliate. The honor was so rare and the position so coveted that no one in the court had anticipated it. In two years, only three girls—including Cyrene's sister—had been placed in the position.

As if the Creator herself was responding, lightning flashed beyond the windows. A crack of thunder erupted overhead. The storm that had been threatening them all morning was about to open up on top of the ceremony.

As gazes shifted to the window, the sky commenced a torrential downpour, hitting the castle in sheets. She couldn't remember the last time a storm with such force had hit Byern. Maybe it never had.

Coming back to the reality of what had just happened, Cyrene returned her gaze to the King in awe. Her heart rate skyrocketed.

He gestured for Consort Daufina to move forward. He held out his hand, and she lightly placed something into his palm. He returned his focus to Cyrene. "Give me your hand."

Cyrene obeyed, holding her hand out to him.

"In your palm I place the Queen's symbol, a circular pin of Byern climbing vines. So long as you have this with you, you will have a piece of your land, our land, and you will be known throughout the world as one of our own."

Cyrene closed her fingers around the small circular charm that she had been waiting for her entire life. "Thank you, My King."

She stared at the symbol of the Affiliate, and her heart fluttered. The pin was an incredible piece of craftsmanship. The filigree pendant was intricately woven into a circle of gold leaves, as if the artist had plucked real climbing vines right out of the garden, with a clasp that she could attach to any of her garments.

King Edric addressed the awaiting crowd, who had finally quieted down, "Thank you all for attending Affiliate Cyrene's Presenting. There will be a customary ball in her honor tonight to welcome your newest Affiliate."

At the end of the ceremony, the crowd cheered one more time, and then courtiers began dispersing.

"Affiliate Cyrene," King Edric said, drawing her attention away from the commotion, "we need to speak with you before you can leave the castle."

Cyrene glanced over at her parents. Beaming, they addressed the line of nobles congratulating them. Two Affiliates and a member of the High Order in one household. It was almost like breeding well-trained horses.

"Yes, My King, of course." She trailed behind the royal procession and entered a small anteroom far removed from the previous one.

A large ornate desk took up the majority of the far side of the wall, and several high-backed chairs were placed around it.

"Sit." King Edric gestured to the chairs as he took a seat behind the desk.

Cyrene sank into the nearest seat. The Queen and Consort both moved fluidly to seats on either side of the desk, neither looking at the other.

"After today, your belongings will be moved into the Queen's quarters," King Edric informed Cyrene. "As your Receiver, Queen Kaliana will make sure everything is taken care of for your new position as an Affiliate. You will report to the Queen tomorrow morning for instructions on proceeding with your regimen. Of course, you are equally responsible to Consort Daufina, who might have additional directions. Do you have any questions?"

Cyrene's mouth went dry. She had a million questions, but one was more pressing than the others. "What happened to Rhea?"

"You may speak with your family regarding other Presenting ceremonies, but now is not the time. Do you have any further questions?"

She wanted to know more about what they had discussed during her Presenting and what had made them come to the conclusion to make her an Affiliate. *If it had taken them so long to decide because I went off script, why did they decide to make me an Affiliate?* Staring between Queen Kaliana and Consort Daufina, it was clear that they disagreed with each other. The Consort must have spoken in her favor and the Queen against her. *The last thing I want is to make powerful enemies.*

None of these thoughts were something she could vocalize.

"No, My King," she said quickly.

"Very well. Your family has instructions on the festivities for the evening," he said. They all stood. "Congratulations, Affiliate Cyrene."

"Thank you, My King." She dipped a low curtsy and darted out of the room.

The ballroom was now mostly empty, except for her family and a few stragglers. She descended the stairs and threw herself into Reeve.

"Congratulations," everyone cheered.

Reeve wrapped her in a big hug, clearly having forgotten their earlier altercation. She was passed from sister to sister before reaching her parents.

"We're so proud." Herlana bawled with tearstains on her cheeks.

"Oh, Mother," Cyrene said.

"And a whole ball in your honor," her mother murmured as if this wasn't the case for every member of the High Order or an Affiliate. "We'll have to find you something suitable to wear."

Cyrene's family bustled around her out of the ballroom. Considering how doomed she had felt only a short while ago, she couldn't have been happier. The King had made her an Affiliate!

They approached the castle doors that would lead them out to their carriages when Cyrene stopped abruptly at the rain-splattered steps. "Where is Rhea?"

Her family stared at the floor, at the ceiling, outside at the rain—anywhere but at her face.

Cyrene's hands began to shake. "Mother? Father? Reeve, Aralyn, Elea…please."

They all purposely looked away.

"She…she made First Class, right?" Her voice trembled.

Elea finally stepped forward and took Cyrene's hand in hers.

The tears Cyrene had been holding back all day sprang to her eyes. "No, no, no, no, no."

24

"She has been selected into Second Class," Elea whispered. "Her new Receiver is in Albion."

"Albion?" Cyrene spat. "By the Creator, that's a hundred leagues away!"

No one spoke. Everyone already knew what this meant to Cyrene.

She had been given everything in one day, yet the most precious person in her life had been torn away from her.

4

The
PROMISE

As soon as Cyrene returned to her home, her mother whisked her upstairs to be fitted for her new ball gown. She didn't question how the seamstress, Lady Cauthorn, one of the most sought after in the city, had been acquired for an in-home creation in the span of an afternoon or the price it was costing her parents.

She simply stood stiffly as the seamstress poked and prodded her while she listened to the constant babble of her family. They surely thought their words were comforting her against the pain at the loss of Rhea. They all talked about how she had finally gotten the position she always wanted, how important her future work at court would be, and how her life would be so busy with all her new duties.

So, she wouldn't have time to miss Rhea—though they never said that.

When they thought she wasn't paying attention, her parents whispered about how she would get through this and make new friends, how the pain would pass, that this was why everyone took the Oath of Acceptance, and how Selecting was the best process even if it didn't feel like it now. None of those words were much comfort either.

Unable to coax much life out of her, they left her alone with the seamstress.

Several hours of intense labor by the seamstress and two of her assistants produced a dress fit for the Queen herself.

"All done," Lady Cauthorn said. "Take a look."

Cyrene stepped stiffly onto the box in front of the trifold mirror, and her mouth dropped open. The softest red silk draped across her fair skin in the most flattering manner. Thin straps on her shoulders led to a sharp V-cut neckline between her breasts. The back mirrored the front, revealing the soft contours of her back. The dress cinched at her slender waist with a thick ribbon tied at the base of her spine. From there, the silky material cascaded like a waterfall over her narrow hips before pooling at her feet on the ground. She had never seen such a bold design.

She knew one thing for certain. She would make a splash at the ball tonight.

"I love it, Lady Cauthorn." Cyrene turned slowly. "I would like to pay you for this."

Lady Cauthorn shook her head. Her mouth was set in a bright smile, and her eyes glowed at her creation. "Your parents commissioned the dress. They will pay."

Cyrene wrestled with her newfound position. "As an Affiliate, I will make plenty to cover the costs."

"Your parents will pay," she insisted.

"What if I pay you from my endowment?"

Lady Cauthorn raised her eyebrows. "Why do you insist on paying?"

"I want this to belong to me and only me."

The seamstress seemed to see straight through her. She tilted her head and continued to examine her. Her eyes turned glossy and far off for a moment, and then she snapped back to reality. "You are meant for great things, Child."

"Thank you," she said automatically. "But in the matter of the dress…"

"The dress." Lady Cauthorn busied herself with cleaning the mess she had made. "It's a gift."

"What? No. Lady Cauthorn, I have the money!"

"No bother, girl." She snapped her fingers at her stunned assistants, and they rushed into motion.

"I cannot accept this," Cyrene assured her. "It's too much."

Lady Cauthorn looked back up at her once more and smiled, but it wasn't a kind smile. It seemed almost calculated. "A gift is a precious thing. Perhaps we could negotiate the price of the dress for a favor."

"A favor? That's it?"

"Yes. Just one favor from you at a time of my choosing."

"I don't understand. This dress must have cost a fortune. What is the favor?"

"Whether a high cost or a low cost, it won't be one you will pay for today." She gave Cyrene a toothy grin. "The dress for a favor. Are we in agreement?"

Cyrene nodded at her in bewildered accord. "Yes, I agree."

"Perfect." Lady Cauthorn walked forward and attached Cyrene's Affiliate pin to her chest. "I'll inform your parents that the gown has been paid for."

"When will you collect your favor?"

"Likely when you least wish it so. Good luck in the lion's den." Lady Cauthorn bowed her head and then exited the room.

Cyrene wasn't sure what to make of the entire exchange. All she knew was, she was certainly indebted to Lady Cauthorn and wasn't entirely sure if that was a good thing.

Cyrene tucked her Presenting letter away into a fold in the gown. It was the only thing she was bringing with her tonight. She touched the wall of her bedroom one last time before leaving the comfort of it behind. She was no longer a little girl anymore. In her place was a woman who would begin a new life as a palace noble.

Tilting her chin, she descended the staircase to a vacant foyer. Her fingers trailed along the climbing-vine pin attached to the bodice of the gown, and a tremor of excitement ran through her. She couldn't believe she had been appointed an Affiliate, especially considering Rhea had not been given the same honor.

Trying to put aside the depressing thoughts, Cyrene opened the front door and stared out to the cobblestone road beyond her home. A light trickle of rain was still falling from the sky. She breathed in the crisp dewy air. The comforting smell reminded her so much of the rainy seasons of her childhood, such as the time when she had kissed a boy in the stable yard to prove to Rhea that she wasn't afraid. After she had been caught, Rhea had crept up into her room and brought her dinner. They'd giggled about it until she had to go home.

Cyrene laughed, but there was a touch of sadness and desperation in the hiccuping sound. They could never be those children again.

At that moment, Rhea stepped out of the shadows. "What's so funny?"

Cyrene started at her friend's sudden appearance. "Rhea!" She rushed out of the doorframe to the covered front porch.

Rhea stepped away from her. "You'll ruin your dress!" She had changed into a much simpler dress with her heavy rain boots and a cape to cover her head, but she was still dripping with water from head to toe.

"Why are you soaking wet?" Cyrene demanded. "You're certain to catch a cold."

"I snuck out." She shrugged off her drenched coat and hung it on a nail. Her long red hair hung down her back. The ends were damp, and the wisps around her face had formed into ringlets.

"And what? You walked over here?"

"It's not that far. I couldn't risk getting caught, and I couldn't leave without seeing you."

"I would have come to see you, but they wouldn't let me out of their sights."

"I know." Rhea's boots squelched as she fidgeted. "But we promised to share Presenting letters with each other, and I thought you would have some idea what mine meant."

Cyrene's smile grew. She had thought the same thing about Rhea.

The only problem was, Aralyn had said Cyrene was not to tell anyone about the letter—save other Affiliates, members of the High Order, and royalty.

Cyrene bit her lip in consternation. "Did your Advisor tell you not to talk about it?"

Rhea eyed her with mirrored trepidation on her face and then shrugged. "Are we going to start listening to other people now?"

"Of course not." Cyrene retrieved her paper from her gown and exchanged it for Rhea's.

Cyrene read Rhea's Presenting letter, and her eyebrows knit together. Rhea's letter made no more sense than Cyrene's own letter with talk of helping those who cannot be helped, submitting to a lost cause, and keeping determination in the face of her greatest fear.

The blank look on Rhea's face was enough to convince Cyrene that neither of them knew what to make of these cards.

"How do we sort out this gibberish?" Rhea handed Cyrene back her letter, likely having already memorized the lines.

"Study, travel—"

"No, Cyrene. How do we sort this out without each other?" Her voice quavered. She cast her eyes out across the lawn.

"I don't know, Rhea." Cyrene's heart hammered in her chest. "Wha-what happened? I mean, in your Presenting?"

The normal soft lines of Rhea's oval face hardened. She clenched her hands into fists at her sides. "Nothing out of the ordinary. We went through the ceremony as planned, like we had rehearsed for hours on end. I don't know how I could have done better. What was yours like?"

Cyrene sighed at the question. "I went off script and...flirted with the King."

"You did what?" Rhea asked in disbelief.

"I know. I thought I would become Third Class, Rhea. I don't know why he picked me," she said, splaying her hands flat in front of her.

"Well, I do," Rhea said. "You're brilliant and beautiful and a loyal friend. You deserve it, Cyrene."

She flushed at the compliment. "Did the King tell you why you were becoming a Second...erm, being put into Second Class?"

"No," she said, her voice clipped. "They most certainly did not. I tried to ask them, but they kept up with ceremonial talk about the Oath of Acceptance and the Selecting process. Either way, by the end of the week, I'll be off to Albion, working for my new Receiver Master Caro Barca."

"Why does that name sound familiar?"

"He's an inventor, supposedly a genius." She dismissively waved her hands. "He studies militaristic development and strategy and is working on some new weaponry plans. He sounds like a raving lunatic in the scant literature I could acquire about him. However, I couldn't find much, and King Edric hardly elaborated." Her shoulders slumped.

"Didn't we read about Master Barca?" Cyrene asked.

"I don't remember the name."

"Are you sure? Didn't he invent Bursts?" Cyrene was pretty sure that was where she remembered him. One of their tutors had been fascinated that something that could produce bright colors in the sky just by lighting a fuse. The inventor had never given up his secret.

Rhea's eyes illuminated in the fading light. "Cyrene, you're right! How could I have forgotten? I don't understand Bursts, but I am certain that Master Barca was the inventor." She threw up her hands in derision and started muttering to herself. After a moment, she turned back to Cyrene, looking aghast. "By the Creator, I am going to be meddling in magic!"

Cyrene burst into laughter at her friend's outrageous statement. "Now, you are talking about fables, Rhea Analyse! You'll certainly gain much knowledge in your work with Master Barca, but magic? Magic doesn't exist! I'm sure Bursts have a perfectly logical explanation that you'll have to tell me about as soon as I am allowed to travel to Albion."

"As soon as you are allowed?"

"I'll not wait one day. You're my best friend, Rhea."

After a moment, Rhea brushed the circular pin on Cyrene's dress. "So, you're really an Affiliate then? You have the luckiest family in the city."

Cyrene received the retort like a slap in the face. She wanted to be an Affiliate more than anything else so that she could travel and find adventure, but she had always envisioned that with her best friend at her side.

"You'll outshine them all, Cyrene," Rhea said. There was no malice in her voice.

Rhea smiled faintly and then began to dictate a course of action regarding their Presenting letters. Cyrene listened to Rhea's plan, desperately wanting to believe in it even with its uncertainties.

"Promise me you'll find time to do the research," Rhea said as if reading Cyrene's pessimistic thoughts.

"I promise."

"Good. I promise, too. No matter what."

Someone called Cyrene's name from inside the house.

Rhea's gaze darted nervously to the open front door, and she grabbed her cloak off of the hook it had been drying on. "I have to go."

"I love you, Rhea."

"I love you, too."

"I'll see you soon," she promised.

Rhea nodded and then rushed off the front porch, around the corner, and out of Cyrene's line of vision. The rain finally halted with Rhea's departure, but Cyrene didn't move. Even when she had gone on holiday with her parents to the countryside, she had never been without Rhea for longer than a few weeks. Most of the time, Rhea had come with her.

"There you are!" her mother gasped. "I had no idea why this door was standing ajar."

"My apologies." Cyrene scurried inside.

"We're to leave soon. Are you ready?"

"Yes, Mother. Let me say good-bye to Elea."

"I'm so proud of you," her mother said, positively glowing with excitement for her daughter. She planted a kiss on Cyrene's cheek.

Cyrene smiled faintly at her as she left to retrieve her husband. Elea rounded the corner from the kitchen, entering the hallway.

"I'm…I'm sorry." Elea bit her bottom lip. "About Rhea. We're all sorry about Rhea."

Cyrene released a heavy breath. Although she knew it was not their fault and that her family was sorry for what had happened, they were not the one losing their best friend in a span of an afternoon…just a daughter and a sister.

"I know."

"Mother simply wants what is best for you."

"And didn't I get it?" She flicked the gold pin on her chest.

Elea grabbed her sister's hand. "Don't deny that this is what you wanted. There was always a chance that one of you wouldn't make the First Class, and it was almost inevitable that you both wouldn't have been made Affiliates."

"I know, and I can't change it. I'm just…"

"Angry and sad," Elea finished for her. She wiped a lone tear from Cyrene's eye. "You and Rhea are my best friends, too, and now, both of you are leaving."

Cyrene grappled with Elea's comments. She had no idea how to respond. "I didn't mean for you…I wouldn't want—I can't make anything right, Elea."

"You would if you could."

Cyrene pulled Elea into a hug.

"Take care of Mother and Father for me?" Cyrene asked.

"Of course. I wish I could attend the ball though," Elea said. "But I suppose I shouldn't even want to stand in the same room as you when you are wearing this. No one else would look at me."

Cyrene laughed. "You'll be an Affiliate next year, and they'll throw a whole ball in your honor! I'm sure no one will look at me twice by then."

"That'll be the day," Elea said disbelievingly. "Anyway, I have something for you."

"You didn't need to get me anything."

Elea removed a small book from her purse and handed it to Cyrene. "It's your birthday. I bought it from an Eleysian peddler in the Laelish Market when I went with Mother and Father to pick out your slippers."

Cyrene's hand slid down the cracked leather spine where minute black letters had been artfully written in a language she didn't recognize. She scrunched her eyebrows together as she attempted to decipher the scrawled words. "Is this Vitali writing?" Her eyes wide, she glanced up at her sister.

"You got it in the first guess. Big surprise." She bounced on her toes.

"Who travels with Vitali translations? Doma books were burned for heresy after the First Dremylon War." Cyrene flipped the book to the front. The only thing clearly legible was a symbol with a stick-straight line parallel to the binding and two additional lines painted at an upward angle. It resembled a tree missing branches on the left side.

"I don't know, but the man was so strange. He kept saying such odd things, like this book was for the Children of the Dawn and the Heir of the Light. Have you even heard of such things?"

Cyrene shook her head as she traced the symbol. It looked familiar, but she wasn't sure where she had seen it. "It's so beautiful. I can't believe he had this sitting out."

Elea sighed forlornly. "I wish there was more to it than the binding, but all the pages are blank inside. I thought it was worth it for the Doma binding at least. I know how you love history."

"I do." Cyrene opened the book to the first page and scrunched her eyebrows together. "You said that it's blank?"

"It is. See?" Elea pointed her finger to the page.

"What are you talking about?" Cyrene turned to the next page and the next. Iridescent glossy ink covered every single one of them.

Elea's eyes narrowed in confusion. "I thought you'd be pleased even if the book was empty."

"You can't see that?" She jabbed her finger onto one of the pages.

"Cyrene, are you all right? Nothing is there."

How could Elea not see the words? They were there. All of them were there, shifting from gold, yellow, orange, red, purple, blue, green, and back to gold. The handwriting was superbly fierce with sharp edges and large looping swirls. Cyrene had never seen anything quite like it, but she felt as if she should know what the words said.

"Cyrene?" Elea questioned, her voice soothing.

Their father stuck his head into the hallway. "Darling, your mother is waiting in the carriage."

"I'll be along, Father," Cyrene said, waving him off.

He nodded and ducked out of the hallway.

Cyrene sharply closed the book, suddenly feeling possessive of the small thing. At the same time, she was frightened of its meaning. If Elea couldn't see the writing, then something must be wrong. Cyrene had no idea what to make of it. *How can I see the words and Elea cannot?*

"You're the best sister. Can you make sure this is sent with the rest of my things?"

"Of course I will." Elea hesitantly took the book from Cyrene and tucked it under her arm.

Cyrene bent down and kissed both of Elea's cheeks. "I'll see you as soon as I can."

"Good luck."

Cyrene left in a daze, her thoughts lost on this strange book and her grief. The best she could hope for was that her duties as an Affiliate would leave her little time to think about the new development and would mask the sadness of leaving everyone she loved behind.

THE BALL

"BY THE CREATOR," CYRENE WHISPERED.

She stared through the massive double doors that opened to the ballroom where her ascension as an Affiliate would take place. The room had curved ceilings and stained-glass windows in beautiful blues and greens. Black marble, imported all the way from across Emporia at the base of the Barren Mountains, tiled the vast floor. A six-foot-high fireplace roared to life at the far end of the room. Multiple black wrought iron chandeliers dangled from the ceiling, illuminating the room with large wax candles.

A string quartet with their quick-paced melodies guided couples across the open dance floor. Dozens of Affiliates and High Order were in attendance, and gold pins glimmered from gowns of nearly every passing woman.

A shiver ran down her. She pushed back the thought of what Rhea's reaction might have been. It wouldn't help Cyrene this evening.

She took a breath and then walked into the room. She had only made it a few steps before someone drunkenly careened into her. She yelped on impact and stumbled forward, reaching out for the nearest person to keep her from toppling to the ground. A faint tear sounded as she seized the sleeve of a man in front of her.

Turning, he snatched her out of midair, twirled her in place, and held her in his arms. Cyrene's cheeks were flushed in horror.

"Are you all right?" he asked, slowly placing her back on her feet.

"Yes...yes, I'm fine." Her head swiveled from side to side, trying to search out the person who had run into her. What kind of mule headed idiot barreled into someone like that? There he was. She watched a disheveled man with dark hair drunkenly lurch through the crowd.

"Affiliate?" The gentleman reached out for her hand.

"Yes. Sorry." She glanced at the man for the first time.

Her world tilted as her eyes met blue-gray orbs shining with concern. He had the same strong jawline, the same broad-shouldered stature, the same eyes. She would have recognized the similarities between the man standing before her and the King any day.

"Uh...I mean..."

A knowing smirk crossed his face. "I don't believe we have been formally introduced." He reached for her hand and softly kissed it. "I am Crown Prince Kael Dremylon."

Crown Prince.

The formal title felt like ice throughout her bones. *How could I have been so stupid as to tear the Prince's garment?*

She dropped a hasty curtsy. "Your Highness, my apologies for tearing your garment. I am Cyrene Strohm...Affiliate Cyrene Strohm."

"Ah, the newest member of court, I see," he said with a laugh in his voice she didn't understand. "You may rise, Affiliate Cyrene. The ball is in your honor tonight, is it not?"

"Yes, that it is, uh...Your Highness."

Prince Kael raised her chin. She could smell his heady musky scent, and she felt a small zap of electricity pass between them. She swallowed hard but didn't look away.

This close, she could tell the differences between him and King Edric. The King was roughly shaven with high-chiseled cheekbones, cropped short hair, and strong, hard features. Prince Kael was more beautiful than handsome with a smoothness that showed he was a youth of only eighteen. But it was the smug smirk on his mouth, the arrogant set of his shoulders, and the daring, almost brazen look in his eyes that truly set him apart from his brother. He looked much more like his mother, Queen Adelaida—the Creator bless her soul.

There was an underlying deviousness she found herself attracted to despite herself.

"Kael will suffice, if you please."

"Of course, Your High—Kael." She couldn't believe she was addressing a member of the royal family by his given name. "I am terribly sorry about your dress garments. Do allow me to replace them."

"Nonsense. All I'll require from you, Affiliate Cyrene, is the first dance." He formally bent forward, offering her his hand.

Cyrene's head swam with delight. The Prince was asking her for the first dance of the evening. The honor was typically reserved for a queen or consort. At the very least, royalty would bestow their graces on men and women of their high circle. But he had picked her!

She lightly placed her hand in his own, and he wheeled her toward the dance floor. The quick jig ended and flowed into the smoother melody of "Haenah de'Lorlah," one of her favorites. The movements slow and deliberate, the intimate dance was meant to appear as if the couple was floating effortlessly above the surface.

Prince Kael was by far the best dancer she had ever partnered with. Leading her around the room with ease, he made the steps seem as if they were actually floating. It shouldn't have surprised her, given he was royalty, but having never experienced such an incredible match, she could hardly keep the shock and exultation from her face.

He swept her along, passing a blur of faces she neither recognized nor cared about in that moment. Thoughts of the exotic dress draped across her frame and the firm embrace of the Crown Prince of Byern were lost to her as she kept up with Prince Kael's graceful footwork.

Their feet stilled on the black marble surface at the close of the song. With a flourish, Prince Kael bowed deeply, and Cyrene sank into a graceful curtsy.

As the emotions of the dance had taken over, her breathing had turned ragged. While the steps had not been difficult, she felt as if she had somehow poured more of herself into the movements. The feeling was exhausting yet exhilarating. She was on fire, and she needed water to even begin to douse the flames.

Cyrene broke from her reverie by the sound of faint applause. She tore her eyes from Prince Kael's and realized that guests were openly staring at them.

"Cyrene, you are an intoxicating dancer." Prince Kael drew her away from the crowd.

"Thank you," she breathed unsteadily. "You are quite good yourself." She hid the true weight of her statement behind hooded eyes and a coy smile.

"Allow me to get you a refreshment."

He reached for two goblets of wine, and she gratefully took the glass out of his hand and took a sip. She didn't drink often, but the wine was extremely high quality, and she could hardly resist.

Cyrene noticed when Prince Kael's attention was diverted. Following his gaze, she jumped slightly in surprise, nearly slopping the wine out of her glass.

King Edric.

Cyrene fell into a deep curtsy. "Your Highness."

"Affiliate Cyrene." King Edric inclined his head as she rose. "Kael," he brusquely acknowledged his brother, grasping his forearm. "You seem to be capturing all of Cyrene's attention at her own ball."

If Cyrene didn't see the sneer cross Prince Kael's face, she would never have believed it were there when he addressed King Edric.

Prince Kale's demeanor seamlessly shifted into an aloof front with a mocking smile. "How could I not steal the attention of such a beautiful woman?"

"I certainly cannot blame you."

She hastily took a sip of her wine to avoid the heated gazes of the men staring down upon her. Her heart was still thumping from the dance, and the magnetic pull she felt from both of them kept her even more off balance. *How did I end up between the two most powerful men in the kingdom?*

"You are quite the dancer, Cyrene," King Edric said with a mischievous glint in his eye.

"You flatter. My dance skills are perfectly adequate."

"On the contrary, you and my brother ignited the floor." His gaze shifted from her to Prince Kael, who was hiding a steely glare behind his own blue-gray eyes.

"I thank you very much. However, I must give credit where credit is due." She lightly laid her hand against Prince Kael's shirtsleeve and smiled at both men.

"Then, perhaps you will allow me to show you the steps of a king." King Edric held his hand out for her.

Cyrene slowly removed her hand from Prince Kael and placed it in King Edric's. Her throat tightened. She was about to dance with the King of Byern. She couldn't believe it.

Affiliates associated with the queen and consort on a regular basis. *But the king?*

King Edric turned his attention back to his brother. "Kael, I do hope you would do Queen Kaliana the same honor you bestowed upon Affiliate Cyrene and entertain us with the next dance."

Prince Kael nodded, his jaw set. "Of course," he said with a stiff bow. He strode across the room to where the Queen stood, surrounded by a cluster of brown-nosing Affiliates.

"After you," King Edric said.

Two columns of dancers formed in the center of the floor, men on one side and women on the other. King Edric took the head of one, and Cyrene fell into place across from him. Queen Kaliana placed herself opposite Prince Kael on the other end. Cyrene tore her gaze away from the other dancers and laid her eyes on the man—the *King*—standing before her.

King Edric snapped his fingers at the string quartet, and they immediately straightened, drawing their bows.

Violinists seductively strummed the opening chords of "Cat's Cradle," and men bowed as the women demurely curtsied. The dance was intricate with elaborate weaving patterns, opening and closing circles, and partners swapping at specific times.

The King seemed much at ease with the steps as he flawlessly led her through the first weave.

"You're wearing that color again," King Edric said.

"I thought you quite liked it."

"Have your eyes failed you tonight?" He twirled her around another couple.

"What could you possibly mean?"

"I've told you once before that no one wears such a color in my court." He eyed the cut of the dress rather deliberately.

"I guess I will have to return the commission I ordered today." She knew she had to act quickly as the time in the dance where she would be swept from person to person was approaching, and then it would be over. "I informed my seamstress of your affection for the color, and she redid my entire wardrobe in the bright hues, My King." Or at least, she would do so when she left.

King Edric looked down upon her face, his expression as near to shock as Cyrene had ever seen on him. He recovered swiftly, clearly determined to set her straight on his opinion about her attire, but at that moment, she was pushed into the arms of a member of the High Order. As she was carried from person to person throughout the dance, she hardly remembered their names. Some of the men were simply adequate, and others spun her in circles that made her neck ache while one or two more were nearly on par with King Edric and Prince Kael—though certainly no one would suggest it.

A moment later, she was thrust back into the King's arms, and she smirked up at him.

"You really do wear that smirk all the time, don't you?"

"I said I did at my Presenting. Are you inferring that I would lie to Your Majesty?"

"No more than your insinuation for having an affinity for the weather," he countered.

Cyrene almost laughed. She had been joking of course when she had told the King that Elea thought Cyrene could predict the weather.

As the music changed, they filed back into the two lines in which the couples had initially stood. She dropped her curtsy to the men's side, and the King nodded in acknowledgment. The dancers broke off and returned to the circle of friends they had left behind.

King Edric approached her once more with a smile for the watching courtiers. "A fine dance, Affiliate Cyrene," he complimented openly.

"You do me a great honor." She tilted her head in acceptance of his praise.

"I do wish you good luck in your training tomorrow."

"With your blessing, I am certain I will do all I can for Byern," she murmured.

He stared at her thoughtfully for a second before he turned and strode away to his Consort. Cyrene had no idea how she had garnered this much attention or what it all meant.

6

The COURTIER

WITH THE CROWD'S EYES HOT ON HER FACE, CYRENE promptly exited the dance floor. Retrieving a glass of wine from a passing waiter, she searched out the family she had all but forgotten after Prince Kael's request to dance. She could pick Reeve's towering figure out of any crowd, and she seamlessly maneuvered around the ballroom to his side.

"Cyrene," Reeve boasted, throwing an arm around her.

He staggered forward against her, and he reeked of alcohol. She had never seen her brother in such a state before.

"Hello, Reeve."

"Congratulations again, little sister."

"Thank you."

She glanced around at the array of men standing before him. All of them wore the Dremylon crest on their chests.

"Let me kindly introduce you to my good men of the High Order—Brayan, Surien, Rhys, and Clovis." He pointed out each man as he called each one by name. "Gentlemen, meet my sister and now Affiliate Cyrene."

The level of intoxication among the mix was on a level that she didn't even deem worthy of a curtsy.

"Pleasure is ours, Affiliate." Rhys dipped slightly at the waist.

"Thank you," she said, trying to remember her manners and not his demanding looks.

"Have any of you heard from Zorian?" Clovis asked. "He was supposed to be back for your sister's Presenting."

"I haven't heard from him." Brayan took a swig from his mug.

"I'm sure he'll turn up," Reeve said.

"Yeah, he told me he would be in from Carhara," Surien confirmed.

"Must have ended up with one of those Carharan women. I've heard the ones in the capital city work you—" Rhys began.

Reeve smacked Rhys on the chest and threw his head in Cyrene's direction. The weight of the men's gazes landed on her, and she tried not to feel vulnerable in their midst. Something in their nature reminded her of a pack of wolves stalking their prey.

Cyrene searched for a way to exit the conversation. She didn't know this Zorian, nor did she have any interest in hearing about his adventures with Carharan women.

"Have you seen Aralyn?" she asked Reeve.

"Aralyn?" Reeve asked in disbelief

Reeve's friends laughed at the suggestion.

"What would anyone want with that prude?" Clovis asked.

Rhys chortled drunkenly next to him. "I could think of a few things."

Reeve shook his head, but he was laughing at his friends' indecency. "I don't know, Cyrene. The ice queen sticks to her Ambassadorial snow castle in Kell. She probably has her nose in a book somewhere."

Reeve might as well have punched Cyrene in the stomach. *How could he speak in such a manner about their sister and let his friends laugh at her?* They had always had their differences since Reeve was older, more boisterous, and more outgoing where Aralyn was austere, studious, and rather particular about everything around her.

Apparently, Cyrene had quite a few things to learn about court life. If she had it her way, she would certainly unlearn this lesson from Reeve.

"Well, I'm going to go find her," she said. She snaked out of his embrace and stumbled away from their circle. She tried to block out their snickers as she left.

Eventually, she located Aralyn sitting with one other woman. They were just removed from the entrance to the grand hall.

"Aralyn, I've been looking for you."

"Hello, Cyrene," Aralyn said with a small smile. Her wavy light-brown hair was dead on the ends, and she had circles under her eyes. Her shoulders seemed too tight with tension. The travels the Queen requested of Aralyn had obviously taken a toll on her.

"You seem to be in a better mood than when I left you. Could it be because Prince Kael and King Edric asked you to dance?" Aralyn suggestively arched an eyebrow.

"That could have something to do with it."

"Oh, forgive me," Aralyn said. "This is Affiliate Leslin. She works for the Queen's library division."

"Pleased to meet you," Cyrene said.

A disturbance at the entrance cut off further conversation. All eyes in the hall turned to the broad double doors as two men of the High Order hauled a man up off the ground and shoved him forward. The man threw expletives in such a slur that Cyrene only understood half of what he was saying.

As they approached where she was standing, she recognized this man. Of all the people she had met tonight, she could distinctly remember this person even if she had no clue of his name. He was the man who had run into her when she first entered the room.

They forcibly threw the man out the doors, and he landed heavily on his backside and rolled a pace before lying still.

"And stay out there, Ahlvie," one of the men yelled.

"We've had enough of you tonight," the second one chimed in.

Cyrene winced, and a twinge of pity hit her.

Several women gasped in outrage at the treatment, but Ahlvie slowly righted himself. He glared at the two members of the High Order and tossed a few more choice swear words in their direction.

"I've go-got to ge-get out of here." He staggered to his feet. "Too many damn ru-rules in this forsaken pl-place!" Ahlvie staggered away from the hall, all the while muttering to himself.

"He is insufferable." Leslin shuddered.

"A bit of a drinking problem?" Cyrene asked. She knew full well he had been beyond drunk when he careened into her earlier.

"A bit? If that…that man comes into my library again with a drop of alcohol in his system, I'll murder him myself. I don't care if he is a genius. His behavior is uncalled for."

"Decidedly uncalled for," Prince Kael agreed, walking into their conversation, unannounced.

Cyrene's back had been turned, and she jumped at the sound of his voice.

"Perhaps I'll have a word with him."

Aralyn and Leslin looked at Prince Kael as if he were a large mythical Indres with huge talons and a body twice the size of a wolf.

Prince Kael acted oblivious to their bug-eyed expressions. "I'd hoped for another dance, Affiliate Cyrene. Will you oblige me?"

"Of course she will," Aralyn said without thinking for once. "We were just leaving. Weren't we, Leslin?"

"What?" the older woman squawked. "Oh, yes. Yes, we were just"—she cleared her throat—"leaving."

Cyrene didn't know whether to be grateful or humiliated by their hasty departure. Prince Kael stood before her with a humorous look on his face.

She linked arms with Prince Kael, and he escorted her back to the dance floor.

Prince Kael moved to the beat of the music and pulled her along for the ride. He would dance with her once or sometimes twice in a row, and then he'd hand her off to another gentleman. When they had completed their circuit, the man would promptly return her to Prince Kael's arms. Some dances, they would speak of nothing, content to let the music carry them through. Other dances, they would chatter about such a variety of subjects that Cyrene began to wonder if she would be tested later.

At the close of another dance, Cyrene plopped down into a nearby chair and fanned herself with her hand, dizzy from the energy of the night. The exhaustion of the day was settling in. After hours upon hours of dancing, her poor feet were sore. It was so late now that the room had all but emptied of people.

Arriving at her side, ever merry, Prince Kael offered his hand to her once more. "You look drained. I would hate to keep you from your beauty sleep. Please allow me to escort you back to your room"

Cyrene stood with his assistance. "I'm not even certain where they are."

"Then, you are lucky you have me here to guide you."

Prince Kael directed her out the double doors. Cyrene didn't even care how it might look to the remaining attendees. She only wanted to find her new living quarters and sink into her bed.

"How do you know where my room is?" Even in her state, she found that odd.

"There's a directory," he said nonchalantly. "We'll cross by it before we reach the Vines."

"Oh." *Why did no one tell me about the directory?*

Prince Kael stopped at a corner where one of the biggest books Cyrene had ever seen sat on a podium. He easily opened it and found her name within the contents.

"This way." He led her down a hallway took a few turns and then ended up in front of an archway with climbing vines that mirrored Cyrene's Affiliate pin. They had found the Queen's chambers, the Vines.

She marveled at the entrance for a minute and then followed Prince Kael through the corridors. After a few more twists, he stopped in front of a door where her name was written in a swirling green script.

Affiliate Strohm

"Thank you very much. I would never have found it without you."

"It is my pleasure." He held the door open for her as she entered.

"I can't see anything."

Prince Kael let the door close behind him. He struck a match and lit a lantern sitting on a wooden table. The dim glow cast light across the space, revealing a lovely sitting room complete with a brocaded silk sofa and soft-pink-and-cream armchairs. Tapestries in complementary colors lined the walls, and a beautiful braided rug took up a large part of the floor.

Prince Kael leaned one hand against the table, watching her.

"It's beautiful." Her quarters were incredible.

She couldn't wait to see what the bedchamber looked like!

She turned to face Prince Kael, heat rising to her cheeks. Those intense blue-gray eyes looked back at her as if he knew exactly what she was thinking.

He prowled toward her. "You're blushing, Affiliate."

Cyrene swallowed but didn't respond. The same current, an inexplicable connection, zapped between them just as it had earlier.

Then, without warning, Prince Kael's lips were on hers. His strong arms circled her waist, and he pressed his chest tight against hers. She could feel every solid inch of his abdomen as his fingers dug into the silken material of her dress.

He pushed her backward against the wall, wedging her body between him and the hard surface. Her heart seized with panic when she realized there was no escape. She was at his mercy, and he used this to his advantage to snake one hand up into her hair.

He tried to coax life out of her as his other hand moved further and further down her waist, grabbing at her through the thin material. At this moment, the utter shock of the moment wore off, and Cyrene wrenched her head away from him, gasping in horror.

"What are you doing?" She shoved roughly against his chest.

He only grabbed her hair harder and pulled her lips back to his own. She muttered a few choice insults, which he swallowed through his kisses. Ignoring her protests, he kissed down her neck, across to her ear, and over her exposed collarbone. She breathed in quickly, both at the feeling of his mouth on her and the astonishment of being in such a position.

He had no right to kiss me in such a manner without my permission!

His knee moved up between her legs and drove them apart. Cyrene redoubled her efforts, not caring that her hair was ripping from the roots.

"Kael!" she screamed. "What are you doing? Get your hands off of me!" The shriek gave her an inch of leeway, and she stumbled sideways, away from him.

Breathing heavily, Kael narrowed his eyes.

Her entire body trembled. She swallowed hard to try to hide her terror as best as she could. "How dare you touch me!"

"How dare I—" He broke off with a snarl. "After I danced with you all night and escorted you back to your room, you turn me aside?"

Cyrene's eyes were storm clouds, her jaw set in stone. "Turn you aside? You say that as if you were a suitor." She couldn't believe he could be so cavalier after he had forced himself upon her. "You certainly know nothing of being a suitor."

Kael's eyes lost the pale blue color that accentuated his features and turned a formidable slate gray. "I know nothing of being a suitor? I have roamed these castle walls my entire life. I have seen more courtiers come and go than you could imagine in your lifetime."

"Then, you should leave the walls more often!" The fury of the incident still scorched through her veins. "You seemed to have lost your sense of reality if you believe that escorting me back to my bedchamber would suffice."

Anger flared up in Kael's face, but Cyrene did not regret her words. She might be making a grave mistake by angering the Prince, but she damn well was not going to be treated like a common whore. She didn't care who the man was. This was not acceptable behavior!

"For all the education they give you women, I would think they would have taught you something of society, outside of your parents' four walls," he sneered.

"And for all your education, you seemed to have forgotten the appropriate behavior between a man and a woman."

His mocking laugh unnerved her. "You're a beautiful woman, Cyrene," he said, the seductive tone of his voice returning. "I won't be the only man vying for your good graces. You'll learn soon enough that I've treated you with much honor by being here tonight."

He stepped forward again and stroked his hand across her cheek.

"Have I made myself unclear?" She slapped his hand away from her. "Have I shown you one morsel of interest since you made *your* intentions clear? I think not."

"It is hardly your words that have enticed me onward. It is the soft blush against your skin—from your cheeks to your ears and down to your breasts," he softly murmured the last word as he glanced down at her supple curves peeking over the top of her dress. "The increasing heaviness of your breathing as we speak, and—might I?" He drew his fingers to her neck, and she pulled away from his touch as if he were a viper ready to strike. "The rapidity of your heartbeat as we stand so near together."

"Leave now, Prince Kael." She added the formality to place a barrier between them.

Kael was handsome and did tempt her, but the manner in which he had approached her and the cutting edge of his voice at her refusal forced her hand. His presence in her room was nothing less than humiliating to her, her family, and their good name.

"Cyrene—"

"Affiliate Cyrene," she reminded him.

He ground his teeth at the correction.

"Do not expect to receive an invitation again," she said. "I now know what an invitation entails. Thank you kindly for instructing me in my first lesson in society." Her narrowed eyes told him if he made one further move, she would not be as considerate for his position as she had been thus far.

"I hope you are so kind to your other suitors," Prince Kael purred. "May your nights be as warm as the one before you."

He bowed with excessive flourish, and with that, he thundered out of her living area. The door crashed shut behind him.

Cyrene's heart fluttered wildly, but it was not from fear. It was pure anger. If he weren't the rightful Prince of Byern, she would have gone straight to the nearest member of the Royal Guard and had him arrested for indecency.

She collapsed on her new sofa, pulled up her feet to hug her knees to her chest, and let a lone tear fall down her cheek. For what felt like the hundredth time that day, she wished Rhea were here with her.

7

The MASKS

HANDS FELL HEAVY ON CYRENE'S SHOULDERS, RIPPING HER out of her sleep. Her eyes opened wide with terror. A forceful scream escaped out of her lungs. Adrenaline coursed through her body, and she pelted out another ear-shattering shriek.

A hand clamped down over her mouth, smothering her shouts. Cyrene struggled against her assailant in the pitch-black room. Another pair of hands pushed her out of her bed, but Cyrene clawed at the hands and kicked out. Her foot connected with something hard, and a person cried out. The hand covering her mouth wavered, and Cyrene took the liberty to bite down hard.

Her captor yelped and withdrew the hand from her mouth. Cyrene hopped out of bed and made a break for the door. Before she could even make it out of her bedchamber, hands latched on to her on both sides. Another scream was cut off mid-cry as a hand slapped her across the face, hard enough to turn her head.

Cyrene gasped in shock as her vision blurred. She had never, ever been hit before, and she was glad for that because the whole side of her face stung like nothing she had ever experienced.

"Move along," someone said gruffly, pushing her through the door.

Cyrene jostled out of her room. Her feet were bare, and she was wearing nothing but her thin white shift. Her hands fisted in the material. She hated that anyone could see her so exposed.

She was pressed forward into the hallway of the Vines, and she received her first view of the captors. They wore oversized masks shaped like grotesque animals and mythological creatures. It was as if she were at a disturbing re-creation of a masked ball. She hadn't been to one since she was a girl, but even then, people had worn beautifully constructed masks to shape their faces with glitter, feathers, and painted designs. The captors' masks were nothing of the sort.

A giant spotted hyena's face appeared next to her. The wearer shoved her down the hallway, and she collided into another person, who turned around and snatched up her hands. Staring back at her was an otherworldly snarling Indres with a fake like a wolf with large fangs protruding over out of its mouth.

"Watch where you're going!" the Indres screeched.

"What are you doing to me?" Cyrene demanded, hysteria taking over.

"You will speak when spoken to," another voice growled. It belonged to a Leif-masked figure, standing nearly the same height as Cyrene. Strawberry-blonde locks fell out of one side of the mask that was all glittering smooth skin with high-pointed ears. The Leif was a deceptively beautiful creature prone to stealing children in the middle of the night.

"No! You will answer me immediately! I am a Queen's Affiliate," she said, brandishing the title like a weapon. "You will stop this at once."

Laughter filled the corridor.

"Be quiet, little girl."

Something sharp jabbed her in the back. Her feet stilled as the knife punctured her skin. She sucked in a harsh breath at the pain shooting through her body.

"Keep your feet moving, or I'll use this on your throat." The hyena cackled in her ear.

Terrified, Cyrene clamped her mouth shut and followed the strange masked troupe. The torches along the hallway had been extinguished, and Cyrene couldn't make out the route they were taking through the Vines.

Suddenly, the Leif came to an abrupt halt, and Cyrene barely kept from running headlong into the person. The Leif pressed against a nearly invisible door in the pitch-black hallway, and it creaked open. Cyrene bit her lip, trying to rein in the fear threatening to burst out of her.

Her captors shoved her through the pitch black entranceway. Cyrene helplessly stumbled forward and went down a few stairs. At the last second, she latched on to a railing and saved her body from smashing on the hard stone steps.

The group huddled together and descended the steep flight of damp stairs. They seemed to drop farther and farther beneath the castle, spiraling endlessly, and she became dizzy from the descent.

An eerie glow appeared around the next bend. Cyrene's legs shook with the effort, and she was thankful to finally leave the stairs behind even if it meant they were that much closer to wherever her kidnappers were taking her.

Once they reached the bottom step, someone nudged her to keep moving. Through her terror, she put one foot in front of the other. They traveled through a maze of corridors before entering a room.

Upon closer examination, Cyrene realized it was actually a monstrous cave with ruby-red stalactites dripping dangerously from the ceiling and crystallized stalagmites precipitously shooting up from the floor. From her location on a raised stone platform, a flat black lake stretched out before her across the cave. As Cyrene's eyes adjusted to the darkness, she noticed several large boats docked at a distance, and a few smaller skiffs were tied near her. The lake must empty out of the castle on the Keylani River, which ran along the city's perimeter.

She turned away from the lake to the matter at hand and steeled herself for whatever was about to come.

Two rows of fiercely masked faces in high-backed black chairs sat before her. They were absolutely still, staring at her and quietly waiting.

But for what?

Suddenly, ice-cold water cascaded down on her head. The water drenched her hair, matting it to her face, and soaked through her thin shift. As the frigid water hit her skin, Cyrene cried out in shock. She brushed her hands over her eyes to dispel the water. Almost at once, another assault crashed onto her, soaking her to the bone. She had just enough time to close her eyes and mouth before more water rained down.

"What in the name of the Creator is going on?" she screamed through her chattering teeth.

Someone jabbed her in the ribs with a knife blade, and Cyrene flinched from the touch.

"You will speak when spoken to," the person said, repeating the Leif's mantra.

"How dare you!" She held her arms around her body to try to retain a semblance of modesty.

A fourth torrent of water poured on top of her head, and she doubled over in an effort to block herself from the frigid water. Her whole body trembled, and her fingers and toes curled in on themselves. Her white shift did nothing to cover her body, but the cold was so all-encompassing that she almost didn't care.

Cyrene waited for more water to fall, and when it didn't immediately come, she took a moment to brush her hair back. She stood as regally as she could muster. Staring her captors down, she defiantly tilted up her chin. She didn't know who these people were or what was going on, but she would not be broken.

"Do what you will."

"Little girl, you will learn your manners," a person said from behind her.

A gloved hand shot up in the air, staving off the next surge of water.

"That will quite do." The man was wearing a terrifying depiction of a Dragon, the fearsome warriors in the Age of the Doma. "Do you think yourself worthy to wear the climbing-vine pin of an Affiliate?"

There. She had been spoken to.

"Of course!"

"Then, you must prove it," a squat, short individual with a rather fitting dwarf mask said.

"I do not have to prove my worth to anyone. I am an Affiliate. I was selected into receivership to Queen Kaliana. There is no going back."

"There is if you're dead," a peacock-masked individual trilled.

Cyrene blanched. Were they here to kill her? Had they dragged her to this place to send her remains down the Keylani River?

"Enough," the Dragon rumbled.

Cyrene shivered. She had always feared the tales and fables that included the fire-breathing creature that could level a town with a swish of its tail.

After a short pause, a dreadfully emaciated individual wearing a terrifying Braj mask spoke up.

Braj were even more horrifying to her than dragons. They were vicious killers, who were all but invisible in the shadows. It was said that if a person ever saw the true face of a Braj, it would be the last thing they would ever see. The monsters would carve off the faces of their victims and wear them as a prize.

"Did you know that Affiliates and High Order were once warriors?" the high-pitched voice asked.

"Warriors?" she asked. She had not heard such a thing before.

"Oh yes."

"That's not right. After Viktor Dremylon destroyed the Doma, he created Affiliates and High Order for the restoration of Byern. He wanted the country to flourish, and he used the Class system with his new Affiliates and High Order at its head to bring about the peace the citizens all so desperately desired," Cyrene told them.

"Yet what exactly were they restoring?" a man in a fierce lion mask asked.

"They were restoring the lands for the prosperity of Byern," she said tentatively. "They were restoring education and knowledge for the people. They were restoring order to the world that they now ruled."

What else would they have been restoring? The Doma had ruled for too long. They hadn't seen the plight of the everyday people. Viktor Dremylon had saved Byern.

"And how do you best restore order?" the Braj-masked woman asked.

Cyrene blankly stared forward. It took her a second to piece together what the Braj had meant. After Viktor had pushed the Doma out of Byern, he'd had to restore order and implement his Class system. She had never thought to question how he'd done it. And now that she was, it dawned on her.

Oh Creator! She had been backed into a corner.

The best way to restore order after rebellion was surely through…force.

"He used his warriors to restore order," she said, understanding it for the first time. "The first generation of Affiliates and High Order were people he could trust through and through. They were Viktor Dremylon's…warriors."

The Dragon laughed. "Yes, it is true, and now, you know it. The answer we must know is whether or not *you* are a warrior."

"You want to know if *I'm* a warrior?"

"Yes, and you must prove it to us now," the dwarf squeaked out, "as we do not believe you belong among us."

"How can I—"

"You will prove it!" the Dragon called out. "You will prove that you are worthy of such a title."

"We will leave in a moment and lock the door behind us," the peacock interrupted. "You must find a way to exit this cave and return to your quarters. *If* you make it, speak of this to no one. *If* you make it, then you can consider yourself a warrior, an Affiliate, in truth."

"Be warned. You are not the only *thing* in the room." The Braj giggled.

Cyrene stared at them in utter shock. She was supposed to escape this cave, wearing only her shift, in the dead of night with something else in here. *Are they absolutely mad?*

"What if I choose not to?"

"Then, you *will* die," the peacock said with bloodlust in her voice.

8

The ESCAPE

SLOWLY, THE TWO ROWS OF PEOPLE STOOD AND CROSSED the room to the door. A lock clicked in place, and the sudden all-consuming feeling of being alone wrenched itself over her heart. Panic seized her consciousness, and she forced herself to breathe in through her nose and out through her mouth. She needed to keep her wits about her and think.

A torch glowed in a metal slot next to the door, and she jerked it from where it hung. The flame skittered along the lakefront as she searched for something, anything that might help her. She walked half the length of the cave floor and found nothing but water through the entire room. Thrusting the torch out in front of her, she gazed out into the depths revealed by its light. The flames showed no more than a few additional feet in front of her. She gnashed her teeth together in frustration.

How in the name of the Creator do I get out of here?

Still shivering in her soaked nightgown, she returned to the center of the room. *What did I see when I entered before they had humiliated me, pitched me in darkness, and left me to die? Red stalactites, the lake, the river, the boats—*

The boats!

Cyrene rushed back in the direction of the entrance and gazed out across the flat lake. She would no doubt be unable to man the huge boats alone, and she did not think that she had the skills to do so. The skiffs though were closer and smaller. If she could find an oar among them, then she could paddle her way out of this dank hellhole, regardless of what the river current might be outside of the cave.

Unfortunately, the skiffs were tied quite a bit farther than she had originally thought. *It wasn't too far to swim by any means, but can I even get in the water? What is the thing the Braj had warned me about?*

Beyond the depths of the Keylani River, Cyrene had never seen so much water. With the Fallen Desert creeping closer and closer on the other side of the river, scant water survived a summer season. She knew what could be within the depths for she had studied aquatic life, but the real question was if anything could survive in such an endlessly dark lake under the Taken Mountains.

Running the torch along the edge where the mountain met the lake, Cyrene searched for footholds or a ledge that could help her cross. A ridge on the opposite side led up to a dock, but she didn't know how deep the water was, and she certainly couldn't jump that far.

She cursed under her breath, smashed the torch back in its holder, and paced in circles. She didn't want to believe that the masked figures would have put her down here in a hopeless situation. There had to be a way out, and she would find it.

If only the stupid lake would just recede!

A spark lit in her chest at her thought. She felt a tug back to the waterline. Staring at the ledge on the other side, paces away from where she was, she resigned herself to the fact that there was no other way to get out of the cave than to get to those boats.

Cyrene grabbed the torch once more and returned to the edge. She swallowed hard before placing her toe in the water. Surprisingly, it was warm, nearly the temperature of bath water. She sank her foot deeper into the depths, silently praying she might reach the bottom or at least something that would help her get to the other side.

When she was knee-deep in the water, her foot jarred roughly against a jagged rock. She cried out. Wheeling backward, she pulled her leg out of the water. The cut across the ball of her foot was shallow but bleeding more than she would have liked.

Gritting her teeth, she shoved her foot back into the water and found the rock again. She tested her weight on it, and it didn't budge. She sighed happily and eased her other leg into the water. She carefully kicked her leg out in front of her, and to her relief, she found another rock. Ignoring the pain in her foot, she nearly giggled when she located another and another.

A ripple pulsed in the water.

Cyrene froze stiffly. There it was—another ripple. Her heart hammered against her chest.

What's out there?

She was as close to the ledge as to where she had started. She had to risk it. A ripple closer than the last steeled her nerve, and she dashed across another group of stones as fast as her feet would carry her through the black water. She didn't dare look across the lake as she searched desperately for secure footing.

The ledge was up ahead, and all she could hear behind her were snapping jaws. Her breath came out ragged as the sounds approached faster and faster, gaining on her. Without a second thought, Cyrene dived for the ledge. Narrowly making it, she landed roughly on her right side, skidding against the rough stone. As she rolled away from the lakefront, she lost her torch in the process.

Her face shot up from her crouched position in time to see a pack of feral fish with red scales and razor-sharp teeth jumping eagerly out of the water toward her. She screamed and skittered farther away from the edge. Several flapped against the ledge, ferociously snapping their jaws before crashing back into the depths.

Rising uneasily to her wobbly legs, Cyrene forced the image of dying by flesh-eating fish out of her brain.

She had torn her shift in several places, and massive bruises blossomed on her hip, knee, and shoulder. In addition to scrapes on her leg and shoulder, a trail of blood ran down her right leg from her knee. Ripping off a piece of her nightgown, she tied it around the injury as best as she could. She would deal with it when she got out of here.

Striving not to put pressure on her right side, Cyrene teetered over to the edge of the wall and grabbed another torch, this one dim and barely flickering. Blowing on it brought the flame back to life. She tried to open the only visible door, but it was locked, so she moved back to the docks.

She yanked an oar out of the smallest boat, the only one she might be capable of rowing by herself, and untied it from the end of the dock. After seating herself within, she shoved off and allowed herself to drift out on the open waters.

Tentatively, she dipped the oar into the water and waited for the little monsters to come back.

Nothing moved in the cavernous lake.

Breathing a sigh of relief, Cyrene painstakingly rowed herself toward the large arch exit. She didn't waste her time with the other doors, assuming they would also be locked.

After what felt like an eternity, Cyrene approached the huge carved doorway, molded with gray-and-black stone that was similar to the interior of the castle. She rowed under the arch, and the boat collided with something, emitting a loud gong-like sound. She sprawled backward onto the planks of the boat. Her small boat swayed from the force of the impact, and she waited until it stilled.

Cyrene righted herself and let her fingers graze a smooth metal surface. No wonder the inside of the cave was black as night. It was closed off from the outside world. Her gaze scoured the archway and found a thick worn iron chain. She grappled with it and gave it a tentative tug. A creak set the hairs on the back of her neck on edge, and the water rippled around the door where it moved marginally away from the wall.

The heavy metal chain tensed her shoulders as she pulled it, hand over hand. Voices sounded over the drone of the metal door screeching against the rock archway, and Cyrene rested her cracked hands as she craned her neck and listened. She hadn't thought anyone else could access the cave.

The voices picked up again, but Cyrene couldn't decipher what they were saying. She couldn't see anyone, yet the voices were getting clearer. Then, her gaze landed on something in the water. Her stomach sank through her body, and she held back the nausea that threatened her.

A Skrivner snake.

Even though she couldn't make out the entire outline of the body, she was sure of it, and she wasn't going to wait around for it to get any closer. A Skrivner was the deadliest water snake. Its three-inch-long fangs caused hallucinations as the snake feasted on the blood of the victim. Plus it could mimic human sounds, and if she was right, then that was where the voices were coming from.

Ignoring the sharp pains in her hands and the blood she'd left behind on the chain, Cyrene wrenched it with every ounce of strength she had in her aching muscles. The metal door seemed to move even slower than before, as if her efforts were becoming more futile. She muttered every curse word her father had ever used as she heaved the chain putting her shoulders, back, and legs into the motion of yanking on the insufferable chain.

She glanced over her shoulder just once. The Skrivner approached fast, his crimson eyes bright with bloodlust.

Finally, the door opened far enough for her to be able to maneuver the boat through. She quickly tied off the chain, sank back down, picked up the oar, and paddled like the prize of becoming consort waited on the other side.

Tonight was not her night to die. She had too much to accomplish. She still had to see the world!

With one final push, she glided forward through the archway, and a fast-moving current seized her boat. She swiveled around in her seat to see the Skrivner strike out at her, but it was just out of reach, so it slithered back into the black lake.

"By the Creator!"

Tears trickled down her face while blood boiled under the surface of her skin. She had never felt happier to be alive.

At the first turn, she paddled off the current. The river flowed more smoothly down this path. Her head swelled with curiosity as rowed past several more turns. *Where did they all lead?*

Her mind focused on the bits and pieces she knew of the underground passageways within the castle. Hidden doors wound up to the rooms above, and some even led to the grounds themselves. Finding one that might be open was her only chance.

She traversed the pathways, passing doors with giant iron locks on the outside. Someone had been down here long ago to prevent intruders from infiltrating the castle. Cyrene panicked at the thought. *If they are all locked up tight, then how can I find a way out?*

A spark ignited in her chest, and out of it, a thought flickered to the surface. *Believe in those whose honor doth shine.*

Where did I read that? Cyrene didn't have a clue, but somehow, it felt right. It just *felt* right.

Her heart beat in her temples, her bloodied fingers, and her splintered feet as she searched out the inscriptions on the doors before her. She didn't want to think about how many doors lay within these walls or of the possibility that none of them would lead her out of here or what would happen if she encountered another Skrivner, feral fish, or the mouth of the Keylani.

Then, as if she had conjured it up from nowhere, a door without a padlock appeared with words gleaming on the surface. She could just make out the words *shine* and *honor*. She didn't have another option. This one had to be it.

Groaning in weary relief, she rowed toward the ledge. She barely made it as her throbbing arms worked against the current. After tying up the boat to a peg stuck in the ground, Cyrene exited the boat, reached forward for the door, and recited the words that she felt were her saving grace, "Believe in those whose honor doth shine."

The door easily swung open at the touch of her fingers, and she entered into a small dusty room, empty of all belongings. This entrance had surely not been used for years.

Her legs felt like lead as she followed a winding flat pathway upward for what felt like an eternity. Finally she reached a large cellar door that blocked the passage in front of her. She pushed it open with her shoulder. Hay exploded all around her, sticking to her skin that was slick with water, blood, and sweat. Cyrene coughed at the sudden onslaught and shielded her eyes with her arm against the brightness. Light filtered in through the slats of the stable, but thankfully, Cyrene didn't see anyone else.

After stepping through the cellar door, she closed it and covered the area over with hay again. Since the door had clearly fallen into disuse, the last thing she wanted was for people to notice it.

As she started to walk cautiously away from the door, she hit something sturdy and toppled forward. Gasping, she landed hard on a solid body. Her eyes flew open, and she struggled to get away from the man beneath her. When he didn't move, she lightly nudged him with her uninjured foot. After everything that had happened to her tonight, she prayed to the Creator that he wasn't dead.

A gargling noise came from the man, and she blew out a breath.

As he sat up and stared at her through bleary bloodshot eyes, she scrambled to her feet. He didn't look much older than her, but he already had the body of a sturdy hunter. He had haphazardly tousled dark brown hair intertwined with hay. Blood and dirt caked one side of his face where he had been lying down. His clothes weren't in a much better state. One sleeve hung almost completely off, and he had a gash across the stomach of his shirt. It looked as if it had been sliced through with a knife, but she saw no blood. His pants were frayed at the ends, and he had somehow managed to lose just one boot.

"What ya want?" he grumbled, closing his eyes and pressing his hand to his head.

"For you to get your putrid stink away from me," she said with no tolerance for anyone after this night's events.

Cyrene was surprised to find her voice unchanged. After running, rowing, pulling, and climbing her way away from her own death, she'd thought it would have changed somehow, yet she still sounded strong, maybe even stronger.

He roared with laughter and then covered his mouth as he leaned away from her. He held his side and coughed into his hand. After a minute, he turned back to face Cyrene and really seemed to look at her. His eyes bulged, and he whistled lowly. "What in the Creator's name happened to you?"

Cyrene blushed despite herself. She didn't even want to know what she looked like in her torn white shift. Her body was relatively numb at this point, but she knew the extent of her injuries—sliced open foot; bruised everything; aching and cramped arms and shoulders; bloodied hands and fingers; stiff legs—but it was better than being dead.

"What happened to you?" she countered.

He looked nearly as bad as she did.

A rueful smile crossed his tanned features. His mischievous eyes were deep dark brown with rings of gold around the pupils.

"Too much fun," he said with a shrug.

"I see. Remind me never to have fun with you."

He laughed again, harder than before. This time, he turned and vomited out the contents of his stomach. Cyrene's stomach seized at the sound and smell, and she nearly wretched herself.

"Sorry," he moaned. He wiped his mouth with his sleeve.

"I have to return to my quarters."

"Wait, you never said what happened to you."

"Too much fun," she said bitterly.

She pivoted on her heel to walk away from him.

"You're Cyrene, right?"

She stopped in her tracks. "Yeah, I am." She was surprised he knew who she was.

He stood and leaned against a wooden beam that had been driven into the ground. "I'm Ahlvie. Ahlvie Gunn, at your service."

"Ah, the drunk," she murmured, remembering how he had gotten thrown out of her Presenting ball.

By the Creator, was that only yesterday?

"If the shoe fits."

She nodded at him and staggered forward to leave.

"Might I be of assistance? I'm quite good at getting through the castle without being seen. And if I were you, I wouldn't want to be seen like *that*."

Cyrene looked down at her torn nightgown that was wrinkled and splattered with her blood. He was right, of course. She couldn't be seen like this.

What if the King saw me? Or even worse, the Queen? Cyrene couldn't bear it.

"Please."

Ahlvie smiled crookedly at her. "This way."

She followed him through a back passage that wound all through the castle. As soon as Ahlvie got her into the Vines, unseen, she thanked him, and then she rushed to her room and slammed the door with force.

Cyrene threw her ruined shift in a heap on the ground and buried her naked self under the goose down comforter. A rustle of someone passing by her door made her get up to investigate to make sure she had locked it. She didn't want to be disturbed ever again.

As she reached her chamber door, a piece of paper stamped with the royal seal slid underneath it. She ground her teeth as she snatched it off the ground and jerked it open.

WELCOME TO THE RANKS, WARRIOR.

She didn't know who had subjected her to this torture and then left this note, but she hated them. She would always hate them. She would hate them with every fiber of her being for making her suffer through that, for making her risk her life for some ill-brained cause. She was not a warrior, nor would she ever consider herself one.

But if they wanted to believe they had won the battle, she would show them that she could win the war.

9

The DRUNK

AHLVIE WATCHED CYRENE DISAPPEAR DOWN THE HALLWAY to her rooms before tucking back into the secret corridor. He didn't know what had possessed him to help her. He wasn't particularly susceptible to damsels in distress or the like, but something in her eyes had spoken of determination. He actually believed she would have gone strolling around the castle, looking like a beat-up drowned rat.

She reminded him a bit of himself when he had first arrived in this Creator-forsaken castle. He hoped that she could keep up the rebellious nature, but he doubted it. This place could leech the life out of a person.

Pushing the new girl out of his mind, he contemplated returning to his quarters to change before vanishing from the castle grounds once more. He jerked on his sleeve, and it ripped the rest of the way off. If he'd managed to keep both boots last night, then he wouldn't have to return to the High Order quarters. He would make it quick though.

He navigated the empty morning corridors with ease and then crashed into his barely lived-in room. He opened his wardrobe and saw that someone had laundered his clothing. Hopefully, the person hadn't gotten all the bloodstains out of his clothes from home. Every other article of clothing had the High Order logo attached to it.

How did anyone expect me to move around so easily in the city with a Dremylon D *plastered on to all my clothing?* Not a single person in

Low market would talk to a High Order. Half the people in the Laelish wouldn't either.

After pulling on newish boots and a slightly less destroyed dark blue shirt, he left his room in a hurry. He careened around the corner and slowed his feet when he saw the hallway was occupied.

"Creator," he grumbled.

"Ahlvie," Reeve called down the hallway.

Reeve was the nicest of the High Order around Ahlvie's age, but he hung out with the pigheaded idiots—Rhys, Clovis, and Surien. Ahlvie cared little for other people at court in general, but those guys were the foulest lot.

"Have you seen Zorian this morning?" Reeve asked as he approached.

"Is he back from Carhara? Tahne is a rough sort of city," Ahlvie said of the capital city of Carhara.

"Came back last night."

He skirted around Reeve. "Perhaps he is still as intoxicated as I am."

Reeve narrowed his eyes. "You don't look too bad."

"You mean that you've seen me look worse."

"That's not what I meant," Reeve said, exasperated. "If you see Zorian, will you send him my way? We have an outstanding dice game."

"Dicing?" Ahlvie's eyes lit up. "Let me know when you play."

"I would if I wanted to lose."

Ahlvie smirked at him. "I'll tell Zorian about the dicing if I see him, and we'll find a time to play."

Reeve shook his head, but Ahlvie knew that Reeve would dice with him later. Ahlvie's fingers itched for his own dice to throw. He thrust them into his pockets and ignored the inclination.

He swung around to the back entrance to the High Order quarters, which the guys called the Flames. Guards were stationed at the exit. Most of them knew him by sight. Still, he could sneak by them at night. Considering the security of the castle, it could be done a little too easily, but it was convenient for him.

Ahlvie left the grounds on a path that ended in an unpleasant steep descent into the capital city. He wasn't sure how he had come back this way last night while completely obliterated. As he skidded down the slope, he saw a large body passed out in the middle of the path.

Ahlvie laughed out loud and jogged down toward the man. Apparently, he hadn't been the only person sneaking in and out of the castle while inebriated.

"Hey!" Ahlvie called out. "Had a bit too much to drink, my friend?"

Rolling the man over onto his back, Ahlvie got a clear look at the man and then stumbled backward a few steps in horror. He fell onto the rocks and wretched up whatever was left in his stomach.

Most of the man's face was…missing.

10

The
REGIMEN

CYRENE AWOKE THE NEXT MORNING, ACHING ALL OVER. She had tended to her wounds last night, and she was surprised to see her injuries were healing remarkably fast. She was still stiff and sore, but after a few steps, she managed to walk without flinching.

Two servant girls in long-sleeved white gowns arrived to help her dress in a sky-blue gown with cream lace sleeves. They placed a plate of toasted bread, seasonal berries, and a hard-boiled egg on her table along with a fresh pot of tea. She graciously thanked them before they departed.

After taking the last sip of her tea, Cyrene placed the porcelain cup on the matching saucer and stood from the sofa in her sitting room. She eased her damaged fingers into her plait and tried to loosen some of the strands. She had already woken up with a headache that morning with the memory of what had happened the night before still fresh. She shuddered at the thought of Kael and the warrior ceremony and hoped that no one else would find out about either incident.

Trying to push that out of her mind, she focused on her fast approaching meeting with Queen Kaliana. Cyrene would be given her official duties as an Affiliate today.

Cyrene wasn't certain where she was supposed to meet the Queen. Despite her fears, she opened the door to her chambers and gazed out into the empty hallway.

Her heart sank. No one was there to direct her, but at least there weren't masked figures. She wished she had thought to ask the servants. The next best thing would be to hunt down the directory from last night.

As she was about to start wandering the corridors, the door next to her room opened, and a petite girl no older than Cyrene with stick-straight blonde hair walked out in a pale yellow gown, her nose buried in a book.

"Um...excuse me," Cyrene called out.

The girl stopped abruptly and looked up from her book in confusion. "Yes?"

"Sorry to bother you, uh...Affiliate. I'm supposed to have a meeting with Queen Kaliana. Do you think you could direct me to her rooms?"

"Oh. Yes, of course, I can," she said with a bright smile. She closed the book and held it against her chest. "If you want to follow me, I can take you there myself."

"That would be most helpful. Thank you."

Cyrene fell into step next to the girl. She had eyes that were a little too big for her face and a splatter of freckles across the bridge of her nose. At the same time, her appearance was far from distinct, and Cyrene was sure her eyes would have slid easily over the girl in a crowd.

"I'm Affiliate Cyrene, by the way."

"I know. I was at your Presenting yesterday." The girl set a hasty pace as they walked down the corridor.

"I'm Affiliate Maelia Dallmer."

"So nice to meet you," Cyrene said.

"What kind of path do you hope for your Affiliate duties?" Maelia clutched the book tighter.

"I'm not certain what is available," she began carefully, "but I'd prefer to be placed somewhere I'll be able to travel. My sister is the Ambassador to Kell for the Queen and is fortunate enough to be able to travel the world. Do you know Aralyn?"

She smiled meekly and shook her head. "I'm afraid not. I've been here less than six months."

"Oh. Then, you're not that much older than me," Cyrene murmured in relief.

She knew there were going to be girls around her age, but she hadn't thought she would be lucky enough to find someone on her first day. The girl's soft demeanor reminded Cyrene so much of

Rhea. Maybe once Maelia broke out of her shell, she would also turn out to be someone Cyrene could be friends with.

"Are you from the capital city? I apologize for not remembering seeing you anywhere."

"No, this city is still foreign to me. I was raised in Levin. My family are Seconds." She used the slang term without a trace of emotion about being taken away from her family in the northern mountainous Byern city to enter into the First Class.

Cyrene dealings with the Second and Third Classes had been all but limited to the Laelish Market. She had been freaked out enough about moving into the castle without being transplanted into an entirely different city. On top of all that, Maelia had had to learn to adjust not only to an Affiliate's lifestyle, but also to the First Class.

"Well, maybe I can show you around some, if we can find the time," Cyrene offered.

"I'd like that." A genuine smile crossed Maelia's face.

She turned them down another hallway with more decoration than the previous one. Oil paintings hung on the wall. The first one showed a beautiful countryside with rolling hills and gorgeous oak trees. Another one revealed what looked like the foothills of their very own Taken Mountains and the Keylani River running through the mountain pass. The next showcased an oceanic scene with rippling waves, soft white sand, and palm trees blowing in the breeze.

While staring at the beach scene, she could almost hear the waves crashing on the bank, feel the gentle sea breeze, and smell the salty air thick with sea spray even though she had never even seen the Lakonia Ocean. She lightly shook her head, trying to rid herself of the strange emotions rolling through her body. She must have read about the paintings in a book prior to this moment.

With difficulty, Cyrene tore her gaze away from the incredibly detailed designs plastered on the walls, and she continued her conversation with Maelia.

"Let's arrange to meet after I receive orders from the Queen."

Maelia fidgeted with her book as they approached the enormous wooden door at the end of the hallway. "I hope she lets you off easy. I'd love to see the city."

"Is she particularly stern?"

"*Stern* is not the proper word." Maelia's voice dipped to a whisper. "The Queen is power hungry on a good day, and today might be even worse. Perhaps I should not say so though." Her hazel eyes glanced anxiously at the closed door as if someone might hear her critique of the Queen.

"Why is she more so today?" Cyrene mirrored Maelia's soft tone.

"I've heard," Maelia murmured, drawing closer to Cyrene, "that the Queen is with child, and she announced such circumstances to His Majesty."

"Why, that's wonderful news!" Cyrene boomed. Maelia's hesitant peek at the doors made Cyrene lower her voice. "Isn't that wonderful news?"

"It's hard to tell. The last one ended in a miscarriage."

Cyrene's mouth popped open in shock. "She lost the baby?"

Maelia nodded solemnly. "So, you can see why today might be worse. The baby is good news but only if she can hold on to it. I think she fears she cannot."

"How terrible. Thank you so much for telling me. I would have hated to go in there blind."

"Good luck. I'm sure my warnings were unwarranted." Maelia placed her hand on Cyrene's shoulder. "You'll do great. King Edric and Prince Kael both seemed to like you after all."

Cyrene blushed. *Had they been that obvious?* "I'm sure they were both performing their duties in welcoming me as the newest Affiliate."

The coy smile on Maelia's lips told Cyrene that had not been the case. "I'm sure."

"I'll find you afterward. Will you be in your rooms?" she asked to divert the subject.

"Most likely. It was really nice meeting you, Cyrene. I can't wait for our adventure."

"Me either. It was so nice to meet you as well, Maelia."

The girl scurried back down the hallway and around the corner.

Cyrene didn't know what it was, but she already liked Maelia. With Rhea gone, Cyrene had been afraid it would be a while until she made friends. She had heard stories of all the Affiliates being close, but those were countered with just as many tales of them hating each other and battling for favored positions.

Cyrene heaved the heavy wooden door open and entered the Queen's compartments. For all the inactivity of the corridors, people were bustling in the Queen's chambers. Affiliates and servants alike milled around inside—some speaking rapidly to one another, others with their noses buried in books, and still more writing furiously on loose sheets of parchment. The room reminded her of a beehive with a large round central room and other rooms branching off in various directions. A stained-glass mural overhead depicted a fabled land with unnaturally beautiful individuals with wings sprouting out of their backs.

An athletically built woman with a face covered in freckles flowed gracefully toward Cyrene. "Hello, Affiliate Cyrene," she said with a bright smile. Her pale green dress brought out the stark quality of her frazzled fiery-red hair, which hung loose to her waist. "Pleasure to finally meet you. I'm Affiliate Catalin, Director of Internal Affairs for Her Majesty, Queen Kaliana."

Cyrene dipped a small curtsy to the woman. "Good day to you, Affiliate Catalin."

She had heard her mother complain frequently enough about the woman who had been the DIA under Queen Adelaida for King Maltrier. DIAs expected nearly as much respect as the queen and the consort, but they frequently abused the authority vested in them.

"Queen Kaliana is meeting with His Royal Highness, Prince Kael, at the moment."

Cyrene tried to keep the tightness from her mouth at the mention of his name.

"I am to begin with your training until she is ready for your assignment. Follow me, please." She briskly walked across the marble floor.

After crossing the busy foyer, Cyrene entered an immaculate small square room on the far end of the chamber. Books lined the built-in shelves of one wall in descending height order. Sheaves of paper were stacked carefully in neat piles, and emerald-green feather quills were perfectly aligned. A practical wooden desk sat against the far wall, and two matching wooden stools stood before it.

Catalin took a seat behind the desk and gently folded her hands on the desk. "Please sit," she offered graciously.

"Thank you very much."

"We'll get right down to business then, yes? I'm sure you are aware of much of what I am about to tell you, what with your family's impeccable First Class background, but procedures must be followed."

"Of course."

"I'll start at the beginning." She cleared her voice. "Congratulations on being selected into the First Class and having the luxury of being appointed to Her Royal Highness, Queen Kaliana, as a Queen's Affiliate."

With a quirk of her mouth, Catalin said, "As you know, Viktor Dremylon set in place a new government with three Classes to allow the people a chance to have better lives. With the new system, Viktor Dremylon put in place the High Order and Affiliate program to bring the best and the brightest together. You have been admitted into this prestigious role."

Catalin continued, "We expect you to begin your educational regimen on your first day. You answer to Queen Kaliana and offer assistance for any requests she might have. Your unhesitating acceptance is required. Her Majesty always has a larger picture in mind than you might be aware of. Do you have any questions?"

Cyrene hesitated. "Yes, Affiliate Catalin. What of Consort Daufina? I realize you did not mention her."

She couldn't think it was an accident that Catalin had left off information about the Consort. Cyrene knew from her lessons that Affiliates were expected to have the same deference to the consort as to the queen. In nearly every right, except for blood, the consort was royalty.

Catalin's sneer confirmed Cyrene's beliefs. "You are not bound to the Consort. You'll do well to remember that you work for the Queen, first and foremost. Upon request, the Consort can work with you if you are not already busy with the Queen's orders."

It simply didn't work that way. Cyrene knew it, and this woman knew it.

Either way, Cyrene smiled sweetly as if she did not know that Catalin had blatantly lied about the mechanics of the business.

"As I was saying, you have obligations as an Affiliate, other than your education. The King has plans to travel on procession to Albion, and you will likely be asked to accompany the court on the expedition. Additional duties might arise throughout your time as an Affiliate, and as always, you are expected to accept these responsibilities with grace and goodwill. Are there any further questions?"

Cyrene opened her mouth to tell Catalin that she understood her responsibilities when a figure burst into the room.

"Affiliate Catalin!"

"Jardana!" Catalin rushed to her feet and glared at the girl.

Cyrene craned her neck around to take a look. The girl was dreadfully thin with honey-blonde hair pulled high off of her face, similar to the Queen's fashion.

"There's been an attack!" Jardana cried dramatically.

"An attack?"

"King Edric sent me directly for Prince Kael."

"Slow down, child. What has happened?"

Jardana bristled at the use of the word *child*. "High Order Zorian was found dead this morning. His face..." She swallowed hard. "His face had been ripped off."

Cyrene paled. *A death of a member of the High Order had occurred in the castle?* That was unheard of. *And why does that name sound familiar?*

"Not Zorian," Catalin said, tightly clutching the desk. "He just returned from Carhara."

By the Creator!

That was the man who Reeve had wanted to introduce her to last night at her Presenting. His friends had joked about Zorian engaging with Carharan women, but he had been...killed.

"Follow me. I must tell the Queen at once," Catalin said.

The group exited Catalin's office and went back into the round common room that was still bustling with Affiliates. They stopped in front of a pair of double doors worked with the Queen's intricate climbing vines. Catalin entered without waiting for an invitation. Cyrene and Jardana swept in after her.

Propriety still in order for the DIA when addressing the Queen, Catalin fell into a deep curtsy. Cyrene's blue eyes raked the room as she also curtsied before Queen Kaliana, next to Jardana. When Cyrene met Prince Kael's smug look from his seated position before the Queen, she stared icily back.

"What in the Creator's name do you think you are doing, barging in like this, Catalin?" the Queen demanded.

"My apologies, Your Highness," Catalin said, hastening to stand.

"Well, explain yourself!"

"Your Highness, Affiliate Jardana has arrived with some most troubling news this morning," Catalin began.

"May we speak about this after my new Affiliate appointment, Catalin?" Queen Kaliana snapped. She lounged back in her chair inlaid with gold and clasped her narrow long fingers together in her lap. She was swathed in the finest gold silk, her long-sleeved dress fitting tightly across her chest, and tied around her neck was a faintly shimmery gold lace ribbon.

"But it comes directly from King Edric," Jardana cut in.

Queen Kaliana set her cold and calculating blue eyes on Jardana, who kept her back ramrod straight. The Queen's blonde hair was pulled sharply off of her face, which only gave her a more severe appearance. This was not a woman to be underestimated.

"Please remember whom you are speaking with, Affiliate."

Jardana nodded her head. "Your Highness."

"Now, be quick with this matter, Catalin. I have business to attend to, and I'm in no mood this morning."

"High Order Zorian was found dead this morning, Your Majesty."

Queen Kaliana breathed in sharply. Cyrene watched Prince Kael's lips thin, and then she quickly diverted her attention.

"Affiliate Jardana was sent here from King Edric for his brother, Prince Kael," Catalin added.

"She was sent here for the Prince?" the Queen asked, her words as sharp as a razor blade.

"Yes, Your Majesty," Jardana whispered.

"Very well. He will leave at my discretion. In the meantime, Catalin, do hurry along to my Edric and let him know I will be there to deal with this as soon as I am finished with my new Affiliate."

"Yes, Your Highness." Catalin bobbed a curtsy and then rushed from the room.

"As for you, Jardana," the Queen began, "you will wait outside for Prince Kael."

"There's no need for Jardana to wait while we speak with the new Affiliate. I can find my way," Prince Kael said.

Jardana's jaw set at the dismissal. "Of course, Your Majesties."

She swept out of the room like a thundercloud, and the door slammed shut behind her. Cyrene had been standing back, observing them throughout the entire encounter. She was surprised to find that neither Prince Kael nor Queen Kaliana seemed to be in a rush to find out more about the dead man. In fact, Queen Kaliana seemed to be purposely stalling the Prince from leaving.

"Affiliate Cyrene," Queen Kaliana said.

"Good morning, Your Majesty," she murmured with an uneasy smile.

"Indeed." Queen Kaliana contemplatively turned her attention to Prince Kael.

"You slept well, I hope," Prince Kael said. A sly smile played on his lips.

"Quite well in fact. Nice and warm." She clenched her hurt hands at her sides. "Thank you for asking."

Prince Kael's smile widened.

Queen Kaliana suspiciously eyed them. "Prince Kael was just telling me how kind he was to direct you back to your chambers last night. I'm not certain how you'd missed the information to get there on your own, but you're here now, so you must have received the instructions I sent to your rooms this morning."

Cyrene maintained her outward calm, but all the while, she was seething on the inside. The woman had sent no such instructions last night, and she had not done so this morning either. She wondered if Queen Kaliana was the reason for the vile warrior ceremony in the first place.

But Cyrene needed to play along. There was surely some reason for all of this.

"Yes, they were most helpful, My Queen."

Cyrene would have to find proper directions on her own. She would not be caught unaware again.

"We're very glad you arrived in time," Prince Kael said.

"Kael," the Queen snapped. "I believe you have other matters to attend to. Did we not just receive news that a High Order was killed?"

Prince Kael slowly dragged his gaze away from Cyrene. "Of course, Your Royal Highness. I was waiting for your leave."

"You have it. Tell my husband that I will be there to help in any way I can."

"As you wish. I do hope you save me the pleasure of your delightful company another time."

The Queen's stare never wavered, even as his tone openly mocked her in front of a new Affiliate, one of her own. Cyrene could tell she would have flailed him alive if he had been anyone but royalty.

"Thank you, Kael. You may go."

Prince Kael rose smoothly from the chair, stretching out his lean-muscled body. He swept the Queen a deep bow, and then he managed one only a bit less regal for Cyrene but with an even bigger smile.

Courtier indeed! She wished he hadn't bowed so low even if the gesture did honor her.

The Queen would surely see it as a slight against her from Prince Kael.

As he walked toward the exit, he stopped right before Cyrene and directly looked her in the eyes. "I would be careful about leaving the grounds, Affiliate. We don't know what's out there. You should keep yourself safe."

Cyrene's eyebrows rose. *Is the Prince worried about me?* She had a hard time reconciling this with the man who had been in her room only last night.

He smirked once more, and her eyes followed him as he barged out of the room, letting the door slam behind him. Cyrene didn't know what to make of him. He was a bit of an enigma.

"What an animal," Queen Kaliana mumbled. "Always carrying on and slamming doors. You would never guess he was related to my Edric."

Cyrene didn't know what to say, so she focused on the room instead. It was nearly twice as large as the foyer outside the chamber and similarly round with two concealed doors on either side of the room. Several hundred-year-old tapestries hung without a day of fading or wear. One showed dancing, another revealed a circle of multicolored mushrooms, and a few appeared to depict an enchanted forest habitat alight with activity. Large colored glass orbs hung from the ceiling and cast a rainbow across the room that was brightly lit from an overhead sunroof. The effect was dazzling.

"Well, let's make this quick. As you can see, my day is full of important matters." Queen Kaliana reflexively brushed a piece of hair off her face. "Sit, Cyrene. We need to come to a decision."

Cyrene sat gracefully in the chair Prince Kael had vacated.

"I've been reviewing your file to make a decision about your educational regimen. It seems you have excelled in nearly all your subjects, and you have received positive marks from your tutor.

But where to put you?" She slapped her hands down on the table, spreading her fingers wide, and then she rose before positioning herself in front of her desk.

After a couple of minutes of silence, the Queen said, "As you know, an Affiliate's educational regimen is *the* most important aspect of your First Class life. You will become an expert in whatever is decided, and you will make a great contribution to Byern. As your Receiver, it is my job to find a proper placement for your career…somewhere you will flourish." She gave a wry smile. "Lucky for you, my husband spoke to me about you this morning."

"He did?" Cyrene gasped out. Her mouth popped open, and her blue eyes grew wide. *Why did the King speak on my behalf?*

"Indeed he did," Queen Kaliana said. "You act surprised."

"I beg your pardon, Queen Kaliana, but it is not an act. I have no idea why King Edric would have spoken of me or about me."

"While I'm sure that is true," the Queen said as if she believed no such thing, "he still spoke to me about his opinion regarding your Affiliate duties. He mentioned that you have quite an affinity for the weather, even suggesting heretical things such as predicting it."

Cyrene's face blanched. *Oh no!*

"You don't deny it?"

"No, Your Majesty," Cyrene began carefully. "I did mention that to the King, but it was in jest."

"That would be a useful quality."

Only If I want to be burned for witchcraft or cast out for madness…

The Queen stalked over to a gorgeous standing cabinet. The top half was lined with shelves and covered in glass to protect the priceless artifacts within. The bottom half was covered with solid wooden doors and round doorknobs protruding from each one.

Queen Kaliana opened one door to reveal a stack of papers over a foot tall. She eased the loose papers out of the cabinet and heaved them across the room. She quivered under the weight of the documents.

Cyrene jumped to her feet. "Do you need assistance, My Queen?"

"Sit," she barked.

Cyrene nearly fell back into the chair. The Queen slammed the papers onto a blank space on her desk with a sigh of relief. The papers were black around some of the edges, and other pieces looked like scraps.

Queen Kaliana stared into Cyrene's blue eyes, searching.

For what, Cyrene had no idea. She wished Rhea were here for strength or to help her determine what was about to happen.

"I've taken my husband's wishes into consideration," she began.

Cyrene felt like sinking into the seat.

"Additionally, after looking at the various positions that have recently opened up, I have come to a decision."

The weight of the Oath of Acceptance Cyrene had taken only yesterday morning was already weighing heavily on her shoulders.

"One of the most trusted and oldest living Affiliates among us, Affiliate Lorne sadly passed away. She had been working in her field for more than seventy years. Unfortunately, Lorne's house was burned to the ground before we could retrieve her life's work from her residence. This stack here"—Queen Kaliana placed her hand on the enormous pile of papers—"is one of four that we were able to recover before the fire consumed everything. You are to read through everything Affiliate Lorne left behind and write a detailed report on her discoveries...if any."

"What was her life work on?" Cyrene asked warily.

Queen Kaliana smiled. "Foreign agriculture."

Cyrene's heart sank. If she was stuck in agriculture her entire life, then she might never get to leave. She would never see the world. All her dreams of traveling were shattering before her eyes. This could not be happening. She was supposed to have an Ambassadorship.

"My Queen, are you quite certain that *agriculture* is the best use of my abilities?" Cyrene asked, trying to sound confident. "Do you not think I would be better served in some other field?"

The Queen smacked her hand back down on the stack, crumpling the paper on the top of the pile. Her face was set in a stern scowl, her mouth bunching up, and her eyes seething. "Do you dare contradict what I have decided?"

"No. Of course not, Your Highness."

"I thought not." She released the paper from her hand. "Your *abilities* will be best utilized in the field I have chosen for you, and you will receive no further training until you have completed the task I have set forth for you. Do you understand?"

"Yes, My Queen," Cyrene said, meeting the Queen's gaze. "I understand perfectly."

She understood that the Queen, for some reason, felt threatened by her. She understood that the Queen did not like her husband speaking on anyone's behalf, and clearly, she thought this was some sort of punishment for him doing so. She understood perfectly this was a means to get her out of the way.

But Cyrene wouldn't be pushed aside so easily.

She was meant to see the world, and she would find a way to do so, one way or another.

11

The
DEATH

CYRENE'S HANDS WERE BLEEDING AGAIN WHEN SHE MADE it back to her rooms.

The Queen had made her stagger there under the weight of the enormous stack of papers. She'd nearly tumbled headfirst into ten different people within the Queen's common room alone—not to mention, the number of other people who had finally woken up and were strolling through the castle.

Over the next couple of days, the castle was occupied with the death of High Order Zorian and the preparations for his funeral, which everyone in the castle was required to attend. Cyrene spent the time leading up to that attempting to glean anything of value from the wreckage of Affiliate Lorne's life's work and learning her way around the Nit Decus castle. At some point, she returned to her room to find servants had deposited the remaining three stacks of paperwork in her room, and she despaired over ever finishing.

One day, on her way back to her room, Cyrene found Maelia waiting for her in the hallway. Cyrene had been so occupied with her studies that she had forgotten her promise to the girl, the only friend she had made in the castle.

"Cyrene," Maelia said in greeting. "I have been looking for you."

"Hello, Maelia. I haven't seen you in days."

Maelia nodded. "I have been...held up. I'll tell you all about it."

Cyrene walked beside Maelia the remaining way to their rooms. Cyrene opened her door and found that her things had finally arrived from home. Books lined the once empty bookshelf, jewelry dangled from an open box, and a multitude of clothes burst from her wardrobe.

"I see you've been given your full orders." Maelia eyed the hundreds of pieces of paper neatly arranged on the sitting room table. "What was decided?"

"Foreign agricultural division." The last thing Cyrene wanted to discuss was her dull research. She wandered over to the bookshelf and thumbed through the titles.

"Oh."

"It's as bad as it sounds." Her finger landed on the book she had been looking for, and she extracted it from the shelf. She stared at the funny symbol that was like a tree missing branches on one side.

"It will get better. The first week is the hardest."

Cyrene flipped open the mysterious volume and saw that Elea had added a note to the inside.

ASK FOR BASILLE SELBY AT THE LAELISH.

Interesting. Well, at least she had some sort of starting point.

"So, what took you away?" Cyrene snapped the book shut and replaced it on the shelf. The journal with its strange words made her nervous all over again. She had a strange urge to hide it under the floorboard when Maelia left.

She turned back toward Maelia and found her chewing on her bottom lip, her eyes watery.

"Are you all right?"

"Yes. Sorry. I just feel so torn"—she glanced at the closed door—"between the Queen and the Consort. I probably shouldn't say anything, but I didn't know who else to talk to."

"What happened?"

"Isn't it obvious? The Queen is my Receiver. I should want to do as she orders, but the Consort has procured me to work with medicinal herbs. I find myself...drawn to the Consort and to the tasks she requests of me. Have you ever felt such a way?" Maelia's hazel eyes widened.

"Yes, I know perfectly what you are describing. Have a seat, and I'll ring for some tea."

A pang of jealousy hit Cyrene at the thought of Maelia working for the Consort, but it quickly passed. She must deserve it if she was getting the privilege.

A few minutes later, a servant woman rushed into the room with a silver tray, a still hissing teapot, and a pair of cups with matching saucers. Cyrene thanked the woman and poured her friend a spot of tea out of the kettle.

Maelia thanked her, and after letting the beverage cool, she drank warmly from the cup. Once she seemed comfortable again, she began to talk, "I was raised in a militaristic household. My parents were both in the Royal Guard. A Receiver is your commander. You follow the orders perfectly and without question. One order is no different than another."

Cyrene couldn't imagine such a life—to never question, to never feel the freedom of your life since it was constantly shaped for you.

"This world here is very different. Court is not as I expected. The Queen expects me to work as a Treasury assistant, as if I've had more than a few coppers to my name in my life."

"Maybe that's why she has trusted you with it," Cyrene offered.

Maelia softly shook her head, the wisps of her nearly white-blonde hair brushing against her youthful round face. "I don't presume to understand Queen Kaliana's agenda. And if that was the proper course, then why do I find myself enjoying my medicinal training under the guidance of Consort Daufina more than I ever have in the Treasury?"

"Well, I've wanted to travel the world my entire life, and now, I'm stuck with this." Cyrene spread her hands for Maelia to see the stacks and stacks of papers she had to dig through. "I'm not sure we are always assigned to a program that suits us completely. I think we're meant to adapt—just as you're adapting. There is nothing wrong with that."

Maelia seemed to weigh Cyrene's words as she drank more of the tea. She slightly chewed on her bottom lip in a way that made Cyrene think of Elea.

"You don't have to come to terms with it overnight," Cyrene said. She knew that it would take herself a long time to get over being relegated to the agricultural division. In fact, she wasn't sure if she would ever be okay with it. "How about we schedule a time to go see the city to take your mind off of it?"

Maelia nodded. "I'd like that."

Everyone in the castle had been given two days off before the funeral for High Order Zorian. Cyrene would have preferred to keep working on her assignment, but she and Maelia had agreed they would go into the city.

While waiting in her bedroom for Maelia before they were to leave, Cyrene removed the leather-bound book from its new hiding place under the floorboard in her bedroom. She felt uneasy about having it in her hands, but she hoped to get answers from the peddler Elea had said she had purchased it from.

Why am I able to see the words when Elea hadn't been able to? Maybe if she tried to read it, she would know what it said, and then she could go from there.

Taking a seat on the sofa in her living quarters, she opened the book on her lap. She inhaled deeply and stared down at the pretty pages. Cyrene had never seen anything like it. Something demandingly tugged at the back of her mind, but for the life of her, she didn't know what about the font was familiar. Her fears were creeping in all around her. Since Elea hadn't been able to see the words, Cyrene believed that something was…wrong with her. *What could it mean?*

Her eyes roamed the page, wondering what the secret language would unlock. Sighing, she pondered how much time she had before Maelia would show up. She probably still had twenty minutes. Cyrene shrugged and focused on trying to decipher the first sentence.

A second later, Maelia rushed into the room, breaking Cyrene's concentration. Cyrene snapped the book shut, not wanting to risk Maelia seeing it.

"Sorry I'm late," she said with a huff. "Got caught up in the corridor. Are you ready?"

Late?

Huh. Cyrene had thought she had twenty minutes. *Strange.*

Oh well.

"Yes, let's be off." She hastily placed the book in her satchel and followed Maelia out the door.

They weaved their way out of the Vines and back through the main corridors, angling toward the stable yard. As they got closer and closer to the entrance, they noticed that Affiliates clustered together. Cyrene recognized one of the girls as Jardana, but she did not know Jardana's three friends. Maelia and Cyrene shared a confused glance and moved closer to the group to listen in.

"That's right. High Order Zorian's death wasn't an accident. It was murder!" Jardana exclaimed.

"But who do they think did it?" another Affiliate asked.

"The Queen wants everyone to know they are perfectly safe, and they will figure all this mess out, but I know they took in High Order Ahlvie for questioning. He was the one who found the body."

Ahlvie? No, that didn't make sense. He had helped her when she came out of her warrior ceremony. Then again, he'd had blood splattered on him, and his clothes had been cut apart.

She blanched at the thought.

Cyrene pulled Maelia away from the other Affiliates.

"What do you think about High Order Zorian's murder?" Maelia asked.

"I don't know. I was with Ahlvie that night," Cyrene admitted.

"What? You were?"

"Yes. He showed me how to get to my rooms. I never suspected—"

"You have to tell someone, Cyrene!"

Cyrene sighed. "Do you think so? I wasn't involved."

"But what if he brings it up?"

"Then, if I'm brought in to answer questions about it, I'll answer honestly, of course. I hope it was all an accident," Cyrene said as they reached the stable yard.

"Me, too. The Royal Guard always said that death was an unfortunate necessity that should never be taken lightly. I pray the Creator carries Zorian's soul peacefully from this life." Her friend's cheeks flushed.

Cyrene nodded. "As She always does."

Still, she wondered what was happening to Ahlvie if he was being accused of murdering Zorian. A gut instinct told her that he hadn't done it, and she always relied on that instinct. *But what do I really know about Ahlvie anyway?*

The sun beat down on them as they took Cyrene's horses out of the castle stable yard and into the city. Maelia borrowed her chestnut-brown horse, Astral, while Cyrene took her gray dapple, Ceffy. The pair trotted leisurely out of the castle gates and onto the cobble path that led into the inner city.

Cyrene weaved them down the main path, passing First Class stone houses along the way. She pointed out some of the large stone homes, like her parents', that housed the wealthiest citizens among them. The houses became smaller and more tightly packed together as they neared the second tier of the city. The crowds grew dense, pushing Maelia closer to Cyrene. Then, they entered the main road, and the path widened considerably.

"This is Broad Street, our largest avenue to the Laelish Market," Cyrene said.

Guards strode by them. Their leather breastplates were ablaze with the Dremylon golden flames, a scripted D lying across their hearts, and steel blades with a matching emblem hung at their sides. Women and men alike called out to each other in passing, dragging their children behind them while keeping them from dipping their hands in candy booths. Giant signs announced inns and taverns.

Cyrene guided their horses behind the well-established Winespring Inn, a sturdy-looking stone building with a waterfall of wine displayed on the hanging sign out front. She tossed the stableman a few copper coins to take care of their horses.

Once the boy had a hold of Astral's and Ceffy's reins, the girls left the stable and walked back to Broad Street. Their first destination was a simple two-story house off the main stretch. No decorative sign hung from the doorway. No welcoming host burst from the entrance upon their arrival.

Cyrene walked up the small staircase to the main door of the building and knocked twice. Not more than a minute later, a woman appeared at the door and frowned when she saw Cyrene.

"What are you doing here, girl?" Lady Cauthorn asked.

"I've come for a commission, of course," Cyrene said. "Lady Cauthorn, this is Affiliate Maelia. Maelia, this is my seamstress, Lady Cauthorn."

"How do you do?" Maelia said.

"Yes. Yes. Fine. Come in then."

The girls followed Lady Cauthorn into a sitting room. An assistant hurried in with a pot of tea and some tarts from the kitchen.

"Tell me about this commission."

"I've made a list," Cyrene said.

She retrieved a sheet of parchment from her bag and handed it to the seamstress, who read through the items listed.

Cyrene wanted eight new gowns—one ball gown in the same design as her Presenting attire, three everyday silk dresses with embroidery, two dresses in a sturdy cotton wool, and two riding habits with divided skirts. She had told the King she would commission a new wardrobe, and she would see it would be done.

"Fine," Lady Cauthorn said after a moment. "I require half payment up front. I'll have it all completed in four months."

"Can you not do it any faster?"

"Eight new gowns, and four are in silks with full embroidery." Lady Cauthorn ticked off on her fingers. "You'll be lucky if it's done in three."

Maelia's mouth dropped open. "What do you need all of that for, Cyrene?"

Cyrene didn't want to tell Maelia her reasoning just yet—that she was doing it in part because of the King and in part because she wanted practical riding gear in case she was able to travel. Neither was something she could impart on someone she had only recently met.

"I know you can do it faster. I want them for court. I need to make an impression," Cyrene said. "Six weeks."

"Cyrene," Maelia hissed.

Lady Cauthorn shook her head. "Only for you, girl. Just don't forget that favor."

Cyrene swallowed and nodded. She hadn't forgotten, but the look on Lady Cauthorn's face made her pause. *How much will I regret the promise of these favors?*

"I haven't forgotten."

"Good. Then, six weeks will be feasible for all, except for the ball gown. It will have to suffice for that to come after."

"I understand. Thank you."

She heard Lady Cauthorn mutter some unsavory comments as she and Maelia exited the house, but Cyrene ignored them. She had gotten what she wanted after all.

Cyrene and Maelia walked back to Broad Street and then approached the entrance to the Laelish Market. An inner and outer circle of multicolored booths was compactly pressed together, and patrons busied themselves in the densely populated location. Objects of various sizes, shapes, and functions rested on tables, sat in carts, and dangled from overhangs that blocked the sun. The royal banner hung from a tall flagpole at the center of the market. The smell of freshly caught fish hit their nostrils along with the sweat of the horde surrounding them. Summer was already beating down, and the heat radiating off the Fallen Desert carried through the city.

They picked their way through the crowds, stopping at nearly every shop along the way. All the while, Cyrene searched for Basille Selby, the merchant Elea had claimed sold her the mysterious book.

Cyrene walked by a couple discussing the merits of various types of tea leaves when someone brushed against her shoulder. She turned quickly to make sure no one had tried to pickpocket her, but she didn't see anyone suspicious. She checked her bag, and everything was still there. As she started walking again, someone whispered something to her, but she couldn't quite decipher it. She pivoted but found no one close enough to her.

What in the Creator's name?

Pushing past a group of Carharan merchants waving jewelry at her, she heard the whisper one more time. Like an idiot, she did a full circle in the middle of the market.

Nothing.

Something about this felt...wrong. It made the hairs on the back of her neck stand on end, and her pulse quickened. She suddenly didn't feel safe being out in the market with Maelia while a murderer was on the loose. Maybe it wasn't safe outside of court after all.

"Maelia"—Cyrene caught her arm when she came out of the next tent—"I feel like...someone is following me."

Maelia's eyes widened to saucers. "Do you want to go?"

Cyrene looked around at the crowd one more time, but she still didn't see anyone. "I just need to look at one more tent."

"All right. I'll wait for you in this one then."

Cyrene nodded and then checked out one of the last canopies in a hurry.

"Excuse me," she anxiously called out.

A rather bulky man with scars on his almost leathery tan hands and arms was seated in a chair. He had streaks of gray touching his temples, but his eyes were ever vigilant.

"Hello. Sorry to disturb you, but I was looking for Basille Selby. Do you know him?"

"Was it ta ya?" he drawled in his thick Eleysian accent.

"Master Selby recently sold me a book, and I had a few questions about it."

"He won't take returns if tha's wha' you're af'er."

"No, no, I don't want to return the book. I wish to speak with him."

"He ain' here. He went ta Levin. Said da pickin's good," the man said.

"Do you know when he will return?"

He shrugged. "Coupa weeks. He say he be back when he be back."

"Wonderful," Cyrene murmured dryly. "Thank you for your assistance."

As she left, she tried to be relieved that she hadn't come back empty-handed. She was determined to return to meet Basille Selby as soon as she could, and hopefully, she would receive some answers about this damn book.

"Find anything?" Maelia asked when Cyrene reappeared.

"Not a thing. Ready to go?"

With excited eyes, Maelia glanced around the market once more, soaking it in, and then she nodded.

The girls retrieved their horses and then trotted back onto the castle grounds.

As soon as Cyrene handed over the reins to a stable hand, a guard appeared before them.

"Affiliate Cyrene?"

"Yes," she said, stepping forward.

"King Edric requests to speak with you."

"What is this in regard to?" she asked. Anxiety hit her in the stomach.

"High Order Zorian's murder," he said. "Please follow me."

Cyrene saw that Maelia's shocked features mirrored her own. The guard had confirmed what they had heard earlier today.

Murder.

The
ACCUSATION

"HONESTLY, YOUR MAJESTY, DO YOU THINK I'M AN IDIOT?"
Ahlvie asked in exasperation.

King Edric sighed and turned his head away from Ahlvie. He
impatiently tapped his foot. Frustration was written on every line
of his face.

Prince Kael simply looked ready to punch Ahlvie in the face.
That, at least, Ahlvie could handle. He had been in fistfights before.

However, this absurd accusation about Zorian…well, Ahlvie
wasn't sure what to do about it, except continue to rebuff them.

"Yes. Yes, we do," Prince Kael grumbled.

He stalked across the room and slammed his hands down on
the sides of Ahlvie's chair. His blue-gray eyes were menacing, but
Ahlvie laughed in his face.

"Find something funny?"

"This whole situation actually."

"Zorian was a good man, and now, he's dead because of you."

"Kael," King Edric said sharply, "that's enough. We need
proof before we can incriminate High Order Ahlvie."

Prince Kael shoved away from Ahlvie. "He brought Zorian in.
He has no alibi, and a servant found his clothes bloody and torn.
How much more evidence do we need, Edric?"

Ahlvie raised a finger to interject. "I have an alibi."

King Edric dragged his hand down his face. "Let's start at the
beginning, Ahlvie. Where were you last night? Who were you with?
What were you doing?"

"Like I said before, I went out on the town, as I do on most other nights. I left through the side exit by the High Order quarters around midnight. Two guards saw me leave—Maurus and Brenner. I was at the Howling Raven, dicing and meeting a lady I fancy. You can speak to people there to confirm that."

"Yes, we'll send someone down there," King Edric said.

"Anyway, a man accused me of cheating."

"Were you?" Prince Kael interjected.

Ahlvie shot them a toothy grin. "I would never."

Prince Kael blew out his breath. "Right."

"Continue," King Edric said.

"All right. We got into a fight. He pulled a knife on me, which explains the condition of my clothes. I returned late through the gate, and then I passed out in the stables."

"Can anyone attest to where you were you left the Howling Raven until you reported finding Zorian?" King Edric asked.

Ahlvie sighed and sank further in his seat. "This whole thing is insane. I've been at court for over a year. Why would I suddenly start killing off people now?"

"That's what we're trying to figure out," Prince Kael said. He crossed his arms and stared down his nose at Ahlvie.

"If I killed a guy, do you think I'd be stupid enough to bring forward the evidence? I made it into First Class because I'm a genius." He cracked a smug smile. "I wouldn't suddenly slip up and do something this moronic. Whoever killed Zorian was either sloppy or wanted to be found."

"Exactly what the killer would say," Prince Kael said.

"You're wasting your time!" Ahlvie cried.

He leaned forward in his chair and rested his elbows on his knees. He didn't care how long they kept him in here. He wasn't going to suddenly confess to a murder that he hadn't committed. He didn't think the King even believed that he had done it. They just needed someone to pin it on.

"We might be," King Edric conceded. "But first, answer the question. Did you see anyone else after you supposedly left for the stables?"

"Okay. Fine. Yes, I saw that new Affiliate. What's her name?"

"Cyrene?" King Edric and Prince Kael asked nearly at once.

"That's the one."

Their eyes met, and something passed between them. If Ahlvie didn't know better, he'd say it was almost…jealousy. But while the Prince bedded nearly every Affiliate who walked, the King normally steered clear of them. Ahlvie wondered if they'd be looking at each other like that now if they had seen the drowned rat wandering around the stable yard before he had helped her.

"What was she doing out on the night of her Presenting?" King Edric asked. His hands fisted at his sides, and he blatantly ignored the hard stare from his brother.

Ahlvie shrugged and analyzed the two of them with interest. "No idea. I didn't ask questions. Just helped her back to her rooms, changed my clothes, talked to Reeve for a minute, and then left."

"High Order Reeve? Cyrene's brother?" King Edric asked.

"Yeah, sure."

The King sighed heavily. "We'll have to bring them both in to confirm this. Kael, have a guard bring them in and send someone down to the Howling Raven to inquire about Ahlvie's dicing."

The Prince glared at his brother's command, but he left the room without a word.

"Let's hope that all of this holds up," King Edric said to Ahlvie candidly.

"What good would it do for me to lie?"

"*That* is an excellent question and one I intend to get an answer to."

The
QUESTIONING

CYRENE TRUDGED BEHIND THE GUARD. AS SOON AS SHE had overheard Jardana talking about how Ahlvie was somehow involved in the death of High Order Zorian, Cyrene had known she was going to get summoned.

It was by complete chance that she had found Ahlvie in the stables that morning. She had been so happy when he offered to help her back to her rooms after her warrior ceremony. It was hard to believe the man who had vomited at her feet from intoxication would have had enough coherence or forethought to murder someone. He seemed an unlikely candidate, but she would wait to pass judgment after hearing what he had told the King.

The guard finally stopped in front of a plain wooden door where two more guards stood in position. "Here you are, Affiliate." He opened the door and leaned inside. "Affiliate Cyrene has arrived."

"Let her in," King Edric called.

The guard creaked open the door the rest of the way and allowed her to pass. Cyrene entered a rectangular room bare of decoration, save for a few hard wooden chairs and a small square window.

The King sat regally, facing a lone chair. Prince Kael stood against the far wall. He followed her every move as she glided inside and curtsied.

"Your Majesties."

"Affiliate Cyrene," King Edric said with a broad smile.

His blue-gray eyes rested on her face, and her heart lurched. *How can I be so nervous about the investigation and still have this electricity surge up through me at his nearness?*

"Cyrene," Prince Kael said.

She startled at the familiar tone, and her eyes darted to his face. His lips were pressed into a firm line, but he perused her face with an intimacy that was unsettling.

She returned her attention to King Edric.

He gestured in front of him. "Please take a seat. This shouldn't take too long."

Cyrene crossed the room and sank into the seat facing the King. She crossed her feet at her ankles and lightly rested her hands in her lap. She wanted to look relaxed, not as stressed as she felt.

King Edric began speaking, "We want to ease your mind about the circumstances. We are just going to ask you a few questions regarding your whereabouts since you've become an Affiliate."

"Okay," she said uncertainly.

"Do you mind telling us where you were the night and morning after your Presenting ball?" King Edric asked.

She peeked up at Prince Kael and then down at her clasped hands. Her cheeks heated. She tried desperately not to think about the Prince escorting her back to her room and pressing her up against the wall with his lips and hands on her, but it only made her think about it more.

King Edric's eyes moved from Cyrene to Prince Kael and then back to her. She swallowed and ignored the Prince's smirk.

The door burst open in that moment, saving her from answering.

"Edric!" Queen Kaliana cried.

"Kaliana?" the King said, his voice holding a hint of confusion.

All traces that the Queen had rushed over here out of nowhere were wiped from her face as she flowed into the room. "I'm here for the questioning of the Affiliate as I'm sure you were not going to do it without her Receiver present," Queen Kaliana said.

She sank effortlessly into the seat next to King Edric, who looked nonplussed at her appearance.

"Edric would never do anything without speaking with you first," Prince Kael said with enough sarcasm to make Queen Kaliana narrow her eyes at him.

King Edric cut in, "We had simply asked Affiliate Cyrene about her whereabouts the night and morning after of her Presenting."

"Yes, Affiliate, do tell us where you were," Prince Kael prodded.

Cyrene wanted to glare at Prince Kael, but she held her composure. She couldn't seem frazzled. It was even more pressing now that the Queen was there.

"After my Presenting ball, I returned to my rooms to sleep. I was awoken in the middle of the night and went through the warrior ceremony."

The royalty before her stiffened.

"The warrior ceremony?" King Edric asked cautiously.

"Um…yes," she said. "I was left on a platform in the underground lake and had to find a way to escape."

"Kaliana," the King snapped. He glared at her with open disdain. "You said they had stopped."

"I'll take care of it," she whispered.

"I won't have any more of these pranks taking place," he told her.

"I said I'd take care of it."

"Good," he said dismissively.

Cyrene tried to remain outwardly calm throughout what had just occurred. *But had they honestly said that what I had gone through was nothing more than a prank?*

"A prank?" she asked in disbelief.

"Other High Order and Affiliates have been known to play tricks on each other on the night of their Presenting. It's almost an initiation into their ranks," the King explained.

I could have died that night! All for a stupid prank. Just thinking about it made her blood boil.

"I see."

"My apologies, Affiliate. Please continue with your story," King Edric said.

"Of course," Cyrene said, covering up her frustration. Then, she recounted the tale of how she'd found Ahlvie in the stable yard, the state of his attire, and how he helped her home.

"Yes, but why did he do that?" Queen Kaliana asked. "He could have just helped you with the hopes that he would have someone to act as an alibi after he'd already committed the murder."

"Pardon, Your Highness, but if you had seen the state of his intoxication, then you would not think he would have had the forethought to use me for that. Not to mention, I had been there entirely by chance."

"But," Queen Kaliana said, facing the King, "she confirmed the state of his dress, including the blood on him, and that she wasn't there the whole time. He could have killed Zorian the night before and then pretended to find him the next morning."

King Edric listened to his Queen without a word and then turned back to Cyrene. "What do you think, Affiliate?" he asked.

Cyrene swallowed. King Edric was asking for her opinion on the matter. Queen Kaliana looked at her in a manner that said Cyrene had better agree with her, and Prince Kael stared at her as if she were a puzzle he was trying to figure out how to put together.

"To be honest, I can't see how Ahlvie had anything to do with this. The evidence is circumstantial at best. Ahlvie and I are only recently acquainted, but I don't think the killer would have brought forward the body."

Queen Kaliana raised her nose in disagreement, but the King just nodded.

"Without more evidence, I'm going to have to agree with you. Thank you for your time, Affiliate. Hopefully, this case will be closed before High Order Zorian's funeral."

Cyrene took that as her cue to go, and she hurried out of the room. She had only made it a few steps before she heard someone following her. She turned around and nearly jumped out of her skin.

"Why are you following me?" she snapped before she could think better of holding in her temper.

"I simply came to make sure you were all right," Prince Kael said with that devious smile. "It's not every day you're involved in a murder investigation."

She shivered. "I'm quite all right. Thank you."

He took a step closer until he was speaking only for her ears despite the fact that they were nearly alone in the corridor, "Why have you not heeded my advice?"

"Your advice?" She arched an eyebrow in question.

"You left the grounds. You went into the city when you knew it was not safe."

Cyrene took a step back. "How do you know that?"

"I'm well-informed on what goes on in and out of the castle."

"Did you have me followed?" she demanded. *Did I scare myself in the Laelish Market over nothing?*

He smirked but ignored her question. "Just stay in the court like a good little Affiliate," he said, patting her shoulder.

She slapped his hand away from her, but he just laughed.

That was answer enough. He'd had someone follow her in the market. She couldn't believe it. No wonder she had felt like someone was watching her. *Someone had been watching me!*

Before she could say anything else, he retreated to the investigation room where the King and Queen still remained. Cyrene shook her head in disbelief at her afternoon. She just hoped that, after today, she could put this whole messy business behind her.

Rain fell in sheets on the High Order and Affiliates congregated in front of the gravesite outside of the castle grounds. Cyrene had the hood of her cloak held high as she shivered in the downpour. Maelia stood at her side in the crowd. She was even paler than normal and kept clutching at her cloak.

King Edric had announced the night before the funeral that the killer had not been located and anyone with news of Zorian's death should step forward. She wondered what had become of Ahlvie—if they were still holding him or if he had been let go.

As a holy official intoned sacred language over Zorian's body, her mind kept slipping back to the night of her warrior ceremony. She hated second-guessing herself. Ahlvie had been in a poor state, but she didn't want to think that someone she had trusted could have done this.

A brush at her elbow made her jump, pulling her out of her thoughts. She turned to find that no one occupied the empty space, and she narrowed her eyes in confusion.

Cyrene took a step closer to Maelia and tried to tune back into the ceremony.

"The Creator shine down on…"

Another brush made her heart stutter. No one was moving around her. It was as if the person flowed through the water-streaked shadows.

"Don't fight."

She shivered and inclined her head to the left where the voice had come from. It had been just a faint whisper, but the voice made her skin crawl. Taking a deep breath, she waited a heartbeat before looking to see if there was anyone nearby. Nothing moved, but it felt she could feel eyes on her from a distance.

She shook her head, realizing she was just chasing ghosts. With all the talk of death swirling around Zorian's untimely demise, she was simply scaring herself. It was probably the person Kael had sent to follow her in the Laelish Market. That was the reason she felt like she had eyes on her, and the whisper had been a figment of her imagination.

How could I possibly hear a whisper over the sound of the rain beating down on me?

She took another step to her right anyway until her cloak was brushing against Maelia, so she could feel the safety and security of another body near hers.

Cyrene spent the remainder of the ceremony with her head bowed, speaking to the Creator to bring Zorian peace and ignoring the tingling feeling on the back of her neck.

At the end of the service, the crowd dispersed down the path over the mountainside, heading toward the castle.

Someone grasped her cloak, and she nearly jumped out of her skin.

"Easy, Affiliate," a voice said softly. "A little tense?"

She breathed out in relief that she hadn't made up someone touching her. "Ahlvie."

"At your service."

"I am a bit jumpy. I did just come from a funeral."

His hood was covering most of his face, but she could see him nodding in understanding. "Thank you."

"For what?"

"I know you told them that you didn't think I did it."

"I simply told them what I believed was the truth."

"Not many others would have done that. So…thank you."

AFFILIATE

He stormed off then, and she was left to wonder about him. *Did I just make another friend? Is he a friend I'll come to regret having?*

The
RESEARCH

WITH ALL THE COMMOTION AROUND HIGH ORDER Zorian's death, Cyrene had had little time to work on her Affiliate studies. So, she fell headlong into Affiliate Lorne's papers while still attending to court duties, feast days, and appointments with the Queen. After another week of slaving over the agricultural materials, Cyrene pushed the papers away from her in frustration. There was still so much to do, but her brain was turning to mush.

Walking into her bedroom, she loosened the floorboard that hid her Presenting letter and the book Elea had given to her on her birthday. She grasped the sheaf of paper and reread the note. Aralyn had said Cyrene could speak to other Affiliates about the letter if need be. Maybe it was time to pay her a visit.

Cyrene strode out of her room and then navigated the Vines until she found her sister's room. She rapped on the door twice and waited. After several minutes, Aralyn opened the door. Her brown hair fell forward in front of her face as she stared at a book.

"Can I help you?" she mumbled.

"Aralyn, it's Cyrene," she said, trying to attract her sister's attention.

"Oh, yes, Cyrene. Come in. Was I expecting you?" Not even looking up at Cyrene, Aralyn just left the door open and retreated back inside.

"All right," Cyrene grumbled, following her, "you weren't expecting me, but I wanted to pay you a visit."

"Lovely."

"Aralyn"—Cyrene waved her hand in the air—"can I have five minutes here?"

Aralyn sighed and then glanced up at Cyrene. "Sure. What is it?"

Cyrene withdrew the Presenting paper and handed it to her sister. "I was wondering if you could help me with this. It's my Presenting letter."

"Let me take a look." Aralyn opened the paper and read through the contents. She bit out a harsh laugh. "This is gibberish, Cyrene. Don't waste your time on it."

"What?" Cyrene gasped. "You were the one who told me it was important."

Aralyn handed back the paper. "It was part of a script I was given. I found nothing of use in my letter. You should focus on your Affiliate duties."

"So, you won't help?"

"There's nothing to help, Cyrene. If you must investigate this, go dig through the library, but you're wasting your time."

"Fine," Cyrene snapped.

She stuffed the paper back into her bag and stormed from the room. She couldn't believe that Aralyn had just laughed at her after telling her how important it was in her Presenting. Cyrene knew there was something to these letters.

Cyrene left the Vines in search of the library. She had been inside the archives at the center of the castle several times, but she'd only looked at the agricultural volumes.

Her head swam with ideas as she walked in through the enormous circular doorframe. Filling the room, hundreds of rows several stories high were full of books stacked as far as the eye could see. It smelled like old leather, musty paper, and aging ink. She breathed in the aroma and then decided to start looking through Presenting materials.

After an hour of wasted time, she got more creative and looked up riddles and their interpretations, deciphering meaning from the text. The whole time, she wondered if Rhea had decrypted anything about her Presenting letter while she'd been in Albion. Cyrene had received no word from her friend, but she hadn't sent any word either.

At least the King was preparing himself for the procession traveling to Albion, which meant she would get to see her best friend again soon. *Hopefully, I'll find some answers by then.*

"Not finding them now," she grumbled to herself as she slammed another massive volume back onto the shelf.

With a sigh, she left the stacks and went in search of an Affiliate. Perhaps someone could point her in the right direction.

She walked up to the first woman she found and smiled at the familiar face. "Affiliate Leslin," she said in greeting to the woman behind the massive desk.

Leslin had been with Aralyn the night of Cyrene's Presenting ball.

"Ah, Cyrene." Leslin smiled up over her work. Her hair was frazzled, and she had an ink spot across the bridge of her nose and another on her dress. "Hello. How can I help you?"

"I am doing some research on Presenting letters and their interpretations. Do you happen to know where I could start? Or maybe, do you know who writes them, so I can speak with him or her?"

Leslin smiled pleasantly. "All the Presenting letter information we have is in aisle seventy-six, section three thousand forty. We always have new Affiliates and High Order coming in and asking questions about them. As for who writes them, it is an Elder of the First Class who was once a High Order or Affiliate. However, no audience is permitted with the Elder. Would you like me to look over your letter to help you with it?"

The letter in her bag was like a brick weighing her down. She didn't feel right showing it to Leslin after Aralyn had just laughed at her. "No, thank you. I'll keep looking."

"Let me know if you change your mind. I'm going to be on holiday for a short time to visit my daughter in the countryside, so I won't be in the castle for a bit."

Leslin's eyes narrowed considerably, and her otherwise pleasant faced turned sour. "I'm in desperate need of a holiday, what with a murderer walking in our midst."

Cyrene turned to see what she was talking about and saw Ahlvie striding into the library. She pursed her lips at Leslin's reaction. Ahlvie hadn't been convicted of anything. King Edric had let him go, but Leslin was judging Ahlvie based on an accusation.

He nodded his head at Cyrene when he noticed her and then looked at Leslin. His smile turned mischievous, and his youth showed through. He might have even been handsome, if he didn't look like he was going to cause trouble.

"Hi ya, Leslie!"

"It's Affiliate Leslin, High Order Ahlvie. There is an *n* attached, as I have told you the last hundred times you set foot in my library. What do you want?"

"Oh, Leslin. Right," he said as if he hadn't already known. "Just swinging by to get some more books."

"What did you do with the other ones you borrowed?" she demanded.

"I read them," he said, giving her a blank look.

Cyrene stifled a laugh behind her hand. Ahlvie flashed Leslin another grin, but Leslin just scowled at him. Cyrene saw this going poorly.

"Are you ever going to bring them back?" Leslin asked.

"I suppose—at least the ones that I didn't lose." He shrugged nonchalantly.

"Lose?" she cried. "Those books are invaluable. You...you...you man! It's not enough to act like a drunken fool in my library and then murder a High Order. Now, you *lose* books?"

Ahlvie scrunched his eyebrows together. He looked bemused, but there was also a touch of anger at the accusation that he had been cleared of. "I never murdered anyone. It was only an investigation," he reminded her. "And, hey, I'm not drunk now!"

Leslin pointed her finger to the door. "Get out of my library."

"What? It doesn't *belong* to you. I'm here on High Order business."

"Get out!" She stood and hit her hand on the desk. "And don't come back until you bring back the books you lost, or else do not return *at all.*"

Cyrene's eyes widened at Leslin's outburst.

Ahlvie ran his hand back through his hair. "Is this all because I called you Leslie?" His eyes twinkled.

"Out!"

Ahlvie shrugged and started walking backward. "Fine. I'm out of here. Crazy old loon."

Leslin sank into her chair once more and covered her head with her hands.

"Are you all right?" Cyrene asked.

She thought that Leslin had been harsh with Ahlvie, but perhaps she was just on edge from the murder. Ahlvie hadn't helped anything by needling her.

"Yes. I simply need that holiday," she said.

Cyrene nodded at Leslin as if she understood, but her eyes were fixed on Ahlvie's retreating form. For once, she felt a twinge of pity for the man everyone dismissed as a drunk.

The
ROSE GARDEN

"FEAST DAYS ARE SO MUCH LESS OVERWHELMING THAN A Presenting ball," Cyrene said.

A few hours after her encounter with Ahlvie and Leslin in the library, Cyrene's hand was wrapped around a goblet full of wine. The black marble ballroom was lit with a thousand candles floating in chandeliers above the room. Affiliates and High Order were dancing to the sounds of the string quartet while Cyrene and Maelia stood apart from the group near the enormous fireplace.

"I danced with no one my entire Presenting ball," Maelia told her with a bitter laugh.

"You still dance with no one," Cyrene reminded her.

"You're not much better. The last three balls, you've danced with no one but a few suitors and the King himself. How terrible to be in your position." Maelia pressed her hand to her forehead as if she were going to faint.

Cyrene wanted to tell her that was only because she had been avoiding Prince Kael at every turn, but she had yet to tell Maelia of the events that had occurred. Cyrene wasn't sure how much longer she could evade him.

The King was another matter though. He rarely danced more than once or twice with anyone, save his Queen and Consort, of whom he divided his time equally. Maelia seemed to think he always chose Cyrene for the longest dances because he favored her, but she wasn't sure she believed that. She wasn't sure she wanted to believe that.

"I've no idea what you're talking about. I have no suitors, and I have received no extra attention from the King."

Maelia giggled and then pointed across the dance floor. "As if plucked from the heavens at your request. Who knew you were lucky enough to receive a third dance tonight?"

Cyrene followed Maelia's gaze to the King striding dutifully in their direction. His figure was draped in the finest black velvet shirt with bridged sleeves. His riding boots covered his snug-fitting black pants up to his knees. A forest-green cloak tumbled off one shoulder and reached nearly to the floor. It was held in place around the neck by a heavy chain of gold square links with the royal seal artfully designed into each piece.

He was handsome, frustrating, desirous, stubborn, and most of all, dangerous. His presence put her on edge. One moment, she would feel an electric pull toward him, completely forgetting his rank, and treat the King just like anyone else. The next, she would realize her mistakes, remember that he was the King, and have to quell her biting tongue. It was a never-ending battle to please.

"Affiliate Cyrene," King Edric said with a charming smile, "I hope the feast day is to your liking."

"My King," she murmured, bobbing a curtsy. "It is most enjoyable as always. You do remember my good friend Affiliate Maelia, yes?"

"Yes, of course," Edric said, making a poor show of acting like he remembered Maelia.

He had been introduced to her more than a handful of times, and still, he couldn't seem to place her. Something about her made everyone pass over her, even in plain sight.

To her credit, Maelia dipped a curtsy, honoring the King's station, as she pretended that she did not care that the King never noticed her. "Your Highness."

Cyrene prepared herself for the oncoming invitation to dance. She had already danced with the King twice tonight, and she was sure this would draw more notice from Queen Kaliana.

"Would you do me the honor of taking a walk with me?" King Edric asked.

Cyrene's mouth opened ever so slightly. *A walk?* That was so much more intimate than a dance as they would be away from the rest of court. She felt the King's gaze on her as he waited for her response—as if she could reasonably turn him down, as if she would want to.

"I'd be delighted, Your Majesty."

He extended his arm, and she touched her hand to the inside of his sleeve. Cyrene's heart fluttered, and she was having difficulty keeping her breathing even. A request to walk and have a private audience with the King—unencumbered by the dance, the music, and other prying eyes and ears—made her giddy. Maybe Maelia was right. Maybe the King did favor Cyrene after all.

The King slowly maneuvered them off the marble floor and out onto the gray-and-black stone balcony overlooking the inner courtyard. Byern climbing vines corkscrewed around the stone columns and up the handrail of the spiral staircase. Rows of fully grown apple trees lined the exterior of the castle. Bushes bursting with roses—white, yellow, orange, red, purple, blue, and even a minty green that nearly blended into the leaves—threaded along the pebbled pathway. In the large circular courtyard, a giant sculptured fountain stood as the centerpiece, its water flowing freely from the mouth of some stunning sea nymph.

"Do you enjoy the view?" King Edric asked.

"The rains have made the gardens bloom, and it warms my heart to see it so."

"It is good to know that the gardener approves of the work."

Cyrene laughed lightly. "I have not gardened in a month's time. I fear I can no longer call myself a gardener."

She remembered when she had told the King of her interest in gardening at the last feast day almost a week ago. After that dance, Queen Kaliana had added a list of plants to Cyrene's assignment, forcing her to reread every page she had already dredged through for information. It had wasted two entire days.

"Perhaps I could change that," he offered.

He directed her down the staircase and into the courtyard lit solely by the setting sun in the distance.

Her stomach churned at the thought of him offering assistance to any of her needs. It was like what she had read in her children's books of the tales of Leifs and how one request would necessitate a much larger sacrifice. Her biggest sacrifice at the present moment was time. She wanted nothing more than to finish her work on agriculture and prove that she should get moved somewhere that involved traveling and adventure.

"On the contrary, My King, I am fully enthralled in my Affiliate duties, and I believe that gardening would only distract me from my work."

"You cannot spare one afternoon to spend in my gardens?" His blue-gray eyes searched her face. "If you have half the green thumb you suggested, then it would be delightful to have you on the grounds."

She swallowed. "I really have much work to accomplish before we go on the procession."

"I could speak to the Queen and request it to be lessened," he whispered into the evening air.

It was the first time he had ever admitted to discussing her with the Queen. Hearing him say it aloud made her voice come out strangled. "No!"

Cyrene missed her footing on the pebbled path and stumbled forward a pace. Edric steadied her. He turned his body to face her in the middle of the garden, and her breath caught at the sight of him in the setting sun.

"You do not wish for me to speak with the Queen?"

"I spoke out of turn. Please forgive me."

"I cannot forgive that which I do not understand. Has the Queen somehow offended you?"

Cyrene shook her head. "I fear that the Queen does not... like me."

Edric laughed softly, taking one of her hands in his own. "Oh, Cyrene, I believe that the Queen likes no one but herself."

Cyrene found that she, too, could laugh at his comment.

"Now, tell me what the Queen has done to make you believe that she dislikes you."

"It's nothing, My King." She turned her face away from his. She couldn't possibly tell him the real reason.

"It's enough to infuriate you, which is enough for me."

When she looked back up into his blue-gray eyes, she felt that same magnetic pull between them. Somehow, she had not realized how close they were standing to one another. His hand felt warm against her bare skin. His body was only a few inches away from hers. His breath was hot on her face.

Her heart contracted in her chest, but she forced herself to respond, "She speaks of...of your interference...as if...as if you..."

Time stretched between them, and for a split second, she thought he might move even closer to her. She was rooted in place, captivated by his gaze.

"Yes?"

His other hand drifted to her waist, and she was suddenly on fire.

Their breaths mingled together as she murmured, "As if you favor me."

"And do you think that?"

"I..."

"Yes?" he asked, stepping closer.

She couldn't breathe. He was so close. His fingers tugged her body toward him. She felt the hard contours of his chest through her thin dress. His head tilted downward, and she rose up ever so slightly on to the tips of her toes, arching up to him. Her gaze landed on his lips, and she knew any second that something was going to happen that she could never reverse.

"Cyrene," he whispered, their lips nearly touching, "do you think that I favor you?"

Her eyes fluttered closed, but she couldn't keep the words from spilling from her lips. "I think you have Your Queen."

The spell was broken. King Edric took a step back, and Cyrene quickly found the roses incredibly interesting.

She couldn't believe what had just happened. *Had the King been about to...kiss me? Had I been about to let him?* It seemed unfathomable.

"I shall refrain from commenting about you to Her Majesty again," he said coolly. "If you believe that will make your life easier."

"Thank you, Your Majesty," she said. Her heart was still beating out of her chest. She was sure he could hear it. "I believe it will."

King Edric let the silence lapse between them as he directed her back along the rose-lined path.

As they ascended the spiral staircase to return to the party, he stopped her. "Affiliate Cyrene."

She looked up at his beautiful unlined face, strong jawline with a five o'clock shadow, dark hair cut short, and shining blue-gray eyes. This feeling blooming between them was dangerous, but she didn't know how to stop it.

"Yes, My King?"

"I'd prefer for you to call me Edric."

Cyrene's cheeks heated. She couldn't believe the King wanted her to use his given name.

"Of course…Edric."

He smiled down at her once more before escorting her into the ballroom.

Cyrene walked to where Maelia still stood beside the fireplace in a haze. Maelia had a million questions about her foray into the courtyard with the King. The court was buzzing with rumors and speculations about what had happened, some as good as idle conversation and others as bad as copulation.

"Copulation?" Cyrene asked, shaking her head. "Honestly."

"Well, what happened?" Maelia asked.

"We walked around the rose garden and talked about how I enjoy gardening. Positively boring."

Cyrene knew that she was glowing from the encounter, but she was too happy to care at the moment.

"Right," Maelia said, unconvinced.

When they reached their rooms in the Vines, Maelia finally stopped badgering Cyrene for answers.

After entering her room and undressing to her shift, Cyrene fell into an easy slumber. She dreamed peacefully of dancing with Edric in an empty ballroom as he told her to use his given name, brandishing it like a caress.

16

The
HISTORY

CYRENE AWOKE IN A DAZE. WHEN SHE OPENED HER EYES, her head pounded, and her vision blurred. She lifted herself out of bed and then plopped back down. A wave of nausea crashed over her.

What is wrong with me? She certainly hadn't had enough to drink last night to feel like this.

Tingles traveled up her arms, starting at her fingers, as if they had been asleep and were now waking up. The tingles turned into pinpricks, and then the stabbing pain moved from her arms to her chest, down her stomach, and to her legs, like a wave washing over her skin. She gasped when it finally passed, and she breathed in the wet stale air.

Her eyes flew open.

Wet stale air?

Her rooms were in the interior division of the castle, and there was nothing wet about being encased in a mountain. She eased into a sitting position, the dizziness slowly subsiding. Cyrene couldn't see anything in the pitch-black room. She just felt the small bed beneath her. Swinging her feet over the edge, she landed on soft compact earth.

What in the Creator's name?

Is this another test? Edric had been clear that he didn't want any more pranks. Her nerves prickled. *Am I not supposed to have said anything? Are the masks punishing me for getting them in trouble about the ceremony?*

She hardly cared about what might have happened to the people who had done that to her. They deserved their punishment, but she didn't want retaliation—or worse—for speaking up.

Plus, Zorian's death was only a couple of weeks behind her. At the thought of this being another attack, the hairs on the back of her neck stood on end.

She noticed a slit of light across the room. She rushed to the wall and felt along the stone until she found a door handle.

She took a deep breath, turned the knob, and pulled. Expecting some kind of resistance, she yanked on the handle harder than necessary and shuffled backward a few steps when it opened with ease. The way ahead of her revealed nothing but a dirt path covered on either side with high hedges illuminated by the moon and stars above.

Placing one foot in front of the other, she left the small room behind and walked the length of the path, which ended at a wrought iron gate with climbing vines snaking around the intricate design. She unlatched the gate and pushed it open to reveal a large circular pavilion.

Well-manicured bushes enveloped the perimeter, leaving only one exit directly opposite her. The pavilion was set up in a series of concentric circles from the bushes to the pathway and up to the marble slab patio before landing on a flat-topped dais. Thick wax candles had been set up in a semicircle, lighting the patio and casting a silhouette on four individuals.

Cyrene swallowed hard. *Not another ceremony.*

She couldn't believe they were about to put her through something else after her warrior ceremony and everything she'd had to deal with regarding Zorian's death.

With a sigh, she stepped across the circular garden until she reached the patio. She couldn't keep the shock off her face as the four individuals came into focus—King Edric, Queen Kaliana, Consort Daufina, and Prince Kael. They were all clad in ceremonial Dremylon green and gold.

Her gaze found Edric's.

He had been so kind and charming in the gardens earlier this evening. *Is there some ulterior motive with him as much as his brother?* The whole situation was too confusing.

"Affiliate Cyrene," King Edric finally broke the silence. "Welcome to the Ring of Gardens, a place of peace, loyalty, duty, and acceptance."

Queen Kaliana spoke next, "When King Viktor Dremylon first came to rule Byern, where he rightfully belonged, the Ring of Gardens was a constant place of solace. He believed, to truly nurture and grow the most valuable aspects of his subjects, he needed to set the example."

"The time before the Class system is not well known among our citizens," Consort Daufina said. "The Doma are our history, our example, yet much of what transpired has lapsed into folklore. This has been our own doing. We have purposefully let it be forgotten by the every day person."

Cyrene stared forward, her eyes growing wider. They had let history become folklore *on purpose?*

"King Viktor Dremylon chose to stamp out the memory of the Doma and everything they had done to torment our people and our lands," Daufina continued. "He left a glimmer of a reminder with his heir and his most trusted High Order and Affiliates of what could happen if we allowed his Class system to fall or fracture. He didn't want the leaders of our world to forget what was possible under that kind of rule."

"So, King Viktor left it to his best and brightest," Prince Kael said, his characteristic smirk gone, his eyes like stone. "He didn't want those who had the most influence over the structure of the new regimen to forget. The scholars, ambassadors, and inventors were the backbone, his Affiliates and High Order."

"Back to the first group of Affiliates and High Order, the King tested those who wished to remain in his service," King Edric said.

Cyrene's blood ran cold. *Is this why he forbid the warrior ceremony? Because I would have to undergo another such test?*

"And he tested the very qualities that the Ring of Gardens represents—loyalty, duty, and acceptance," King Edric spoke severely, as if the Doma's subjugation still pained him to this day. "Affiliate Cyrene, do you wish to continue in my service as an Affiliate of Byern?"

Is that even a legitimate question? The thought of relenting her position, even after all that had happened, was heartrending.

"Of course, My King."

"Then, we must put you forward to the test of the Ring of Gardens. Loyalty to the throne, duty-bound to your lands, and acceptance of the structure of the system were the three qualities King Viktor believed to be required of a true subject."

"Should you choose to continue," Queen Kaliana said, "know that the trials might be difficult. The outcome, should you fail, might be as simple as removal from the Affiliate program or as severe as death. Once you start, there is no going back."

Cyrene held her chin high. She wouldn't have the Queen scare her off. Surely, it couldn't be as difficult as the warrior ceremony.

She glanced once into Prince Kael's eyes. He held the same stony expression, but something about him seemed to be pleading with her. *What is he thinking?*

She didn't know, and she couldn't hesitate.

"I accept."

King Edric walked two paces into the center of the pavilion and produced a small glass vial. He placed it on the center of a small table and gestured for Cyrene to walk forward.

Cyrene blankly stared down at the liquid. She couldn't show any signs of weakness. To her core, she knew that she would need to remain strong or else she would surely fail.

"There will be three tests. The first is your agreement to begin and to drink this," King Edric said, gesturing to the liquid.

"Do you agree?"

"Yes," she said strongly.

He pushed the vial a fraction closer to her.

"What will it do to me?"

"It has a different reaction to every person who drinks it. If it doesn't kill you, you'll enter into another world of what could have been…and maybe even what could be. It is your risk to take," the King stated simply before taking two steps back to stand between his Queen, Consort, and the Prince.

Cyrene steeled herself, took the small vial in her hand, and weighed it.

Loyalty. Duty. Acceptance.

She just had to drink it and trust that it wouldn't kill her. She just had to step off the ledge and hope she had a soft landing on the other side. This was what they wanted from her. This was what she had to give them.

She unstopped the vial and set the cork down before pressing the glass to her lips and tilting her head back. The liquid ran down her throat and settled in her stomach. Cyrene placed the glass next to the stopper and looked at the four people standing in front of her, waiting.

Is something supposed to happen?

Then, it hit her like a fire scorching and burning away her skin. Worse, it was like poison turning her blood to sludge and pressing against her veins. She felt near to bursting. It was like jagged glass was dragging against her entire body.

She sank to her knees as tears sprang to her eyes. All she wanted to do was scream, but her lungs wouldn't cooperate, and she could only open her mouth. She was a picture of agony and strangled desperation. She closed her eyes and rocked back and forth, wondering if it would ever end, if she would die.

Think!

There had to be an explanation.

The push of the poison coating her insides made thinking almost impossible. She tried to settle herself and ignore the pain, but it was a constant battle.

What am I even doing here? Where am I?

She couldn't open her eyes to tell. All she felt was the all-consuming agony that would surely equal death.

Loyalty.

The word appeared in her mind out of nowhere, and she held on to it like a drowning person reaching for a raft.

She was loyal. She'd drunk the vial. She was forfeiting her life for the good of the country.

At her Presenting ceremony, she had told Edric that she was his most loyal subject. The thought made her smile despite the pain.

Then, it was replaced by numbness.

And then, there was nothing.

Cyrene stood in the side room she had been escorted to immediately after her Presenting.

King Edric sat behind his desk, impatiently drumming his fingers against the stack of papers in front of him. Consort Daufina leaned against a bookshelf, impassively staring at the shelf. Queen Kaliana's lips were set in a severe straight line, and she looked as tightly coiled as the bun on her head.

How did I get here?

A perfectly snug pale blue dress embroidered in cream fit her to perfection. Pins dug into her hair where they held it back off her face. Even her feet were in her favorite pair of dark blue slippers, not the black she typically wore.

"Affiliate, are you even listening?" King Edric snapped.

"Yes, of course, My King."

Cyrene dipped a curtsy to cover her shock at his tone rather than to show deference. The potion must have done something, made her forget everything that had happened before this moment.

"We're concerned about your performance with your work as an Affiliate thus far," King Edric said. "The Queen said you've disobeyed orders, refused to listen to her, pushed against her commands, and even requested to be assigned to the Consort for no reason whatsoever. Is this all true, Kaliana?"

"It has been dreadful to work with her. I would hate to have to put her off on Daufina. I don't know what we were thinking when we accepted her into my service," the Queen said, her voice controlled.

"If she is this much trouble, then I don't see how I could work with her either," Daufina said harshly. "Even her own friend said she hides behind others' brilliance."

Cyrene stared at her in disbelief. Her stomach plummeted. She had been stubborn and opinionated, but it was certainly nothing to make her endure this kind of treatment.

When she had spoken with King Edric about Queen Kaliana's interference, he had seemed to understand what was going on. *Had that all been a ruse?*

"That settles it then." King Edric signed a document on his desk.

"That settles what?" Cyrene asked.

She froze under his heated gaze. His blue-gray eyes were normally alight with affection and hidden mischief. She was sure she had misconstrued those looks now that he was staring at her so solemnly...as if she were incompetent.

"We're moving you to the Third Class."

Cyrene gasped. Her hand flew to her mouth, and her knees weakened. She nearly fell, but she grasped on to the desk in time to stay upright.

"Your sparse knowledge of agriculture should assist you with the farming out on the banks of the Taken Mountains, past Levin, where we are reassigning you," he continued.

He didn't seem to notice or care about her discomfort.

"Reassigning me?" she asked softly.

"Yes, we feel that perhaps this was not the best fit for you." The King looked up at Queen Kaliana and nodded.

"Edric," Cyrene whispered, pleading.

Everything happened at once. Queen Kaliana hissed through her teeth and stood abruptly, her chair scraping against the stone floor. Consort Daufina strode across the room, her eyes hard, her expression nearly as cross as the Queen's. But the King…he blankly stared forward, his mouth set in a line. His fingers had ceased their drumming, and he clenched them into a fist.

"You will not call the King by his given name!" Consort Daufina scolded.

"My apologies," Cyrene stated quickly, straightening and trying to look demure.

"Third Class," King Edric said. "Straight away. You spoke the Oath of Acceptance, and you'll follow the orders set forth in our Class system. You are no better than anyone in the Third Class, as they are no better than anyone in the First. Do I make myself clear?"

Cyrene nodded. _The Oath of Acceptance._ Yes, she had agreed to abide by the King's requests.

Duty.

She plucked the word out of thin air. She was duty-bound to her Class, and she would do as he instructed.

Slowly, as if she had the weight of the world on her shoulders, Cyrene sank into a curtsy, nearly brushing her head on the stone floor. She didn't peek up. She didn't stagger or sway.

She just stayed there and whispered, "As you wish, My King."

Cyrene stood, her head full of reluctance, her body aching from the heartbreak. *Third Class*. She was to be reassigned to the Third Class. Never once had she ever dreamed it possible.

She brushed at the tears pooling in her eyes. Tears would do her no good. She had pushed too far and broken the thing she had wanted most.

She was no longer an Affiliate.

With a start, she realized that she wasn't in the castle but in a master bedroom that resembled the one in the house she had grown up in. It had the same sturdy stone walls and wide open room. But it couldn't be her parents' house.

"Darling!" someone called from outside the room.

Cyrene's heart fluttered at the voice. *But who is it? No one calls me darling.*

Yet her stomach felt as if she had butterflies in it. She couldn't keep from biting her lip, and a smile broke out on her face.

He's home. It was like she had known him all along.

At the sound of his voice, she burst out of the room and stared all around at the house she had called home for many years. She gripped the railing and flew down the flight of stairs to the foyer.

A man stood in the entranceway. He was stunning with dark blonde hair and dark eyes, and his smile set fire to her insides. He was strong and sturdy and dependable. He was her cure, her relief, her true solace. Nothing else mattered when she looked upon his face.

Cyrene rushed to him.

He picked her up around the middle and swung her in a circle. "Oh, I have missed you," he breathed into her neck.

He smelled of timber, ink, and the clove soap her servants used in the wash.

"I missed you, too," she murmured.

He set her back down on her feet and kissed her full on the mouth.

She could never remember a time without him. She could never remember a moment in her life when it wasn't him that she wanted most of all. This was her life, a perfect life.

"My darling"—he softly kissed her once more—"this arrived for you."

Cyrene scrunched her brows together. She took the envelope out of his hand and stared at the royal seal. *An invitation from the*

King! Surely, this would be for the royal wedding. She had heard rumors of the engagement of Prince Kael to an Affiliate, but she wasn't certain when it would be official.

"I'll just be in the study," he said, rubbing his knuckles against her jawline. "Don't be too long."

Cyrene stared up at him, entranced, the letter already forgotten in her grasp. She watched him walk down the hallway and into their study. They would take the next hour to read together before sitting down for supper and attending to houseguests. She smiled dreamily and then tore open the envelope.

A crisp cream letter fell into her hand, and she read it, her eyebrows rising.

> AFFILIATE CYRENE,
>
> IF YOU FIND YOURSELF IN COMPANY WHEN READING THIS LETTER, PLEASE PROMPTLY REMOVE YOURSELF BEFORE CONTINUING.
>
> YOUR LIFE IN THE FIRST CLASS IS AT RISK. THE LIVES OF THE AFFILIATES AND HIGH ORDER FOR THE ENTIRE KINGDOM ARE AT RISK. WE NEED EVERY PERSON TO RETURN TO THEIR RIGHTFUL PLACE—BESIDE THE KING. YOUR COUNTRY NEEDS YOU, AND THOSE WHO ARE LOYAL TO THE THRONE MUST COME BACK TO COURT AT ONCE.
>
> TELL NO ONE YOUR INTENTIONS TO LEAVE. YOUR ABSOLUTE DISCRETION IS NECESSARY.
>
> DESTROY THIS LETTER AFTER READING.
>
> KING EDRIC
>
> HIS ROYAL HIGHNESS

A sob escaped her throat, and she choked back on the cry that would be certain to bring her love back into the foyer. She swallowed the pain rising in her chest.

I can't leave him! What about the way he looks at me when he comes home and the husky smell of him after work?

No, the court couldn't ask that of me. They shouldn't have!

She had given them her time and devotion. Now, she was settled down and happy just to be with him. She didn't deserve this request.

She read through the royal demand one more time, running her finger across the King's indented signature. He had pressed too firmly in such haste.

Cyrene walked to the study and peeked through the open door. Her wonderful man was sitting in a chair, engrossed in an age-old book. Deep in study as he read, his brow crinkled between his eyes.

A smile touched her face. At least she would always have that—the one last image of him, the man she was madly in love with.

She retreated from the study, pulled open the front door, and began tearing the paper into a million little pieces.

She would do what was right. She had to help save the kingdom. If the King needed her, then she would follow. She would always follow.

She brushed the tear from her eye and hurried out of the house.

Cyrene took off at a sprint down the pebbled street. Her sturdy boots clattered and squished her toes. She would never have made it this far if she had worn slippers. Her hands clenched her dress, so the ends wouldn't drag in the dirt. The roads were particularly wet and muddy this time of year, and a wrong footfall or a catch on her dress could result in her twisting an ankle.

The Royal Guard was close behind her, but she had to get there first.

A vague memory of a man with brown hair and deep dark eyes needled her, but she pushed it away. She had never known such a man. All she could think about were the beautiful blue-gray eyes she had been staring at all these years.

Her breathing was raspy, and she was getting a stitch in her side, but she kept running. It wasn't much farther. She turned the bend and saw the small thatched cottage at the end of the lane. A strained smile touched her lips, and she surged forward.

Cyrene pushed open the door to the cottage and burst into the stifling hot room. "Where is he?" She stared at the maid sitting in a rocking chair in the corner. "Where *is* he?"

The maid cowered. "Right…right here, Your Grace."

"What are you waiting for?" she snapped. "Get him ready. Bring him to me. We must be on our way."

"Yes, Your Grace. Where are we taking him?" The maid jumped up and stuffed belongings into a bag. Then, she hoisted a little baby boy in her arms before swaddling him in blankets.

"Away. As far away as we can. Quickly!" Cyrene all but shrieked, staring at the door in worry.

There was a trap door that led into a tunnel. Since they had so little time, they would have to take that.

Cyrene brushed aside a chair and the dirt covering the trap door, and she wrenched it open. A darkened set of stairs descended under the cottage. She yanked a lantern from above the hearth and handed it to the maid. Cyrene took the little baby out of the maid's hands, and with a sigh, she gently cradled him in her arms. It had been too long, far too long, since she had seen him. Planting a kiss on his soft forehead, she ushered her maid down the stairs, so the woman could light the way ahead.

As she took a step down the stairs to follow, the front door slammed inward.

"Halt! In the name of the King!" a guard called. His plume denoting him as Captain of the Guard waved about.

Cyrene swallowed and tried to keep her feet moving. She almost made it down the stairs when a guard grasped her by the back of her cloak and ceased her progress.

"Let me go!" she shrieked.

"Your Grace, you know I cannot."

"You show up here, yet you still call me Your Grace."

"I'm doing my duty as Captain of the Guard. Come with me."

He marched her back up the stairs. She struggled against him the whole way.

Queen Kaliana strode into the quarters, and her eyes filled with hatred. Cyrene had never actually expected her to show up.

"Hand him over," Kaliana spat.

"No."

"Hand *him* over!"

"Never! I'll never hand him over."

"By order of the King," she growled. "He has denounced you. Everyone has denounced you."

"Then, he is all I have left," Cyrene snarled.

"The King said he would take pity on you, if you gave the boy up."

"You wench! I don't care about his pity. I will never give him up!"

"You swore an oath. Do you not remember? You swore fealty to the King, to your lands, to your people. If you keep him…then you will truly have lost everything," Kaliana said, her eyes hard.

"What will you do with him?" Cyrene asked, the oath weighing down on her.

Loyalty, duty, acceptance—the words came to her like a rushing torrent of water, as if she had stepped into a hurricane.

"That is none of your concern…or mine. He is a Dremylon heir. The last male Dremylon heir. One day, he will become the king, and to him, it will be as if I was always his mother. If you are truly an Affiliate of this realm, then you will give him to *me*."

"I know what I am," she spat back.

Tears streamed down her face as she stared at the little baby boy in her arms. He was the most beautiful thing she had ever seen in her entire life. She had never expected a baby. She had never even really wanted one, but this boy, this wonderful baby boy, was a part of her now. *How can I lose a part of myself?*

"He should not be king," Cyrene whispered.

"That is not for you to decide."

Cyrene felt the oath as if it were a crushing boulder falling upon her from thousands of feet up. "Just because you could never produce an heir does not mean that you have to steal the only living one!"

"I'm not stealing. You did your duty, and now, you are to *leave*. That is the next King of Byern. If you are loyal to anyone but yourself, then you will give him to me, so I can raise him as a proper prince." Kaliana stepped forward and put out her hands. "Give him to me, Cyrene. You can no longer provide what he needs."

Tears ran like a river down her face as Kaliana reached forward, removed the baby from her arms, and walked out of the room.

Cyrene sank to her knees feeling dead inside.

Arms gripped Cyrene on all sides as they helped her stand. She heard whispers all around her.

"She fainted."

"She must be unwell."

"I heard she is with child."

Her thoughts seemed to swirl all around her. *Did I actually faint?*

All she could remember was Kaliana taking her baby, her beautiful baby boy. He had his father's eyes, those same blue-gray eyes. Her throat tightened.

Then, it slipped away. She didn't have a child. *Why did I think I had one?*

Cyrene shook off the hands still pestering her, and the people scurried away. She straightened and raised her head high to survey her surroundings. She was in the throne room, but it was empty, save for a splatter of Royal Guard, a few flustered courtiers, and the King seated on the throne before her. He was whispering to the Captain of the Guard with huge green and gold plumed feathers in his hat.

There was no Queen and no Consort. It was just the King.

"Affiliate, are you quite all right?" the King asked.

Cyrene sharply looked up at that silky smooth voice. *Kael.* Her heart began beating in overdrive at the man she had not expected to be seated on the throne, wearing the crown while dressed in Dremylon green and gold. He even had the linked gold chain of the Dremylon line attached to his forest-green crushed-velvet cape.

As she tried to speak, her mouth went dry, and she found she could not articulate words.

That jawline, those blue-gray eyes, the almost black dark hair— he was so beautiful but in a way that she always associated with a predator tracking his prey.

"Do you need some water?" Kael asked with that heart-stopping smile.

"No. I mean, no, thank you," she corrected, quickly dipping him a curtsy befitting a king.

Why did it feel wrong? By the Creator, it feels wrong.

But she could not pinpoint the exact reason for feeling that way.

"My lady, surely you need a minute before we continue the proceedings," Kael said.

He stood and gestured for the courtiers to be seated. They flitted away like they were used to following his orders on a whim.

"Come along. I'll see that you are restored to health before we proceed."

Kael stood and strode to Cyrene. He offered her his arm. She walked with him across the ballroom. The Captain of the Guard held the door open for them, and she followed Kael inside a small office.

"I'll keep watch. I've stationed men at all the exits," the Captain spoke gruffly.

Kael nodded, and the Captain shut the door.

Cyrene had so many questions. They bubbled up out of her from places unknown but dissolved into the wind just as quickly.

"Water?" Kael walked to a full pitcher on the other side of the small room.

With a start, she realized that she was in the room she had waited in before her Presenting. It had been draped all over with rustic colors with too many throw pillows tossed about.

"No. Really, Kael, I'm fine," she said, using his given name like she always had.

He set the pitcher down and returned to her side. His hand trailed the length of her face and down her neck before circling her waist and pulling her closer. "You know I look out for your comfort, Cyrene," he said, her name falling off his lips like a caress.

She swallowed hard. Goose bumps broke out across her skin, and she tried to push away the pestering feeling of wrongness in the air. Her mind flew to the first thing that might bring her to reality.

"Edric," she whispered.

Kael stiffened and pulled away. He looked hurt, and she immediately wanted to comfort him, but she wouldn't move.

"You really must have fainted. Did you hit your head?"

She remained silent.

"Edric has been gone for a year, Cyrene. I know it was hard for all of us, but that is why we are reinstating our vows—swearing fealty to the throne, to the Dremylon line, to me."

He reached out for her again, bringing his lips down onto hers. Her first instinct was to struggle, but she didn't.

What was she doing? And why couldn't she place why all of this felt wrong?

Kael broke the kiss with a smile. He was clearly pleased because his face showed only delight and smugness. "I want so much from you, but I'll start with your Oath of Acceptance," he said. "We can go from there."

Everything seemed to swirl around her at once. Edric was dead, gone. Kael was king, but he wasn't. He couldn't be. She could *never* swear fealty to him.

She wrenched backward, out of his embrace, and landed on a divan stacked with pillows. Her hands trembled. He wanted her to be his queen. She knew it with every fiber of her being. *How could he think I would do that with Edric having been gone for only a year?*

Kael assessed her with a look of concern. "Are you sure you'll be all right after that fainting spell?"

"Yes. Quite," she said.

"Then, I should probably bring you back into the throne room to finish the proceedings before the entire court is up in arms." He offered her his arm.

Seeing no other option, she begrudgingly took it and followed him back out into the throne room. The courtiers reassembled, and Kael returned to his place on the throne.

"You have been selected as an Affiliate of the realm. You have been announced to your Receiver and placed in her charge for proper training. Do you accept the circumstances of your Selecting?"

Cyrene defiantly stared back at Kael. She could not swear her fealty to him. She couldn't do it. Her loyalty rested with Edric, with Byern, with her people.

"Cyrene," he growled softly.

She stared up into those blue-gray eyes and tried to understand what she was supposed to do. *How can I trust Kael?*

Acceptance. She had to accept him. She had to accept him as the next in line on the Dremylon throne. She had to give her life to the line as much as to the land, the people, and the King.

She gritted her teeth and braced herself to answer him even though it was the last thing she wanted to do. "However I am fit and however I am able."

"Kael," Cyrene groaned into the silence.

Her hands were covering her face, and she was lying facedown on a hard flat surface. Tears ran down her cheeks, and her body shook when she remembered everything she had gone through—Third Class, love, family, fealty.

She wiped tears from her eyes, unsure of how she looked or if anyone would be around. Her head throbbed, but she slowly pushed off from the marble patio and stood on shaky legs. Chairs had been set up before the small platform, and King Edric, Queen Kaliana, Consort Daufina, and Prince Kael all sat, staring at her with wide eyes.

With horror, Cyrene remembered that she had spoken Prince Kael's name when she first regained consciousness. She couldn't even look at him, but she could feel his eyes on her.

King Edric stood stiffly and walked to the flat podium where the glass vial still rested. "Affiliate Cyrene, you have completed two of the three tests of loyalty."

Two of the three? She almost wept.

"The final is the easiest to request and the hardest to follow. We have already required deference and dedication. Now, I ask discretion of you. Swear that you will speak of what you have seen in this test to no one."

Cyrene placed her palms flat on the marble table before her. She never wanted to speak of what she had seen with anyone, and she never intended to. Perhaps discretion was hardest for some, but it would not be for her.

"I swear," she murmured, staring into the King's blue-gray eyes. She let her gaze travel to the Queen Kaliana, Consort Daufina, and then finally rest on Prince Kael seated behind him, and repeated herself. "I swear."

She felt a jolt run through her body, and she clutched onto the table for support. Whatever that was…it was powerful.

"Congratulations, Affiliate Cyrene," King Edric said with a smile, not seeming to notice her momentary paralysis. "You have passed the Ring of Gardens. You are now bound by your loyalty to Byern and the Dremylon line."

Cyrene sagged with relief. "Thank the Creator."

"You have had a long night. The Royal Guard will escort you back to the interior of the castle. Congratulations once again. It is great to have you as one among us."

Cyrene dipped a deep curtsy before walking past the royalty, toward the opposite entrance from which she'd come. As much as she'd sworn that she would never tell about the things she had seen, she would not soon forget the bitter taste of reassignment, the deep ache of losing a lover, the crushing blow at the loss of a child, or the Oath of Acceptance to a king she did not trust or believe in.

The
PRESENT

"WHAT IN THE CREATOR'S NAME ARE YOU STILL DOING IN bed?" Maelia demanded.

Cyrene opened her eyes. "Why are you in my bedchamber?"

"I've been knocking at your door for fifteen minutes. Just because you walked with the King in the gardens doesn't mean that you can sleep through our study time."

"What time is it?" Cyrene groaned.

"Half past noon!"

Cyrene threw the covers off of her, aghast. "I can't believe that I was still asleep."

"Me either. Get dressed, and let's go down to the pavilion to work. It's beautiful out today."

"I just had a dreadful night."

Maelia raised her eyebrows. "What do you mean? We walked back to the Vines together."

Cyrene conspiratorially glanced around the room. "I know I can't talk about what happened, but I passed."

"Oh. Oh! Wasn't it horrible?" Maelia asked. "I had nightmares for weeks."

"Yes, it was horrible and emotionally draining, but nothing as bad as the warrior ceremony," Cyrene admitted.

"Really? I thought King Edric had put a stop to the warrior ceremony."

"Yes, well, he wasn't happy when he found out."

"I'd think not after he'd given a direct order," Maelia said. "What happened to you? I was locked in the highest tower overnight and left to wonder if anyone was going to let me out."

Cyrene recounted her story about the underground lake to Maelia and watched her gradually grow paler.

"I've never heard of a warrior ceremony so gruesome. Did you tell Queen Kaliana what happened?" Maelia asked.

Cyrene laughed. "I would never bring anything to the Queen that I did not have to."

Maelia colored and looked down at her feet.

"I'm sorry, Maelia. I know how you feel about authority, but the Queen *hates* me. I would rather be in your shoes, working for the Consort."

Maelia appeared flustered and changed the subject. "We'll get nothing done if we sit here and talk all day. Come on. You have packages waiting for you."

"Packages?" Cyrene asked, her eyes alight.

Cyrene grabbed her dressing gown and pulled it over her head before rushing out of her bedchamber like a child on the morning of the Eos holiday. She walked past the table in her sitting room, cluttered with notes and papers from Affiliate Lorne's research, to the entrance table. The smaller package on top had no note or signature, and she moved it over to examine the second one, which was signed by Lady Cauthorn. Cyrene tore open the brown paper, revealing seven dresses, three in red, two in blue, and two in gray. She was still waiting on the ball gown and couldn't wait to get her hands on it.

After leaving the gowns carefully folded on the table for the servants to hang in her wardrobe, Cyrene returned to the smaller package. Her eyes gazed upon the nondescript wrapping. Coming up blank, she eased the paper back and gasped.

Inside laid a hooded cloak made of the finest crimson velvet and lined with white ermine. Her hands splayed across the brilliant fabric before tenderly pulling it from the wrapping. The cloak fell in folds to the ground, and Cyrene threw it over her shoulders. It was simply gorgeous and seemed to ripple and move with her. She tied the red leather ribbon in the front where a gold leaf hung at the end of each cord.

"That is gorgeous. Did you commission that from Lady Cauthorn?" Maelia asked.

Cyrene shook her head. "No. I have no idea who sent it. It had no note."

Maelia ran her hand down the smooth material. "Whoever sent it has good taste."

"Indeed," Cyrene agreed. She wondered who her mysterious benefactor could be, but she couldn't think of anyone who would have sent her something this exquisite. She wondered if it was because she had passed the Rose Garden test. It was the only explanation that made sense to her. "Let me change, and then we can go study."

Cyrene slipped into a cream lace gown with a tight bust and a free-flowing skirt, and then she draped the exquisite cloak over it. With her work tucked under her arm, she hurried out of the chambers with Maelia.

The girls settled their work down inside a stone gazebo surrounded by hundreds of flowers blooming in the summer sun, next to an easy-moving creek. Maelia was busy researching herbal treatments while Cyrene stared at Affiliate Lorne's life's work. The woman had researched every region, every environment, and practically every species of plant in the known world.

Cyrene had spent hours working on a chart system that showed specific agricultural plants and how they grew based on region, climate, and various other properties. Then, she had supplemented that list with a note on whether or not she thought the plants would grow in Byern and how to implement a plan for new crop rotations. The burdensome report to the Queen was becoming almost too long.

Cyrene and Maelia had been working in the gazebo for a couple of hours when they heard voices approaching. Jardana rounded the corner of a large hedge with her three lackeys, and they started walking toward Cyrene and Maelia.

Jardana stood at the center of the group. She wore a sky-blue corset dress that made her look emaciated. Her waxen blonde hair was styled in a severe bun on the top of her head, the same fashion as the Queen. The girl on her right nearly towered over the other women. She had stick-straight light-brown hair hanging to her waist and a snub-nosed face with beady little eyes. A pudgy short girl with dirty-blonde hair and a round face with an open demeanor scurried her little feet double time to keep up with her companions.

The only thing Cyrene could make out about the girl behind them was her untamed strawberry-blonde locks. Cyrene's eyes narrowed at the color. She had seen a girl with strawberry-blonde hair at her warrior ceremony. This woman must be the masked Leif.

As if feeling Cyrene's eyes upon them, Jardana halted their progress and smiled up at her. "We did not mean to disturb you," she said with a high-pitched voice and a wicked smile.

"No bother," Cyrene said with the warmest smile she could muster.

She wasn't sure how she hadn't noticed the similarity before. Jardana had been the masked Braj. She doubted this woman was quite as dangerous, but with ambition, there was always danger, and Cyrene could tell Jardana had ambition in spades.

She wanted to know these girls and why they had performed the ceremony against the King's orders. "Would you care to join us?" Cyrene asked.

The two girls on either side of the Braj looked startled, and both glanced toward Jardana.

"We'd be delighted. Wouldn't we, girls?"

Cyrene cleared away her work and put it back in its leather folder as the girls took seats on the other benches. She didn't care that the warrior ceremony had just been a prank. She wanted retribution for the hell they had put her through.

"I'm not certain we've been formally introduced. I'm Cyrene. This is my friend Maelia."

"Nice to see you all again," Maelia said.

As expected, the Braj spoke up first, "Pleasure to see you both. I am Jardana, and this is Nyasha." She gestured to the taller woman who reminded Cyrene of the peacock.

"Cheala," Jardana said, pointing out the short woman, likely the dwarf.

"And Adelas."

The Leif.

"Well, I'm very pleased to meet all of you. Will you be accompanying the King on the procession to Albion?" Cyrene asked. "Maelia and I were both offered invitations."

Jardana sat up straighter on the bench with a self-importance and arrogance that could rival the Queen. "Of course we're attending the procession. We're to be on the Queen's own vessel as I am the assistant to the DIA."

"The Queen does not travel with His Majesty?" Cyrene asked, widening her eyes with innocence.

She knew the answer, having seen the King travel for the procession to Albion down the Keylani River her entire life. She even remembered when King Maltrier used to travel. The men always preferred the company of their consorts to their queens.

Jardana kept a forced smile on her face. "Consort Daufina has been offered the privilege of riding alongside His Majesty for this procession."

"But Prince Kael has decided to accompany the Queen," Adelas said.

Jardana's eyes snapped to Adelas and struck her with a fierce glare.

"That's wonderful," Cyrene cried, pretending not to notice Jardana's glower. "I know how much Her Majesty favors him."

"Yes, it is," Jardana responded slowly.

"Prince Kael is so very charming," Cyrene said.

She pushed her luck. Maelia looked at her in confusion, but Cyrene just smiled back at her, silently begging her friend to play along. Maelia's eyes widened in understanding.

"And attractive," Maelia said with a giggle.

"Very," Adelas agreed.

Jardana seemed to be warring with herself. "Do you know where you will be stationed?"

"Surely, with your newly acquired Affiliate status, you will be placed on one of the smaller ships with other Affiliates," Nyasha offered, her eyes gleaming.

"Oh, surely," Cyrene agreed good-naturedly. "As long as Prince Kael doesn't request I be moved."

"And why would he do that?" Jardana asked. Her high voice was as tight as a whip about to crack.

"Now, I trust you ladies," she said, "so I know you will speak of this to no one. Prince Kael has requested I call him by his given name...as if we're equals."

Nyasha, Cheala, and Adelas slowly turned and peered at Jardana. She seemed to be boiling over, ready to combust at any moment. Maelia covered her mouth with her hand.

"How wonderful," Jardana snapped.

Just then, Cyrene noticed a figure walking toward them on the grass path she had taken this morning. The four other women turned around when they noticed her looking.

A smile spread across Cyrene's features. She had never been more pleased to see the Prince. An image of a crown on his head popped into her mind, and she had to remember that it had just been a dream, a reality that would never occur.

Even from the distance, he was devilishly handsome. His Dremylon green silk shirt fit perfectly on his muscled chest. Muddy brown leather riding boots reached the knees of his chestnut-brown pants. His hair, which was a bit too long for royal custom, was tousled, and his cheeks were flushed, like he had recently been on horseback.

Jardana and her friends preened as he walked slowly up the steps into the gazebo.

"Ladies." Prince Kael swept them a deep bow.

"Prince Kael," Cyrene said with a heady flirtatious smile and hooded eyes. "So nice of you to join us."

To the Prince's credit, he didn't even skip a beat. "It is always a pleasure to spend time with such beautiful women."

"You flatter us," Jardana murmured, her high-pitched voice straining.

"You give me much to flatter," he said. His blue-gray eyes met each woman before returning to Cyrene. She could see the questions in his expression, but he was too much of a skilled courtier to speak of any of them. "I've never seen so many attractive women congregated in one place."

"To what do we owe the pleasure of your company?" Jardana asked hastily.

"Consort Daufina has requested an audience with Affiliate Cyrene," he announced as if the news would not strike a chord with the entire group.

Cyrene always wanted a proper audience with the Consort, and the other girls were as devoted to the Queen as Cyrene was against her.

"Really?" Cyrene breathed.

He inclined his head in the affirmative. "I was out hunting with the King and Consort. When we returned, I offered to come and find Cyrene myself as I knew she liked to study in the gardens."

"Well, thank the Creator you are so well acquainted with Cyrene's whereabouts," Jardana murmured under tightly veiled anger. "The girls and I were just leaving anyway. Weren't we, girls?"

The girls tripped over themselves to rise and agree with Jardana.

"I was about to leave as well. Consort Daufina paired me with a member of the High Order, and I am to meet him shortly," Maelia said.

When Cyrene met her gaze, Maelia winked. Cyrene would have laughed at Maelia's made-up excuse to leave, thinking Cyrene wanted to be alone with Kael, but in actuality, it was the last thing she wanted.

"Until next time, Cyrene," Jardana said. She waggled her fingers at Cyrene and turned to Prince Kael. "Your Highness." She dipped a low formal curtsy and then stalked out of the gazebo with her entourage hot on her tail.

Cyrene's false smile fell away as the girls disappeared around the corner, and she was left with Prince Kael.

"Do you wish for me to accompany you?" the Prince asked, providing his arm for support.

Cyrene retrieved her leather folder and tucked it under her arm. "I don't want to go anywhere with you."

"And here I thought you had a change of heart. Court has transformed you since that first night. It appears you can play the game well enough now," he remarked snidely.

"I'm nothing like you."

"On the contrary, I think you played that even better than I would have." His face clouded with desire.

"You are sleeping with her, aren't you?" Cyrene accused.

He laughed and reached out for her slim waist. She dodged his approach, rushed past him out of the gazebos, navigating the gardens with him hot on her heels.

"What gives you that idea?" he called out to her.

"You're vile."

The Prince yanked on her elbow, pulling her to a standstill. "You're so feisty, Cyrene," he said with a soft chuckle.

Still holding on to her elbow, he forcefully pulled her against him. She gasped and glared up into his blue-gray eyes as she tried to wiggle free from his tight embrace.

"Tell me why I should not be with her. Is it because you secretly harbor a desire for me? Is it because you long for me to return to your chambers?"

"Never," she snarled.

"Then, why did you speak my name at the Ring of Gardens?"

Cyrene froze. "I am to speak of that to no one."

"You said my name when you left the dreams. I was there. I heard you cry out. Was I there in your future?"

"You will never know," she snapped. She placed her free palm on his chest and shoved away. "Now, leave me alone." She stalked away from him, continuing through the gardens.

Kael followed behind her, ignoring her request. "Come now, Cyrene. You can't avoid me forever."

He caught up to her again and latched on to her cloak billowing out behind her. The tug stopped her in her tracks once again.

She glared at him and crossed her arms over her chest. "I'm not avoiding you. I have somewhere to be."

He ran his fingers over the soft material. "Where did you get this?"

Cyrene pulled it out of his grasp. "It was a gift."

"From whom?" he asked.

"I assumed it was a present for completing the tests." She hadn't even spoken that thought aloud to Maelia, and now, she was telling the Prince of all people. The man could get under her skin.

Prince Kael barked out a short derisive laugh, but his face looked anything but happy. "Presents are not given for completing the Ring of Gardens."

Cyrene absorbed the information. She knew that she had been grasping, but she had wanted to brush aside the expensive gift as nothing more than a present for her accomplishments. She didn't want to read into what Prince Kael's eyes were suggesting.

"It doesn't matter," she said, pulling the cloak out of his hands. That wasn't the truth though. If the gift wasn't for completing the tests, then she could only imagine a few people who had access to such rich material.

No. I'm not thinking about that at all.

Cyrene glared at him one more time and then started to walk away. She didn't want to have this conversation anyway.

"I wouldn't let Kaliana see you in that," he called after her. His laughter followed her out of the gardens.

18

The
CONSORT

PRINCE KAEL PUT HER ON EDGE.

Now, she had thoughts swirling through her mind about her mysterious cloak. She had waited for this moment her whole life, and now, she couldn't even concentrate on the fact that she had been summoned to speak with the Consort.

Cyrene reached the room where the Consort conducted her business. The noise and hectic behavior of the Queen's rooms were replaced with laughter and the strumming of a harp. Only a select few Affiliates and members of the High Order lounged within the rectangular hall. It was a communal place of educational advancement, deep philosophical discussion, and entertainment that resulted in enlightened attainment.

An elaborately painted mural covered every inch of wall space from floor to ceiling. It was as if she were entering a forest with hundreds of trees, gorgeous green undergrowth, and birds in the brightest colors imaginable. A panther stalked the forest floor on one side. Dozens of monkeys swung on the branches high above their heads.

Candles floated around the otherwise dim room, illuminating the atmosphere. A tiered fountain produced the faint sound of water trickling from the canopy. Affiliates rested on forest-green settees, and countless pillows that resembled a pebble-bottom river ran through the moss-blanketed room.

The men of the High Order sat in hard-backed oak chairs around a matching table that appeared to be coming out of the largest painted tree in the room. It was an unbelievably big oak that stretched beyond the wall and into the ceiling.

The most striking aspect of the mural was that the leaves only grew on one half of the tree. It gave the appearance of the tree being perpetually stuck in both summer and winter seasons— forever half alive and half dead. She could feel the power coming off the mural. It spoke of caution, the duality of nature, and perhaps the duality of the human condition.

She shook off the thoughts that had come over her and tore her eyes from the mural. Thus far, no one had noticed her appearance in the Consort's chambers. She hated to interrupt the few people who were deeply involved in their work.

Suddenly, a door materialized out of thin air, peeling back one of the larger trees as it sprang open against the far wall. Consort Daufina stood regally in the open doorway. She was as majestic as the last time Cyrene had set eyes on her. She wore a gown with multitiered skirts beginning at her waist with the palest of lavenders deepening to the darkest amethyst at her feet. The tight corset dress interwoven with amethysts rose to a sweetheart neck, and soft sheer lace covered her arms and buttoned at her neck. Her midnight-black hair hung loose over her shoulders.

"Affiliate Cyrene," she said cheerfully. She waved Cyrene into the alcove she had just vacated.

Her study mirrored the outside forest, and the Consort reclined in a cushioned chair placed at a small circular table. As Cyrene took the seat next to her, as directed, she realized there was no head to the table. The thought made her smile.

"Would you care for some tea?" Daufina's bracelets jingled on her arm as she motioned toward a teapot sitting over a burning fire.

"No, thank you, Consort Daufina."

Consort Daufina chirped with laughter. She seemed much more relaxed than any time Cyrene had seen her outside of these walls.

"Please, no need for formalities. This is my sanctuary, my escape. I refuse titles here. You will simply be Cyrene, and I will simply be Daufina."

"Of course, Daufina." It felt strange to say her name aloud.

Cyrene had only ever been around the Consort at her Presenting, on feast days, and during the Ring of Gardens ceremony.

"See? We're already close friends," she said. "I'm sure you are wondering why I requested your presence this afternoon."

"I am, Daufina."

"If you keep saying my name like it's a title, then I'm going to make you call me Daffy for the rest of our meeting. You'll get over the title quite snappy then." Daufina smiled.

Cyrene giggled into her hand. "Has someone really called you Daffy?"

"I'll have you know that my father did until I was seventeen. It was nearly impossible to get him to cease once I made Affiliate. He still starts all his letters to me with 'Dear Daffy,'" she said with dismay. "At least he addresses me as Consort while he's at court."

Cyrene had never thought about what the Consort's past had been like—whether she was happy or how her friends and family treated her before or after her title.

"I think I'll stick with Daufina. It's rather beautiful, if I do say so."

"Thank you. It's a family name. Every first daughter across the generations has it. Can you imagine what it is like to get the entire clan together?" She rolled her eyes.

"No wonder your father called you Daffy."

"Yes, I suppose that was one reason." Daufina laughed along with Cyrene. "But enough about my embarrassing history. I would like to make a request from you."

"Oh?" Cyrene lifted her eyebrows.

"I'm not sure if you are aware, but I ride alongside Edric during the procession. It is part of my duty as his Consort to entertain him. I'd heard the chore was burdensome, but I find it delightful. Edric is a wonderful man and ruler to his people. He cares for each one of them, and he makes it easy for me as he has many interests. And I believe *you* are one of those interests," she said with a smile reminiscent of a feline.

"Me?" Cyrene gasped.

"Indeed." Daufina examined Cyrene rather closely. "For instance, that cloak you are wearing on your shoulders, where did you get it?"

Her mouth went dry. "It was a gift."

"I've seen that craftsmanship before." She reached out and touched the soft material between her multi-ringed fingers. "It is

149

the work of none other than a royal seamstress. Edric sent you that cloak himself, if I had to guess."

Cyrene's stomach dropped. It was one thing for Kael to have suggested that the King had sent her a gift, but it was quite another for Daufina to confirm it.

"You must be mistaken, Daufina."

"I am not," she stated simply as a matter of fact. Her tone suggested she should not be second-guessed again. "Now, I've made accommodations for you to be on board upon Edric's craft destined for Albion. Do you find this suitable?"

"What's in this for you?" Cyrene couldn't help but ask.

Daufina's green eyes narrowed almost imperceptibly and then returned to their congenial nature. "I would tell you that it is only to procure Edric's entertainment for the trip, but I can see you are a woman of reason. I'll be frank then. You have not been afforded the privilege of being around Edric nearly all his waking hours. I have that privilege, and I believe I know him better than anyone else. Probably better than he knows himself. I see the way he looks at you, and I can see how he feels about you." Her eyebrows knitted together.

Cyrene's mind flashed back to when she had been so close to him last night, certain he was going to kiss her. *Did he always look at me like that? How many others had noticed?*

Daufina continued, "I saw it the first time he set his gaze on you in the Presenting hall. I voted for your acceptance as an Affiliate because of that, whereas Kaliana voted against it for the same reason. Kaliana saw you as a threat, but I saw you as an asset."

"Yet Kaliana is my Receiver and not you," Cyrene spoke boldly.

"Yes," Daufina said with a sigh. "I believe Kaliana wanted to keep tabs on you."

So, Cyrene had been right about the Queen all along. She liked Daufina better than Queen Kaliana, yet they both wanted to use her in some way.

"You suspected some of this?" Daufina asked.

"It is hard to mistake the Queen's dislike," Cyrene told her.

"Yes, Kaliana is one not to be reckoned with, even on her best day," she said through gritted teeth. "She is infuriating, that one. I'd steer clear of her if you can."

"Easier said than done."

"I could have you moved into my duties," Daufina offered, seemingly offhand.

As much as Cyrene wanted to work with the Consort, she couldn't accept Daufina's offer. She would just be switching hands from one woman to another, and both wanted to control her. At least Daufina was open about it, but it still didn't excuse the fact that the women had similar agendas.

"While I appreciate the offer, I think I will stay with the Queen—at least until I finish my latest assignment."

"As you wish. The offer is always open to you. Now, the matter with Edric. I think his interest in you goes beyond your physical beauty. He does not dole out his affection lightly, and if you are important to him, then you are important to me."

Cyrene had no idea what to say. *I'm important to the King?*

"You will join us on his vessel?"

She knew that she couldn't actually refuse, but Daufina wouldn't be asking if it wasn't important, which meant she had some bargaining power.

"Can Maelia come with me?" Cyrene asked.

"Maelia? My Maelia?" Daufina asked in surprise. "I did not realize you two were acquainted."

Cyrene could never figure out how no one ever saw Maelia when they were together. "Yes, we're together all the time."

"Well, I don't see why not. I'll change it to two rooms then. Is there anything else you'll require?" Daufina asked dryly. A note in her voice said Cyrene was pushing her luck if she kept trying to negotiate.

"No, Daufina. Thank you for considering me."

"No, Cyrene, thank you. I cannot wait for our procession together." Daufina clasped their hands together.

Even though Consort Daufina had given her much to think about, especially regarding what entertaining the King would entail, the only thing on her mind was how to let Jardana and her minions know that she was going to be seated with Edric on his vessel while they trailed behind on the Queen's ship.

Cyrene laughed to herself as she thought about Jardana's comment about Cyrene being on a smaller vessel than the Queen's.

A smaller ship indeed, thanks to my newly acquired position.

The
WAR ROOM

WITH A SIGH, DAUFINA WATCHED THE GIRL LEAVE HER office. Cyrene was too young to be dealing with this sort of court maneuvering. Though she wore her strength like Edric's cloak around her shoulders, she had so much to learn. Daufina worried about subjecting her to this, to breaking the innocence of a girl who had just come into adulthood, but she would do what was necessary for Byern, for Edric. She always had done so, even when he had been the King at only fifteen and lost and confused without his mother or father.

Well, he was not that child anymore. When he had come of age, he had shaken off all his father's advisors, who had attempted to take control. She was the only one he'd let in, and she would rest the weight of that on her shoulders to make this country run.

Exiting through a secret passage in her study, she walked directly into Edric's war room. She could have taken the same route to his bedchamber, but she was certain she would find him buried under a mountain of paperwork as he prepared for the procession.

His head snapped up at her entrance.

"Ah, Daufina, come in," he said distractedly.

She floated across the room and then stood next to his desk, taking a peek at the trade negotiations he had before him. "News from Eleysia?" she asked.

Edric ran a hand over his face and then leaned back in the chair. "They will close the borders to all Byern citizens if we do not comply with their demands. Queen Cassia is sending her son as an emissary for me to meet with once we arrive in Albion."

"Are they still requiring that import taxes be lessened?"

"Yes. They're also asking that there be no goods searches. I can't stomach it. These safety measures have been in place for two hundred years, and they levy similar taxes on our goods."

Daufina clasped her hands behind her back and stared off in thought.

"What do you counsel?" he asked.

"Speak with their Prince. Perhaps you can come to an accord. If no compromise is available, then severe action will be necessary, Edric."

He pushed the papers away from him. "This is not the reason you came to see me."

"No, it is not."

He sent her a questioning look, urging her onward.

"You sent the Affiliate a cloak."

"Would you like one?" he asked.

His eyes were bright, and she saw a trace of the boy she had once thought she would love. Their relationship had lapsed into more of a casual affair when she realized that she had only ever loved the throne.

"You know that is not why I mentioned it."

"Then, why did you mention it, Daufina? I have a thousand things to do, and you're concerning yourself with one Affiliate."

"You have made it my business to concern myself with her."

"I've done nothing of the sort," he said, standing to his full height and looking down upon her.

"I see the way you look at her, Edric. Your eyes follow her, you dance the longest dances with her, and now, you're sending her presents. I've known you too long not to know that this is unlike you. You're not Kael. You don't fraternize with the Affiliates who parade themselves in front of you, hoping for a scrap of your time. Yet here you are with this Cyrene. What is she to you?" Daufina asked.

At her question, Edric paced the long room. She watched him through the silence and wondered what he was thinking.

"You told me once that you would inform me if you wanted to take a mistress—"

"I do *not* want to take a mistress," Edric snapped.

Daufina straightened in surprise. He never raised his voice with her.

"I apologize," he said with a sigh. "I didn't mean to startle you."

"Just talk to me."

"Would you believe me if I said that I didn't want anything to do with her?" His eyes were pleading.

"No," Daufina admitted.

"No," he agreed. "No, I wouldn't either. I keep telling myself that I'm acting like a fool, Daufina, but then I see her again." He stroked his chin as he tried to find the words. "She has this pull. When I'm with her, the throne slips away, and I'm just a man with a beautiful woman. It both intrigues and terrifies me." He splayed his hands before him. "I can never be anything but the king...but when I'm with her, I want to be."

20

The
PEDDLER

CYRENE SHIELDED HERSELF FROM THE HARSHNESS OF THE blazing summer sun and hurried toward the shade of the booths in the Laelish Market. Many of the foreign merchants were missing from their shops, and she worried that Basille Selby might have already come back from Levin and then gone on his way. She breathed a sigh of relief when she found the tent still up. The flap draped over the entrance, indicating that it was closed but not empty.

As Cyrene drew closer, she heard raised voices inside, and she sighed in relief. *Someone is here.*

"Excuse me," she called. "I'm trying to find Master Basille Selby."

The voices suddenly broke off, and then she heard rustling, followed by a crash and cursing. The flap flew open, and a man's huge form filled up the space.

"Who's askin' fer Master Selby?" He fixed her with a sharp look.

She recognized the man from the day she and Maelia had come down to the market all those weeks ago. She had just forgotten how big he was.

"So nice to see you again," Cyrene said.

"We met?"

"I was here several weeks ago, trying to locate Master Selby about a book he sold me." She shot him a charming smile.

"I thin' I do 'member ya now." He scratched under his stubbly chin with one scarred leathery hand.

"Wonderful. Has Master Selby returned from Levin?"

"I 'aven't seen 'im."

"I heard you arguing with someone before I arrived. If that was not Master Selby, then who was it?"

"It wa' nobody. Now, clear out. I gots work ta do." He shooed her away.

"I can't leave. I have to speak with Master Selby about a book. I'm leaving on the procession in a week, and I don't know when I'll get a chance to speak with him again," she desperately told him.

Gather's eyes bulged. "Youse one of dem-dem people? An Affiliate?"

"Yes. I'm an Affiliate, so I won't have another time to get down here."

His jaw set, and he spit off to the left. Cyrene reflexively stepped back at the fire in his eyes.

"Basille don' deal with youse kind," he growled. His already daunting figure reached an additional height.

She gaped at the fierceness of his scowl. No one had ever reacted so negatively to her title.

"I've no idea why you despise Affiliates, but I don't mean you or Master Selby any harm. I merely want to ask about a book." She reached inside the small bag she was carrying and pulled forth the book. "This book. Please, if you could, take this to him and tell him I have questions about it. That's all I'm asking. I swear by the Creator, I'll never bother you again."

He seemed to be weighing his mistrust of the situation with what she was saying and the book in her hand. "Youse people 'ave broke promises before."

"I don't." She looked him dead in the eyes as she shoved the book into his burly chest.

"I'm 'a regret this," he mumbled, taking the book from her and closing the flap in her face.

She huffed irritably as she baked in the afternoon heat. His reaction worried her. Every other time she had uttered her position, she had been shown much respect and deference. Her parents were always shown similar esteem. In fact, she had become accustomed to it. But this man had not only been angry with her, something in his face had shown that he was actually scared of her.

What could an Affiliate have done to that man to make him scared of me?

Cyrene mopped her forehead with a handkerchief and waited.

A short while later, he returned, looking none too pleased. He suspiciously eyed her up and down. "I dunno why he's lettin' ya in, but if ya cause any trouble, I be throwin' ya out," he warned her. "Here's ya book."

After tossing her cloak off her head, she grabbed the book out of his hand and followed him inside the tent. Under the confines of the tent, the drop in temperature was startling. She gazed around and saw that more than half of the books were missing from the tables, and a large portion of the remaining knickknacks was gone, but a few Levin-made products were on display.

"He's in da back." He pointed to a back room covered by a magenta curtain.

"Thank you," she responded politely. She braced herself and walked through the curtained wall.

The back room hosted a mountain of half-empty boxes on top of a surprisingly clean brown rug. A small desk stood off to the side, covered in rolls of parchment, a few pouches—one that had toppled over and spilled a handful of gold Byern pences—and two large maps Cyrene couldn't make out. The back flap of the tent opened to reveal a covered wagon hitched to a pair of brown steeds.

In the corner, rifling through one of the boxes, stood the man she had been looking for. He was exceptionally tall with an almost stringy, lean body.

"Excuse me, Master Selby."

He swung around to face her with a flourish. He wasn't exactly what she was expecting. Some might have considered him handsome with his slicked back dark hair, manicured beard and mustache, skilled long fingers, and general fluency of his movements.

"I did not mean to interrupt," she said.

"Not at all, Affiliate. Not at all," he said with a beautiful flowing Eleysian accent. He swept her a deep bow that would have befitted the Queen. "It's always a pleasure."

How interesting, considering the other man's revulsion at the title.

"The pleasure is all mine. Please, do call me Cyrene."

"Cyrene it is then, and I am Basille Selby, a humble Eleysian merchant," he said with a crooked smile. "At your service. Now, how can I be of assistance?"

"It's a matter of this book." She showed him the cover. "My sister purchased it from you as a birthday gift for me."

"Fine gift there. Fine gift," he amiably told her.

"Yes, yes, it is. She said that when she purchased it from you, you said the book was for the Children of the Dawn. I was curious. Who are the Children of the Dawn?"

Basille, until that moment, had seemed every bit the cool, composed businessman, but at the utterance of the name, he intently stared at her with his sharp chocolate-brown eyes. He reached his hand out to take the book from her. He skimmed through the blank pages, his muscles tensing at the movement, and then he quickly returned it to her.

"Why are you interested in the Children of the Dawn, Affiliate?"

"Please, call me Cyrene," she reminded him. "You were the one who told my sister about these Children, and I don't know who they are, nor can I find any information in the libraries about them."

Basille snorted. "Of course you can't, Affiliate. Not in Byern libraries at least. The Children of the Dawn are no longer spoken of in this world...or many other worlds either."

Cyrene had a sudden flashback to the Ring of Gardens. The royalty present at her ceremony had said that they had held back the histories of their lands for protection. *Could this be part of that history?*

"What do you mean?"

"No...nothing. You shouldn't even be here, asking about the Children. Forget I ever mentioned it to your sister." He began ushering her out.

"But I cannot, Master Selby! This has something to do with me." Cyrene ducked under his long arms and moved deeper into the back room, clutching the book to her chest. "You don't understand. I have to know."

He wheeled around to stare at her. "Why do you have to know?"

Cyrene ground her teeth in frustration. The last time she had revealed what she knew about the book, Elea hadn't been able to see the text. Cyrene had thought that she was crazy for it, and she didn't know if she was ready to feel like that again.

"I...I can't explain," Cyrene murmured, turning away from the peddler.

"You're going to have to try, Affiliate. I have quite a bit of work to complete before I leave the city."

Cyrene turned to face him. "Where are you going?"

His eyes narrowed almost imperceptibly. Either he noticed her sidestep, or he did not like her questioning his whereabouts. Likely, it was both.

"It does not concern you. I am Basille Selby. I travel to the farthest reaches of our land and beyond."

"Where have you been? To Lake Mische, the Barren Mountains, the haunted Drop Pass? All the way to Bienco and the far reaches of the Lakonia Ocean?" she asked in a rambling tone.

Basille chuckled softly at her enthusiasm. "I have been to all those places and more that you should never know of. Have a seat, Affiliate. With all these questions floating in the air, it seems I won't be getting much more done at the moment."

Cyrene plopped into the nearest seat by the desk as he gracefully folded himself into one adjacent from her.

He crossed a leg over the other at the knee and interlaced his long fingers. He stared a moment before asking, "What are you really doing here? You have one of the best positions in your land. You seem to have the world at your feet. What are you doing down in the dregs of the Laelish, carrying on a conversation with a peddler? Even if I *am* the best."

Cyrene warred with herself about opening up to the man. After all, it was why she had come down to meet with him. He would soon be out of Byern. *Who knew the next time they would meet—if ever?*

She opened the book to the center of the supposedly blank pages. The shimmery gold font mockingly stared back at her. It teased at the back of her mind, as if she should know what the words said, but she couldn't understand them. It made even less sense than her Presenting letter, and out of fear of the unknown, she hadn't spent any more time studying the book.

She placed her finger on the page. "Is this page blank to you?"

Basille visibly shook as he looked at the page. "Yes." His voice wavered, yet he was rapt with attention.

"And this one?" She turned to the next page.

He nodded.

"All of them?" She ran her hand along the pages and flipped through them.

"Yes, they are all blank."

"They're not to me," she whispered as her eyes rose to stare into his face.

Basille's chest rose and fell rapidly, and he rubbed his palms against his linen pants, leaving sweat marks behind. He gulped hard, his whole body moving with the effort. His eyes rapidly moved back and forth, but he stared off into the distance, not meeting her gaze.

As if possessed, he jumped up from his seat and began shoving books, knickknacks, and loose ends into random boxes with seemingly no order. "Time for you to go, Affiliate." He rushed past her and tossed a handful of books into a box.

"What?" She jumped to her feet in surprise. "I don't understand."

"Go. Go on. Get out of here." He grabbed more books and repeated the movements.

"Where are you going? And aren't you going to help me and answer my questions?"

Basille frantically shook his head. "No, no, no. I can't get mixed up. I'm sorry. I like you, but I can't."

"You can't answer my questions, or you can't help me?"

She reached out to try to still him. He flinched away and collided into a towering bookshelf that came toppling down on his head.

The man from the front appeared immediately through the curtain. "Everythin' okay back ther'?"

"Yes, Gather. Thank you." Basille hauled himself out of the pile of books. "If you would, please escort Affiliate Cyrene out."

"Master Selby, you didn't tell me anything. Who are the Children of the Dawn? What is this book? Why can I see the writing?"

Gather forcefully grabbed her elbow. "Come on. Don' botha 'im no more."

"Please." She pushed against Gather's meaty arm. "Tell me something, anything!"

Basille suddenly turned to her. "You'll *never* find answers here. Go to Eleysia. You must go to the Eleysian capital city and ask for Matilde and Vera. I cannot help you, Cyrene, but they can."

Cyrene's breathing was ragged as Gather all but threw her out of the tent with garbled swear words. She stared, starry-eyed, at the closed curtain for a moment, trying to grasp what had happened. Basille had quaked in terror at the mention that she could see the gold lettering, but he had been afraid before she had said anything. Something had been off about him from the beginning.

Did he know someone else who could see the lettering? Could these Matilde and Vera see it? Is that why I must go to Eleysia?

The number of new questions piling up infuriated her enough to almost return and demand answers from him.

Almost.

She couldn't muscle her way past Gather, and there was no guarantee Basille would be free with information. She should feel lucky she'd gotten as much as she did out of him. He could have already left Byern, and she would have never known that she needed to go to Eleysia or seek out Matilde and Vera.

Perhaps this was the thing she was supposed to find, as described in her Presenting letter. After all, she was searching for something she didn't know about. Not that having a destination helped her any because her Presenting letter riddle had said that what she was looking for couldn't be found.

Cyrene retrieved Ceffy and swung up into the saddle. Resigned to the idea that she wasn't going to get any more answers today, she kicked Ceffy into a trot as she began to formulate a plan.

Cyrene returned to chaos.

Affiliates were rushing around the grounds, clustered in small groups and holding on to each other. One girl was crying into a friend's shoulder. A group of High Order talked in mournful whispers. The Queen's DIA, Catalin, was going from group to group with a piece of parchment in her hand.

Cyrene trotted Ceffy to the stables, threw the reins to a man on duty, and then went in search of answers. She hadn't been gone from court for more than an hour or two. She wondered what she had missed.

As she rounded the corner, Maelia came running straight for her. Maelia threw her arms around her and hugged her tight. "Oh,

Cyrene! You're all right. When you couldn't be located, we thought…"

Cyrene pulled back and held Maelia at arm's length. "You thought what? I just went down to the market."

Maelia's face paled. "You haven't heard?"

"Heard what?"

"Affiliate Leslin was found dead in the same spot as Zorian. Her face had the same mutilation," she whispered.

Cyrene's hands flew to her mouth. *Not Leslin!* She had gone to look for the librarian today. Leslin had been on holiday, visiting her daughter, and now…she would never return.

21
The
PLAN

CYRENE SANK TO HER KNEES IN THE MIDDLE OF THE courtyard.

Leslin was...dead.

She covered her mouth as a sob racked her body.

Aralyn. Oh no.

How did Aralyn react to finding out that her friend is dead?

Cyrene hadn't handled the news that Rhea had made Second Class very well. She couldn't stomach thinking about something worse happening to her friend...or never seeing her again.

"Maelia," Cyrene gasped.

"I know, Cyrene. It's so terrible. When you were gone, I thought the worst had happened. I'm so glad that you're all right."

"I just...can't believe this." Cyrene brushed aside the tears that had fallen on her cheeks, and she slowly rose again.

"Me either. More guards have been called to duty around the perimeter and in the city, and the King instated a curfew. No one is allowed to be out after dark."

"But Leslin wasn't out after dark. It was the middle of the day," Cyrene said.

Maelia nodded. "I know, but what else can they do?"

Cyrene didn't know. She had never experienced anything like this. *Who is killing people and for what purpose?*

"I have to find my sister," she told Maelia. "She was friends with Leslin."

Was. It sounds so final.

"I'll go with you. I don't like the thought of you walking around here on your own," Maelia admitted.

Cyrene didn't even disagree with her friend, which really showed the severity of the situation. Her head was full of the news of the death of an Affiliate, but still, she couldn't stop thinking about Basille's demands for her to go to Eleysia. She needed to leave the castle, find Matilde and Vera, and get answers to her questions.

But how would that be possible when the castle is in such turmoil? And would I even be safe? Certainly not alone...

They strode through the Vines, past the clusters of Affiliates huddled together as they discussed the news, and stopped at Aralyn's room. Cyrene knocked twice and waited. Aralyn answered almost immediately. She looked exactly like the last time Cyrene had been here. Her nose was buried in a book, her brown hair was pulled off her face, and her dress had been immaculately pressed.

"Aralyn," Cyrene said softly.

"What is it, Cyrene? I'm in the middle of something," Aralyn said.

Cyrene shared a look with Maelia. "We came to see how you were doing."

"I'm quite well. Just about to leave for Kell on official business. I have much to do before I depart."

She started closing the door, but Cyrene put her hand out.

"Have you not heard the news?"

"I don't follow castle gossip," Aralyn said. She finally closed her book and looked up at Cyrene with an exaggerated sigh. "What is it?"

Cyrene wet her lips and let the unsaid words hang in the air. She hated being the one to tell her sister, but she had to.

"Aralyn, I don't know how to tell you—"

They heard footsteps stomping down the stone hallway, and all three girls turned their heads to see who was coming forward. Maelia yelped and jumped sideways as if someone were coming to attack her.

"Reeve," Cyrene whispered.

"I came as soon as I heard," her brother said.

"Oh, honestly, what are *both* of you doing here?" Aralyn asked. Her eyes were narrowed at Reeve.

Cyrene knew that they hadn't been getting along, but it was strange to see them this way.

"You haven't told her?" Reeve asked Cyrene.

"Just spit it out," Aralyn said, crossing her arms.

Reeve gave Aralyn a sympathetic look. "Aralyn...they just found Leslin's body."

She tilted her head at him in confusion. "What do you mean, *found* her body?"

"She's dead," Cyrene whispered.

"What?" Aralyn asked aghast. "She was on holiday to visit her daughter."

"They think it was related to the attack on Zorian," Reeve said. His voice was strained at the mention of his friend.

Aralyn's face crumpled as she realized that what they were saying was reality. "I...I don't," Aralyn mumbled. She looked like she wanted to cry but was holding back her tears.

"Come on," Reeve said, placing his arm around her shoulders. "Let's go sit down."

Cyrene and Maelia followed Reeve inside. They busied themselves with trying to comfort Aralyn, making tea, and helping her pack her things for Kell. Cyrene wasn't sure how much help she was, but she didn't want to leave her sister when she was an emotional wreck.

Hours later, when Aralyn finally passed out, Reeve ushered them out of the room to get some rest.

She and Maelia walked solemnly down the hall, back to their rooms.

Helping Aralyn had gotten Cyrene's mind off of Basille's warnings, but now that she was away, everything kicked back into overdrive. She had a plan. She simply needed to implement it.

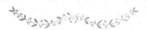

The next morning, the castle was buzzing with the news that Ahlvie had been called into questioning for a second time. Cyrene couldn't believe that he was being accused again when there had been no evidence to indict him with Zorian. She still didn't think that Ahlvie had killed anyone and hoped that his disagreements with Leslin wouldn't come back to haunt him.

She had no affiliation with him this time around, so she didn't think she would get called in for questioning. She hoped he knew how to get himself out of this again.

Thankfully, she had very little time to contemplate the deaths. It was on the tips of everyone's tongues, but she kept herself cloistered in her room, digging through the final pages of Affiliate Lorne's agricultural work. Procession was only a week away, and she had so much to attend to before then.

Two days before she was going to leave on procession, she had all her bags packed and ready to go. The day before, Cyrene had requested an audience with the Queen and she was impatiently awaiting that appointment.

Cyrene couldn't keep from bouncing up and down on the balls of her feet. It had been nearly six weeks since she was this nervous for anything, but her Presenting already felt like a lifetime ago.

She dressed quickly and simply in a pale blue dress. Then, she plaited her hair back and knotted it into a bun with a navy-blue satin ribbon. She wanted to look presentable but not over the top.

It was unfortunate she hadn't been able to include Maelia in on her plans. Cyrene wanted to make sure all the pieces were in place before discussing it with anyone. If all went according to design, she would be able to tell her this afternoon.

She grabbed her leatherwork folder from her coffee table and traipsed out of the room with her retinue trailing behind her. Cyrene's steps faltered as they entered the typically hectic atrium to the Queen's quarters. The room was almost completely silent, and the few Affiliates who remained in the vacant chambers were spaced far apart. No one even gave Cyrene a second glance.

Regaining her confidence, Cyrene hurried across the deserted room to the DIA's small office. She knocked twice and waited.

A moment later, the door opened, and Cyrene tried not to hiss at the figure standing before her.

"Cyrene," Jardana said with a slow poisonous smile.

"Jardana," she said, curtsying politely. "Is Affiliate Catalin not in today?"

"She is with Her Majesty, and I am acting DIA at the moment." She stretched her neck to its limit and stuck her nose in the air, giving her the appearance of a giraffe. "What can I help you with?"

"I sent word yesterday, requesting an audience with the Queen," Cyrene plainly told her.

Jardana fluffed her blonde hair and retreated into Catalin's office. Cyrene had no choice but to follow, leaving the servants in the common room.

"It's simply not possible," Jardana uttered once she had made herself comfortable at Catalin's desk.

"I sent word yesterday."

"The Queen is not well," Jardana said. Her light-blue eyes were wide with concern. "And she will see no one today."

Cyrene's stomach plummeted to the ground. The Queen had to be well. She had done too much already for her not to be able to speak with the Queen. "What is wrong with her?"

Jardana fixed her now cool eyes upon her. "That is hardly your concern. Her Majesty needs some rest. That is all. You may go." She fluttered her manicured slender fingers at Cyrene.

"Very well." Cyrene was determined to find another way in to see the Queen. Jardana was very likely lying. "I'll see you at the procession."

Jardana's eyes narrowed to slits at the words. Until that moment, Cyrene hadn't been certain that Jardana knew that she would be on the King's ship. Jardana's sneer only made Cyrene smile wider.

But when she turned toward the Queen's doors, her elation at besting Jardana slipped away. She couldn't just barge in on the Queen, especially if Jardana had in fact told the truth.

Something banged loudly against the wooden door in the Queen's study, and Cyrene jumped back a pace in shock. The walls were half a foot thick of solid wood, yet she could hear the Queen shrieking. She was trying to make out the words when the door sprang open in front of her.

Affiliate Catalin scrambled out of the room. Her fiery-red hair was even messier than normal with chunks of it pulled out of her braid, giving her a manic appearance.

"Affiliate Catalin," Cyrene chirped.

"Cyrene," she said, barely looking at her.

"You promised me an audience with the Queen," she said loud enough for her voice to carry into the chamber. She knew it was a bad day to address the Queen, but she couldn't go back now.

"I...what? No. No audiences today." Catalin shook her head.

"You promised an audience, Catalin?" Queen Kaliana shrieked, hurling what looked like a small glass orb at Catalin's head.

Catalin ducked as the glass flew through the space where her head had been and exploded against the far wall.

"I wouldn't, Majesty," she whimpered. She rose infinitesimally from her crouched position.

"Oh, let her in, you cow," Queen Kaliana cried. "Get out! Get out of my sight!"

Catalin hurried to obey orders and murmured softly to Cyrene, "You want her. You can have her. May the Creator be with you."

Creator, give me strength.

Cyrene entered. The Queen's face was paler than normal, and her eyes were rimmed with red, as if she had been crying. Her perfect blonde hair fell loose from her bun, and a few strands framed her face. She looked younger and more vulnerable. However, the set of her ice-blue eyes revealed the Queen was otherwise unchanged.

Cyrene stopped before Queen Kaliana's desk and curtsied. The four servant girls, who had been standing away from the cross fire, followed after Cyrene. The first girl walked forward, and without hesitation, she placed a rather large stack of papers near the front of Queen Kaliana's desk.

"What is this about?" Queen Kaliana asked as the woman turned and went back to stand by the other girls.

The next three girls placed an equally large pile of paperwork on the Queen's desk. When they were finished, the women curtsied deeply for the Queen and whispered their formalities before disappearing behind the wooden door.

"What in the name of the Creator is all of this?" Queen Kaliana glowered openly at Cyrene.

"My report, Your Majesty." Cyrene sauntered forward and placed the stuffed leather folder on top of the wall of paperwork.

"Your report on what?"

"On Affiliate Lorne's life's work regarding foreign crop development. You will find a full detailed list of everything that she studied that could be of use to Byern. Also, in advance, I constructed a plan of implementation for several of the more important foreign agricultural developments."

"You've only been here a couple of weeks," the Queen said.

"Six weeks," Cyrene informed her. "And I've completed everything you requested of me with satisfaction."

"Mmm," Queen Kaliana said noncommittally.

Cyrene took a deep breath. "I would like to request a leave of absence."

Queen Kaliana's mouth was agape, and her blue eyes stared uncomprehendingly. As quickly as the surprise registered, it passed, and she once again resumed her regal authority.

"You wish to be granted a leave of absence?" the Queen asked.

"Yes, Your Majesty."

"What exactly do you need this leave for?"

"I need to travel to further the interests of Affiliate Lorne." She kept her voice level and controlled.

"The interests of a dead woman?" the Queen asked incredulously.

"She was unable to travel to the distant lands she researched to study the crops in their natural habitat, and if I am to become an expert on foreign crop development, I need leave to visit these locales," she told the Queen as passively as she could muster. Her palms sweated as the lie slipped from her mouth, but she refrained from wiping them against her dress.

"Affiliate Lorne did quite well without ever leaving Byern, did she not?"

"She succeeded beyond measure," Cyrene began.

Queen Kaliana smiled.

Cyrene continued, "For someone who was not afforded the opportunity to fully study the subject she was enthralled with."

"No." Queen Kaliana leaned back into her enormous rosewood chair.

"What?" Cyrene asked, losing all sense of formality.

"You have my answer, Cyrene. You may not have a leave of absence. You will journey on the procession bound for Albion tomorrow, and I will continue with your training and education henceforth." She crossed her hands over her stomach.

"But, Your Majesty, I must leave Byern to study—"

"Cyrene! Have we not discussed your back talking previously? You will do what I say as I am your Queen and your Receiver."

Cyrene's stomach turned as she remembered her Ring of Gardens ceremony when Edric had moved her to Third Class based on such a statement.

"Of course, Your Majesty, but may I ask *why* you will not let me leave?" She knew the Queen begrudged her because of the King's affection, but it could only benefit the Queen to send her away.

Queen Kaliana shakily rose to her feet, pressing her hands on the edge of her desk. Streaks of blonde flew before her eyes as she leaned forward and pursed her lips. "I need no reason," she said cold and steady. "I am your Receiver, your Queen. You do as *I* say. When I command you to remain in Byern and never leave the city, you curtsy and smile like the good little girl you are. When I demand you study foreign crop development, you study the material until *I* tell you that you are finished." Queen Kaliana shoved the paperwork off the desk, letting it scatter aimlessly across the open floor around Cyrene's feet. "Do I make myself clear?"

Cyrene's eyes never wavered from the surge of hate radiating from the Queen. She kept her head level and her chin slightly raised, as if she would not succumb to the Queen's torments. She had been through worse, lost in a nightmare while trapped in the recesses of the castle's underworld. They had thought they would break her, but she had survived and come out stronger than ever.

"Very," Cyrene said.

"You're dismissed." Queen Kaliana collapsed back into her chair. "Send in that vapid woman, Catalin, on your way out."

"Yes, Your Majesty." She gritted her teeth as she curtsied, walked across the paperwork she had slaved over for hours, and left the Queen's quarters.

22

The SETUP

CYRENE WAS SEETHING.

The thought of being alone in her room debilitated her, and she made her way toward an open window to gaze out across the garden grounds. She tried to find composure from the Queen's outburst, but none came to her.

Knowing that Maelia typically studied medicinal herbs this time of day, Cyrene skipped down the stairs in search of her friend. It was about time to clue her in on Cyrene's plans.

After striding down a row of twelve-foot bushes, Cyrene came to a stop at the rustic metal gate blocking the entrance to the medicinal gardens. Her hands trembled as she unlatched the gate. She sighed before pulling it open, and she peered inside the garden looking for Maelia.

Her heart stopped when she saw the Prince first. *What is he doing here?*

She eased back out. The last person she wanted to run into when her temper was high was Prince Kael.

Narrowing her eyes, she looked past him and saw Maelia's pale face staring up at him. Her face was a mask, but then again, it always was. A lump formed in Cyrene's throat at the thought of the Prince trying any of his antics on her friend. Cyrene was a tempest ready to unleash at the drop of a hat, but Maelia was so timid. She obeyed authority like any militaristic Second. Cyrene would throw a fit if he used that to his advantage, and the man used everything to his advantage.

Whatever they were discussing had clearly come to a close, and before Cyrene knew it, Prince Kael was advancing directly toward her at the exit.

Taking the handle in his hand, the Prince wrenched the gate open. "Affiliate," he said with a smile as he angled around her.

"Prince," she murmured, holding back her rage.

He hadn't done anything yet. She could handle this.

"Are you ready for the procession? On the King's ship, no less." A muscle twitched in his jaw.

He was jealous. She would have laughed at him if she wasn't in such a wretched mood.

"I'm so fortunate."

"I'd say my brother is the fortunate one."

"He is the King."

"I was right." He took another step around her.

"About what?" She edged out of his way.

"That I wouldn't be the only one courting you," he responded with a smirk.

Her mind flashed back to her first night in the castle, and she shuddered. She couldn't believe he was even bringing it up again.

"No one is courting me," she responded through gritted teeth. "Least of all your brother."

Prince Kael chuckled. He bridged the distance between them. Cyrene stood stiff, wanting nothing more than to wipe the smirk clear off his face.

"My brother was raised alongside me. He is a courtier through and through." He softly ran his hand across her cheek. "You'll do well to remember that."

Cyrene turned her face away from him. "Good day, Prince Kael."

"It always is when I see you," he said as he strode away.

Cyrene forced herself to take a deep breath before entering the garden.

Maelia quickly turned around and broke into a smile. "Good to see you, Cyrene."

"Did you see the Prince?"

"Yes, he was just in here," Maelia said.

"What did he want?"

"He was discussing the procession with me," she said.

"Why? I've never seen you two speak before."

"Cyrene," Maelia whined, turning back down to the garden, "please don't make me say."

"Oh, come on, Maelia." Cyrene managed a smile. "You can tell me!"

Maelia shook her head from side to side, clearly debating with herself. "You cannot let him know."

"I'll never breathe a word of it," she vowed.

"He was questioning how we got onto the King's ship for the procession, but he told me not to tell you about it. He…he fancies you, Cyrene."

Cyrene sighed. She had been more afraid that the Prince was going to press his luck with Maelia.

"I'm sorry he's asking you questions. Did he pressure you in any way?" She hated asking, but she had to know.

"He…well, you know how he is. He puts me on edge, Cyrene. I don't know why it upset me so."

"I do," Cyrene said. This was the moment. "The first night I was here, before you and I met, Prince Kael held me down against the wall and tried to take advantage of me in my chambers."

Maelia gasped, staring up at Cyrene in horror.

"And when I forced him to stop, he didn't back down, and he has been pursuing me ever since. I've told no one but you."

Maelia reached out and grasped Cyrene's hand. "He didn't!"

Cyrene bit her lip and nodded.

"Oh, I'm so sorry. How…how vile!"

"I know. He's never going to stop, and the Queen is worse."

"The Queen?"

"She hates me, Maelia. She thinks I want to take over."

"But you've never done anything to make her think that!" Maelia cried.

Cyrene glanced around the garden, making certain that no one else was listening. "Nothing, Maelia? With King Edric asking me for walks through the garden and Prince Kael chasing after me like a hound?"

"What are you going to do? You have something in mind. I can see it."

And that was when Cyrene knew the Queen's resolution about her performance, about her behavior, about her very existence in the castle didn't matter. Nothing would stop her now.

"Yes, I have a plan."

"Could we get in trouble?"

"Yes."

"Is it worth it?"

Goose bumps broke out across her skin, and she swallowed. *Is it worth it to leave everything on the whim of a peddler?* Yet it felt like more than that. The book called to her. She needed to find out what it meant. She needed to know why she could see the words when no one else could. She needed to find out why he had gotten hysterical when she told him about it. It terrified her, but she couldn't ignore it…even if a killer was on the loose.

"Yes," Cyrene finally answered. "I need to leave the castle."

"What?" Maelia asked. "There have been two deaths, and you want to leave the grounds?"

"Not the grounds. The country," she whispered.

"Is this about Zorian and Leslin?"

"Partly. It's complicated." Cyrene sighed. "I just…do you trust me, Maelia?"

Maelia paused and then nodded. "Yes."

"Then, know that I have to do this, and I'll tell you everything as soon as I can," Cyrene finally said.

"All right. I trust you," Maelia said. "Whatever it is, I'm in."

Cyrene heavily breathed out in relief and then began to fill Maelia in on her plan. With Maelia on board, this might actually work.

She left Maelia to finish packing and entered her rooms to make sure all preparations for the procession were close to completion. Her clothes had been properly folded and placed into traveling bags. Someone would come to take them to the boats soon enough.

A new package sat on her dresser. She cautiously took it in her hands. A note fell to the floor. She hastily retrieved it and saw the scrawled handwriting of her seamstress, Lady Cauthorn.

A smile broke out on her face. She tore into the brown paper and let the gold gown fall elegantly to her feet. It was exquisite in the same fashion as her Presenting ball gown but in a color fit for a Dremylon. Her fingers ran over the silky material. She didn't imagine she would have anywhere to wear it on the procession and lamented leaving it behind.

After hanging up the dress, she retreated from her rooms and went in search of Reeve to ask about Aralyn. After she had first found out about Leslin, Aralyn hadn't wanted any more visitors. The funeral for Leslin was tomorrow afternoon, and Cyrene hoped to speak with her after that.

Cyrene rushed to the High Order common rooms, anxious to see Reeve. A few minutes later, she found him in his room. The door was cracked open, and she raised her hand and knocked.

"Come on in," Reeve called.

She peeked inside. "Hey."

"Hey, Cyrene. What are you doing here?"

She bit her lip. "Just dropping by to ask about Aralyn."

"You just missed her," Reeve said. He shook his head. "She left for Kell this morning."

Cyrene's mouth dropped open. "She left already? She isn't even staying for the funeral?"

"Yes, well, it's Aralyn," Reeve said.

Sometimes, she couldn't understand her sister. She had thought that Aralyn would want closure on the loss of her friend, but instead, she'd just left as soon as she could. *Then again isn't that what I'm planning to do as well?*

"I heard you're on the procession."

"I am," Cyrene said, still surprised about Aralyn's departure.

"And on the King's ship."

"Indeed."

"What did you do to get there, Cyrene?" He took her elbow and drew her closer.

"Nothing." She wrenched herself away from him.

He sighed. "Did you sleep with him?"

Cyrene sputtered, absolutely floored by the turn of the conversation. She had always been close to her brother. He had doted on her when she was younger. Not in a million years had she thought he would suspect her of such a thing.

"That is none of your business!"

"Cyrene, this is serious. I know how things are around here, but I can't help you without answers."

"I don't need your help! I can't believe you would think so lowly of me."

"Everyone has seen you with him, and now, this. What do you expect?"

"I expected better from you," she said before she turned and fled the room.

Cyrene left the High Order's corridors at a jog, desperate to escape the pressing prison cell in which she found herself trapped. She broke through the nearest doors, heading out into an open courtyard. She stopped to catch her breath and ran a hand back through her tangled dark hair. The pathway reflected back at her in a glittering cracked glass prism, darting from white to yellow to orange and then red, purple, blue, and green.

The trail led to the stables. She walked down the pathway and through the stable doors. The motto carved into the entrance reminded her all too well of her warrior ceremony.

BELIEVE IN THOSE WHOSE HONOR DOTH SHINE.

Cyrene wandered over to her dapple, Ceffy, who whinnied at her approach. She stroked her nose and tried to forget everything that had happened recently.

"Come here often?" a voice sounded behind her, breaking her from her solitude.

She turned and saw Ahlvie walking toward her. He was unsteady on his feet, but his eyes were still alert.

"A little too often. I keep running into you, don't I?"

Ahlvie smiled, holding out a brown leather wineskin. "You look like you might need this more than I do."

She eyed it. "I'm guessing that's not water."

"What's the fun in that?" He took a swig himself.

"I think I'll pass."

"Your loss."

"I heard that they called you in for more questioning." She returned her attention to Ceffy. "So, you might need it."

"They don't have anything on me, but it doesn't keep them from banning me from leaving the premises."

"Why do they think you did it this time?"

"Don't you know?" he asked, pitching forward. "Leslin and I argued."

"She obviously disliked you more than you disliked her though. I thought that was clear," Cyrene said.

"Yeah, well, go tell them that." He thrust his hand out at the castle and shrugged.

"So, if you are banned from leaving, then you're not going on the procession?" she asked.

"Nah. I wasn't going anyway. Byern is better without court, but now, I can't even leave the castle to enjoy myself." His eyes twinkled mischievously.

She doubted they could keep him locked inside.

"Don't you ever want to just be free of all of this?" she asked.

Their eyes met, and for a second, it was almost as if he understood something about her that she didn't even have to speak aloud.

"More than anything."

"Then, I'd find a way to get on procession."

23

The
PROCESSION

As soon as the Keylani River hit the docks of the capital city of Byern, it transformed from a swift and dangerous mountain pass into an easy flowing broad body of water. The voyage from Carhara through the deep cutting passageway was treacherous and had abated aggression between the Eastern and Western worlds for generations. Once the river swept out of the mountains, it led smoothly to the mouth of Byern's trade networks in Albion.

Cyrene stood on the deck of the King's ship with Maelia and watched the hustle and bustle below them. Adults and children flooded the docks and stone roads that looked across the great flat ships tethered to the berth. Even with the increase in guards keeping watch over the general populace, a sense of merriment was in the air. People were calling out well wishes to the passengers, and vendors were selling candy and streamers for children.

She leaned forward against the wooden railing in awe at being on the other side of the cheering. Right now, she was just enamored with the wind in her hair, the wooden deck under her feet, the Dremylon green flag flapping overhead, and the knowledge that she was leaving Byern for the very first time.

The wind was steady, and the sails dropped, carrying them upstream into the oncoming breeze. Behind them housed the five other ships with the remaining court.

Maelia reached out with her left hand and grasped Cyrene's hand where it rested on the railing. Cyrene tore her eyes away from the crowd to look at her.

"We're really going," Maelia said, her voice almost disappearing into the wind.

"Isn't it exciting?"

Maelia's eyes cut to the crowd. "It's all a bit overwhelming."

"That's what makes it an adventure." She squeezed her friend's hand.

Maelia smiled forlornly as she watched her second home disappear.

Their ships breezed past the Laelish Market with its brightly colored tents, the leveled stone roads, and the city skirts as they gained speed. Soon, even the lowest stones of the outer ring of the city passed from view. Only flatlands, gently rolling hills, and mountains lay in the distance.

"Let's go below. I've heard there's nothing more to see for a while."

"Have you never been to Albion?" Maelia asked.

"No. Did I not mention that? My parents preferred not to travel, and over holidays, we would just go to the countryside. This is the farthest I've ever been outside of the Byern city limits." She bounced on the balls of her feet.

"Byern was not what I expected after seventeen years in Levin. I hope you like Albion more so."

Cyrene hoped so, too.

They quickly darted below deck to Cyrene's chambers. She had accommodations fit for a woman above her status at court. The bed was large and plush, and she had a full vanity, dresser, and wardrobe. A richly colored Aurumian rug covered the floor, and a decadent silver wash bin rested by the vanity.

"I still can't believe you got this room," Maelia said.

"Isn't it grand?"

"Are you going to tell me how you acquired it, or should I even bother?"

"The Consort offered it to me."

"You're in contact with the Consort now? Why am I even surprised? Will you ever share all your secrets with me?"

Cyrene had the good sense to look sheepish. She still had secrets a plenty that she wasn't planning on sharing with anyone— not now, not yet.

A knock at the door pulled both girls away from their discussion of adventure and secrets.

Maelia crossed the room and opened the door.

"Sorry to disturb you, Affiliates," the gentleman said.

Cyrene observed the High Order logo on his garb. He was attractive enough with dark features and an open smile.

"Now that we're past the outer banks, His Majesty has requested your presence for lunch."

"Thank you," Maelia said, not hiding her awe at the invitation.

"It is my pleasure. Would you mind if I escorted you myself? It has been some time since I've been in the company of such beautiful ladies." He addressed Maelia with the latter statement, and then his gaze shifted to Cyrene before immediately returning to Maelia.

Maelia's cheeks heated, and she stared at the floor. "That would be most appreciated."

"Let us freshen up, and we'll be right out." Cyrene walked over to the door.

"I'll gladly wait," he said with a smile.

She closed the door in his face and instantly turned around. "Well, *he* was taken with you!"

"Oh, nonsense, Cyrene. No one notices me when you're in the room," Maelia said dismissively.

"He was staring directly at you," Cyrene insisted. "He hardly looked at me."

"Well, it doesn't matter with the journey ahead anyway," Maelia announced somewhat defensively.

"Perhaps not, but it is a fine time to flirt nonetheless."

Cyrene grabbed Maelia's arm and pulled her toward the door. Their escort was waiting for them on the other side.

"If you'll follow me," he said, offering each of them his arm. "I'm afraid I know both of you, but I haven't given you my name. Too long out of court, and I've forgotten the pleasantries. I am High Order Eren."

"Pleasure," Cyrene said as Maelia dipped her head in acknowledgment. "You said that you were out of court. Where were you?" She loved learning about other lands from people who had actually been there.

"Not far. I was an emissary to Carhara in the Tahne court for some time, and prior to that, I was stationed in Levin where I was raised."

"I was raised there as well," Maelia said.

"Really? In which foothold were you?"

Maelia made a swift hand motion that Cyrene didn't follow. Eren nodded and made a motion back. Maelia laughed and leaned into his arm.

Cyrene gave her a questioning look. She had no idea what had happened.

"Forgive me." Maelia straightened. "The Guard has a signaling language that they use to discuss military matters."

Interesting. Now that she thought about it, she had seen the Royal Guard around Byern make slight hand motions.

There seemed to be more and more things that she didn't know. There was an endless amount of information that she could never hope to acquire.

"Here we are." Eren released the two women and opened a door.

Luxury seemed to follow King Edric wherever he went. The long rectangular table with seats for a dozen filled the room with a plush green runner. Decorative silver candelabras cast a bright glow among the seven attendees already settled into high-backed chairs carved with detailed carpentry work.

But what drew Cyrene's attention were the blue-gray eyes of King Edric staring at her from the far end of the table. Her breathing hitched at the weight of that gaze and the spark of electricity that always seemed to flash between them. He looked ruggedly handsome, stripped out of his ceremonial attire and clothed instead in a loose green shirt and brown pants.

"Affiliates, thank you for accompanying High Order Eren. Please have a seat," King Edric said.

Eren prompted Cyrene to sit to the left of the King, and the Consort sat to his right. Cyrene thanked him as she sat down, shocked at the reception. She knew the Consort had wanted her on board for the King, but she was woefully unprepared for this.

The ten members of the King's inner circle toasted to Edric's good health.

With so few in the room, Cyrene had the strangest feeling of importance come over her. She had been selected for this. What *this* was, however, was yet to be determined.

Servants placed a banquet of delicious lunch choices before them, and everyone dug into their food.

Cyrene picked at a soft roll and watched everyone's interactions.

"My good friend, Eren," King Edric said, "it is a pleasure to have you back in Byern. Tahne has taken you from us for too long."

"Thank you, My King." He tipped his head. "It's a pleasure to be back."

"It is unfortunate the circumstances surrounding your return. I extend my sympathies at the loss of your brother, and I hope that we can work together to discover the means of Zorian's passing."

Cyrene glanced at Eren. "Zorian was your brother?"

"Yes. His research Trinnenberg, Tiek's capital city, had come to some manner of completion. So he traveled north to stay with me in the Tahne court for he last fortnight. He had intended to be back in Byern in time for a Presenting."

"That was your Presenting, Cyrene," King Edric said with an easy smile in her direction.

"Yes, I remember," she said softly.

Eren's smile seemed to widen when he looked upon her next, and Maelia sank into her seat.

"You must be Reeve's sister then. Zorian did mention him. I remember now."

"Yes, I am."

"Zorian spoke fondly of your brother. I'm sorry he didn't get to see Reeve again before—" Eren broke off and looked away. "I just regret not being able to make it in time for his funeral."

King Edric nodded solemnly. "We'll discover what happened to him and Affiliate Leslin. In the meantime, let's turn the matters away from such dour subjects."

The conversation shifted course as Consort Daufina began discussing procession activities. Cyrene had other plans for her time off this ship, but she listened intently to block out thoughts about the strange deaths.

Lunch ended with the Consort's insistence for rest after the stress of preparations.

Maelia stood as if to leave and then immediately sat back in her chair.

"Are you all right?" Eren asked, concerned.

Cyrene looked at her friend who had been all but silent throughout the meal. The paleness of her face betrayed her disposition.

"I think resting sounds pleasant." Maelia covered her mouth and attempted to stand again.

"No sea legs for you it seems," Eren said. "Perhaps you'll allow me to escort you back to your quarters."

"Yes, that would be most helpful, High Order Eren." She grasped his arm for support, not moving her hand from her mouth.

With worry creasing her temple, Cyrene turned back to thank the King.

"No fear," he said. "She'll recover after she rests for a time."

"I hope so. I didn't realize the sea could cause such distress. I find it comforting."

"I think it's convenient and quick, but I prefer the mountains." He smiled back at her. "Cyrene, do you mind walking with me back to my study? I have matters to attend to, and I would appreciate your company."

"I...of course," Cyrene murmured.

"Wonderful. Eren, please see me after you've attended to the Affiliate. I'd like to discuss this business with Zorian and Leslin."

"Yes, Your Highness." Eren bowed slightly at the waist before escorting a distraught Maelia out of the room.

Consort Daufina dipped a low curtsy with a smile that made Cyrene uneasy and then departed with another Affiliate at her heels.

King Edric offered Cyrene his arm. She gingerly placed her hand on it and followed him out of the room. Her mind was whirring. She wasn't sure that accepting the Consort's invitation onto the King's ship had been advisable.

They walked through a corridor and passed the set of wooden stairs that led above. A guard posted in front of a room at the end of a hallway signaled to the King, and Cyrene wondered if it was the secret language Maelia and Eren had been discussing.

The guard opened the door for them, and King Edric allowed her access to his private office. A hulking desk was the centerpiece, and it was covered in maps, scrolls, strange gold objects, and inkblots. The rest of the room had papers and books scattered about along with two overflowing bookshelves.

As the door closed behind them, Cyrene realized she was completely and utterly alone with the King of Byern.

"You must forgive my mess, Cyrene." It seemed as if a stone had been lifted from his chest, and he smiled openly as he sat down in the desk chair.

"I believe I can oblige you," she said with a smile, not knowing where to sit. There were two wooden chairs with green cushions, but one was piled with books and the other had a stack of dusty papers, so she stood instead.

"I feel as if I will crush you with this next question, and I do not mean for it to be so," he said quickly. "Do not take offense."

"I hardly ever do with you," she whispered. Her heart hammered in her chest.

"While I am very glad to have you aboard my vessel, I am curious as to the means in which you acquired your passage."

Cyrene raised her chin. Her ego was quickly bruising. "I do not understand."

"Please, take a seat."

"There are no seats." She raised an eyebrow as she locked her hands behind her back.

"Ah, my apologies," he said, jumping up.

Yes, the King of Byern actually jumped up. He cleared off one of the chairs for her, depositing the stack of books on an already too crowded bookshelf.

Cyrene swept her red dress aside and slowly sank into the chair before Edric. She softly placed her hands in her lap, trying to appear demure beneath the seething humiliation she was withstanding.

King Edric sat back in his chair and plainly stared at her. "I want you here."

"That's disappointing. I was hoping you would throw me overboard." As the realization of what she had said caught up with her, she covered her mouth.

King Edric burst into laughter. "Well, I certainly can't throw you overboard now."

"I should hope not."

"I mean no offense. I hardly have cause to laugh this much in court. How was I fortunate enough?"

"Did no one tell you of my presence aboard your ship?"

"Ah, you got me." He crossed his ankle over his knee and lounged back. "I did know you would be aboard, and I had heard that Daufina approved it. I didn't stop it."

"Then, what else would you like to know?"

The King leaned forward over the clutter of his desk and stared at her, seemingly waiting for something, but there was no more to the story. The Consort had invited her, and she had accepted.

"So, you didn't request this spot or—"

"What? Of course not," Cyrene said.

King Edric smiled and stared at her like she was a pawn in a chess game.

"Not that I do not want to be here," she corrected.

He stood regally and walked around the desk to face her. She stared up at him, wondering what his end game was. They'd had a moment in the gardens, but after the Ring of Gardens ceremony, she had seen little of him, yet here she was on his boat at the Consort's request. Staring into his eyes, she found that she didn't want to be anywhere else.

Edric extended his hand to her, and she stood before him. He didn't let go of her, and they moved a step forward until there was little room between them. He raised her hand to his lips and gently placed a kiss on the top. His eyes never left her face, and she felt flushed.

"I think it will be quite a pleasure to have you on board, Cyrene."

"Thank…thank you, Your Highness," she said, striving to put some distance between them.

"Edric. Please, call me Edric."

"Edric," she whispered, withdrawing her hand.

"I'm sure you need to rest as well." He walked her toward the door.

"Yes, I believe I do need to rest."

He stopped her before they reached the door though. "Cyrene?"

"Yes?" she asked. Cyrene's stomach fluttered as she stared up at the King of Byern.

"If I send a maid to your quarters, will you come to me tonight?"

Whatever part of her that might have denied him vanished from her mind. "Yes."

"Good," he said with a smile. Edric rapped on the door once, and the guard member swung it open. "Good day, Affiliate."

Seeing Eren standing on the other side of the door sobered her girlish pretenses. She straightened and then left the room.

"Come on in, Eren." Edric signaled once more, and the guard closed the door after Eren had entered.

Cyrene raised her chin and started down the hall. As soon as she was on her own, she all but dashed back to her room. She shut the door and threw herself on her bed with a heavy sigh.

Edric wanted to see her later. Nerves pricked at her, but more than anything, she felt excitement. She rolled over, and something crinkled under her. She reached beneath her and extracted an envelope that she hadn't noticed when she came in. She stared down at the Dremylon green wax seal.

How did this get here? Did a maid leave it for me while cleaning? Or did someone deliver it here for a purpose?

With trembling hands, she broke the royal seal on the back of the envelope and pulled out the letter.

After carefully unfolding it, she stared down at the finely scrawled handwriting of Prince Kael and nearly cursed aloud.

REMEMBER...

COURTIER THROUGH AND THROUGH.

THROUGH AND THROUGH.

—K

The
INVITATION

KAEL WAS RIGHT.

Cyrene *hated* when he was right.

When she had been lost in Edric's gaze, she had forgotten everything but that moment between them. But he had done exactly what Kael had said. Edric was playing a game like any other courtier. He had been raised to be the King of Byern, but he had also been raised alongside Kael. Edric knew exactly how court life worked.

Of all the games for Kael to play, he'd had to choose this one. And he had the advantage of not even being on her ship so that she could give him a piece of her mind. He'd had someone else deliver the message. *The arrogant, self-righteous, pompous*—she didn't even have enough words for her anger. *Why did he have to ruin this?*

She tossed the useless envelope onto her bed and flopped backward into the down comforter, infuriated by the man and his words. His meaning was glaringly obvious, and it fit with the conversation she had been delighted to have with Edric only minutes earlier. If Edric had the chance, he would take it. He had said as much in his study when he had invited her to his chambers…and she had agreed.

She didn't know what she felt for the King. He had more power than she could ever dream of, yet when she looked at him, she saw something else…something more…something that could never be.

That thought infuriated her further, and the anger welling within her pushed her off the bed and into action. She had more to do in her lifetime than be cast about at the King's whim. She needed to be irreplaceable if she was going to hold any weight in court. *How many other Affiliates stood in my position, feeling the misplaced importance?*

Something in the back of her mind prodded her to *feel* her own importance. Stiffly, she walked to her bags on the other side of her room. Only one had been unpacked for the voyage. A few dresses hung in the wardrobe, and undergarments were tucked away in the dresser. At her insistence, the servants had left her largest bag tightly packed.

She bent down, hovering over the bag. Her hands shook as she undid the buckle and extracted a small leather satchel from its hiding place.

Cyrene sat on the cushioned green chair and set the pouch on the table. From within the small bag, she removed the cracked leather book with the strange symbol that looked like a tilted F on the front.

She released a deep sigh, reminding herself that it was just a book after all. They provided information, stories, and maps but nothing more than that.

Everything in her world had an answer.

She would find it.

Elea's handwritten note on the inside made her smile. A pang touched her heart. She missed her sister. Before leaving for the procession, she hadn't even gotten a chance to say good-bye. It was disappointing.

ASK FOR BASILLE SELBY IN THE LAELISH.

Yes, a lot of help he had been.

Cyrene had no idea what to make of him. He had been terrified of her...of the book. *What could this book possibly hold to make him act that way?*

Turning to the first page, Cyrene stared down at the iridescent swirly font. The one time she had tried to read the font, Maelia had interrupted her, and then she had been too afraid to pick it up again. The knowledge that Elea and Basille could not see the font had shut her brain down. *How can I see something that others couldn't?*

But there it rested, still as captivatingly stunning as the first time she had laid eyes on it.

She attempted to piece together what the strange font said, but it was unlike anything she had ever seen. Yet, in the back of her mind, she felt a familiar tugging, as if she should know what it said. The faint tickle in her mind seemed to tell her to try harder...to just know.

Her eyes narrowed, and her brain worked overtime to try to discover what it all meant. She broke into a sweat as she stared endlessly at the font. Frustration creased her temple, and her lips puckered. She let out a disgruntled groan and flipped the page, hoping that maybe she would have better luck.

Now, two pages of the dazzling shimmery font taunted her, and she was no closer to understanding its meaning, no matter how much she felt like she *should* know what it said.

Crying out in irritation, she slammed the book shut and stood. Disappointment crushed her, and she had to restrain herself from flinging the useless thing across the room. What was the point of being able to see it if all it did was mock her with its impossibility?

She grabbed a kerchief from her vanity drawer and wiped her brow. *How did staring at that thing cause me so much distress?* Red splotches marred her cheeks. She was practically out of breath.

This is ridiculous. It's just a book.

Steeling her determination, Cyrene sat down and opened it back up to the first page. She decided she would try a different approach. Before, she had concentrated until she felt like her temples would burst. Now, she would try not to concentrate too hard. The shimmering font revealed itself again, and she waited. She didn't want to push herself or force it. Maybe it would suddenly make sense. *By the Creator, it should make sense!*

Despite her change in approach, the font never made any more sense. It remained eternally useless, the knowledge of how to read it hanging just out of memory. Her heart sank for a second time. She pushed the book aside again, defeated. But she would get it...eventually. What had terrified her shortly before now left her with a stubborn resolve. *I will figure it out.*

A quick rap on her door made her jump.

"Just a minute," she called out, replacing the book into the leather pouch. She hastily positioned it back into the pocket of her bag.

She jogged across the room and opened the door to see a maid waiting for her. Her stomach churned at the thought of the King's earlier comment.

"Good evening, Affiliate," the maid said meekly, dropping her chin in deference. "It appears you never received your dinner invitation. The afternoon storm must have upset your stomach, quite like the others on board."

She stared at the maid in surprise. *What did she mean?*

Cyrene had only been in her room for an hour at the very most. *How could I have missed a dinner invitation? And what storm?* Their send-off from Byern had included a cloudless sky, and the ship hadn't rocked at all since she had locked herself in her room.

The maid continued, "If you will follow me, King Edric has requested your presence. I believe he has prepared a small meal as well."

What in the Creator's name was this girl talking about? I just ate. Just as she had the thought, her stomach growled noisily. The maid held back her smile, but Cyrene looked astonished.

"This way." The maid began to walk down the hallway.

Cyrene's mind locked on the sudden loss of time. She numbly followed the maid through the passageway before stepping out onto the main deck. When she looked up at the pitch-black night sky with stars twinkling all around them, her mouth dropped. Her silk slippers struggled to find purchase against the slippery deck. Clearly, a storm had hit the ship while she was safely under.

How did I lose time? She had been reading the book, and suddenly, *poof. Did the book...steal the day away from me?*

The maid broke through Cyrene's thoughts while ushering her down a flight of wooden stairs separated from the rest of the ship that led to the King's quarters. At the far end of the hallway, the maid knocked on the door and announced Cyrene's presence. She gave Cyrene an encouraging smile before backing away and allowing her to pass.

Upon stepping inside, it was apparent to Cyrene that the King had spared no expense. To say Cyrene's rooms were extravagant compared to the King's would be like comparing a puddle to the ocean. Interchanging rugs covered the floor, creating a carpeted appearance. Gilded frames held portraits on the walls. A deep mahogany table in the center of the main room was set for four with an assortment of dinner items.

Through an adjoining door, Cyrene could see an enormous bed draped in Dremylon green and cream. She flushed and looked away.

"I wasn't sure what you wanted for dinner," King Edric said. "So, I had the kitchen staff bring a bit of everything, including some of my favorites."

"Thank you," she whispered, still standing in the doorway.

"Please, come and sit."

Cyrene found a place at his table. They didn't speak as she ate small portions of the roasted chicken, thick stew, and rolls. She hadn't noticed that she was hungry. Then, she had felt like she was starving. She took a sip of wine, hoping to calm her nerves.

"You seem out of sorts," the King said finally. "I hope your seasickness has passed."

"Quite," she said, meeting his gaze.

"That is good to hear." He leaned his elbow against the table and smiled.

By the Creator, he is handsome.

For the first time, she let her mind consider what the Consort had meant when she said that Cyrene was here for the King's entertainment. Her eyes darted to the silky large bed once more, and she quickly tried to banish that thought from her mind.

Edric carefully watched her. "Come here, Cyrene."

She swallowed. She was in the King's bedchamber, they were alone, and he was addressing her plainly. This was the King of Byern. She didn't want to disobey.

"Yes, Your Highness," Cyrene whispered.

Kael's warning be damned, her walls were falling all around her. She stood on shaky legs, and her feet carried her toward him.

"Edric," he reminded her. "Please call me Edric."

"Edric," Cyrene repeated, feeling his name on her tongue.

"That's better."

He stood to face her, and the flickering candlelight dilated his pupils, reflecting back the ring of blue-gray in his eyes. She noticed all the endearing little things about him—the stubble on his strong jawline, the light smile that tugged on the corners of his mouth, the way his hair curled lightly at his ears. She reached forward and brushed it back. Then, she caught herself and retrieved her hand.

"My apologies," she breathed. *What tethers me to him? How did I always make such mistakes?*

He reached out and took her hand in his own. "No need to apologize." He slowly traced his thumb over her knuckles, and then he drew her in closer.

She kept her eyes down, focusing on the heat spreading through her from her hand to her arm and down into her chest. This was bad, so bad, yet she couldn't find it in herself to withdraw from him. Her body trembled lightly in both fear and anticipation. She wanted him to move forward, but she didn't know what would happen to her if she gave in.

"You're shaking," he said.

"I..."

"What is troubling you?" He brought his hand up to her chin and tilted her head so that she would look at him.

"The Queen—"

"Is not aboard my ship."

Cyrene bit her lip. "She is still my Receiver," she whispered. The words fell flat.

"She is what she is," Edric said dismissively, clearly not wanting to discuss Kaliana.

"Your Queen," Cyrene said. "She is your Queen."

"A queen who does not fulfill her duties is no queen at all."

Cyrene startled. She didn't know what that meant. *What duties is the Queen not fulfilling?*

Edric sighed and closed his eyes. "Forgive me. I've had a lot on my mind."

She held her breath expecting him to pull away, but when he opened his eyes and stared down at her, she melted. There was such passion and warmth and desire trapped within. His eyes pleaded with her to understand, to feel the depth of what was passing between them. Her heartbeat picked up, and that same spark that always ignited between them flared. The cord binding them together was the fuse, and every touch and look and emotion was the match igniting the flames.

He took a step toward her until their bodies were nearly pressed together. His eyes held a question in them.

"Cyrene," he whispered.

Their breaths mingled in the space between them. They were so close that their noses almost brushed. His hands came around her waist, and then his lips fell lightly, ever so lightly, on her own.

Time froze.

Her eyes fluttered closed, and the taste of him consumed her. His lips were tender and appreciative, covering her mouth and perfectly fitting against her. He drew her against his broad chest, and she circled her arms around his neck.

The kiss intensified. Their mouths moved in time together, leaving her head dizzy. She wobbled on the tips of her toes as he held her in place. He started walking her backward into the bedroom. His hands dug into her dress, bunching the material around her waist. Her knees hit the footboard of the massive bed, and she could barely breathe as she realized where this was all going.

And still, she didn't stop. The spark had turned into an inferno, flames engulfing them, and they were trapped in the blaze that was their passion.

His hands slid up to cup her face before easing into her hair. "Cyrene," he murmured between kisses, "stay with me."

She pulled back from his lips and stared in disbelief at what he was so boldly asking. The surge of emotion welling inside of her shocked her. Sensation seemed to build up and then ripple out through her body. Her breathing was ragged. Even the tips of her fingers tingled.

"Stay?"

"Here. Tonight."

She closed her eyes to try to calm her racing heart and get the echo of his words out of her mind. She couldn't do this. She couldn't be his mistress. She deserved more than that.

"I...I think I should leave," she stuttered out.

"You should stay."

She shook her head and stepped around him. "No. No, I should go."

"Cyrene..."

"It's improper," she muttered, wishing for nothing more than his lips to be on hers again. Even as she backed away from him into the entryway, she couldn't look at the bed behind him.

"To hell with propriety!"

Her gaze wavered briefly and then held. He had kissed her! She had been kissed before, but none of them were anything compared to this. Her very insides had quivered at the touch of his lips on hers. The King of Byern had given her the best kiss she had ever had in her entire life.

197

Yet she couldn't continue like this.

She *could* not be his Queen, and she *would* not be a mistress.

Her skin crawled at the thought.

"I'm sorry, Edric. I can't."

"I cannot force you to stay."

She didn't believe that.

"But I would prefer it if you did. I have only four days without an entire court full of people watching my every move, four days with only Daufina to judge me."

"Four more days until the gossip begins, you mean," she said softly, taking another step away from him.

"Just by your mere presence on my ship, the gossip will ensue whether you want it to or not."

Cyrene turned her face from him. "Please do not make me, Edric."

He strode across the room and took her hand. "Tell me you do not feel as I do."

"My feelings are inconsequential."

He brushed his lips against her knuckles. "Never."

Cyrene looked up into his pleading eyes.

He could have forced his hand at any point. As the king, he could have commanded her to do what he said. He could have used her. He didn't need to consider her feelings to get what he wanted.

Yet he was.

She said the words anyway, "You are the king. You have a queen and a court and a country to run. I have nothing to offer."

"You."

Her eyes begged with him to be reasonable. "I cannot give you that." She turned to leave.

"Your time then," he said, reaching for her once more.

"My time?" She slightly turned her head to the side to judge his words. "Just my time?"

"I require nothing further."

Could he hold to that bargain after that kiss? She wasn't certain *she* could.

Time with him would only endear her to him more completely. Perhaps he knew that. His offer was tempting. She enjoyed his company, making it difficult for her to hold any kind of resolve. He might be the courtier Kael insisted he was, but he hadn't pushed past any boundaries she hadn't consented to. Edric was asking to get to know her. *Is that such a bad thing?*

"What else do you have to do during the next four days?" he asked with a smile.

The next day, Eren stopped in when Cyrene was with Maelia. Cyrene told Maelia that she would return to check on her later and left the two of them alone with a sneaky smile.

Maelia's sea legs never returned, and without much effort, Cyrene found herself fulfilling the request the Consort had made of her. She and Edric paced the deck, discussing everything from geographical formations to ancient history to gardening. Over meals, they found themselves contemplating various cultural differences between the cities of Byern, and at night, they practiced languages and read aloud late into the night. They listened to a minstrel on board, danced their favorite jigs, taught each other card games, and watched the sun set over the Taken Mountains.

Cyrene felt alive again for the first time since she had become an Affiliate. The Queen had sapped the life out of Cyrene with the boring agricultural regimen and forced paralysis in her education. Suddenly, she felt like all the studying and tutors had been worth the effort. Edric, in particular—if not the other courtiers aboard—found her interesting and knowledgeable.

"You bloom like a rose," Daufina said in passing one evening.

Edric was dancing with Affiliate Neila, a favorite of Daufina's. He kept glancing in Cyrene's direction and smiling. It was hard to keep the euphoria from her face. They hadn't kissed since that first night, but it was times like this when she wanted to ignore the rationality of her mind and listen to the thrum of her heart.

"Thank you," Cyrene said, tearing her eyes from the King's lingering gaze.

"I believe Kaliana made a mistake in placing you in agricultural studies. It is such a waste when you would make a wonderful Ambassador or court advisor."

Cyrene's cheeks heated, and she smiled. She couldn't disagree. From day one, she had believed the Queen was wasting her talent.

"Thank you, Daufina."

"It's a shame that Kaliana lost the baby, or else she might care less about Edric's affections," Daufina said offhand.

Cyrene startled forward. The glass she was holding jarred and splashed wine onto the deck. "What?"

Daufina assessed her. "Have you not heard?"

"No," Cyrene whispered.

Suddenly, Edric's words the first night came back to her. *"A queen who does not fulfill her duties is no queen at all."*

The Queen had failed to produce a Dremylon heir. *Is that the duty he spoke of? Is that the reason she had been ill and infuriated the day when I went to ask her to leave?*

Despite it all, jealousy hit her in the stomach. Edric had his Queen. He belonged to her so long as he needed an heir to secure his line on the throne.

But Cyrene didn't want to have those thoughts or at least, she told herself she didn't want them. They led to a slew of concerns that she couldn't do anything about. It only frustrated her more.

"If you'll excuse me," she whispered.

"Cyrene, I didn't mean to upset you," Daufina said.

"I'm just going to check on Maelia."

"Shall I tell Edric you will see him tonight?"

Cyrene swallowed. *Oh, how I want to get lost with him on our last day on the procession. When would I get the chance to hold his undivided attention again?*

But she couldn't. Not with the reminder of the Queen hanging over her head.

"No. I'm going to bed early. I need my rest before we get to Albion."

Daufina sighed and nodded. If anyone knew the war raging within Cyrene, it was Daufina.

Cyrene left the deck and stopped in front of Maelia's room. She knocked once, and Eren opened the door.

"How is she feeling?"

"Today is the best day so far," he said. The day before, Eren had told Cyrene that this was one of the worst bouts of seasickness he had ever seen. "Though she hasn't been able to eat that much. Perhaps you could persuade her to try."

"Thank you so much for your patience and attention."

"Of course. I would help anyone under such poor conditions."

Cyrene smiled, certain that he was being extra thorough because he liked Maelia. She passed him and stepped into the cramped quarters, taking a seat in the chair next to Maelia's bed. She heard the door click shut when Eren left.

"How are you feeling? Eren said you're not eating."

Maelia was beyond pale, but she sat up. "What have you been doing with the King?" she demanded.

"Spending time with him."

"That's quite obvious." She folded her hands in her lap. "The entire ship is buzzing about you two. Even as sick as I am, I have heard the maids discussing it. Do you wish to draw this much attention to yourself? How do you expect us to do anything with the *King* falling all over himself because of you?" Her eyes were stern.

Cyrene winced at her harsh yet true words. "Is he falling all over himself?"

"Cyrene! That is not the point!" Maelia snapped.

She actually snapped.

"It was only in jest."

"Do not forget what we are risking. Just imagine how much more you would be risking if the King catches us," she said. Then she sighed heavily. "I'm just worried. Tell me I don't need to."

"You don't need to worry."

It felt like a lie.

25

The
WHITE CITY

THE NEXT MORNING, CYRENE SHOT OUT OF BED AND hastened up the steps onto the deck. Her feet skidded across the planks until she was at the railing with her mouth agape. Still leagues ahead of them—glistening, pale, and gorgeous in the morning sunrise—stood Albion, the White City.

She had never dreamed Albion would be so breathtaking. Krisana, the central palace, had been constructed to be seen from nearly anywhere in the city as it sat high above the surrounding buildings. Rumors suggested seashells that had been laboriously crushed, molded, and reconstructed into a smooth, flawless matte surface constituted the entirety of the castle. The sectioned off neighborhoods within the city walls called Vedas that were built around the castle were whitewashed in the same fashion, but none gleamed quite as gloriously as the palace or stayed as perfectly white. The city branched out into a maze of roads and crossroads of white flattop houses and shops. From a distance, it gave the illusion that the city was one white dot on the surface of the Earth.

Their ship rounded the last great bend of the Keylani River leading into Albion and revealed the Lakonia Ocean in all its expansive beauty. Cyrene had never seen the ocean, and a knot formed in her throat at the sight. It was truly an experience that could not be equated with anything else. She had lived her life in the Taken Mountains, believing them to be the most magnificent and imposing thing in existence, and then the Lakonia Ocean shattered every preconception she had ever had.

"It's beautiful, isn't it?" Daufina asked, coming up behind Cyrene.

Cyrene startled, not having heard her approach. "Stunning."

"You would think it wouldn't be as beautiful returning to a place you lived for seventeen years, but it gets more and more so each time I return."

"You grew up in Albion?"

"You can't see my parents' house from here, but it is in one of the oldest of the Vedas surrounding Krisana."

"Were your parents in the inner circle?"

Daufina gave her a secretive smile, as if the question was controversial.

"Sorry. I don't mean to pry."

"No, it's nothing. Just old scandal." Somehow, she managed to look gloriously regal, even with her dismissive hand motion. "My father was in the High Order, and my mother was working as a seamstress's apprentice in the Third Class when they met. He was supposed to marry an Affiliate, but they wed. After my grandfather passed, my father left court to return to Albion to take control of the Birket House."

"Sounds like a hopeless romantic."

Daufina laughed. "That is my father. Probably the truest reason he was placed in the High Order."

Cyrene wasn't sure how that made any sense since it was all based on one's education and what was best for the person and society. There was something about the whole ceremony that was beyond comprehension. It certainly made little sense to her why someone like Jardana had been raised to be an Affiliate. If anyone had deserved it, it was Rhea.

At the thought of her best friend, Cyrene's excitement returned in full force. She would soon be reunited with Rhea, and she couldn't wait to see her. A pang hit her heart at the weight of her absence.

"Come along. We'll be there shortly." Daufina paced the length of the deck and took a seat at a small table.

Cyrene sat across from her, staring at the White City as they approached.

Edric appeared shortly after, freshly shaven and already in his finest outfit. He smiled brightly at the two women.

"Fine day to arrive in Albion. Not a cloud in the sky."

Breakfast along with morning tea was placed before them. Cyrene was too anxious about their arrival to engage Edric and Daufina in conversation. Her mind was elsewhere—on the city and what she would be doing once she got there.

Maelia finally made it to the deck at the end of breakfast. Her complexion was still pale, but Cyrene was just happy to see her on her two feet.

The girls went to the railing to watch as the procession ships maneuvered into the dock. Edric and Daufina joined them, smiling down at the small entourage waiting on the dock.

Cyrene observed their welcome party. Besides the guards stationed around the docks, only fifteen in total greeted them. It was a far cry from the hundreds waving their farewell earlier that week.

As they stood on the deck, Edric brushed against her arm, and his fingers slid on top of hers. Her heart sped up a million miles a minute. She was met with a quick glance of blue-gray, and she saw a mix of emotions wash over his face.

She tucked her hand under the railing, and he laced their fingers together.

He leaned in closer, whispering so that only she could hear, "I wish we could stay."

"You're the king," she reminded him.

He could make them stay if he wanted.

Edric extracted his hand and nodded grimly. His lips were set in a straight line. "Yes, I remember."

Cyrene swallowed. She hadn't meant to push him away, but this ship had been a dream, and they were about to walk the plank back to reality.

The boat shuddered to a stop. Edric walked forward with Daufina following close behind him. He didn't look back once. Cyrene told herself it was for the better in the long run. He knew that nothing could happen. After she spent a minute trying to convince herself of that, she trailed them to the gangway.

Cyrene landed on firm ground again. Maelia stepped off after her, clutching her arm, as she seemed to rock back and forth a few times. Cyrene reassuringly squeezed her arm, and then they caught up to the rest of the group.

"Cousin"—Edric grasped the forearm of the burly man with a full-grown beard and a round belly at the lead of the party—"it has been too long."

"King Edric, you bless our family with your gracious ruling. May your honor forever shine upon Byern."

Edric chortled, bringing the man into his chest for a hug. "Come, Duke Halston of Albion. Let's make peace together over this fine day in the White City."

Cyrene glanced over the shoulder of Daufina and stared at Duke Halston. She knew about him and his brother, Duke Wynn of Levin. They were the sons of Edric's aunt, Princess Saldana, and Duke Reagles.

Cyrene remembered her parents speaking about how if King Maltrier had died without an heir, then their father, King Herold, had wanted to ensure a Dremylon still ruled, and the alliance had formed. They carried Dremylon blood but weren't in contention for the throne as long as there was a Dremylon son in line.

For the first time, she truly understood Edric's fear about the Queen's miscarriages. She buried her dark thoughts and focused on the matter at hand.

A plump woman in a lavender gown stepped forward. She had a genuine bubbly smile, joyful round face, and a good-natured bounce in her step. "Consort Daufina." She bobbed a short curtsy. "I have deeply missed your presence in the court at Albion. It is a great honor to see you back in the White City and looking as ravishing as ever."

"Duchess Elida, it is always a pleasure to be in your company. I look perfectly ordinary next to you in full bloom." Daufina touched her belly. "Not much longer I believe. A month or two?"

"Two!" she squeaked, proudly putting her hands under her belly.

"Wonderful! I do hope the King and I can make a trip down through the rainy season to greet your new boy," Daufina said, paying her the highest compliment.

"One can only hope." She practically bounced up and down.

Daufina introduced Cyrene, Maelia, and the other Affiliate Neila, who had just walked onto the dock. Duchess Elida welcomed them to her home and introduced an Affiliate of her own, Karra, a tan woman with dark features and a pleasant demeanor similar to the Duchess.

Duchess Elida linked arms with Daufina and walked them toward the waiting carriages. "Come along. Can't keep the men waiting now, can we?"

The carriages were large white spectacles, big enough to comfortably fit six. Enormous all-white horses standing nearly seven feet tall with extensive feathering on their lower legs drew the carriages. While used to the guard steeds, Cyrene had never seen ones of this size look quite as elegant or as snowy white.

The horses took off, bustling the women through the city, followed by the remainder of the people who had been on board the King's ship. The horses, luggage, and additional items that the court would need while traveling would follow them up to the castle shortly afterward.

Albion's streets were narrower than Byern's and packed with city folk calling out to the carriages as they passed. Merchants and peddlers flocked to the crowds, trying to sell their wares.

As they neared the Krisana castle, her eyes remained trained on the crowds, and her smile was bright on her face. Children tossed flowers at their carriage. Others danced and laughed in the streets. Girls wore flowered crowns on their heads and waved ribbons in the air. A few of the boys jabbed at each other with wooden swords. This procession welcome was a merry place with cheerful music.

A chill ran up her spine, and her eyes cast around her surroundings to figure out where the uneasy feeling was coming from. She distinctly felt like she was being watched. *But how would I know when there are hundreds of eyes on me?*

Cyrene's gaze drifted to a man standing among the onlookers. With a plain brown cloak, a matching rumpled shirt, and large brimmed hat, he was much taller than the women and children around him. Unlike everyone else, he wasn't smiling. Maybe it was just the severity of him that had chilled her...

As he faded from view, Cyrene shrugged it aside. She didn't even know why she had noticed him or why she was thinking such grim thoughts.

They passed through the final bend of the city and reached the great white gates that allowed them entry to the inner gardens of Krisana.

Up close, the castle rivaled Nit Decus, the Byern castle, in size and grandeur. Without the mountain obscuring its immense depths, the castle seemed endlessly tall with hundreds of balconies shooting from round-topped spires.

Their carriage traveled over a wooden drawbridge. Krisana had seen more battles than any other Byern city in history and had never fallen. The white exterior was reinforced with a strong fortification that had never yielded to an enemy. The entire city could crumble, and Krisana would continue to stand regally.

The carriage carted them around a circular travel-worn entranceway and stopped before mother-of-pearl double doors. They glistened and shined in the afternoon sun in such a gorgeous fashion that perfectly fitted the castle's namesake. Krisana was the ancient word for pearl.

A man immediately appeared to help them out of the carriage. Cyrene took his hand and followed behind Maelia onto the grounds of the White Castle.

The double doors to the castle opened, and the whole party moved through the inner foyer that had a mile-high round ceiling with intricate mother-of-pearl molding, arched trellises, and a rug with baby-blue, cream, and gold colors running the length of the room. The royal throne room was at the end of the hallway and matched the foyer in construction. Interchanging white and mother-of-pearl tiles were visible on the floor throughout the room, and several glass murals of the ocean cast natural light into the center of the room. The focal point rested on the five chairs set on a pedestal, all ornate and all draped in Dremylon green.

"As Regent of Albion," Duke Halston said, standing inside the throne room, "I happily present to you, King Edric, the great throne of Byern set forth in the White City."

"Much thanks, Duke Halston," Edric replied. "I trust that the city has been successful in the hands of my kin, and I will be happy for you to continue as Regent when I return to the capital."

"It is an honor." Duke Halston bowed at the waist.

"Now, this matter you mentioned in the carriage—" Edric began.

"Terrible thing." Duke Halston swallowed hard, his Adam's apple bobbing visibly in his throat. "I almost fear suggesting it in front of the women."

Daufina raised an eyebrow at Duke Halston, and the remaining women all looked shocked at his impropriety. To think that a woman would be any less capable of handling whatever terrible matter the Duke was about to describe than a man was outrageous. They might as well regress their society and break down the Affiliate program entirely. *What is the point of having a consort as an advisor to the king if she wasn't as capable as any man?*

Duchess Elida popped her hand against the Duke's arm. "Halston!" she said shrilly. She shot him a disapproving look.

"No offense meant, Consort." He had the decency to look sheepish.

"Daufina presides over all matters of state," Edric said.

"Yes, well, I meant no harm. It's just—"

"First things first, Halston," Daufina cut him off, holding up her hand. "I believe we should excuse some of our audience before speaking about these matters."

"Of course, Consort." He bobbed his head. Even as Regent of Albion, cousin to the King, and a duke, his position rested below the Consort.

The room emptied of servants, and Halston ushered out the Albion court. As everyone was leaving, Queen Kaliana strode into the room with Jardana and Catalin close on her heels. Her eyes immediately settled on Edric, and Cyrene did everything in her power to remain calm and not panic. The Queen couldn't know what had happened on the procession ship.

Then, Edric glanced up and met Cyrene's gaze. They both smiled, as if sharing a secret. It was only for a second, but it was enough.

Queen Kaliana shot daggers at her. Any chance that she didn't know something had gone on between them slipped away.

"What is going on in here?" Queen Kaliana asked.

"Duke Halston has brought forward some news," Edric said. "There have been two more deaths here in Albion."

The room fell silent at the proclamation. *Two more deaths? How can this be?* Cyrene had thought that they had left the killer behind in Byern.

"Two more?" Daufina asked. "Who?"

"High Order Grabel and Affiliate Pallia," Halston said.

"Don't you think we should only speak about such matters in front of members of the inner circle?" Queen Kaliana asked sharply. She turned her eyes to Cyrene.

"I believe we *are* among the inner circle," Edric countered. He ignored her rebuff and turned his attention away from her. "Back to the matter at hand. We cannot ignore what has happened. Zorian, Leslin, and now, Grabel and Pallia. It doesn't seem coincidental."

"I knew Pallia," Daufina said. "She was as skilled with a sword as any man."

"Grabel grew up in the Royal Guard. He, too, knew the way of the sword. He was a formidable opponent," Duke Halston told them.

"Where were they last seen?" Queen Kaliana asked.

"For several months, Pallia and Grabel had been overseeing and assisting the river city Strat in Aurum," Duchess Elida said softly. "They returned a couple of weeks ago to meet the procession. A good friend of Pallia's had told her that her sister would be on the procession, and Pallia was interested in meeting her. I believe the friend was...hmm...Aralyn. That sounds right."

Cyrene's vision blurred. Aralyn had told someone she was coming to Albion, and that person had turned up dead. She covered her mouth in horror. Zorian had come back for her Presenting, and he had also been killed. Leslin was friends with her sister and had died after Cyrene had gone to ask for her help. Her stomach clenched, and she had to close her eyes. *What could it possibly mean?* It couldn't have anything to do with her.

"Cyrene," Maelia whispered softly.

She shook her head, silencing her friend. She couldn't talk about this right now.

"We must send a team to investigate, especially after the manner of deaths of Pallia and Grabel. No disappearance should go unwarranted, but the signs of targeted murders..." Edric let that thought hang thick in the air.

"I'll get a team together and see what can be discovered." Duke Halston signaled to a High Order.

"I'd love to add my own companion. High Order Eren is quite adept in this field, and unfortunately, he has lost a brother in these circumstances," Edric said.

"Any person you recommend, Your Highness, is of the utmost quality. I am sure of it," Duke Halston agreed.

"I would be honored, Your Highness," Eren said.

"It will be great to have a trusted addition from the King's High Order. This way High Order Eren," Duke Halston said.

The men bowed to the King, and Eren followed Duke Halston out of the chamber.

The nausea that had started at the mention of Aralyn's name wouldn't pass, and the more Cyrene thought about it, the more she feared that she needed to speak up. If it had just been Zorian, then maybe she wouldn't feel the connection, but Leslin, Pallia, and Grabel too? She needed to say something. It might help the investigation.

But she didn't know what connection she had to these murders, and drawing attention to herself in such a manner could be counterproductive. *How could I possibly tell Edric or any of them that I think I'm involved when I had come here in the first place to fulfill my plan?* She was risking much with Maelia, and she needed to think about that first and foremost.

The moment passed in which it would have been appropriate for her to mention her connection, and the conversation moved on to more cheerful matters.

"I believe I'm worn out from the journey," Cyrene spoke privately to Daufina. "I need to go rest."

"Of course," Daufina said with a smile.

Cyrene could feel Queen Kaliana's eyes on her, but she didn't look in the Queen's direction, not wanting to give her the satisfaction.

"You're in the Pearl Bay Chambers," Daufina said. "Elida has maids waiting to direct you to your rooms."

"Thank you, Consort," Cyrene said formally. She dipped a low curtsy, knowing the Queen was watching.

Maelia exited with her. Cyrene's maid approached her, curtsied, and offered herself as an escort to her new quarters. Cyrene politely declined, telling her she wanted to look around some first, and then dragged Maelia away from the woman.

They fell in step together, walking leisurely toward the castle grounds. The circular entranceway now bustled with people arriving from the procession. Affiliates and High Order walked around, speaking freely to each other. A group of horses were tied together and being guided across the drawbridge. Strong sturdy men and a few able-bodied women unloaded carts, carrying everything from luggage to food to furniture.

"I can't believe there were two more murders," Maelia whispered.

Cyrene nodded. "Me neither."

"They were friends of your sisters here to speak with you."

"I know," she whispered.

"What do you think it means?"

Cyrene shook her head. She had no clue.

"Do you still want to continue forward?" Maelia asked.

The words stuck in her throat. Continuing forward meant leaving all she had known behind, including Edric all to find out about a book. A book that only she could see the words, that stole time, and frightened a peddler, who insisted she seek out Matilde and Vera in Eleysia to discover the meaning of it. *Is it worth it?*

"Yes," she responded, answering the spoken and unspoken question.

"Okay."

"With everything going on right now, I think we won't find a better chance."

"You're right." Maelia seemed to stand taller at the thought. "You're right."

"Let's go," Cyrene said, nudging her forward.

While Cyrene's horses were with her in Albion, nothing was organized enough for her to find someone to locate them for her. So the girls found the first available horses, took hold of the reins with purpose, and began to slowly walk them in the opposite direction. No one even seemed to notice them among the chaos of the courtyard. Soon, they were trotting down the narrow lane outside of Krisana's walls, away from the castle.

26

The CROWN

"WHAT HAPPENED ON THAT SHIP?" KALIANA DEMANDED, following Daufina into her quarters after the business in the throne room dispersed.

Daufina sighed and walked away from the Queen. "Business as usual."

"Don't lie to me!" she snapped.

"Kaliana, do you mind skipping to the point? I've had a long journey, and I would like to rest," Daufina said dryly. She took a seat on her divan.

"He was with her, wasn't he?" Kaliana asked. Her voice choked, and then she recovered.

"With whom?"

"Don't play dumb with me. Cyrene. Edric was with Cyrene."

Daufina rested her hands on her lap and arched an eyebrow. "You are his Queen, Kaliana. No more than that."

"Is this because of the baby?" She looked so small and scared—like the little princess who had traveled across the mountains to marry Edric, not the cold and heartless creature who had taken over her since they had wed.

"We need a Dremylon heir," Daufina said. She couldn't tell the Queen that Edric actually cared for Cyrene and not just because he needed to put a baby in her belly.

"If he lays one finger on her, we'll have another death on our hands," Kaliana growled.

Daufina hopped up and strode across the room. "Do not overestimate your importance, Kaliana. Your threats have no

K.A. LINDE

weight, and belittling the deaths of the fallen is disgusting. Leave Cyrene out of your politics, and get the hell out of my room!"

Kaliana raised herself a few extra inches, tilting her nose in the air, and then whirled around. She left the room in a swirl of Dremylon green and gold. Daufina sagged at her exit. She hadn't meant to snap at Kaliana. It did nothing to improve their ever-crumbling relationship.

At the same time, she couldn't take Kaliana's threat lightly. She couldn't take the chance of Kaliana acting out against Cyrene and having it coming back negatively on Edric.

With a heavy heart, she navigated the corridors of Krisana until she reached Edric's room. She tipped her head at the guard before the King's room and then entered without knocking. She found him stripped to the waist with a broadsword in his hand. His back muscles flexed as he swung the powerful weapon, running through the series of exercises to keep his body and mind in top shape.

She cleared her throat behind him, and he turned quickly, the sword ready. It rested only six inches away from her heart before he dropped the blade to his side. He was breathing heavily, and a slick sheen of sweat coated his body. For a moment, she remembered why she had loved him in the first place.

"Daufina, I wasn't expecting you."

"No. I hadn't intended to come see you," she admitted.

"Is something on your mind?" He sheathed his sword and found a towel to wipe his brow.

"Kaliana."

Edric huffed and turned away from her. "Something on your mind that I actually want to talk about?"

"She's not blind, Edric."

He tossed the towel on his dresser. "Am I still the king?"

Daufina pinched the bridge of her nose and walked away from him.

"You put her on my ship. You sent her to my chambers. You let her take your place for four days, Daufina. Did you expect that I wouldn't fall for her more each day she was there?"

"I thought you would be smart about it. You said you didn't want a mistress, and then you went and—"

"Nothing happened," he said, grabbing a shirt and throwing it over his head.

Daufina laughed. "I'm sure."

214

"I'm serious."

Daufina looked at him sharply. Her brows knitted together, trying to see if he was telling the truth. She couldn't believe it. The man who could have whatever he wanted hadn't taken what he wanted?

"Why?"

He ran a hand back through his hair and then walked across the room to her. He brushed aside the dark locks that tumbled over her shoulder. "Because I want her to want the man behind the crown."

Daufina couldn't meet his gaze. It drew her back to a time before when they could have been happy like that. "Then, be careful with Kaliana. She will do everything in her power to not let that happen."

The
INQUIRY

THE ROADS HAD CLEARED OF PEOPLE, AND THE HORSES' hooves crushed the fallen flowers lining the way to the castle. Despite Cyrene's and Maelia's best efforts to blend in, the people on the streets still smiled, waved, and curtsied as they passed. Being a spectacle in the city was a strange thing. In Byern, it wasn't uncommon to see Affiliates out in the city. Albion had a diverse environment since it was on the shore, but the majority of the citizenry were Thirds.

About halfway to their destination, they passed a plain all-white pub with a swinging wooden door and a sign hanging on only one hinge from the framework. Rowdy customers caused a small crowd to form out front, and Cyrene and Maelia brought their horses to a halt.

"And stay out!" a guy cried. He pushed another man through the open door.

The man stumbled backward out of the bar and landed roughly on his hands and backside. His head dropped forward, and his hair fell into his face. A dust cloud sprang up, coating his already mussed clothing and settling into his hair.

"We don't cut cards like that here!" the guy yelled.

The man slowly pushed off his hands and stood, facing the tavern.

Cyrene gasped when she recognized him. *Ahlvie.*

A smirk crossed Ahlvie's face as he pocketed a small bag he'd collected from the ground and then dusted off his pants. "Good afternoon then." He flourished a deep dignified bow, but it crumpled mid-bend, tipping him forward.

"You cheat someone else!" The guy slammed the door.

The crowd began to disperse, but Cyrene maneuvered their horses toward Ahlvie.

"Cyrene," Maelia said, reaching out for her. "You know who that is?"

Cyrene nodded. After speaking with him, she hadn't known if Ahlvie would actually go on the procession, so she hadn't told Maelia.

"Only a few hours in the city, and you're already making friends," Cyrene said to Ahlvie.

"I have enough friends. It's enemies I prefer to collect," he replied.

"Well, you're awfully good at it."

"I haven't scared you away yet." He swept her the bow he hadn't managed for the tavern owner. In that moment, he looked far less like the drunk he had appeared to be seconds before. He really was a cheat.

"Cyrene," Maelia whispered frantically, "come on. Let's go."

"Just give me a minute."

"Where are you fine Affiliates off to in the middle of the day?" Ahlvie asked pointedly. "The procession just docked, and I notice you're riding His Grace's horses."

"Cyrene," Maelia whispered again.

"It's all right, Maelia." She gave her friend a confident smile.

Cyrene dismounted and strode before Ahlvie. He was a good head taller than her, and she had to tilt her head up to look at him.

"I made it on the ship," he said.

"So you did."

"You spoke of freedom."

"I didn't expect you to make it aboard."

"I said I would," he responded gruffly, "and I always do what I say."

"Always?" She narrowed her eyes. Maybe she should be second-guessing herself, but something about him reassured her.

"Always."

"Fine," she said, having already made her choice back in Byern. "Then you're with us." She knew he wasn't a killer, and she might need a man where she was going. She gestured to her horse. "Help me back up."

He laughed at her but hoisted her up onto her steed anyway.

"Maelia, this is Ahlvie. Ahlvie, this is Maelia."

"Nice to meet you." Ahlvie tipped his head to her.

Maelia smiled halfheartedly and glanced at Cyrene with an uneasy glint in her eye.

"If you give me just a moment, I'll go get my horse." He held up a finger when Cyrene began to speak. "One minute."

Cyrene sighed as he rounded the corner of a building. She looked over at Maelia in apology.

"Cyrene, what are you doing?" Maelia demanded. "You know he killed Zorian and Leslin!"

"No, he didn't. He was called in for questioning. That's it."

"You can't trust him!"

"He's helped me before."

Maelia shook her head. "You've never even spoken of him to me."

"I know. I know, but…"

Before she could finish, Ahlvie returned with a horse in tow. Maelia clamped her mouth shut and glared at Ahlvie.

"Where did you get him?" Cyrene asked.

"I didn't steal him, if that's what you're insinuating." Ahlvie threw his leg up and over the horse. "Just spent some of my earnings."

"The money you cheated people out of?" Maelia spat.

"I would never cheat anyone out of anything they didn't already cheat themselves into from cheating others." He tied the sentence around into knots that couldn't possibly make sense. Then, he smiled at their confusion and heeled his horse into the lead.

"You don't even know where we're going," Cyrene called.

"Well, wherever it is, no Second or Third is going to talk to either of you while you're dressed like royalty, wearing your Affiliate pins, and prancing around on Albion-prized steeds."

"Why?" Cyrene narrowed her eyes.

"Because, my fine Affiliate, these people lead different lives than you…or me," he added grudgingly. "And you'll only do more damage if you try to do everything your way. So, let me take the reins, and I'll do what I do best."

"Drink?" Cyrene quirked her eyebrow.

"There might be some of that. It helps."

"I'm sure it does," she said dryly.

"Tell me what you're up to. You want out? Tell me how can I help you help me." Ahlvie sent her a crooked smile.

"Cyrene," Maelia said, reaching out and touching her arm, "are you sure?" Her voice dipped lower. "Can you trust him?"

Cyrene's mind returned to that night when she had been trapped in that dark cave, and against all odds, she had somehow found her way out while bruised, scraped, beaten, soaking wet, exhausted, and most of all, angry. When Ahlvie had seen her in such a weakened state, he had never judged her. He had simply offered her assistance. Every interaction after that had made her see more and more that he was stifled and mistreated in his surroundings, and like her, he needed an escape.

"Yes," she finally answered. She turned her attention back to Ahlvie.

He wore an old green shirt with patched elbows, dusty brown pants, and solid brown riding boots that reached his knees. He hardly looked the part of a member of the High Order. Perhaps he knew what he was talking about.

Cyrene quickly filled Ahlvie in on their plan—or at least the part that would directly concern him. He would have to get them out of Albion and on a ship bound for Eleysia.

As they continued forward at a leisurely pace, he listened, nodding along at some points and snorting at others. He mulled over the idea before taking a turn down a crossroad into a different Veda.

"Where are we going?" Cyrene asked.

"Following your plan. Just trust me."

Maelia sighed loudly.

The horses' hooves clattered against the cobblestones in the Veda, and after a few rather strange turns, they found themselves on a lane along the coast. When Cyrene's eyes cut across the harbor, she found the giant procession ships off in the distance, and she frowned. They were even farther away from the docks than she had thought.

"What are you doing, Ahlvie?" she asked.

"Improvising."

"This isn't part of the plan."

"We should just go back." Maelia pulled back on her reins.

"Your plan made no sense. You want to get out of the harbor?" he demanded, staring down the two women.

They both stared back, stony-eyed.

"You're not going near the King or the Duke or any other royal boats, not even close. So, listen closely. Do as I say, and we'll be out of here faster than you could get to those ships."

"What are you going to do?" she demanded.

He shrugged as if he didn't have a care in the world. "Make an inquiry."

With that, Ahlvie continued forward down the lane.

"You're the one who trusts him. You follow him," Maelia spat.

Cyrene held back and leaned closer to Maelia. "Don't be angry with me."

"You invited him along without telling me! I don't trust him, nor do I understand why you would."

"Don't you ever just know?" she asked.

"No." Maelia looked away from her in frustration. "We aren't supposed to just know. We are supposed to follow through with the plan as we set forth."

"Life isn't always like the Royal Guard, Maelia. Sometimes, you have to take risks to see outcomes! I'm taking my risk on Ahlvie. You took your risk on me."

Maelia sighed. "This is your plan. You make it or break it."

Cyrene nodded as her friend started forward after Ahlvie. They caught up with him as he stopped before a dirty narrow alleyway. He motioned for them to halt as well. He dismounted and tied up his horse to a post at the mouth of the alley.

"You should probably come with me," he said to Cyrene. "Two of you might put them on edge, but one might give me some leverage."

Cyrene hoisted herself off the horse and began to tie it up.

"You're actually going to follow him?" Maelia asked.

"Please watch the horses," she pleaded with her friend.

Maelia hopped down and tied up her horse as well. "If you're not back soon, I'm going to come find you. If I don't find you, I'm going to the King," she pointedly told her and Ahlvie.

Cyrene flushed at the mention of Edric, and a knot formed at the pit of her stomach. She didn't want a reminder that she was leaving him behind for this.

"Deal." Cyrene lightly grasped her hand before following Ahlvie down the alley.

"Quite a trusting one, isn't she?" Ahlvie glanced not so discreetly over his shoulder.

"Give her a reason to trust you."

He shrugged noncommittally, and she sighed. "Just follow my lead, and don't let on that I'm a High Order. Whatever I tell them, don't act surprised. They'll be looking for that."

"Who exactly are *they*?" She crinkled her forehead.

"Doesn't matter. An acquaintance but not one who freely gives information out. You'll follow my lead?"

She nodded, wondering what she had gotten herself into.

"Don't fight me."

Cyrene swiftly turned around. "Did you hear that?" she asked.

"Hear what?"

"I don't know. I thought I heard something."

"Let me in."

Cyrene jumped again. "I think maybe someone is here."

"I don't see anyone," Ahlvie said, glancing around.

She shuddered at the creepy whispers she had heard. *Where did I hear it before?* She couldn't remember, but with a killer on the loose and all the deaths leading back to her, she suddenly didn't feel safe walking the streets.

"Let's just hurry," she told him.

They reached the end of the alley in a rush, and Ahlvie knocked on the door.

It swung open part of the way, and a fierce-looking woman with sharp eyes, straight long black hair, and a busty dark dress peered back at them. "What's your business?"

"Haille Mardas at your service, Mistress Bellevue." He bowed lower than any bow Cyrene had seen him give to the King or Queen.

"Did you say Haille Mardas?" She opened the door a little bit wider.

"In the flesh."

"The last time I heard that name, you owed me five gold pences," she said casually.

"Ah, such a misunderstanding." He swept his hand into his pocket and retrieved a few things from the small bag. "But as it turns out, I have three Aurumian gold trinkets. If you consider, they are the same thing." He removed the three square trinkets and showed them to her.

"Five Byern gold pences, Haille."

"Four trinkets," he countered, making another piece appear from thin air.

The woman snatched them out of his hand and stuffed them into her bodice. Cyrene tried not to appear scandalized.

"Come right in then. I do remember now. It was four Aurumian trinkets."

"I thought you might." He followed her through the door with Cyrene at his heels.

The room they entered was pitch-black, save for a few candles. They walked through that room and entered one only slightly brighter.

Two women with dark makeup passed them in low-cut corseted tops and revealing sheer skirts. Their hips swayed in an enticing dance.

One of the girls ran her hand along Cyrene's shoulder. "Mistress, is she new?" the girl asked. Her dark eyes were hooded, and her lips were as red as blood.

"She is not," Ahlvie said. He quickly removed the girl's hand.

Cyrene stared at Ahlvie in disbelief. *Where in the Creator's name did Ahlvie take me? Are we in some kind of harem house?*

The girl giggled and turned back to her friend. Mistress Bellevue arched an eyebrow, and they scurried away. She flicked a key into a locked door, and Cyrene kept her attention on that and nothing else. Ahlvie touched her arm, and Cyrene hastened after Mistress Bellevue. She escorted them up a small flight of stairs and into what appeared to be her private study.

The room had blood-red walls and furniture to match. Soft white pillows sat atop the two settees, and a delicate white desk looked striking against the contrast of the walls. A dozen or more wax candles were lit around the room, and black and maroon curtains had been pulled back just enough to cast some natural light in from the harbor beyond the window. It was stunning, if not so overdone.

"Feel free to have a seat." Mistress Bellevue brushed aside her long skirt and sat on the divan facing the window. When she crossed her legs, her skirt fell over her knee, revealing a thigh-high slit and more leg than Cyrene deemed appropriate.

"I believe I'll stand." Ahlvie gestured for Cyrene to sit down across from her, which she did.

"Who is your charming friend, Haille?" Mistress Bellevue asked.

"An Affiliate seeking counsel. She wishes to remain anonymous, which I'm sure you can understand. She came to me seeking answers, and I have half the knowledge that you and your master possess."

"Hmm." She cocked her head to the side and stared at Cyrene. "An Affiliate, you say? Yes, I see the pin right there on her breast, displayed like a prized jewel." She smiled coyly. "What sort of answers can I give you?"

"We're simply looking for a tidbit of information from your master."

"He's not in," she responded.

"We're on a tight schedule. Do you think you could check the dock schedules yourself?" Ahlvie asked.

"The dock schedules?" Mistress Bellevue considered it. She raised her hand, palm up, and waited.

Ahlvie grumbled something under his breath that Cyrene didn't catch and then pulled out another Aurumian trinket from his purse. "Far too much," he said. "We're looking for any ship bound for Eleysia, preferably direct."

"I will see what I can do." She slid the other trinket into her corset and then rose.

She left through a side door Cyrene hadn't noticed earlier. As Cyrene opened her mouth to speak with Ahlvie, he silenced her with a shake of his head.

A moment later, Mistress Bellevue returned with a small piece of paper in her hand. "You're in luck."

Ahlvie approached her and said something swiftly in a low voice that Cyrene couldn't pick up from the distance. He snatched the piece of paper out of her hand when she responded with a cackle.

"I do hope to see you soon, Haille. You're always so much fun."

"Let's go."

He grabbed Cyrene's arm and dragged her through the strange house. Soon, they were back out under the afternoon summer sun in the deserted alleyway. Maelia was pacing a path into the dirt next to the horses and jumped when she saw them exiting the house.

"You're back," she chirped when they reached her. "What happened?"

"Can we get away from here first?" he asked, untying all their horses as swiftly as possible.

"What? Why?" Maelia asked, glaring at him.

"Maelia!" The tone of Cyrene's voice made Maelia immediately get on her horse.

They followed Ahlvie away from the strange alleyway. They made it to a small tavern, The White City Pub, before Ahlvie stopped his horse.

"We're going in there?" Cyrene glanced around. "Isn't there somewhere else we could go?"

"We can talk in here without risk of being overheard."

Cyrene and Maelia apprehensively glanced at each other before sliding off their horses and following Ahlvie. The pub looked the same as any reputable place Cyrene had set foot in in Byern with its low-beamed ceilings, a half-dozen wooden tables, and wine and beer kegs resting behind a bar. A full-bodied woman in a brown-and-white apron poured drinks, placed them on trays, and carried them out to the few patrons seated in the establishment. The men spoke jovially to the woman, and they all seemed to be friends.

The trio took over a table near the empty pitted fireplace.

The woman almost immediately came to their side. "Afternoon," she said, leaning against their table with the tray propped up on her hip. "What'll ya have?"

Ahlvie ordered a mug of beer, but the two Affiliates declined service. When Ahlvie had his beer in hand, he extracted the piece of paper from his pocket and placed it on the table.

"What does it say?" Cyrene asked impatiently.

"It seems there have been problems in the harbor," Ahlvie told them. "They're not allowing passage into Eleysia unless on an Eleysian vessel."

"What?" they both asked at once.

How ridiculous.

Sea travel had never been tightly guarded, and anyone was allowed passage, if they could pay the fare.

"We're in luck though. It appears there is one Eleysian ship in dock with plans to leave tonight."

"In the dark?" Maelia asked.

"Eleysian voyages traditionally begin at night. Seriously, do neither of you read?" he asked condescendingly. "If we want to be on that boat, we need to find the captain and make arrangements now. There's no other one for at least a fortnight unless you count the Eleysian royal ship coming into port." Cyrene opened her mouth to say something, but Ahlvie shook his head. "No. We're not considering the royal vessel. That would be impossible to get on, and we could go there and be back by the time they allow another ship to leave port."

"So, tonight then?" she asked. She hadn't thought it would all come together so soon.

"Tonight," Ahlvie confirmed.

"But I don't have any of my things," Cyrene told him.

"We can get things once we get there," he told her impatiently.

"I'm sorry. There are things I need from the castle that I can't leave behind," Cyrene said softly.

She had thought that many more ships would be leaving for Eleysia and that they would have enough time to get their belongings from their rooms. They hadn't had access to their bags since someone else had unloaded the ship. The book, the letter...she couldn't leave without them.

"Well, hurry now then. If you rush, I think you can make it. Meet me at the docks by sundown with your *things*, and I'll have made the arrangements."

Cyrene nodded, rising from the table alongside Maelia.

"Cyrene," he called before she could disappear, "don't be late."

28

The DOCKS

THERE WASN'T ANOTHER OPTION.

If only one Eleysian ship would be leaving Albion, then Cyrene had to be on it.

As much as she wanted to see Rhea, she no longer had the time to wait. Her heart ached at the thought of coming all this way and not seeing her best friend.

Maybe she could get a letter out to her friend in time. But what would it say? That she was here? That she was leaving? That she wanted Rhea to come with her, but she couldn't explain why?

Rhea would never go for that. She would need a good explanation. Cyrene didn't feel comfortable explaining the situation in a letter either. Rhea would just have to trust her.

The hardest part about getting back to the castle was trying not to rush. She and Maelia couldn't raise suspicion. Keeping easy smiles on their faces as they walked down the long lane to the castle was even worse. With worry creasing her smooth forehead, Maelia glanced anxiously at Cyrene while fiddling with her reins, making her horse jumpy. Cyrene had to remind her to stop it. One misstep, and they'd miss that ship.

When they reached the entrance to Krisana, a Royal Guard member waved them through after catching sight of their Affiliate pins. As soon as they reached the stable yard, Maelia hopped off the brown steed and dashed away from Cyrene to get everything she would need. Cyrene directed the stable hand to have the horses saddled and ready to go before sundown.

Once out of the boy's sight, she took off into a full sprint, hoisting her skirts in her hands, and darted for the main entrance. She burst through the pearl doors, entering the foyer of the castle. Thankfully, a maid walked through the room, carrying a white porcelain water jug.

"Excuse me," Cyrene called, trying not to give away how out of breath she was from her mad dash.

The woman stopped and turned around. "Yes...yes, Affiliate?"

"I've forgotten the way to my quarters, and I was hoping that you could be of assistance in directing me." Cyrene clasped her hands in front of her to keep from shaking.

"I'm sorry, Affiliate." The woman dropped a small curtsy as she held the jug between her hands. "I must take this to Queen Kaliana herself. She requested it of me, and I would be out of line to decline her request. I would be happy to show you the way afterward, if that suits you."

A smile broke out on Cyrene's face. "The Queen you say?"

"Yes, Affiliate."

"I do believe that my quarters are of a more delicate matter than that water jug. The King himself has ordered my rooms. Queen Kaliana will hardly care to wait a few extra minutes at her husband's request," she said boldly. Any other night, she wouldn't have been so forthright, but she didn't have any other options.

The woman looked like she was going to drop the jug at Cyrene's words as she dipped into a royal curtsy. "My-my apologies, Affiliate. If the King has requested your rooms, then I will certainly show you to them," she stammered. "Follow me."

Cyrene sighed. She didn't like pulling rank on this innocent. This woman didn't need to be pulled into the web of lies that permeated court life.

"Were you informed as to what chamber you would be living in while staying in the White City?" the servant asked meekly, walking toward Cyrene.

"I believe I was told that I would be staying in the Pearl Bay Chambers."

The servant immediately stopped sloshing some of the water out of her jug.

"The Pearl Bay Chambers? Are you certain?" She dabbed at her wet gown.

"Yes, that was what Consort Daufina informed me."

The girl stuttered forward, then stopped, and then directed her down a corridor. "I-I wasn't aware."

"What's wrong with the Pearl Bay Chambers?"

"Nothing!" she squeaked. "Nothing at all. They are gorgeous."

"Then, why are you shaking?"

"Well..." She anxiously glanced at Cyrene. "I assumed you would be in the Affiliate quarters, and you are staying"—she swallowed—"next to the King."

"What?" Cyrene cried despite herself.

"My apologies, Affiliate," she whispered, ducking her chin toward her chest as she picked up the pace.

It was one thing to be on Edric's ship but quite another to have her quarters next to him in the castle.

When they finally reached her new quarters, she had a headache that felt a bit like someone had been probing her brain all day. She wished that she could just take a nap, but there was no time.

The maid pushed open the door to the Pearl Bay Chambers, allowing her inside. The room was massive, and Cyrene's eyes enlarged to saucers when she walked inside. She jotted off a quick letter to Rhea for the maid to deliver in a hurry for her.

The woman dipped a curtsy and rushed out of the room, leaving behind Queen Kaliana's water jug. Cyrene laughed and then jumped to her feet. She darted into the bedchamber, and her feet stumbled forward as the beauty of the bedroom hit her with the force of a lightning strike.

A four-poster white bed with white curtains hooked to each post took up the majority of the room. White furniture with sterling silver candelabras atop them was placed artfully around the room. The walls were the same seashell white with gorgeously designed filigree pearl molding from which Krisana received its namesake. It was so exquisite that she faltered in her resolve for a moment...just one moment.

Then, she shook her head and steeled herself for what she was doing. Beautiful things weren't what mattered in her world.

She wrenched open the white wardrobe. At the bottom sat her bag, still untouched as far as she could tell. She was glad that she had left detailed instructions with the servants who had followed them into the castle. Her other two bags had been unpacked, and many of her gowns hung in color order. A few pairs of her slippers were neatly arranged on a stand. It would be so easy to stay. *So easy.*

Breathing out heavily, she removed her leather bag from the wardrobe. When she found the book and her Presenting letter still tucked inside, she hoisted the bag onto her shoulder. Beyond the large bay window, the sun was falling on the horizon. She was nearly out of time. Hopefully, Maelia was ready.

Cyrene's hand was resting on the door handle when someone knocked from the other side. She jumped quickly and stashed her bag behind the nearby chaise. The knock sounded again, and she groaned softly.

Go away. Go away. Go away!

"Just a minute," she called. She walked back to the door and pulled it open. Her heart sank when she saw who was standing in front of her. "Your Highness."

"Affiliate," Kael said, his tone soft. He leaned his hip against the doorframe, his eyes eager, and his demeanor showcasing the typical prince she had grown to love to hate.

"Kael, I don't have time."

"Time for what?"

"For this." She gestured between them.

"I don't know what you mean."

"For us. I don't have time for us to argue."

"So, there is an us?" he asked with a smirk.

She rolled her eyes. "I don't have time."

"I didn't come to argue."

"You never do," she said dryly.

"Can I come in?"

"I learned a long time ago not to let a courtier in my bedchamber." She kept the door securely in her hand. "Now, please go."

"Is that so?" His hand pushed gently against the door. "Would you prefer to come to mine then? I've heard you follow court rules that way."

She glared at him. *How dare he come here and talk about Edric like that!* Nothing had even happened on the ship.

"Have you been drinking?"

"Yes," he said with a shrug, "but not much." He forced the door open despite her hold.

She stepped back and let the door loose enough for him to stumble through. "There! Are you happy? You're inside."

He smirked as he closed the door behind him.

She needed to throw him off balance if she was going to get out of here in time. "Have you ever been in the Pearl Bay Chambers before?"

He smiled even bigger. "Of course."

She walked backward, slow and seductive. His eyes followed the movement, and he cocked his head to the side. He cautiously followed her, judging the movements.

"And the bedchamber?"

His eyes narrowed, and he licked his lips. "Of course."

"So, you know about the beautiful white bed?" she asked. Her voice was teasing as she entered the bedroom, and her heart hammered in her chest as she taunted her prey.

"Much too big a bed for one person."

Her eyes darted to the bay window, but she made sure that she looked at the bed, too, hoping to reassure him. Darkness was falling with the sunset.

"Much too big," she agreed. She licked her lips.

His shoulders relaxed with the statement.

She had him then. *By the Creator, it is almost too easy.*

Letting out a slow breath, she reached forward and grasped his wrist in her hand, tugging him forward into the bedroom in front of her. He chuckled softly, and it was a low sexy tone of victory as he walked through the door.

When he passed her and was looking off in the other direction, her fingers tightened around the silver candelabra on the dresser. Then, she reeled back, and with every ounce of force, she could muster slammed the thing into the back of his head. He crumpled to the ground in a heap.

She stared down at the Prince of Byern lying at her feet, knocked unconscious by her own hand. Her hands trembling, she replaced the candelabra, unable to believe what she had just done. Never in her life had she resorted to violence to get what she wanted. It felt unnatural, and she couldn't shake the wobbliness in her knees.

This had better work, or else she would be in some serious trouble.

Despite her shaking hands, she retrieved her hidden bag and bolted out of the castle. She didn't even hold back from breaking into a sprint down an empty corridor. Some of the servants looked at her oddly, but at this point, she had been delayed far too long. She needed to make it to that dock, or she would be stuck in Albion, in Byern, without any answers and an angry prince.

Her feet carried her to the stables, and she was out of breath when she made it.

Maelia sat atop Astral, biting her nails. "What kept you?" she cried.

"No time to talk," Cyrene said breathlessly, attaching her bag to Ceffy. She threw herself onto the saddle. "No time at all."

They heeled their horses into action, heading outside of the inner walls of Krisana and down the drawbridge. Cyrene sent Ceffy into a canter and then a full gallop down the road. The sun sat like a half moon against the Lakonia Ocean.

Only a sliver of the sunset still remained as the horses' hooves clattered against the wooden docks. Cyrene feared that they were too late. Ahlvie stood at the end of their appointed dock with his horse, a small bag attached to the saddle, and nothing else.

"You're late," he called.

"We're not." She stared out at the sunset. "There is still light."

"Quickly then," he said with a shake of his head that looked like defeat.

They reached the end of the dock just as a long ship pulled up its plank. Ahlvie called and waved his hands at the ship.

"Wait!"

"What say you, boy?" the man asked in a thick Eleysian accent. He had a deep scar across the right side of his face, and his head was much too big for his stocky neck, which mostly disappeared into his shoulders.

"I spoke with Captain Lador earlier this afternoon for safe passage for three to Eleysia," Ahlvie informed the man.

The man chortled. "Captain Lador was found dead in the gutter less than an hour ago, boy. You're now looking at the new captain of The Nether Knave, Captain De la Mora," he said, flourishing his last name.

"Captain De la Mora, it's a pleasure. Will my companions and I still be allowed safe passage on your beautiful vessel, The Nether Knave?"

"Two Affiliates and a High Order?" He motioned to a crew member. "I'm sure you can find your own way. I have no room for First Class passengers seeking to infiltrate my beloved country."

"Captain De la Mora, we are seeking nothing of the sort. We are merely interested in visiting your wonderful country and bringing back some of the rich history and culture to our homeland."

The captain scratched his chest hair. "No Affiliates or High Order got any business in Eleysia. You three best remember that."

"Please, sir!" Cyrene pleaded.

"Cast off!" the captain yelled to the crew, walking away from the deck.

"Ahlvie, do something!" she cried.

"What would you have me do?" he asked, his face set. "I did everything I could."

"Captain De la Mora!" she yelled helplessly as the last rope was untied.

The boat began to slowly drift out of the harbor.

Cyrene watched it leave, her heart sinking. After everything she had done to get here, she had lost. No more ships for a fortnight

"What do we do now?" Maelia whispered.

She wished she had an answer. She turned and pulled Ceffy back down the dock.

A dark figure stood at the end of the dock. "What in the Creator's name do you think you're doing?" the person asked as she threw her hood back.

Cyrene broke out into a smile and rushed to her, leaving her friends on the dock. "Rhea!" She wrapped her arms around her friend.

"Cyrene."

They crushed each other in a hug.

"I've missed you so much."

"I've missed you, too, Cyrene."

Rhea pulled back from Cyrene but kept a hand on each of her shoulders. "Now, what is this all about? A cryptic message when you only just got into Albion? I don't understand."

"I was afraid of explaining in a letter," Cyrene sheepishly told her.

"But you were willing to leave without seeing me?"

"No! That's why I sent the letter in the first place."

Rhea opened her mouth to speak and then clamped it shut as she looked over Cyrene's shoulder. Cyrene glanced back to see Maelia and Ahlvie approaching.

"Who are they?" Rhea asked.

"Friends." She introduced them to each other.

Rhea seemed apprehensive. She nodded curtly. "Why did you ask me to the docks? Where are we going?"

"Nowhere," Cyrene said sadly. "The ship has left."

Rhea bit her lip and glanced between all three, who had matching somber expressions. "Come with me. I've already broken curfew, and Master Barca will not be pleased. I might as well bring him a reason for it. Maybe we can figure this all out there."

29

The
REASON

THROUGH THE WINDING ALBION ROADS, CYRENE WALKED
Ceffy next to Rhea. Cyrene hadn't wanted their reunion to go like
this, but there was no other choice under the circumstances. When
Rhea glanced over at her, Cyrene could tell she was thinking the
same thing. She was just so glad to have Rhea back. With her friend
at her side, she was whole again.

Rhea leaned against Cyrene and glanced back at Maelia and
Ahlvie. "Is this about the letter? Do they know?"

"No," Cyrene replied just as softly.

"So, there's something else?"

"Yes. I'll give you the details when we're alone," Cyrene
promised.

"As will I. I have some news," Rhea said when they turned
down another street. "About the letter. I've been digging through
the libraries every chance I get. Have you found anything?"

"Hardly. I've had no chance. The Queen hates me."

Rhea looked at her, astonished by the statement.

"I have a lot to explain," Cyrene added.

"Clearly." Rhea glanced back over her shoulder again.

She didn't trust Maelia and Ahlvie, and Cyrene couldn't blame
her. She had never met them before and didn't know their motives.

"Let's talk in private. We'll have to go to the library anyway for
me to show you," Rhea said.

Cyrene sighed. Now that she had to be here for another
fortnight, she would have time with Rhea, but she would also have

to account for her actions with Kael and put off her journey longer.

Rhea broke her from her thoughts. "Why does the Queen hate you?"

"Because the King doesn't." Cyrene dipped her head to her chin and then glanced back up at Rhea.

"What does that—" She broke off and her mouth dropped open. "The King fancies you?" she squeaked.

"Yes," she whispered. She spoke nothing of her own feelings.

"King Edric fancies you?" Rhea asked again in shock.

Perhaps Rhea hadn't been ready to hear that one. And if she hadn't been ready to hear about the King, she certainly wasn't going to be ready for the unconscious Prince in Cyrene's bedchamber.

"Cyrene, I don't know what to say."

"I still don't either," Cyrene told her honestly.

"Have you... *been* with him?" she whispered, blushing furiously. "I just mean...I know the King has been rumored to...well, you know. I'm not insinuating that you would ever...just never mind." Rhea looked straightforward and continued walking purposely.

Cyrene laughed at her and shook her head. "I haven't."

Rhea blew out a breath. "Good." She squeezed her hand. "Life really isn't the same without you. Thanks for not jumping on that ship and leaving me behind."

"Ugh, I don't even want to talk about it."

"It's all right," Rhea reassured her. "Master Barca's house is around this corner."

They turned one more corner, and Rhea pointed out her Master's residence—a plain white square building with only one window facing the street and a high fence. It didn't look like much from the outside, but it was in a nicer Veda near the castle, so Cyrene had high expectations about the interior.

Rhea opened the exterior door and allowed them to escort their horses through the gate before closing it securely behind her. At the stable yard, an older man took their reins, smiled fondly at Rhea, and even patted her dark red hair. She smiled at him before grabbing Cyrene's hand and pulling her through a back entrance into the house.

The room they entered was dark, and it opened into a well-lit inner courtyard that rivaled the size of her parents' mansion back in

Byern. Rhea's Receiver must be an extremely wealthy man to have such extravagance.

As they walked across the garden courtyard, Cyrene noticed that something was off about it. Where fountains would have been among the flowers, strange metal contraptions stood in their places. Cyrene stared at one giant device with a strange circular piece that rotated around another huge circle. She wondered what that was for.

"Just ignore that stuff," Rhea urged. "I do. It's easier than asking."

Cyrene warily looked at her. "He doesn't tell you?"

"His explanations are more confusing, so I don't bother."

"They confuse *you*?"

Rhea laughed and leaned into Cyrene. "Coming here made me realize how behind I really was. Wait until you meet Master Barca."

They filed into a ballroom filled to the brim with random odds and ends. The room itself was beyond grandiose, but spider webs hung in the corners of the white walls and in between the pieces of cut crystal in the chandelier. Dust settled on the enormous bookshelves filled top to bottom with obscure pieces of metal, old titleless books, strange rocks, and more that Cyrene couldn't even distinguish among the rubble. Piles of loose ends were stacked nearly to the ceiling, and pathways had been cleared, revealing the vibrant blue-and-white crisscrossed tile that had once been a beautiful feature of the room. How anyone could make sense of it all was beyond Cyrene, let alone having someone *live* in this.

"Sorry about the clutter." Rhea guided them through the maze.

Cyrene glanced back and saw that Ahlvie and Maelia both wore similar looks of fascination in their eyes as they walked through.

"You call this clutter?" Ahlvie asked sarcastically.

"I try to help him pick stuff up, but he tells me that he'll forget where he put things if I move them," Rhea said.

"How could he ever know where anything is in this?" Maelia asked the question they had all been thinking.

Rhea shrugged. "He made the piles, I suppose."

She grabbed a lit lantern on the wall and then entered a tidy small office. Cyrene recognized Rhea's handiwork all over the room. A sturdy wooden desk with six chairs around it had stacks of books and drawings of different objects. A banister ran all the way around the room at about hip level, and the bottom half was a soft green color while the top was a light brown. Only one bookshelf sat against the back wall, and Cyrene was surprised to see it all but empty compared to what lay on the other side of the door.

"Take a seat." Rhea pulled out the chair and waited for the others to follow suit. "Now, can someone please tell me *what* is going on?"

Ahlvie and Maelia looked at Cyrene to begin.

Cyrene sighed. "We're trying to get to Eleysia."

"Why?" Rhea lifted her eyebrows.

Cyrene bit her lip. She hadn't told everyone the same information, hadn't even told anyone the whole truth. Maelia knew Cyrene wanted to go to Eleysia to complete her training and that the Queen had refused to let her leave. Ahlvie knew they were leaving, and while he might have had the means to leave on his own previously, he had never had the nudge that he needed to go alone. Rhea, of course, knew about the Presenting letter.

None of them knew about the book. None of them knew about Basille Selby. None of them knew that all her answers rest in Eleysia with Matilde and Vera.

"Because I need to go there."

Rhea narrowed her eyes. "But why?"

Cyrene swallowed and closed her eyes. Then, it all spilled out of her…the whole story. They needed to be on a similar page. She needed to trust them as they trusted her.

She told them about Edric, the unconscious Kael, the envious Kaliana, and the manipulative yet endearing Daufina. She told them about her Presenting letter. She cautiously told them about receiving the book and how she would sometimes seem to lose time when she read it, but she couldn't bring herself to tell them about the strange swirly font. She remembered Basille Selby's apprehension, and she wouldn't repeat that unless she had to. But she did tell them about Master Selby's declaration about how she had to go to Eleysia to get answers.

Finally, she revealed her connection to all the murders. She didn't know how that piece fit into the puzzle, but it felt significant.

"The murders are connected to you?" Ahlvie asked in surprise.

Cyrene nodded. "I just figured it out when we got back. So, you see why I have to leave to find answers. There's something…wrong with me," she said slowly. "I don't know what it is or even how to explain it. I want to make you believe me, but I can't. It's something I don't even understand, but it terrifies me. I've been scared, wondering what is happening, if it will get worse, if something else will happen, if I'll hurt myself or someone else while trying to figure out what is going on inside of me."

A tear fell and then another one. She couldn't stop it. She placed her hands over her eyes to try to quell the storm rising up inside of her.

A minute passed in silence before she could continue, "I wanted to tell you all, but I didn't think you would believe me. So, I'm sorry for deceiving you, even as slight as the deception was, but I need to go to Eleysia. I *have* to go to Eleysia. I'll go with or without you, but I'd rather have you there with me."

She expected disgust, hurt, betrayal, and anger. She expected them to hate her for using her, like Kaliana, Daufina, and even Kael had used her. She hated herself a little bit for it.

All that stared back at her was determination, pity, sorrow, hope, and love. Rhea covered Cyrene's left hand with her own and squeezed like it just like old times. Maelia slowly reached out and placed her hand over Rhea's. She nodded once and then smiled.

Ahlvie chuckled softly and shook his head. "I'll be damned," he said. "Guess I'm in, too."

His hand slid across the table and covered Maelia's delicate hand.

One more tear slid down Cyrene's cheek. They were going to stick by her, even after all of that, even after she had kept secrets from them. She swallowed hard. For the first time in months, the weight slowly eased off her chest.

30
The
INVENTOR

As THEY PULLED AWAY, THE DOOR TO THE OFFICE BANGED
open, and they all jumped apart.

"Rhea!" an old man yelled, walking into the room with his eyes
closed and hands covering his temples. He was incredibly tall with
a great white beard and unkempt long white hair. "Have you seen
that last sketch I made? And the fandangled thing? I used it last
time. Where is it?"

Cyrene stared with her mouth agape. She had no idea in the
slightest what he was talking about.

And Cyrene was slightly shocked by the man's appearance. His
clothes were as disheveled as his house. He wore a long brown
tunic, reaching nearly to his knees, that was threadbare at the hem
and across the seams. He looked like he needed a good scrub down
before he would ever be fit to be seen by the public.

"I left the sketch on your desk," Rhea told him with a smile.
"In the center, on top of your latest concept art."

"What an odd place to leave something!" He turned in a circle,
looking up at the ceiling. "What if I needed to find it?"

"That's what I'm here for, sir," she told him with humor in her
voice.

Suddenly, Master Barca stopped mid-spin, facing the door, and
craned his neck around. "Rhea," he said softly, his madness
seemingly dissipating, "you didn't tell me that we had visitors."

"My apologies," she said with her ever-present easy smile.
"This is my friend Cyrene. We grew up together in Byern before I
moved here. And these are her two friends, Maelia and Ahlvie.

They've just arrived on the procession with King Edric and the rest of the court."

"Affiliates and a High Order, I see."

"Yes, sir," Rhea said firmly.

Cyrene recognized that tone loud and clear. She wanted to giggle because Rhea had used that exact tone with her on one too many occasions. It meant that you should hold your tongue before you got yourself in trouble. Cyrene didn't usually listen, and it didn't look like her Receiver was about to either.

"Well"—he turned in another circle, as if he already forgot what he was thinking earlier—"let's go then. There's much to do."

He barreled out of the room in much the same manner in which he had entered it. Cyrene, Maelia, and Ahlvie stared after his retreating figure.

Rhea, however, had already hopped out of her seat. When she noticed they weren't coming with her, she stopped and turned back around. "Come on then."

They scurried out of their chairs and followed Rhea's hasty steps to keep up with her Receiver.

Muttering to himself, Master Barca led them back through the cluttered ballroom. He turned down a long hallway that was completely blank and then into another courtyard. Row after row of perfectly aligned wooden racks lined the interior of the enclosure.

"Bursts," Ahlvie murmured softly in awe.

The inventor stared off into the clear night sky for a few minutes. When he pulled his gaze away, he looked at Rhea, but his eyes were distance, as if seeing through her to a different time or a different place.

"The King commissioned that lot," he said, pointing to a group covered in a corner.

They all just stared at him.

"You're here for them, aren't you?" he asked.

"Yes," Cyrene responded immediately, having no clue how to transport them but not seeing any other option on how to get them into the castle.

"You'll have to come back tomorrow for the rest. I don't even remember sending word about the first lot."

"I sent word, sir," Rhea jumped in. "I told you earlier today."

"Did you?" he asked absentmindedly.

"You've been busy replicating that explosion you created." She tsked him like a child. "You've forgotten all about it, like the sketch I left on your desk."

"Yes! It is on my desk. Rhea, girl, I know what it is!" He jumped, grabbed a candle off of the wall, and moved to the first Burst on a row.

"Sir, is it really necessary right now? Think about the Veda."

"Oh, let them complain," he said, suddenly lucid and vigilant. As he began to work, his madness fell off of him like a snake shedding his skin, and he immersed himself in whatever he was doing.

No one else moved an inch.

He expectantly reached his hand out to Rhea. She sighed and brought her lantern out to him. He extracted the candle out from the container and touched the flame to a cord at the end.

"Back up!" He jogged awkwardly to the overhang near the door.

They followed behind him and pressed their bodies against the wall.

Cyrene's heart raced. She had never seen one this close, and it had been quite a while since she'd seen the last one. In fact, she couldn't remember the previous time. It was possibly the Eos holiday two years ago.

They braced themselves, smiles growing on their faces as the speck of light traveled farther up the cord. The little piece of paper erupted, shooting out of its holster in the rack and up into the night sky. Cyrene pushed off the wall and stood in the open courtyard.

Then, it happened. With a loud bang, the sky exploded into a million bright red stars that rained down all around them. Cyrene lifted her hands, hoping to catch a star as it fell toward them. But like every other time she had seen them, the color of the Burst disappeared right before touching the ground, leaving the night sky with a smoky haze where such beauty had been before.

So, it wasn't magic. He had simply lit a cord, and the Burst had come alive in the sky, like the fire worked its own magic.

She sighed, slightly relieved that she had been right.

"Argh!" Master Barca pulled roughly on his beard. "It didn't work!"

They all stared at him like he was the raving lunatic that he was. Of course, it had worked! It was gorgeous and had lit up the entire night sky.

He cried out a few more times, striding over to where he had lit the Burst and angrily fiddled with the cord.

Rhea shrugged, as if this were completely commonplace. "Come on. Let's get Rouster, so he can help you transport these."

When they turned around to leave the inventor to his business, they found someone walking through the back door anxiously.

"I heard the commotion," the older man from the stable yard said.

"It's fine, Rouster," Rhea told him. "He's messing with the Bursts again, trying to recreate that same explosion."

"That's normal, Miss Rhea," he said, pushing a piece of paper into her hands. "But the Royal Guard going from house to house, asking for a woman similar in appearance to a woman we have in our quarters, is not."

"The Guard!" Rhea squeaked.

"It says here that Affiliate Cyrene went missing some hours ago. The city is in an uproar, looking for her. The note is signed by both Dremylon brothers. I've never seen anything like it," he admitted shakily.

Royal Guard. City in an uproar. Both Dremylon brothers. Cyrene felt faint. They were out searching for her? *Both of them?* If all had gone right, she would have been far out of the harbor by now.

She finally found her voice. "I am Affiliate Cyrene. I believe it's time for me to return to the castle." She pushed her shoulders back, accepting whatever might come next.

Rhea grabbed her hand. "If they ask, you were here the whole time. I'll swear to it. Don't do anything rash."

Her warning rang in Cyrene's head loud and clear.

Cyrene turned to Maelia. "Stay here and find your own way back. I don't want to raise suspicion."

Maelia nodded, looking sick to her stomach, while Ahlvie stood stoically with his arms crossed.

Two Royal Guard sat on top of enormous black horses when she exited the house. "Are you the Affiliate we seek?"

"Yes. Allow me to get my horse, and I'll come with you." She put on the Affiliate mask that she wore around the castle so aptly. It was a demeanor that few argued with.

She walked with Rouster into the stables and swiftly untied her bag from Ceffy. It would draw unwanted attention. As much as it made her uneasy to leave the book, she moved her bag over to Astral opposite of Maelia's belongings. She trusted Maelia to get it back to her.

Rouster helped her onto Ceffy's back, and a guard directed her to walk her horse between them. *How deep am I in trouble with the royalty for them to fear me so much that the Royal Guard would treat me like a prisoner, forcing me to walk down the street between them?*

She hadn't realized earlier how close Master Barca's house was to the castle. Her stomach was in knots, and she was straining for composure.

Crossing the drawbridge felt like a death sentence when she saw the number of Royal Guard walking around the circular open courtyard and others stationed at every entrance. *How many had they sent out after me?*

The two guards jumped from their horses and walked with her toward the giant pearl doors. They must want to claim their prize for finding the fugitive.

The entranceway was eerily quiet for the amount of activity going on outside. She passed through the foyer, and the two guard stationed at the entrance to the royal throne room opened the door for them. She took a deep breath and walked into the exquisite room, ready to face whatever was coming for her.

Despite the hour, many stood around the thrones. Edric sat in his throne, his hand pressed to his head. Kaliana and Daufina were on either side of him. Kaliana looked triumphant. Duke Halston's arm was slung across the shoulders of his sobbing pregnant wife, who was huddled in an uncomfortable position on her own smaller throne. Finally, her gaze located the one person she hadn't wanted to see in the room, and he was the first to notice her.

Her breath caught at the mixture of emotions in Kael's stormy eyes. Anger was the most prominent, but happiness, desire, and revenge passed across his face in nearly the same instant. As he started toward her, all eyes turned and found her standing in the room. She saw the next few seconds through slow motion.

Kael continued forward until he was standing in front of her. His hand brushed her shoulder as if to make sure that she was real. Edric arrived a second later, nearly knocking his brother out of the way, his soft hands replacing Kael's rough ones. Her eyes locked with Edric's, and all the worry about the deaths being associated with her and the thought of leaving him behind hit her full-on. In that moment, all she wanted to do was sink into his arms and kiss him.

Then, the commotion happened all at once, and the silence turned into deafening confusion. Everyone spoke, and she wasn't sure which question to answer first. In fact, most of the questions didn't even make sense, and she couldn't process them with so much being thrown at her. All she knew was that it sounded like they had been *worried* about her, not angry. And she couldn't fathom it.

Finally, Edric pulled rank and quieted the lot of them, dropping his hands from her shoulders. "Where have you been?"

She raised her chin, regaining her regal composure. "At Master Barca's residence, retrieving a shipment of Bursts."

"What?" Edric cried.

At the same time, Kael yelled, "Really?"

They looked at each other and then back at Cyrene.

Daufina intercepted the two men and stood next to Cyrene. "What I think they mean to ask is, why would you do such a thing?"

"I received a letter instructing me to do so," she stated simply.

"And where is this letter?" Kaliana asked haughtily. She hadn't moved from the throne and was staring at Cyrene as frosty as the ice queen she was.

"I believe I left it at Master Barca's where your guard retrieved me, Your Highness." She smiled as sweet as possible at the woman who wanted her gone.

"Well, thank the Creator, you're all right," Daufina said. "We were all worried about your safety."

Cyrene tried to hide the surprise from her face, but she clearly wasn't successful.

"Why would you go out into the city like that?" Kael demanded. "You've given us quite a headache." He rubbed his temple.

She stood her ground at his insinuation and reminder. She couldn't break in front of everyone else. It didn't seem as if he had told anyone, and she wasn't about to.

But why hadn't he told them? And what price would it come at?

"I didn't intend to give anyone a headache. I was simply following orders and my duty as an Affiliate. But might I ask, why were you so worried?" This was hardly the reception she had been expecting when the guards picked her up from Master Barca's.

Daufina and Edric shared a knowing look.

"Another Affiliate has turned up dead," Daufina said. "In the same manner as Affiliate Pallia and High Order Grabel."

"Another one?" she gasped, covering her mouth.

"Yes," Edric told her.

"That's enough," Kaliana spat, standing and striding toward them. "This is official royal business. She has no right knowing anything further. She's perfectly safe, and she has no idea what we are talking about. Perhaps she should just go to her bedchambers...in the Affiliate quarters," she added.

Edric stared at his Queen blankly. "Kaliana, you've stepped out of line. Have you forgotten who runs this kingdom?" His tongue was sharp.

"How could I forget?"

"Then, perhaps you should allow me to decide who requires information and who does not."

Kaliana smiled, and it was almost worse than when she had glared at him. "As you wish," she said with a tiny bob of her head, "my *husband*."

Cyrene stood still, not wanting to interfere. She had never intended for any of this to happen. All she wanted to do was go to Eleysia and find out what the book meant. She didn't want the King's attention, the Prince's infatuation, the Queen's animosity, or the Consort's help. She certainly didn't want to have to think about the murder of five of the First Class. Not for the last time, she wished she had been on that ship.

Edric ignored the Queen's last comment and turned back to Cyrene. "As I was saying, we had one other Affiliate die tonight. Affiliate Karra was part of the search committee for Affiliate Pallia and High Order Grabel. She pieced together the uncertain coincidence about High Order Zorian returning to Byern for your Presenting and the circumstances of Pallia and Grabel coming to Albion to meet the sister of Affiliate Aralyn. Aralyn is your sister, yes?"

Cyrene's hands were shaking as Edric spoke. Her selfishness was the cause of another Affiliate's death. Her stomach flipped, and she could barely answer, "Ye-yes."

"When Karra discovered you were missing, she went out looking for you herself. Before sunset, she and an Eleysian sailor, Captain Lador, were found dead near the docks."

Cyrene's knees gave out. She closed her eyes. Kael reached out and grabbed her before she could fall. Her head lolled back as she thought about the dead captain that she had so easily dismissed when begging Captain De la Mora for passage on his ship.

How is this all connected?

"Some water!" Edric called to one of the guards standing watch. "Are you all right?" he asked as Kael set her lightly on the ground. "We didn't mean for…"

Water appeared, and a maid tipped some back into her mouth.

She swallowed, and her eyes fluttered open. Her breathing was heavy. She didn't want to think about what he was saying. She didn't want to think about the blood on her hands even if she hadn't killed them.

"I'm sorry to have upset you," Daufina said softly. "We thought you should know."

"When you didn't return," Kael said, "we all thought that the killer had chosen the next victim."

31
The
LIBRARY

HOUSE ARREST.

Or did they call it castle arrest?

Cyrene didn't care because either way, it meant she wasn't leaving. She was trapped behind Krisana's beautiful white walls. She was in a white prison when she had been so close to freedom the day before.

They were doing it for her own good. The killer had followed them to Albion. They couldn't let her wander around until they found out what was going on, but that didn't mean she would enjoy it.

Being stuck, strolling the endless empty castle halls, was the last thing she wanted to do. If she had to remain in Albion this much longer, she at least wanted to see the gardens on the other side of the drawbridge and the ocean. She hadn't even been down to the beaches on the West end. She could dreamily stare out the windows all she wanted, but she wasn't going to be allowed to leave.

Maelia returned and managed to sneak Cyrene's bag back to her room. Apparently, Ahlvie knew passageways through Krisana nearly as well as Nit Decus, and he had snuck her into the building. He wasn't even supposed to be in Albion, so he had decided to stay with a friend in the city.

Guards were posted at every entrance and exit as well as at intervals around the castle, as they had been in Byern. Albion was in lockdown mode, and Cyrene had yet to figure out a way to see Rhea without requesting it from Edric—not that she had seen him since the night in the throne room. It was as if he was avoiding her, and she didn't really blame him…even if she missed him.

With Edric's absence and her forced imprisonment, she was left with one too many days all alone. One of those tiresome mornings, two weeks after her attempted escape from Albion, a soft knock on her door roused her from her boredom. She jumped up and hastily opened the door to her chambers.

Prince Kael stood handsomely on the other side. He looked as if he had just been out riding. The smell of the crisp salty air pervaded him. He stared impassively as he stood before her with his arms crossed, a brown riding crop tucked under his arm.

"Your Highness," she said.

Their interactions had been cold, brief, and few in number. When he looked at her, she could tell he was plotting, but she was nothing but polite. She figured knocking him out had done enough damage.

"To what do I owe the pleasure?" she asked.

"It seems like your freedom has been temporarily granted."

"They found the killer?"

"I wouldn't be too optimistic," he said dryly. "You've been granted leave to visit the library."

"The library?" She had made no such request.

"Do you not wish to leave?"

"I do," she said automatically. "Where do I go? How do I get there?"

"I'm escorting you," he said.

Then, she understood his stony demeanor. He didn't want to be doing this. He didn't want to be near her. That must be it.

"I'll just be a minute." Cyrene rushed back into her room. She threw some powder on her face, added a touch of rouge, and grabbed her blue silk cloak.

Kael was standing in her living room, the riding crop hanging limp at his side, when she returned.

"I'm ready."

He found her hands empty, and then his gaze darted to her face. "You didn't bring a candelabra with you this time?"

She swallowed. "No."

"Then, I guess I won't need this after all."

He made a swatting motion in the air, and her eyes grew wide. He winked at her. "Pity."

"Oh, honestly," she snapped. Her cheeks flushed crimson, and she turned away. *Did the man think of anything else?*

A soft chuckle sounded behind her, and she tried to keep a smile from her face.

"You're fun," he whispered, following her out the door and swatting at her butt.

"Kael! Stop that."

"As ever, your wish is my command, Affiliate."

She grumbled under her breath. She walked through the winding walls of the White Castle and came out into the morning sunshine. Every guard in the city knew her likeness now, and they all stared at her as if to remind her that she wasn't going anywhere.

Two horses were saddled and waiting for them. Cyrene hurried onto her horse and Kael took the one next to her. Just when she thought it couldn't get any worse than this imprisonment, six Royal Guards on their massive black stallions broke into formation around her and Kael.

Yes, parading through the city with armed guards is worse.

"So," Cyrene began as their atrocious display pranced through the main lane of Albion, "why are you escorting me?"

"If you're asking why me and not my brother, you'll have to ask him," he said, looking straightforward.

She had wondered why Edric hadn't come to see her the whole time that she was alone in the castle. After the way he had acted on the procession, she'd thought that things would have been different.

But besides that, she was surprised that Kael was here at all. After she had knocked him out, she wouldn't have thought he would want to be anywhere near her.

"I was simply asking why you and not just six guards? Isn't it all a bit much?"

"Don't you know how important Affiliates are to the kingdom? We can't lose any more," Kael said, every bit of humor gone from his voice. "If this is how Edric wants to stop it, then so be it. He doesn't believe the killer will attack a royal."

"And you? Do you think that?" she asked. She hadn't expected honesty from him.

He shrugged. "I think killers probably don't think too much about it, but I'm not the king."

Cyrene held back her snide comment about him obviously wanting to be the king. He was being polite, and she didn't want to ruin it. It was such a rare occasion.

Being out in the city, even with the unnecessary guards, was refreshing after being cooped up for so long. The library wasn't exactly where she would have chosen for her first time out of the white walls, but she wasn't going to complain.

"So, why the library?" Cyrene asked.

"Master Barca sent a request for you."

"Did he?" Cyrene hid a smile. "What was the request?"

"Something about helping him with an explosion." Kael scratched his head. "I couldn't make much sense of it, but the man is a genius, so we usually oblige him."

Cyrene giggled, ducking her head into her cape. She knew exactly what he was talking about, and she also knew that Rhea was likely the person who had sent that request.

When she glanced up, Kael was staring at her, and she quickly looked away.

A moment later, the guards stopped at a large entrance to the library. Kael dismounted and helped her out of her saddle. She slid to the ground with their bodies nearly pressed together, and then took a hasty step back.

"Thank you for the escort. It was nice to have company," she admitted.

"It was nice not to be unconscious. So, our interactions are improving."

"Yes, well..." Cyrene flushed.

She should apologize. She had been the one to lead him on since she was in a rush.

Just as she was about to, Kael took a step away from her. He tipped his head in her direction and then swung back up into his saddle. "I hope you find what you're looking for in there." He stared off into the distance, his face unreadable. Then, without one last glance, he heeled his horse in the other direction.

"Thank you," she whispered at his back. She wondered if he had wished that she had asked him to accompany her inside. She chewed on her bottom lip and let it pass.

A member of the Royal Guard opened the door to allow her access to a large atrium. A gorgeous painted mural of angels—some floating on clouds, others walking on the thick green grass that she associated with the Byern countryside, and more bathing in the great Lakonia Ocean—covered every speck of wall space. The artist really captured the likeness of the ethereal nature of the angels.

Cyrene entered the main library and found it to be a perfect circle that went endlessly upward toward the domed ceiling. A white marble staircase with a black metal railing wrapped ever upward to the floors above. Books were stacked atop books that were stacked atop more books. They were pushed into shelves, stacked against the wall, and covering once used desks, yet they still managed to be neatly arranged. The soft aroma of paper, ink, and old leather bindings reached her nostrils, and the familiar scratching of quills against parchment made Cyrene feel right at home.

The best thing of all was seeing Rhea's smiling face among the stacks, her nose buried in a book, just like old times.

She rushed down to where Rhea was seated and threw her arms around her friend. "I knew it was you," she murmured against Rhea's auburn hair.

"I had to get you out of there somehow," she whispered.

"Thank the Creator you did! I assume you want to show me what you've found."

She took a seat next to Rhea, too anxious to know what she had discovered. Over two weeks ago, they were supposed to meet in the library to discuss this.

"Yes!" She grabbed two books and stood. "Follow me."

They walked to the first staircase and followed the spiral to the next floor and the next after that. She was a bit dizzy when they finally made it up to the fourth floor. It was much quieter up here, and the books were dustier from neglect. She couldn't even make out the sounds of the gentle markings of the quill by the Affiliate librarian standing at a horseshoe-shaped desk at the center.

Rhea replaced one book on a shelf and then glanced around to see if anyone had noticed them. The guards were staring straight forward, paying more attention to the entrances than to Cyrene herself, and the rest of the people in the room were too involved in their studies. Rhea cocked her head to the side, and they walked all the way to the opposite side of the stairwell before standing in front of a bookshelf that just about looked like every other bookshelf in the place.

Rhea swallowed, glancing anxiously at Cyrene, before pulling down four nondescript books from various locations on the shelves. They all looked rather ordinary to Cyrene.

"Do you have your letter with you?" Rhea whispered even though they were four floors up and no one could hear them.

Cyrene shook her head. She had been in such a rush to get out of the castle that she had left it behind.

"No bother. I have it memorized. I just thought for proof—"

"I know it by heart, too," Cyrene admitted.

"And you hate memorization," Rhea said with a smile. "All grown-up."

Cyrene chuckled, but the laugh died as her nerves escalated.

Rhea licked her lips and then laid the books out across a half-empty table. She opened the book at a seemingly random place until Cyrene noticed the scrap of paper holding the page. She did that for each of the four books. Cyrene bounced on her toes as she stared forward at the pages.

They were each written in distinct handwriting and different languages. The first was written in ancient Helix, which she was proficient in, but her eyes darted to the next book, which was a modern Helix. The third book was barely legible and smeared to the point that Cyrene wondered how much of a hurry the writer must have been in to get this on paper. When she squinted her eyes, she could see it was a Sorpo dialect of some kind. The biggest book of the lot was clearly from the Northern region when Carhara and Tiek had originally been split into multiple counties and then unified under the rule of the Trejcken Empire.

"This is what I've found," Rhea said, gesturing toward the books. "I was looking for riddles and answers to riddles, and I couldn't find anything. Then, randomly one day, when I was cleaning out Master Barca's room, I stumbled across this journal. She pointed at the Sorpo dialect. I was fascinated at first just because of the rare language and the rushed writing. Then, I found this."

Cyrene stared down at where Rhea's finger pointed. She carefully deciphered what she could from the text and then gasped. "But this…this is my Presenting letter."

"I know! I couldn't believe it. Then, I started looking for others like it in the library, which is how I discovered these," she said.

Cyrene shook her head and sat down in an available chair. Dust billowed up around her, and she coughed, swatting it out of her face. "I don't understand."

"Neither do I." She picked up the modern Helix and read through it.

Four different books and my letter in five different languages. All the same thing. All the same riddle. What did any of it mean?

"Do you have a guess? What do they all have in common?" Cyrene asked, hoping for something, anything.

"They're all journals of some sort. One is a collection of letters going back and forth during a battle. Two are daily accounts of their lives, but they have no connection in time or place. One woman is a high-class educated woman, another a beggar who used to do transcriptions and translations but lost his voice in an accident of some sort, one is a farmer, and the other is a sailor. The Helix text is the hardest to piece together, and even then, I can tell that some woman finds it important to write down this passage. She even says so," Rhea said. She pointed at the passage.

"But if they have nothing in common—"

"That is their commonality," Rhea continued. "Their urgency. Three of them, it comes out of nowhere in the middle of another thought, and another, it appears the man had to write it down before he lost it. I just don't know why."

Cyrene touched her friend's hand with a smile. "There has to be more. Why would my Presenting letter be in all these books? It must mean something."

"What if…" Rhea swallowed and averted her eyes. "Never mind. It's even crazy to consider."

"I could use a little crazy right now," Cyrene said with a sigh.

Rhea glanced up. "All right. What if it's all…going to happen?"

"Like…like a prophecy?" Cyrene asked, trying the word out. "But no one can predict the future."

Then again, no one should be able to see font that didn't exist or lose time from looking at a book. Maybe it *was* possible.

"I know, but why else would it be in all of these books?"

Cyrene sighed. "I don't know. Maybe it is prophecy. But then, why do I have it?"

Rhea meaningfully looked up at her. "Maybe you are meant to fulfill the prophecy."

The doors banged open four floors below, and Cyrene jumped at the interruption to the quiet library. She and Rhea glanced over the metal balcony. The imposing figure standing at full height in the center of the entranceway commanded attention with his abrupt arrival, and they weren't the only ones staring at him.

Rhea's hand fell to the railing. "What's the King doing here?"

"I don't know," she answered honestly. She hadn't seen him since the night she returned from Master Barca's residence.

They watched him walk to the Affiliate librarian seated behind her enormous horseshoe desk, buried to her forehead in books. A second later, the woman pointed upward. Cyrene swallowed and watched as his gaze found her among the stacks. Knowing she had no other option, she left Rhea with the pile of mysterious books and walked down the spiral stairs.

"Affiliate."

"Your Highness," she said with a curtsy.

"I thought you might enjoy some company on your way back to the castle."

She hadn't expected to be escorted back already. Rhea and she had just begun. Surely, they could find more clues in this massive library. But she could hardly refuse Edric, and she didn't really want to. Just seeing him this close again sent a spark up through her chest.

"Of course," she said. "Do you mind if I say good-bye?"

"No trouble at all."

She veered back to Rhea.

"I have to go," she said.

Rhea grasped her hand, her expression slightly worried. "I'll get word to you if I find anything else. Hopefully, this whole mess will be cleared up shortly."

"I hope so, Rhea." Cyrene smiled forlornly. "Good luck."

"Cyrene," Rhea said before Cyrene could turn to go, "be safe."

Cyrene nodded and returned to Edric. She followed him out of the library. A command of Guard members sat on their black stallions when they exited. Edric hoisted her up into Ceffy's saddle, and they trotted through the winding city. The Guards took a sharp right at the first juncture, and Cyrene sat up straighter in her saddle. This wasn't the way back to the castle. Her eyes darted to Edric, and he smiled.

"I thought you might want to see the white shores of Albion."

"Very much so, but is it safe?"

"With me you're always safe."

When they finally rounded the bend leading down to the beaches, Cyrene was nearly bouncing up and down. Ceffy pranced, feeling the weight of her owner.

"We'll leave the horses here. Wouldn't want any broken ankles," he said. He dismounted, helped her down, and then escorted their horses to the Guard.

A retinue of guards followed behind them as they set out onto the sandy beach. The waves gently rolled into surf, leaving traces of the white foam across the surface. A soft breeze lingered in the air, cool against her skin. She breathed in the distinct salty smell and listened to the seagulls in the distance.

Cyrene wondered what had possessed Edric to come out here with her this afternoon. After all this time apart, here they were, as if they were back on that procession boat. It was just the two of them lost in this dream of seclusion. She knew that this wouldn't escape the Queen's notice. Nothing did. And while Cyrene hadn't received any instruction since coming on the procession, she was sure Kaliana would cook up something when she thought Cyrene was getting closer to Edric again.

Maybe he had been staying away for her benefit. She really didn't know. She cut her eyes over to him, appraising him, and her feet sank too far into the sand.

"Oh!" she yelped, losing her balance.

She staggered forward, and Edric pulled her close with a steadying embrace. Once he had her in his grasp, he didn't release her. It had been so long since they were this close together, and she had to fight her instincts to keep her eyes from lingering on his lips.

"I've missed you," he whispered.

Her heart sang with the news. She hoped she sounded composed when she spoke next, "I'm sure you've been busy."

Edric sighed. "I have been. The Eleysian Prince should be here soon, and we've been preparing for his arrival, but..."

"But?" she prodded.

"It has been hard to stay away."

Cyrene flushed. She was glad that she was not the only one who felt that way.

257

"Cyrene"—he brushed her dark brown hair out of her face as the sea breeze whipped it around—"I don't want to stay away any longer."

His hand moved to the back of her head, and he drew her lips to his. It was the first kiss they had shared since the night on the procession, and she was shocked at how much she wanted this. She was the one who had made him stop before, but that was now the furthest thing from her mind.

Her whole body stirred at his touch. Their connection shocked through her. Her lips turned desperate. She couldn't get close enough to him. She couldn't find her breath or keep her heart steady. All she needed was this moment here with him. She clutched his shirt, and his fingers threaded back through her hair. He had the same maddening need pushing through every kiss and every touch. The ground seemed to shift beneath them.

They broke apart with a gasp. The heady look that passed between them was a far cry from their innocent looks across a ballroom. She wanted more. She wanted to *feel* again.

Edric removed his shaking hands from her and struggled to take control of his body. She could see the depths of desire pouring through his blue-gray eyes. She was sure that she was a mirror image of him. Slowly, she released his shirt and let her arms hang limp at her sides.

"Cyrene..."

She swallowed. "Yes?"

He shook his head and grasped her hand. Their fingers laced together, and he placed a soft kiss across her knuckles. Her heart hammered from the intensity of it all.

Edric directed her to continue their walk while the time permitted. She had so much going on, so much she didn't understand, and so much she had to worry about, but here, on the beach, the worries disappeared.

She didn't know how much time had passed before they headed back. The sun sank low across the horizon, and Cyrene noticed how high the tide was coming in, covering their early footprints in the sand, wiping them away as if they had never been.

"I never thought it would be so beautiful here," she said with a smile in his direction.

"You're beautiful," he whispered, drawing her to him again. "Come to me tonight."

"Edric…" She knew that she shouldn't do it.

She had to get to Eleysia, which meant far away from him. He had a Queen and so much more that mattered to him.

Yet how can I turn him down?

"Tonight?" he asked before punctuating his request with a soft kiss.

Her eyes fluttered closed. "Okay. Tonight."

32

The
SILVER TRINKET

CYRENE RETURNED SAFELY TO HER ROOM, FEELING HAPPIER than she had in weeks. She couldn't believe the turn in events today. Kael had acted like a human, Rhea had found out about the prophecies, and then Edric…

A shy smile crossed her face at the thought of their afternoon together. She closed the door and stretched out her tired feet. Her slippers were full of sand despite having taken them off several times already. She tossed them to the ground and padded into her bedroom to change out of the clothes she had been in all day.

After throwing her blue cape on the bed, she opened her wardrobe, bent down, and ran her hand against the side pocket of her large leather bag. The book's indent was visible, and she breathed a sigh of relief.

She stood, closed her wardrobe door, and nearly screamed as the shape of a figure materialized in the doorframe from out of nowhere. Her heart beat a thousand miles a minute.

"Shh," Ahlvie said. He put a finger to his mouth.

"What are you doing in here? You scared me half to death."

"Seem to be intact to me."

"How did you even get in here?"

He shrugged. "I have my ways. Where have you been all day? Aren't you on lockdown? I've been searching for you."

"You're not even supposed to be in the castle."

He shrugged, unconcerned.

"I was granted leave to visit the library. I met Rhea there."

"You've been there all afternoon?" he asked as if he already knew the answer.

"Never mind what I was doing. What are you doing in my bedchamber?" She set her stony gaze on him.

"Obviously looking for you," he said.

"Yes, but what for?" She had other plans tonight, and she really would like to clean up before then.

"We have to go."

"Go?" Cyrene asked. "Where? Why? I can't leave the castle."

"You'll have to make another exception."

"Ahlvie, what is this all about? There isn't a way for me to leave. All the guards know who I am."

"I can get you out, but we need to get moving," he said. He was already walking out of her bedroom and toward the exit.

"Wait." She rushed after him. "What about Maelia? Are we bringing her? Do I need my bag?"

"No. You won't need that until later. I can't bring both of you, so you'll have to settle for me tonight. It'll be fun."

She stood her ground. "Where are we going, Ahlvie?"

"Do you have to know everything before you do it? Trust me when I say we need to go now. You didn't last time, and we missed the ship. Now, you're stuck in the castle. So, let's go!"

"Ahlvie, someone out there is trying to kill me," she reminded him.

He shook his head back and forth, as if debating whether this whole thing was a waste of his time. "I think I've found us another ship, but I need a woman's finesse."

"For what?"

"We're going to a bar."

"A bar?" she asked skeptically. "Right now?"

"No time like the present."

"Ahlvie, I can't go to a *bar*. I'm an Affiliate!"

"You won't be wearing your pin."

"That's not the point."

"You want a way out?" he asked. "Then, live a little. Stop caring about others expectations, and live by yours. Are we going or not?"

Cyrene couldn't exactly tell him that she had somewhere else to be tonight. Maybe they wouldn't even be out that late, and she could still see Edric.

"Fine. Lead the way."

Ahlvie knew Krisana as if he were reading a floor plan. She thought her two weeks of wandering the halls had familiarized her with the castle, but he took turns, hallways, and stairwells she had never set foot on. She wished she knew how he was so good at this. Not to mention, he wasn't making any sounds on the stone when he walked. And she hadn't heard him enter her rooms either.

When they turned a corner, Cyrene stopped as she heard footsteps approach. Ahlvie grabbed her, and they ducked into a small alcove. They had made it nearly all the way across the castle, uninterrupted, and she wasn't about to get caught now. She waited anxiously, trying to hold her breath. She was certain whoever was there could hear her heart beating wildly. The footsteps seemed to stop near them, and she listened to the voices for a second.

"We can't go into the Affiliate quarters."

"You wouldn't do that for me?"

Cyrene released a small gasp, and Ahlvie nudged his elbow in her side. She would recognize the seductive tone of that voice anywhere. Prince Kael was trying to convince Jardana to take him back to the Affiliate bedchambers.

Ugh! Swine.

"The Queen would kill me if she found you in there with me."

Cyrene bit her lip as hard as she could to keep from groaning at the sound of that incessantly annoying voice.

"Let me worry about Kaliana. You just worry about us."

Jardana giggled.

Cyrene prayed to the Creator for them to pass by because she wasn't sure how much more of this she could listen to.

"You're talking about us like you don't spend time with that woman," she spat.

"Don't start this again."

"Well, if you didn't make such a public display of it by walking her to the library this morning, I wouldn't have to."

Cyrene closed her eyes and concentrated on breathing evenly. She couldn't believe that Jardana was whining to Kael about her.

"Next time the King of Byern gives me a direct order, I'll tell him you told me to refuse," he said dryly.

"Fine," she groaned. "The Affiliate quarters it is. I can't stand this any longer."

Cyrene actually agreed with her on one thing.

Their steps retreated down the hallway, and Cyrene blew out a breath of relief. Ahlvie rushed to the staircase and opened a wooden door at the bottom, and she followed him through it. He grabbed a lit torch from the wall. The dark stairwell beckoned them downward, and the stones grew colder and colder despite the summer temperatures.

When they reached the bottom, they hurried down an empty hallway. Even with the torch, she couldn't see more than a few feet in front of her. Ahlvie took a few random turns. She sure hoped he knew his way out because she didn't think she could get them back. He hesitated at a three-way intersection and then surged forward down another impossibly long tunnel.

Time seemed to pass endlessly.

As she opened her mouth to ask if he had any idea where they were going, he said, "Aha!"

He clicked a lock and pushed open a heavy stone door. On the other side, the moon shone bright, high in the sky.

Cyrene glanced around at her surroundings. Krisana could be seen from anywhere in the city, but she was shocked by the distance. The tunnels didn't run under the castle. They ran under the whole city!

The alleyway was dark, and she covered her nose to keep from gagging as the rank stench of sewage and manure pinched at her stomach. Wherever they were certainly wasn't the nicest part of Albion, and she wondered what kind of bar they could be going to in this part of town. It would certainly be nothing like the one they had ventured into on the coast.

"Is this the place?" she asked him, trying to breathe through her mouth.

He glanced over at her and laughed. "Never been to the slums before?"

She arched an eyebrow.

"You'll be fine. I'll be with you the whole time."

"Why are we here?" She grabbed his arm and kept him close.

"Just smile a lot and look dumb. They'll think we're together and cut me some slack."

She clenched her hand tighter around his bicep. "What are you playing at?"

He roughly pushed her up against the dirty white stone wall and covered her mouth with his hand. Two guys passed by them and snickered at their position, but they kept walking.

He dropped his hand as soon as they were gone and leaned in close. "I'm not playing at anything." His voice was hoarse. "At the inventor's house, we all agreed that we were going to do this together. If you don't approve of my methods, fine, but that doesn't mean they're not effective. All right?"

She glared at him. "Don't *ever* touch me like that again. You're right. I don't approve of your methods, and I certainly don't approve of you throwing me against a wall. But if this is how we get out of Albion, then let's just get out of Albion." She shoved his body away and gritted her teeth. "What do I need to do?"

"For one, your name is known all over the city, so you need to go by something else, something common. How do you feel about Haenah?"

Cyrene rolled her eyes. "Haenah de'Lorlah? Like the dance?"

"Whatever works for you. The person we're about to meet might appear nice, but he has loaded dice behind every question. He doesn't play fair, and he doesn't answer fair."

"We're gambling, too?" she squeaked, wanting nothing more than to leave this place.

"Yes. He has a penchant for taken women. So, act like you belong to me, and we'll get our answer."

"Taken women?" she scoffed. The skin on the back of her neck prickled, and she briefly glanced behind her, seeing if anyone else were around. She turned back to Ahlvie, angry that the environment was making her chase shadows but even angrier with him. "What exactly are we doing?"

"Trust me on this." He was asking too much all at once.

He offered her his arm, and she rolled her eyes, wondering why on earth she would ever go along with this absurd plan.

"Come on, Haenah."

She sighed and reluctantly placed her hand on his arm. She wondered what the hell she was getting herself into as Ahlvie walked them toward a ramshackle inn with a swinging sign that read, *The Silver Trinket.*

33

The
LOADED DICE

THE SILVER TRINKET WAS THE SEEDIEST ESTABLISHMENT Cyrene had ever entered. It was beyond run-down and packed to the brim with men throwing dice or sitting around beaten-up wooden tables and cutting cards. Women wore dresses showing excessive bosoms and giggling at the men who grabbed them as they passed to bring their beer. Several men slept on the dimly lit bar in the back, and more cheered on a card game. Dilapidated stairs beckoned upward, and a hearth had an enormous cooking pot hanging over it. One of the largest of the serving women walked over to the pot, sloshed some nondescript stew into two bowls, and handed them to men sitting nearby. As she tried to walk away, a man pulled the woman into his lap and started laughing.

Cyrene was horrified. *Who treats women this way?*

Ahlvie tugged her closer, and she didn't leave that position. She scratched the back of her neck and glanced around the room at all the dirty faces staring back at her. Or maybe none of them were staring at her. She didn't know. It felt like it since she was the only clean person in the place.

Ahlvie walked to the bar and ordered a beer. But he held it in his hand, barely drinking any of it.

A few minutes later, when another man wasn't looking, he switched it out with another patron at the bar. His demeanor had changed. He was stooping slightly, like he'd had too much to drink already, and he smiled up at her.

He nodded in the direction of the dice table, and Cyrene angled her body so that she could see.

K.A. LINDE

"Who's he?" she murmured.

"The owner."

The man sitting at the table was surprisingly tall and thin with a trim beard and much cleaner clothing than the men surrounding him. He exuded confidence. She wondered what his importance was in their endeavor as Ahlvie supposedly finished another drink.

Moving closer to the tables, they watched a few rolls of the die. Cyrene didn't know the particular game and stared at it in fascination, trying to determine the rules. When she glanced at Ahlvie, he had a completely different look about him. His eyes were glazed over, and he leaned on one side, but she could see that he was playing the game in his head and waiting for his turn.

When that moment came, he grabbed her hand, barreled forward into the crowd, and slapped down two silver trinkets. "I'm in an' me pretty wife, too," he said. He forced her into a seat right next to the man they were interested in and plopped down next to her.

"We don' 'ave room fer two!" a guy yelled.

"Let them stay," the man said. He matched Ahlvie's two silver trinkets and glanced not so subtly at Cyrene. "What's your name? This doesn't look like your type of establishment."

She smiled, not knowing what her role was supposed to be. "Haenah."

She downcast her eyes and looked over at Ahlvie. He purposely didn't pay attention to her.

"My husband likes to dice."

"And you? Do you like to dice, Haenah?" The man placed the set in front of her.

"I'm no good," she said.

Her gaze darted up and across the table to the darkened stairwell. She could have sworn that someone was standing there a second ago, but no one was there now.

"It's all a matter of luck."

"I'm not lucky either."

"Maybe you will be tonight." He encouraged her to pick up the dice. "I'm Jestre Farranay, owner of this establishment, and I believe you make your own luck."

She swallowed, picked up the dice, and let them loose on the destroyed wooden table. They bounced and rolled a few times before lying still, revealing straight snake eyes. Her heart dropped.

In every game she had ever played with dice, that meant bad luck. But before she even had a chance to frown, the men all around her whooped.

"An unbeatable throw." Jestre pushed the pot in her direction. "Seems you've found your luck."

Cyrene stared down at her winnings in surprise. Everyone else at the table threw in another silver trinket, and the game started all over again. Ahlvie lost the next hand, and Cyrene was pretty sure he had done it on purpose. The dice slid around the rest of the table. Some won, and some lost. After cheering, stomping, yelling, one punch to the face, one triumphant smile from Jestre as he collected from the pot, the dice were placed before her again.

She breathed in before collecting them. Cyrene pushed her hair off her neck and tried to keep the goose bumps from showing on her arms. This place gave her the creeps.

"Only one more for me," she told them. "My husband can play the rest."

She shook the die in the small cup and threw them out on the table. She held her breath as the first one revealed just one dot, then the next, and the one after that. Nearly all of them were showing ones again, and she stared in astonishment as the last one rolled further and further down the table. When the dice finally came to a stop, it stood on its side, stuck in between two wooden boards on the table with a one and a small square mark with a slash through it.

"Break even," Jestre said when it didn't move anymore. "A Braj and a one cancel each other out."

Cyrene sighed. She just wanted to leave. She didn't know what Ahlvie was getting at by bringing her here or what the game had to do with anything, but she was ready to leave—now.

"I'm suddenly not feeling well." She placed her hand to her forehead and stood.

She really did feel warm to the touch. The room was too crowded, and the game was getting to her head.

"Nonsense," Jestre said. "You can't leave yet. You're on a streak."

"One hand is hardly a streak. Anyway, my husband is the gambler, not me," she said with a small smile. "If you'll excuse me."

"The woman requires assistance." Jestre passed the dice to Ahlvie and followed Cyrene away from the game.

Ahlvie hastily passed the dice along and trailed behind them. "A word, Mr. Farranay." He drunkenly grabbed the man's arm.

"I've no time." Jestre glanced at him like he was the scum of the world. "Your wife needs tending to. Did you even notice her fever?"

Cyrene watched as they stared each other down. *What did Ahlvie have up his sleeve? And why is he dealing with a man like this?* He was more than intimidating and towered over them both, and Ahlvie wasn't short.

"I 'ave a bit of a problem, and I thought we could work it out. Me, you, and me pretty wife." He gestured to Cyrene and raised his eyebrows.

Jestre seemed to understand and nodded. "Follow me."

They walked to the back of the bar and into a small room that could pass as an office. It was hardly big enough for the three of them with the desk in the room, but they squeezed in and shut the door. The walls were empty, only a few pieces of parchment were on the desk, and nothing more than a lock cabinet was in the corner.

"What can I help you with?" Jestre stood behind the desk and casually leaned against the back wall.

"We need a boat," Ahlvie told him.

"And how could I help you with that? I am but a simple owner of The Silver Trinket."

"A little birdie told me you have connections to a freighter leaving Albion."

"And who is this little birdie?"

Ahlvie shrugged.

"Right then. Clearly, you've been misinformed. Will that be all? Your wife doesn't look well."

"We need to get on that boat, and we need you to put us on it," Ahlvie continued, unaffected.

"Even if I had a boat, why would I help a drunkard like you? I've seen you in here before, wasting away your time in that mug. Was your wife at home the whole time? Did you think bringing her in tonight would garner you my sympathy?" he asked coldly.

Cyrene gulped. She wished Ahlvie had told her what his plan was. She hated walking into things unprepared.

"By the look on her face, I'd register she didn't even know you'd been here." Jestre had guessed correctly, but it was hardly what he thought.

"Haenah's my concern, and I'm doing best I can by 'er. Albion has nothing left for us, and I need your ship to get out," Ahlvie said, stumbling forward a step and resting his hand on the desk.

For show, Cyrene reached forward and steadied him.

Jestre stared down at Ahlvie. "You're a disgrace. You can run from the booze, but it'll find you."

"I'll dice you for the ride."

Cyrene gasped. "No."

"What do I get when you lose?" Jestre asked with a sly smile.

Ahlvie considered for a moment and then cocked his thumb in Cyrene's direction. Jestre's eyebrows rose, and Cyrene's mouth dropped open.

"Are you mad?" she screeched.

"Done." Jestre held his hand out and shook with Ahlvie. "When you lose, I get the girl."

"I'll not stand for it!" She smacked Ahlvie on the shoulder as hard as she could.

No wonder he hadn't told her his plan. She would never have gone along with it.

What a completely moronic imbecile!

He couldn't wager *her*. He didn't have the right for that. *What if he lost?* She, an Affiliate, would somehow be attached to this…this *man*! If they made it through this, she was going to kill Ahlvie.

They ignored her as if her opinion had no bearing on the matter. She had never been in a world of any sort where her opinion didn't matter.

The two men barreled out of the small room and went back into the main parlor. Jestre cleared off a table and grabbed a container of dice. The rowdy men who had surrounded them before stopped their game to see the commotion in the middle of the room. Tables were eased together, and chairs scraped across the floor, so the men could watch the game.

Cyrene glared at Ahlvie from her vantage point of the game. She wanted to throttle him for bringing her here. He would surely never hear the end of this.

"Two out of three?" Ahlvie taunted.

"One throw," Jestre corrected. "Just one." He pushed the dice toward Ahlvie.

"You first." He shifted them back across the table. "I have more at stake." He chuckled softly.

"No matter," Jestre said with a shrug.

He had an air about him of someone who never lost. He was completely unfazed by Ahlvie's confidence. He was so used to winning that he couldn't even see the signs of inebriation falling off of Ahlvie or his fingers twitching to touch the dice.

Jestre shook the dice once before effortlessly tossing them on the table. They rolled a few times across the table, and everyone in the hall breathed in at once. The anticipation cleared away the anxiety she had been feeling all night. She had been so worked up about where they were, and now, when her mind was focused elsewhere, she realized this place didn't have quite the same edge, quite the same uneasy haze about it.

The dice stopped, and Cyrene covered her ears to hold back the deafening applause from the onlookers. Jestre triumphantly smiled at her in the same way he had when he won the last hand in their previous game. "All but perfect," he informed her. One diamond side of a die marred the perfect snake eyes. "Your roll."

Ahlvie eagerly grabbed the dice, all signs of his earlier drunkenness gone. He swirled the dice in the cup a few times, testing it out. He covered the cup with his hand and shook it back and forth, letting the dice rattle and clink around the container. He smiled at Cyrene and then let them loose on the table.

She couldn't even look.

Her fingers covered her eyes to keep away the disappointment. She didn't want to know. Ahlvie had seemed so confident, but this man diced for a living in his inn. She couldn't believe Ahlvie could outsmart someone like that.

She pried her fingers from her eyes and watched as the last side turned over, twirled on one axis a few times, and then it dropped to the table. All ones. Straight snake eyes. *He'd won!*

Boos and cries were shouted all around them at Jestre's loss. The atmosphere in the room shifted at Ahlvie's win. She could make out a few angry grunts about Jestre never losing a one-on-one game. This wasn't looking good, and they needed to get out of here.

This was a mistake. Even if they'd won, and they had, Jestre wouldn't let them on his boat. They had humiliated him before all of his patrons, and he wouldn't soon forget it.

"You cheat!" Jestre cried, slamming his fist on the table. "You cheated me in my own game. You think you can get away with that in my establishment? You'll never dice again when I'm through with you!"

"Let's go," Cyrene said. She fearfully tugged on Ahlvie's sleeve.

"You promised us a ride!" Ahlvie cried over the noise that was reaching a crescendo among the drunken men.

"I promised nothing to a cheat!" Jestre grabbed the end of the table nearest Cyrene and threw it along with the dice across the room.

Cyrene jumped back in shock at the display of violence and ran into a large man holding a full mug of beer. The beer spilled onto a guy standing next to him, and suddenly, before she was even aware of what was happening, the guy threw his fist in the face of that man holding the mug.

Chaos broke out all around them. Cyrene screamed as a man tumbled to the ground next to her, having just been hit over the head with an old wooden chair. She moved farther away from the scene. Jestre threw himself at Ahlvie, pushing him backward into another table. They brawled, punching haphazardly. Mugs of beer sloshed onto the floor. Tables broke, women ran for the kitchen at the commotion, and blood flowed freely. The mixture of new smells combined with the stench of the bar turned her stomach, and she gagged as she moved out of the way of another swinging fist.

Ahlvie landed a few choice punches into Jestre's stomach, and the bar owner retaliated with his own. A man barreled into her side. She gasped as she fell to the ground, and all the air rushed out of her lungs. Hoisting herself off the ground, she did the only thing she could think of doing.

She ran.

34

The TUNNELS

CYRENE'S SENSES TINGLED AS ADRENALINE COURSED through her veins. She needed to keep moving.

She had been on edge all night, and she had known that something was off, that something was going to go wrong. *How could Ahlvie not feel the shift in the atmosphere as soon as he had started the game?* It was destined for failure, and they should have gotten out before all hell had broken loose.

Cyrene pushed the side door open and darted into an alleyway. Her breathing heaved as she glanced down the dark depths. The alleyway was all mud. Her slippers were already a disaster, but she lifted her skirts to prevent them from soaking through on the bottom.

She edged toward the mouth of the alley, pressing her back against the dirty building. When she touched something wet and slimy, she pulled her hand back and cringed. *Gross!*

Her foot connected with an object leaning against the wall, and she hastily retreated. No other people remained in the alley. She leaned over and saw a box filled with garbage. Without thinking twice, her fingers grasped a large wooden board from the wreckage. Although she knew defensive techniques, she wasn't a soldier and she wasn't going to risk anything. She wasn't stupid.

Board in hand, she walked the last few feet to the edge of the alley and peered around the corner, holding her breath. The brawl had broken through the front door, and men were openly fighting in the streets. The Royal Guard would surely be here soon to break up the quarrel. *Wouldn't they?*

The door to the alleyway burst open before her, and she cried out as men poured out of the building. They tackled each other against the filthy walls, butting heads and drawing rusted swords from their belts. She didn't have time to wait for the Guard now. Swords crashed together behind her, the ringing sound echoing in her ears, propelling her into action.

She darted into the open street. Two men jumped in front of her. One missed the man he was fighting and dropped his sword as the weight of his swing pulled him off balance. The man he had been attacking now stood over him with his sword raised.

Cyrene rushed past them to avoid the bloodshed and then stumbled right into the heart of the brawl. She tried not to see what was happening all around her, but she couldn't stop it. Men lay on the ground, blood pouring from open wounds. Others were wrestling in the muddy street, landing drunken punches and kicks to their friend-turned-foe. A few remained on their feet, jabbing hidden daggers through the open air and cursing each time they missed. Cries, yells, and shouts filled the space, and Cyrene desperately wanted all the noise to stop.

She neared the alley she had entered from with Ahlvie. When she spied an unconscious barmaid, Cyrene's voice wavered as she cried out in horror. A huge blue bruise had formed on the woman's head, and blood flowed from the wound. She stooped to help the woman, and a sword caught Cyrene in the side.

All her breath whooshed out of her lungs as she fell, the board leaving her hands and clattering to the ground a few feet away. She gasped. Pain seared through her. Each desperate inhale sent excruciating pain up her side. The white of her dress darkened under her hand.

Tears burst from her eyes at the sudden all-consuming pain. She pressed her hand harder against her side, hoping the blade had just punctured the skin and not done more serious damage. She didn't even know where the man who had hit her had gone. She just needed to get out of the fight. She needed to get somewhere safe, somewhere she could assess her wound, somewhere she could get help.

As she crawled the last few feet toward the alley near the tunnel door, safety was the only thought in her mind. Her dress trudged through the mud, soaking her to the bone. She clawed her fingers through the mud and locked her mind away, trying to ignore the pain, the nausea rising in her throat, and the swoony feeling of letting go.

She finally found purchase on the wall, her hand gripping the side of the white building on the opposite side of the street from the bar. Her chest was heaving, and she pressed harder on the wound. Adrenaline fueled her forward. She scrambled out of the street and into the alley, her back pressed against the grimy wall. Spending a few precious seconds to catch her breath, she leaned her head backward. She had to move. The door wasn't that far away.

Using the side of the building as leverage, she put the weight on her feet and slid into an upright position. Gritting her teeth, she forced herself to start walking. Unfortunately, the pain didn't ease.

Just a few more feet.

She couldn't die like this. Cyrene steeled her resolve, locking the pain away in the deepest part of her mind, and she rushed forward.

The door was concealed around a bend, and she glided her hand along the wall to find the chink that would open it. Her hand slipped into the small hole, and she pushed. The tunnel door heaved inward, and she stumbled into the dark depths of the underground tunnel system.

Once she closed the door behind her, she collapsed on the ground. From pain and relief, tears streamed down her face. The torch had dimmed from where they left it at the bottom of the small set of steps.

Her fear began to subside the longer she sat in the tunnel entrance. True, her wound hurt worse than anything she had ever thought possible, and she was trapped all alone in a network of tunnels that she couldn't possibly navigate, yet she was safe.

But she couldn't say the same for Ahlvie. *Did Jestre's men gang up on him? Had a knife been pushed into his ribs? Is he lying dead in that disgusting bar?*

No! She couldn't think like that. Ahlvie could handle himself. He was sober and could get himself out of the situation he'd created. If he didn't come find her soon, she would find a way to get back to him.

Cyrene eased herself down the set of stairs and painstakingly stood. She hissed between her teeth, the tears falling faster, as her muddy fingers found the handle of the torch and pulled it from its hook. She gingerly sank back down on the stone step, holding the torch high and pulling back her blood-coated right hand to see the wound in her side.

She gagged at the amount of blood soaking through her dress and looked away, trying not to vomit in the tunnel. After a few seconds of deep breathing, she raised the hem of her dress and found a gouge about an inch in diameter where the edge of the man's sword had nicked her in the side. Blood still trickled out of the gash, and she reapplied pressure. It wasn't clotting. She needed someone proficient in medicinal treatment, like a medic…or Maelia. She replaced the torch overhead and sat again, covering her wound.

Cyrene's next shuddering breath made the hairs on the back of her neck rise. She swallowed, suddenly alert. It was the same feeling she'd had earlier, first in the alley and then in the bar. She had thought it had something to do with their surroundings, but she was safe in the tunnel now.

The atmosphere in the tunnel shifted, morphed, disintegrated, and returned. It became its own being, swirling around her feet and coalescing. Her stomach flipped, and goose bumps broke out across her arms. She scrambled to her feet, her mind groggy and slow. The air pressed in on her as if it wanted to ease the tension in her body. She bit her lip, looking around in the shadows, knowing instinctively that someone else was doing this, whatever this was…commanding the air, telling her what to do.

She knew then that it had happened before—that strange feeling she had gotten at Zorian's funeral, in the Laelish Market, in the crowd leaving the boats when they first arrived in Albion, in the bar when she had won with all snake eyes, and when the fight had broken loose.

Someone was here.

35

The
SOMEONE

CYRENE SWALLOWED. "HELLO? IS SOMEONE THERE?"

"Don't try to fight me."

A wave hit her mind, and she cringed away from the stab. "What are you doing?" she cried out.

"You will give in."

"Not likely," she spat.

Cyrene squeezed her eyes shut and tried to focus on getting rid of the pain. She couldn't handle the jolt in her side and whatever this *thing* was that was going on inside her mind. Without even knowing what she was doing, she pushed back at the whisper in her brain. She prodded it as if it were a living organism invading her mind. She found an edge, imagined a brick wall forming in between it and her mind, then, she slammed the wall down as hard as she could. She pushed, poked, shoved until something clicked. One wall crashed all around her, like breaking ice, and she heard a soft sound, like a yelp, inside her head.

Did I do something? Did it work? She couldn't even comprehend how this was possible, but she didn't have enough energy to think about it. All she did was push her mind harder and fight with all her strength…for she instinctively knew the end result if she lost.

She heard laughter in her mind. The *thing* was still there.

"I am old and powerful, girl. You will lose this battle, and I will relish in your loss."

She grunted at the interruption. It thought that it could intimidate her. She didn't even know what *it* was, but she wasn't about to allow it access to her. She fought back, clawing at the words forming in her head. She would not lose!

She shook her head, as she screamed, "No" in her mind. Whatever it was couldn't have her mind.

"Weakling, you think to defeat me?"

Her mouth fell open at the fierceness of the voice that felt like the edge of a razor blade. Someone shouldn't be able to talk in her mind. The shock gave it an opening, and it came back at her harder, lashing out like a whip and slicing through what meager fortification she had built.

"Your powers have grown stronger since I started tracking you. Thus, it must be extinguished like the flame of a candle."

She didn't understand. *Powers? What powers?*

The voice laughed in her mind again. *"Your reluctance to believe matters is humorous. Yes, you have powers, and no one with powers survives in this world, not while I'm in it. Regardless of your belief, I still must kill you."*

"Kill me?" she cried.

"You act surprised, but it has been coming for a long time."

"I don't understand."

The force of keeping the thing from pushing further into her head hurt like hell, and she wanted it gone. She didn't want it setting up camp where it didn't belong.

"I was summoned to track you ever since you used your powers to bring a downpour. That sparked the ultimate deaths of others with powers like you while I searched for you. Surely, you took notice."

A chill ran up her spine at the softness mixed with the cutthroat sharpness of the voice.

I brought the rain? What did that even mean? Like at my Presenting after I made Affiliate? Had that been the reason for everything else that had spiraled out of control since then? All the...deaths.

Her mind ran through a series of images, starting on the day of her Presenting—Zorian and Leslin's deaths, Pallia and Grabel's murders, Captain Lador, and the poor Affiliate Karra who had been searching for her. They had all been linked to her in some way. This thing that had been hunting her had finally caught up with her.

"So, you remember," the voice screeched in her head, grating on her eardrums.

"Murderer," she growled low, anger welling inside of her.

"I've gone by that name before."

It laughed in her mind, and she lashed out with her mind at its flippant air. It retaliated, slicing at the newest fortification in her mind. She yelped, grabbing her temples. It only made the pain in her side double, and she pushed her hand back at her bleeding side.

"That won't heal."

"Why not?" she spat, clutching her side harder at his words.

"The sword I used to cut you has a poisonous blade. I embedded the venom myself. It prevents blood clotting and is excruciatingly painful."

"You did this?" She applied more pressure as the fear of his words broke through her mind.

"It is too simple to lead my prey to their downfall. I knew you would walk right to me. I simply had to wait for the right time. The others were casualties from your spark of power. Their blood still hummed with energy even though they could not hope to touch it as you do. Now, their blood hums no more. You will have that in common."

"My blood hums with energy? What does that even mean?" she cried. "Why are you doing this?" New tears fell on her cheeks.

"Because I was summoned by the rightful Dremylon heir to fulfill my mission to never allow the Children of the Dawn to resurface after they were extinguished two thousand years ago."

"The rightful Dremylon heir? Edric?" she gasped. "He would never..."

"The Doma and their magical abilities cursed this land. After the Fall of the Light, Darkness now rules, and we will take no chances of you regaining control. If you join the Darkness, you might be spared."

The Children of the Dawn are people with...powers? And also Doma? And I have these powers like the Doma?

She swallowed hard, unable to believe what she was hearing. Nothing made sense. This couldn't possibly be Edric's doing. He was the true Dremylon heir after all, but he...cared for her. He would never have sent this creature to kill her.

It was speaking in riddles all over again, and she had damn well had enough riddles.

"I don't understand anything you're saying! I don't have powers, and Edric couldn't have sent you. Who are you? And why are you doing this?"

The atmosphere around her shifted again. She swallowed and braced herself for what was coming. Any change couldn't be good.

The fog in her mind cleared slightly as faint footsteps sounded down the tunnel hall. She swallowed and went to work in her mind.

She had felt him pull down a wall. She didn't even know how she had built it, but while that thing was briefly preoccupied, she was going to figure it out again.

She thought back to what it had felt like for it to form a wall in her mind against him. Recreating that feeling, she pushed all around her and found the feeblest of walls starting to grow and fortify. She didn't know what she was doing. She only knew that it was necessary to keep herself alive.

As the *thing* drew nearer, she built walls on top of walls as fast as she could. By the time the footsteps approached, she was getting the hang of closing off her mind. Building, weaving, working, constructing—it had to be done.

The presence slammed against her mind again, and she jumped.

The whisper was all but gone, partially garbled behind layer upon layer of brick and mortar in her mind. She concentrated on blocking out even the tiniest of hisses by building one more wall. It had felt easy once she started, but she was now panting.

"Ha!" she gasped out. She was proud of what she had formed in the short minutes while the thing was absent.

The footfalls stopped, and two black boots peeked into the halo of light cast by the torch. She stilled her shaking hand compressing her side. The sound of her steady breaths was the only thing she could hear in the tunnel system.

"You learn quickly but no matter. You are no match for me," the thing said, speaking out loud for the first time.

Somehow, the voice was just as piercing and painful, and she cringed away from the noise.

"What are you? Step into the light!"

The thing laughed a hideous laugh and took one step toward her. She gasped, seeing the face of Affiliate Karra in a mask of horror, as if she had been screaming. But her body had been retrieved from the docks with Captain Lador. Maelia had told Cyrene of the horrific account Eren had given her after the investigation. Affiliate Karra was dead!

So who…or what is wearing her face?

Cyrene wanted to scream, yell, cry out, vomit, claw at the thing before her with the mask of the beautiful face of the woman she had known. But all she did was stare in shock as the thing took another step forward while the curve of his blade reflected back the light of the torch. It had a wicked black handle with a silver inscription and a line of red along the blade itself. It was the most disturbing, grotesque, wrong piece of weaponry she had ever seen. Even from the distance, she could sense the evil about it and its master.

"What…what are you?" she whispered, her voice hoarse.

"I believe your people have termed us Braj."

Her body reeled. Braj were a myth, a scary story parents told to keep their children in check. The evil creatures that went bump in the night didn't actually exist.

"Oh, yes," it hissed, "we exist. We've been well hidden, but we're in your folklore for a reason. We find our marks. We destroy our marks. And we never stop. We will always keep coming."

A Braj. A real Braj.

It was not Jardana, the witch, playing in a mask…but a real live Braj, a trained, practiced murderer.

If this is reality, what else is real?

She swallowed hard and leaned against the wall. Her side was killing her, and this new information weakened her physical fortification. Her mind was still miraculously alert, but her body was losing the poisonous battle.

"Why me?" she demanded.

"The Light no longer shines, and we wish to keep it that way."

"Stop with the riddles! What do *I* have to do with any of this nonsense?"

"The Circadian Prophecy foretold that the Children of the Dawn, led by one with great power, would rise to destroy the Darkness and all those who rule under him. I was sent to ensure that does not happen," the Braj said, its voice grating. "By eliminating you."

Prophecy! Her mouth hung open.

She had used that word with Rhea earlier today. It felt like a lifetime ago.

The Braj believed she had these powers as part of the Children of the Dawn.

Then, the Braj removed the face of Affiliate Karra.

Cyrene gasped. In folklore, to see the true face of a Braj meant that it would be the last thing one would ever see.

The Braj was human, or had once been, but was no longer. Its shape was distorted, mushed, and all wrong somehow. Where normal eyes should have been, only blood-red orbs pierced her with a fiery death stare. The nose was raw to the bone. Elongated teeth jutted from its mouth, hanging down deep into razor-sharp fangs. The skin itself looked like it had been torn off and sewn back on so many times that its elasticity had been destroyed. It sagged and drooped, covering part of one eye and falling a few inches on the left side over the nondescript chin. Its pointed black ears had been stretched, one nearly hidden behind the matted black hair growing unevenly on the top of its head.

Cyrene had never seen anything so hideous or terrifying.

"Good-bye, Light," it blasted into her conscious as he charged forward at her, wielding the curved blade.

Her mental barriers held him back, but the physical one, she could never hope to contain. That blade rushed toward her body, and she didn't know how to stop it, to keep the Braj from slicing through her.

She readied herself for the blow. And all at once, her body seemed to expand and open up even though she wasn't moving. Light filtered into her mind, like a rushing river crashing through her, going down through every inch of her body and then out, like an explosion of energy passing through her very fingertips.

No sound was made. No movement occurred. Nothing happened.

She saw the Braj standing there with its sword in hand. A look of shock passed over its gruesome face.

Then, her vision grew faint and blurry, and she lost her battle to the darkness, crumpling in a heap on the cold stone floor.

36

The
THRONES

CYRENE WOKE UP, HER HEAD HEAVY AND FEELING GROGGY. Gloomy mist settled in her mind, and she had to physically push it aside. She concentrated, trying to force herself to get past the haze. Slowly, it lifted, and the clouds cleared away. Then, her mind was back to normal.

She peeled her eyes open and stared at her surroundings in shock. *Where the hell am I?* One minute, she was facing off with a Braj in an underground tunnel, and now, she was in the middle of some pathway with huge trees all around her.

She must have hit her head pretty hard. She was dreaming, or she was dead. There wasn't another conceivable option. She swallowed back bile at the thought. She couldn't be dead. She felt...fine. She was panicky, but her body was intact.

If she wasn't dead, then where was she?

The packed hard dirt beneath her feet had been trampled smooth from years of travel. In one direction, the path led deeper through the woods, and she could just make out a myriad of stone buildings. In the other stood a castle embedded into the side of a mountain.

She had never seen the trees before, and this path didn't feel familiar at all. But she would know the castle anywhere. It had been a fixture of her world her entire life.

Nit Decus, the Byern castle.

How am I home? It was a four-day trip back to Byern!

"You can stop this!"

Cyrene turned toward the noise in confusion. *What in the name of the Creator am I doing in Byern, talking to a strange man? Did I completely lose my mind?*

The man reached for her hand, and she moved to jerk away. But her body didn't respond. She didn't move at all. Even as she screamed at herself to pull away from this stranger, he wrapped his hand around hers. It was warm and roughly callous.

Terror was setting in. *Why can't I move away? Why can't I move at all? Am I paralyzed?*

No. She could move. Her body was moving. She just wasn't in control of it.

"You know I would if I could," she whispered. The words fell from her mouth, but she didn't command herself to speak, nor was it something she would have said. *What is going on?*

"Then, do it!" He grasped her chin and forced her to look at him. "You know what they will do, what they will be forced to do."

"I know."

Cyrene stared into the face of the man and tried to push down her rising panic. Surely, there was some explanation for what was happening.

She peered at the man and tried to place why he looked oddly familiar. He was young, no older than her, and ruggedly handsome with dark brown hair cut short. His blue-gray eyes stared back at her, filled with anxiety, remorse, and desperation.

"How can you just accept it?" He dropped her hand. "We're betrothed. Does that no longer matter to you, Sera?"

Betrothed! Cyrene didn't know who this man was, and she felt uncomfortable, as if she were intruding on this moment between him and the person whose body she inhabited. It was as if she was role-playing with someone else's life. She was stuck in this limbo where she couldn't do or say anything, only watch as it happened to her.

"It doesn't matter to them, Viktor." She took a step backward.

Viktor? Those blue-gray eyes, that strong jaw, the dark hair, and build.

Could this be the legendary Viktor Dremylon?

"They never mattered to you before." He stomped away from her, throwing his hands in the air.

"That was before. I can't exactly turn them down. It'll happen to me whether I want it to or not. I have to learn to control it."

He stared at the ground as if he thought it might hold the answers. "I wish your powers had never manifested," he murmured under his breath.

She felt the shock register on the woman as if it were the biggest insult she had ever endured. Cyrene didn't feel insulted, but she couldn't believe that he had just mentioned this woman having powers. The Braj had just told her in the tunnels that she also had powers.

"Take it back," Sera said, her voice deadly grave.

"I'll never forgive them."

"We can make it through this." She approached him and took his hands in hers. "If anyone can, surely we can. It isn't unheard of! Please, just fight for me."

"How can I fight for you when you've already given up?" he demanded. He ran his thumb across her hand.

"I haven't given up, but if you love me, you'll let me do this. You'll let me do what I *must* do. I will always be yours even if you no longer believe in me." She resolutely dropped her arms.

"I believe you." He grasped her around the waist and pulled her into him. "I'll always love you, Sera."

Cyrene felt his kiss on her cheek and the blush that followed.

"I love you, too, Viktor," she whispered into his chest. She pulled back, gave him a forlorn smile, and rushed away down the path. Her heart thudded in her chest, and a tear slid down her cheek as she took the left bend in the road toward the castle.

Cyrene didn't know what was going on or who Sera was in relation to Viktor Dremylon, but her chest ached all the same. She had witnessed lovers torn apart because of this woman's destiny. Sera's remorse and loss was heartrending, more painful than the Braj's sword wound. Somehow though, it was worth every moment.

Sera crawled along, clearly not wanting to get to the castle any faster than she had to. She didn't glance back at the man she had left behind. As they approached the castle, Sera glanced up, and Cyrene got a clear image of the structure. Something about it looked off. She couldn't place it until she crossed into the lush blooming gardens and realized they had never walked through a gate, and there was no wall around the castle.

Sera walked through the giant double doors and went inside.

"Serafina?" called a woman dressed in blue, standing at the end of the hall with her hands crossed over her stomach.

Another jolt of shock crashed through Cyrene. There was only one Serafina in their history—the Domina Serafina. *Could Viktor Dremylon have once loved the woman he had killed to right order in the world?*

"Yes. That's me." She curtsied deeply.

"You're late, child," the woman said sternly.

"My apologies."

"No matter. Come along." The woman in blue walked through the corridors.

Cyrene recognized where they were, but she didn't think Serafina knew. It was strange to feel the fear, unease, and nervousness rolling off of Serafina while at the same time feeling perfectly calm and collected. *What am I doing, trapped in the ancient Domina Serafina's mind?* And if this woman truly were the Domina, what atrocities would Cyrene see before she was released from this prison?

The woman in blue stopped before a blank wall. She closed her eyes and pressed the palm of her right hand against the wall. Cyrene watched the woman in fascination, wondering what was about to happen. Suddenly, the wall shifted inward. She couldn't believe that the rock was moving of its own accord and sliding away, leaving a gaping hole.

"Off you go," the woman in blue told her.

Serafina glanced at her with worried eyes. "I go alone?"

"Everyone must at some point. Believe in those whose honor doth shine."

Serafina held her breath and started forward into the dimly lit stone hallway. Cyrene felt like she was holding her breath, too. They walked through the opening, and then the door slid shut behind them. Serafina jumped at the click as it sealed them inside. Cyrene wished she could help Serafina in some way, but she couldn't—at least, she didn't know how.

Serafina inched down the dark hallway. About twenty feet in, she descended a long staircase. When she reached the bottom, her feet touched a slate-gray marble floor. There was just enough light for Cyrene to see that the walls all around her. Even the ceiling was carved and painted with strange glyphs of some sort. A few had real-life painted depictions of all manner of creatures that Cyrene had read about in her folklore books.

Then, the voices began. Cyrene didn't know where they were coming from or who was speaking, but they grew louder and louder to where it was earsplitting. Serafina clasped her hands over her ears, but she couldn't keep from hearing the words.

"Death. Destruction. Murder. Traitor."

The words were accusingly shrieked at her.

"No!" Serafina cried. "I didn't do anything wrong!"

"Murderer."

"No! Please, no." She shook her head and forced herself to walk forward.

"Murderer. You killed him. You will kill them all."

Serafina whimpered as images of the deaths of everyone she knew and loved displayed before her on the walls, and the word murderer kept ringing in her ears.

"Murderer. Murderer. Murderer."

The words blended together, reverberating off the walls and echoing back down the long hall. When she wasn't sure she could take it any longer, the words fell into a whisper.

Her vision blurred, and she tripped as she scrambled forward toward the opening of the hallway. She dug her hands into the hard ground and dragged her body across the marble floor.

"Sera?"

Serafina looked up and saw Viktor standing before her. *How could he be here?* Serafina had left him behind. He shouldn't be in the hall with her.

"Viktor," she whispered.

"You knew it would come to this," Viktor said. He drew his long sword from its sheath.

She hauled herself to her feet and stood before the man she loved. She brushed her hands under her eyes to stall the tears. "What do you mean? Come to what?"

"You made your choice."

"I don't understand. I will always choose you."

Viktor shook his head. "I love you, Sera."

"I love—"

The words died on her lips as Viktor thrust the sword into her body. She gasped, doubling over, as pain seared through her. She felt as if she were on fire, as if the life was spilling out of her body.

"Why?"

"You know why, my love."

Cyrene was shocked. This wasn't how it happened in history. Serafina was the great Domina, and Viktor Dremylon had freed her people. *Is this some premonition?* This couldn't be the end.

Serafina took two heaving breaths before pulling the sword from her body and collapsing on the floor. Viktor impassively stared down at her deteriorating body.

"This is *my* choice," she ground out.

"You chose wrong."

She ignored him and then started crawling the last few feet to the exit. Blood seeped out of her gown, her heart slowed, and she was having trouble gasping in her last breaths.

As soon as her fingers crossed the threshold, Viktor disappeared. Serafina looked down at her tattered dress, only to find it completely whole and her body intact. She was shaken but not dead.

She scrambled out of that treacherous hallway and stood. She ran trembling fingers back through her long dark hair and tried to hide the apprehension of moving forward after what had happened.

She took a minute to compose herself, and then she glanced up, finding herself in a large open auditorium.

Cyrene had never seen anything like this in the castle before. The room was perfectly spherical and made entirely of slate-gray marble. Stairs on either side of the entrance wound upward to empty tiered balcony seating. A small stone podium rested before seven individuals. Four women and three men were seated in ascending glass thrones. Each person was dressed in solid black, except for the woman in the center who was wearing contrasting stark white and the most severe face.

Serafina gulped, and her eyes bugged, her terror palpable.

Who are these people? Why are they dressed in such a manner and sitting on thrones of ice? Cyrene suddenly felt like she was at her own Presenting, standing before King Edric, Queen Kaliana, and Consort Daufina, shaking in her slippers at the thought of not making First Class.

After an agonizing moment, Serafina took the first uneasy step forward. Cyrene empathized with her. The first step was the hardest, and facing whoever these people were wasn't going to be much easier.

Her breathing slowly began to even out, and her steps became steadier. She kept her face staring forward as she stopped before the podium, never dropping her gaze from their scrutiny.

The thrones had an oversized square back with a design of vines winding to the top. At the heart of a circle of flames was a precious gemstone. Each throne housed a different colored stone—yellow, orange, red, white, purple, blue, and green. Their stones matched the diamond pendant on the breasts of the individuals seated on the thrones, save for the woman in white who had a giant white diamond necklace.

The white woman sat up straighter in her enormous throne, and Serafina raised her eyes back to her. Everything about the woman exuded authority and deference despite being much more frail than the rest seated around her. She had more power, wisdom, and authority in one glance than Cyrene had ever seen in another individual.

Then, it clicked in Cyrene's mind exactly who was standing in front of her.

White, yellow, orange, red, purple, blue, green.

By the Creator! It was the Doma court with their diamonds depicting their color ranks, and the dreaded Domina dressed in all white was staring directly into her eyes.

The Doma court was the evil society that had subjugated their people and forced Viktor Dremylon to free the country of their tyranny, bringing peace back to Byern.

She was walking through history before Serafina had ever ascended to the Domina throne, when she and Viktor had somehow been lovers. It seemed impossible, yet she was living it.

"You were brought before us today," the Domina began, "to be tested to the full extent of the Doma Ascension ritual. By walking through the Hallway of Remembrance, you have accepted the discretion of our people and survived. Congratulations." The words hollowly fell out of her mouth.

Cyrene's mind buzzed with the words that the Domina had spoken. The Doma Ascension ritual where individuals were accepted into the Doma circle was one of the few things still taught about the Doma people. The Doma had been exterminated for nearly two thousand years, and she was about to stand through Serafina's own ritual. She couldn't believe it.

"You may proceed with the final task." The Domina gestured to the podium. "The Hymn of Remembrance."

Serafina's gaze traveled down to the podium before her. Cyrene's disbelief at what sat on the podium could have ripped through the entire world at that moment. She had thought she was alarmed by the Domina's comments about the Ascension ritual, but nothing compared to this.

Serafina's hands traveled the length of the pristine leather spine before her with minute black letters and the familiar logo branded to the front—a straight line parallel to the binding and two lines shooting out of it at an upward angle on the right side. It was the *exact* book Cyrene had received from her sister on the day of her Presenting.

Serafina cracked the book open and turned to the first page. The first page revealed the brilliant shimmery font Cyrene had been trying to decipher for months. It shifted gloriously in the light from gold, yellow, orange, red, purple, blue, green, and back to gold. The handwriting had an edge to it, a sharpness and fierceness that cut through the looping swirls of the font.

She inherently knew that Serafina could also see the font, and she was staring at it in the same manner Cyrene had when she first realized she could see it. By Serafina's intense concentration, Cyrene guessed Sera couldn't read it either.

Serafina gazed up at the Domina, silently pleading with her for answers.

"Continue," the Domina retorted.

She swallowed hard and glanced back down at the book. Cyrene could feel her reading, trying to figure out the riddle. She was testing the waters, doing all the things that Cyrene had tried. Cyrene wished she could whisper in her ear about the uselessness of her actions.

Serafina closed her eyes, took a deep breath, and splayed her hands out on the podium. Cyrene didn't know what she was doing, and she certainly didn't know what she was thinking.

After a few minutes, Serafina opened her eyes to the gold shimmery text, and Cyrene saw something she never expected to happen. The font began to move! It swirled around itself like a snake slithering in the Fallen Desert sand. Serafina's mouth dropped open, and she took a tentative step backward from the podium.

The words jumped right off the pages, twisting upward, appearing larger and larger as it traveled toward the ceiling. The pages suddenly began flipping fiercely, the words shooting off the pages faster and faster. The words coalesced into a giant winged beast that flew around the room. Serafina ducked as it soared toward her. Her eyes grew large at the manifestation before her. Then, the creature shot straight into the air and crashed into the ceiling. The words all spilled onto the spherical ceiling until they covered every surface.

Serafina stared up at all the print now written on the walls, and to Cyrene's astonishment, she could actually *read* the words. As plain as her own dialect, the words were written out for her, and it all made sense, complete and total sense.

Serafina bit down on her lip, taking in the room all around her. She absorbed it all, experiencing everything she could, until she was ready to burst. Then, just as fast as the book had exploded onto the walls, it whooshed off of them, each word rushing through her back and out her chest, before crashing back into the book. When the last word returned to the page, it closed with a thud, and Serafina doubled over upon impact.

She was shaking when she was finally able to straighten. She rested her hands on the podium to steady herself. *Did she pass?*

The Doma Court rose and retreated to a vestibule to discuss, leaving Serafina all alone.

A few minutes later, the court returned to their thrones, and all six of the Doma turned and looked at the Domina, raising deference to the highest. The Domina stared at Serafina as if she were no more worthy than a grub to be in her presence, but Serafina didn't budge, and she didn't look away. Her jaw was set and determined.

This was it. This was the moment.

The Domina's severe face slowly broke out into a smile, and she nodded. "Yes."

The six Doma applauded, and Serafina mirrored the Domina's smile, clearly unable to believe what all had just happened.

"Congratulations, Serafina," the lady in red said, who was the highest ranked official after the Domina. "You've successfully completed the task of the Hymn of Remembrance with our highest honors. Your Ascension is complete, and you have been properly selected as a Doma. It has been decided that you will be placed in Receivership with the Domina Valera."

The astonishment was palpable from Serafina. "White?" Serafina asked in disbelief. "But…no one is raised to the White."

"Very few are raised to the White," the Domina corrected. "It means that you have an affinity for all magical elements plus the fifth, ether."

Serafina's mouth was hanging open. "White," she repeated.

"Do you disagree with our decision, child?" the Domina asked. Her voice conveyed that answering incorrectly would be a grave mistake.

"No, of course not. Thank you."

"Good. You will start training with me immediately. After your training period, we believe that you should work with Master Domas Matilde and Vera in Eleysia," the old Domina said. All the other Doma nodded.

Cyrene's mouth would have fallen open in shock if she weren't in some alternate reality at the moment. *Matilde and Vera? Master Domas? Are the people I'm searching out in Eleysia somehow the same people and still alive?*

"Master Domas Matilde and Vera will help you understand the…unique talents we saw in you today. Your regimen will start promptly tomorrow morning to begin training you on how to use and control your gifts."

"Thank you, Domina." Serafina curtsied to the group, trying to contain her surprise and excitement.

"Serafina," the Domina called, raising herself up. "Do be cautious with your abilities. They are a powerful tool, and in the wrong hands, they could be deadly."

"Yes, Domina," she said, her heart bursting with joy.

They had passed.

They were Doma.

37

The
REMEMBRANCE

CYRENE AWOKE WITH A START, SHOOTING STRAIGHT UP, AS she gasped out in a panic. Her side roared with fire, and she crumpled backward.

While her body recoiled from the pain of sitting up, her mind raced ahead of her. She desperately touched her stomach, her side, her face. She was herself again. She wasn't trapped any longer.

It was just a dream, a strange dream.

Or was it?

Her hands rested back down, and she finally realized that she was touching something soft. Her eyes flew open, and she peered around at her surroundings. The room was small with a single bed and two chairs. She couldn't make anything else out in the darkness. *If I'm not in the tunnel and I'm not in the castle, where am I?*

Before she could move to investigate, someone cracked open the door and walked in, carrying a tray with a candle and a bowl. The woman hummed to herself as she set it down on a table and went about rearranging the contents. Cyrene waited until the woman turned back toward her with a wooden bowl and pestle.

"Where am I?" Cyrene pushed herself up on one elbow despite the ache in her side.

"Oh!" the woman cried, jumping and bobbling the bowl. "Oh, honey, you're awake!"

"Where am I?" Cyrene repeated.

"Orden!" She ran to the door. "Orden! She's awake! She survived!"

Orden walked through the door and stared at Cyrene in surprise. "Go wake the boy and his friends," he said, ushering the woman out.

He placed a lantern on the table next to the tray, illuminating the room. The man looked vaguely familiar. She peered at him as she tried to place him.

"Yes. You've seen me before," he answered in a gruff deep voice as he seated himself in the chair farthest from her.

Even when he sat, it was obvious that he was one of the tallest people she had ever seen in her life. She had no idea how she knew him, but he had confirmed her thoughts.

"Where?" she asked.

"Your first day in Albion. You looked right at me when you were riding toward the castle."

"I did!" She coughed at her own exclamation.

I knew that I had seen him! He had stood out to her in the crowd for having such a severe expression. And now, he was sitting here before her, still lacking a smile.

"I didn't think you would recognize me." He leaned backward and stared at her with his deep-set brown eyes.

Orden started to speak again when Ahlvie skidded to a halt in the doorway, still pulling one arm through his shirtsleeve. His dark brown hair was mussed from where he had just woken up, and his eyes were wide. She had never really considered how young he looked until that moment.

"You're alive," he whispered.

He rushed to the bed and threw his arms around her. Pain hit her side, and she cried out. He hastily retreated.

"Sorry. I'm sorry."

"By the Creator, Ahlvie, she just woke up," Maelia said, appearing in the doorway.

A second later, Rhea stepped into view behind her.

"It's all right," Cyrene said. She shifted her weight to lean more into her uninjured side. "I'm just glad to see you all. I really am. But can someone please tell me where I am and what happened?"

"We don't know," Rhea said. "Ahlvie came and got us in the middle of the night. We all thought you...you weren't going to make it."

"We thought you might be able to tell us what you remember." Orden leaned forward in the chair, resting his elbow on his knee.

Everything came back to her in a wave—the bar fight, the dead woman, the sword to her side, the tunnel, the terrifying voice whispering into her ear and clouding her mind, her finding a way to block the voice, the dead Affiliate's face, the Braj and the prophecies and her powers, and then the look of shock on its face when something had exploded out of her.

Then, she had woken up, only she hadn't. She had dreamed of Serafina. *But how could it have been a dream when it had felt so real?* She had seen Serafina walk away from Viktor Dremylon. She had been at Serafina's Ascension ritual before the Doma court. She had been there when the book opened itself to them, and she had realized, just as Serafina had, that she had powers.

Now, she needed to learn how to control them. She needed someone to teach her. She needed Matilde and Vera. Everything finally clicked into place.

"Go on, Cyrene." Ahlvie sat in the chair next to Orden.

She suspiciously eyed Orden. While she appreciated that he was housing her after her injury in the tunnels, she didn't know or trust him.

"He's a friend. He's not going to tell anyone," Ahlvie said.

"I'd feel more comfortable talking without him," she whispered. "No offense."

Ahlvie began to protest, but Orden cut him off, "I understand your concerns, and I respect them. I'm very much interested in your story and how I can help, but until the time you need it, I'll just go see if Younda needs anything." He stood, pushed past the girls, and exited the room without further complaint.

"He's really a friend, Cyrene. You can trust him," Ahlvie said.

"We don't know him like you do," Maelia said. She took Orden's abandoned seat. "We didn't even trust you until…recently."

"Today, you mean."

Maelia shrugged.

Rhea shut the door and crossed her arms. "What she means is that we're a team. We should decide together who else to include in our plans."

"She was going to die!" Ahlvie cried.

"It's okay!" Cyrene interjected. "Can we get back to the matter at hand?"

They nodded, and Cyrene began to fill them in on everything that had happened last night. She didn't tell them about the explosion of energy or the dream. She couldn't trust even her closest friends with that information yet. She didn't know how she could tell them that she had powers.

"Wait…a Braj?" Rhea asked in disbelief.

"Braj are from fairy tales," Maelia said.

"No, really, I saw it!" Ahlvie said, backing her up.

Cyrene shook her head. "You believe…in the Braj?" she asked, a little surprised that he was taking this all so lightly.

"I saw it with my own two eyes down in that tunnel. If I didn't believe in them before, then I believe in them now," he said with a nervous chuckle.

"And did you believe in them beforehand?" she questioned.

Ahlvie glanced away and back. "Yes," he said without elaborating.

She wanted to know why when she hadn't even thought they were real until tonight. But she would respect his silence since she wasn't even telling him everything.

"Okay. It's a Braj," Rhea said, throwing up her arms.

Maelia shook her head like she didn't want to believe it.

"So," Ahlvie said, "you don't know what happened after the Braj attacked you?"

Cyrene shook her head. "No."

Rhea gave her a sidelong look that said, *You're not telling us everything*, but Cyrene just raised her eyebrows.

"Well," Ahlvie said, scratching the back of his head, "I just know that as I reached the tunnel, something like a wave hit me, and then out of nowhere, the skies opened up. I could have sworn it was a cloudless night, but it was an almost instantaneous downpour. I hurried into the tunnel and found you passed out on the ground with a dead Braj at your side."

"Dead?" she squeaked.

"I know! Someone must have killed it. I thought it was impossible, but there it was. I panicked when I saw how much blood you had lost, and I rushed you to Orden's. It's much closer than the castle, and I knew he would understand."

What kind of person is Orden that he expects half-dead people on his doorstep?

"His help attended to you. She said the wound had started to heal in on itself too soon, and she barely had time to withdraw the venom before it closed completely."

Cyrene gingerly touched her side. The skin through her shift wasn't gaping open. Rather, it was a tender puckered bit of flesh. The last time she had looked at it, she had lost too much blood, and the Braj had told her that it wouldn't clot. *How had new skin already covered its place?*

The word hit her mind anew. *Magic.* It still felt wrong to think, but it was the only thing that made sense. It had to have been the outburst of her powers.

"Look, I don't know what happened to you down there, but whoever saved you is one crazy fighter to take on a Braj," Ahlvie said.

"We're really sitting here, contemplating the assumption that someone killed a Braj? That Braj exist?" Maelia asked.

"I'm telling you that's what it was."

Cyrene nodded. "I saw it, too, Maelia. It spoke to me and said that it had killed the other Affiliates and High Order to try to get to me."

"So, a Braj came after you as a mark and killed others in your place along the way? Why?" Rhea asked.

Cyrene sighed as the silence dragged. She bit her lip and considered what to tell them next. "I haven't been completely up front about what happened."

Ahlvie narrowed his eyes, Maelia leaned forward in her chair, and Rhea just crossed her arms.

"I don't really know how to explain it, but it has to do with what I told you guys at Master Barca's."

"About something happening to you?" Ahlvie asked.

"Yes. Well, it happened down in the tunnels." *Magic.* Magic had happened.

"It?" Maelia asked. "What did?"

"I don't know," Cyrene said. "All I know is…I was the only one down in those tunnels with the Braj, and it was about to kill me when it happened. So, I think…I must have killed it."

The next few moments felt like an eternity as Cyrene waited for something, anything—laughter, ridicule, disbelief. At Master Barca's, she hadn't heard it when she first told them about the strange things happening to her, but now, she was saying that she had killed a Braj. The more she put it into perspective with her dream of Serafina, it was the only thing that made sense. No one else had been there to save her, and Ahlvie had felt the explosion she produced from her body, so it must have been powerful.

"Cyrene, I don't want to doubt you, but you're sure about this?" Rhea asked.

"No. Yes. No. I don't know. I think so. That probably doesn't help, but what else could explain my wound? I'm still sore and hurting, but it's healed."

"I saw the hole in your side. If it's healed, then something must have made that happen in a matter of hours," Ahlvie said.

"Exactly. I can't think of another explanation."

Ahlvie seemed to mull this over for a second, as if trying it out for size, like she had earlier. "All right."

"All right? That's it?"

"All right. I believe you. What do we do next?"

She stared at him in awe. *Where had he come from? And why had it taken him this long to get into my life?*

"What do you mean all right, and that's it?" Maelia asked. "A killer is out to get Cyrene. Don't you all realize the most important detail we're missing about Braj?"

"They never stop coming," Rhea filled in.

"That's right. Maybe you're not the real mark, but if you are and they're real, then we need to have a plan to stop them. We need to figure out how they were killed in the first place." Maelia stood and planted her hands on her hips. "We should alert the Royal Guard and let the King know what happened. You know he would be worried for your safety."

"We can't go to the Guard!" Ahlvie protested.

"Or the King!" Cyrene cried.

She remembered all too clearly the Braj talking about the rightful Dremylon heir. She didn't want to believe that it was Edric, but the only other horrifying alternative was that it was talking about…Kael. And if Kael could control Braj…they were all in trouble.

Rhea sighed heavily and shook her head. "I assume you have a crazy plan, Cyrene," she prompted.

"Yes." And it was really crazy after the information in her dream. "I need to get to Eleysia."

Maelia plopped back into her seat in disbelief. "You're honestly thinking of still going there now that you've been *attacked?* The two safest places in all of Emporia are here in Albion and back in Byern. How could you consider leaving?"

"I have to go," she insisted. She was surer than ever before.

"Do you even know what you're looking for?" Maelia looked down like she hadn't wanted to ask it.

"Yeah, I think I do," Cyrene said.

"You think so?" Rhea asked.

"I know how determined you are, but I don't want this to be a wild goose chase," Maelia chimed in.

Cyrene swallowed. If she told everyone the truth, then she was going to sound insane, but she knew it was all connected to that dream. "There are two women in Eleysia who I need to see."

"Who are they?" Maelia asked curiously.

"Matilde and Vera."

Everyone blankly stared at her.

"Who?" Maelia asked.

"How do you know you need to see them?" Rhea asked.

"It's complicated. I met a peddler back in Byern who said that there were people in Eleysia who knew how to help me. He told me to go find them."

Cyrene didn't tell them about the connection to the dream. It felt crazy that they could be the same people as the ones Basille Selby had told her to find.

"How are you even going to be able to find them?" Maelia asked.

"I don't know," she admitted. "I know it doesn't seem like much, but it's all I have."

"Not much? That's nothing," Maelia said. "You're risking your safety on the whim of a peddler."

"It's my safety to risk, Maelia. Are you guys with me or not?" Cyrene said.

Ahlvie tilted his head at her. "I'm in."

Rhea leaned against the wall and nodded, too.

"Maelia? We're going with or without you, but I want you with us," Cyrene told her. She hated doing this. She understood where Maelia was coming from, but this was too important to stay hidden behind the walls of the castle. She couldn't live her life like that.

"I'd like to go down saying this was a bad idea, but I'll not let you leave with this reckless scoundrel," she said, gesturing to Ahlvie. "Plus, you'll probably need a medic."

"I think she likes me," Ahlvie said dryly.

"Look, as long as we're a team, we'll be fine out there. I just don't know how we're going to get there. Our last endeavor to get a ship didn't exactly go as planned."

Ahlvie smirked. "Sorry about that."

Cyrene shook her head. "Does anyone have a better idea?"

"I think we should talk to Orden," Ahlvie told her. "I know you don't know him. I get it. He doesn't exactly look like the trustworthiest guy. But he's going to be our best bet."

Cyrene looked around the group. Everyone seemed apprehensive, but she didn't really see another option. If Orden could help them, then she needed to use his help. She wasn't exactly going to be getting on an Eleysian ship anytime soon.

"All right, Ahlvie."

He stood and exited the room.

A minute later, Orden walked back into the now very crowded small bedroom with Ahlvie on his heels. Orden took the seat Ahlvie had abandoned. He had the appearance as if he had known this was going to happen all along.

Cyrene gulped as she tried to decide how to begin. She glanced at Ahlvie, who nodded at her.

She had to do this her way. "We need a way out of the city, and we need to get out as soon as possible—today preferably."

Orden sat back in his chair.

"We need your help," Ahlvie continued, giving Cyrene a dirty look.

"How can I help you with getting out of the city?" Orden asked gruffly.

"You know your way around Albion, around much more of the world than Albion. You taught me some of the tunnel systems," Ahlvie said. "You can find us safe passage, so we can get a boat and get out of here."

"That's all true." Orden's dark eyes remained stern.

"Please," Cyrene said, her voice lowering, "if you know all these things, can you show us the way out?"

"You kids want out of Albion? Walk right out the city walls. No one is stopping you."

"I would, if every Guard in the city didn't know my face," Cyrene said.

Orden stiffened.

"The mysterious deaths throughout Byern were linked back to me. As a confidant to the King, Consort, and Prince," she breathed, "I was put under heavy guard. They were worried I would be the next target."

"And you were," he said.

She nodded. "The Braj was after me."

"Brajs are always after someone for a reason. What was yours?"

"I don't know. I couldn't understand what it was saying. Everything was jumbled."

"Did it speak into your mind?" Orden asked.

"Yes."

His mouth dropped open.

Did I say too much?

"For how long? When do you remember it first happening?"

"I...I don't know. Maybe as far back as my Presenting...maybe as soon as the procession," she told him softly. "I didn't know it was touching my mind until the tunnel. How did you know that? I'd never read that anywhere."

"When a Braj has touched your mind, you never forget it," he told her stonily.

Silence followed that statement.

"Look, I don't know how you know all of this, but at this point, I don't need all the information," Cyrene began.

"I think you do. If you've had a Braj speak to you, then you're in far worse trouble than I thought."

Cyrene swallowed, but Ahlvie was the one who spoke up, "What do you mean?"

"Braj are killers. You've all heard the folklore saying that they never stop. Well, it's true. One dead Braj doesn't mean the end of it. It means the end of that Braj. I've seen them keep coming until even the best couldn't fight them off. And I saw my master fall under their swift curved blade."

Maelia sent her an I-told-you-so look.

"Cyrene," Ahlvie whispered. His eyes looked fearful.

"I understand what you're saying," she said. "But I need to go to Eleysia."

"What's for you there?" Orden asked. He contemplatively stared at her.

"That's none of your concern. It's my ticket out of this mess, and that's all that is important."

"That's a vague enough answer." Orden narrowed his eyes at Cyrene.

"She needs to go," Ahlvie said. "And we're all going with her, Orden. Will you help us?"

Orden sighed, glancing between them. "All right. On one condition," he said. "Take me with you."

38

The
DECISION

WHEN CYRENE AND MAELIA FINALLY MADE IT BACK TO THE castle to retrieve their belongings, dawn was just peeking over the horizon. Orden had offered a map of the tunnels and a small pony to help them back through the maze of tunnels since Cyrene was still weak. It went faster than Cyrene remembered it taking the night before, but everything had felt like slow motion yesterday.

They left the pony near the entrance to Krisana where Younda had agreed to retrieve it, and then they found the stairs she and Ahlvie had gone down last night.

Ahlvie and Rhea were collecting their belongings in the city while Cyrene and Maelia maneuvered through the castle.

Maelia wrapped an arm around Cyrene's waist and helped her up the stairs. When they reached the strange door Cyrene had entered before with Ahlvie, Maelia released her.

"Wait here," she whispered, holding a finger up. She peeked through the door and looked around into the hallway. A minute later, she waved Cyrene through. "I'll see you in a few minutes to collect your bag."

Cyrene nodded and then hurried out of the tunnels. Her side didn't feel quite as bad as when she had woken up. Part of that must have been from eating something to restore her energy and the nasty concoction Younda had made her drink. Her body was repairing itself at an alarming rate. It was almost like the night after her near death escape in the underground lake.

She moved as quickly as she could handle through the empty corridors. She held her breath as she walked through the castle, hoping that she wouldn't run into anyone. Younda had offered her a clean white dress out of her wardrobe, but it hardly fit like her own gowns, even pinned up. It had to do though. She couldn't have worn the destroyed dress from the previous night.

Cyrene turned the next corner and went into her room, closing the door behind her. She pressed her hand into her side and sighed heavily. It still hurt like hell. The Braj had been right about that.

After walking into her bedchamber, she opened her wardrobe to the sea of dresses hanging perfectly. Her red cloak from Edric was sitting there, untouched. She hadn't had a chance to wear it since leaving Byern. Her fingers moved through the beautiful material. Memories came back to her of the first time she had received this wrapped gift in her chambers.

Her heart thudded. This was all she would have of Edric when she left. She should leave it because she knew that whatever had happened, or had been about to happen, was going to be long over once she left. She hadn't come to his chambers last night and with her gone all would be lost between them. She didn't know how long she would have to be in Eleysia, and she was sure that he would soon forget about her.

Yet as she looked at the beautiful cloak, she didn't think she could do leave it. Even if she was leaving Edric behind, she knew that she would always remember him just like this. The easy smile in the rose garden, the glow of his face in the setting sun on the beach, the desperate kisses on his ship—those were things she never wanted to forget.

With a soft sigh, she finally folded the cloak and placed it into the last bit of space in her bag. While she might not need it, she couldn't go without it. She couldn't leave without taking a piece of him with her.

Cyrene hefted her bag out of her wardrobe with a grunt and removed the leather pouch containing the book and letter. She had a few minutes before Maelia would return to collect her bag. She knew it would be risky, opening the book here, but a part of her desperately wanted to know if the dream had been real.

She was leaving everything she knew and loved behind to go to Eleysia based on this book, the words of an old peddler, and a fantastical dream about the ancient Doma court and Viktor Dremylon. If she could read the words, then she would know that she was on the right path.

Her hands trembled as she held the book. Her future lay before her. For a split second, she desperately wanted it all to be a dream so that she would wake up to find that she had just made Affiliate, and then everything would right itself. There would be no book, no riddles, no strange dreams. Then it passed, and she was desperate to know and understand this power humming just beneath her surface. This power strong enough to kill a Braj…could be strong enough to do much, much more.

With a weighted sigh, she cracked open the delicate binding and stared down at the shimmery sharp font on the first page. She blinked twice, more in shock than anything. This time, she didn't even have to concentrate to decipher the meaning. The words were as clear as day and as beautiful and vibrant as the first day she'd looked upon them, but now, their meaning sang to her as if she had known it all along. It spoke of the Doma society and the magical powers that linked them all together.

This was the proof she had been searching for. Her powers truly existed.

Now that she knew the true importance of the book, she never again wanted it out of her possession. It would be terrifying if it ever fell into the wrong hands. She slid the pouch over her head, so she could keep it on her person.

Jolted out of her thoughts about the book, the door to her rooms creaked open. She rushed out to the main chambers to find Maelia with a small Guard unit bag slung easily over her shoulder.

"We need to get going if we don't want to be seen. The servants are already moving about," Maelia said.

"Yes. You're right. Here's my bag," Cyrene said. She handed over her bag, but she kept the book and letter carefully hidden in her pouch.

"Are you sure this is what you want?"

After reading the Doma book and living through the Ascension ritual with Serafina, she was surer than ever.

"Yes."

Maelia hauled Cyrene's bag over her other shoulder. "Okay. Well, I'll meet you with the horses."

"Thank you for trusting me."

"Good luck in the tunnels." Maelia gave her a quick hug before disappearing through the door.

Cyrene hastily changed out of Younda's dress and into one of her sturdier blue dresses. Her gaze moved around her luxurious rooms as she finished up and prepared to leave. It was hard to believe that she and Edric had walked on the beach just yesterday. It was even harder to believe she had promised to come to his rooms. Everything had changed in one night.

Soon she would be out of Byern for the first time and on her way to Eleysia.

Sorrow choked her, and she swallowed back the tears. She had wanted what Edric was offering her, yet she had made her decision when she left with Ahlvie. She was making her decision again as she was leaving now. In another life, she could have been the girl happy to be at the beck and call of a king, happy to be a mistress. But that other girl wouldn't have heard destiny knocking, and she wouldn't have answered.

She couldn't stay in Byern for Edric. She didn't know what was awaiting her in Eleysia, but she knew that it was necessary to go there. It would lead her to discover the extent of her abilities and find out the truth about this new world she was walking into.

Cyrene carefully closed the door to the Pearl Bay Chambers and whispered, "Good-bye, Edric."

The
DISAPPEARANCE

DAUFINA LOUNGED BACK IN THE CHAIR IN THE COMFORT OF Edric's study. He had been on edge all morning. She could see it in the tension in his shoulders, the way he clenched his jaw, and a million other minute details that someone attuned with his body could see from far off. She wanted to believe that he was just steeling himself for the trade negotiations with Eleysia, but he wasn't normally so ill-tempered when it came to the matters of state.

"Are you going to tell me what's going on?" she asked carefully.

He shot her an exasperated look from where he was standing. He had a spread of paperwork before him, all things he needed to decide on and sign before the Eleysian Prince arrived.

"If you stay in this mood when he arrives, I'm sure he'll be easily swayed to our side with your...charm, Edric."

Edric plunked the quill he had been writing with back into the ink and crossed his arms. "I know how to run this country, Daufina. I was bred for this role, raised to know my place since infancy, and have been doing a good job for the last five years. If you would care to take my place, by all means." He gestured to the pages.

She quirked an eyebrow at his chastisement and sent him a bemused smile. "No one could run Byern as you do. I was just noting that our Eleysian representative might not appreciate the fact that you are sulking."

He ran a hand back through his hair and sighed. "It's nothing. Let it be."

So, she let it be. He would tell her in due time. He always did.

The time passed uneasily. She could hardly concentrate on the text she was reading. She hated that he was so troubled.

"Is it the baby?" she finally asked.

The fact that Kaliana had lost yet another one while Duchess Elida was months away from a baby of her own, in truth, troubled Daufina deeply. They *needed* a Dremylon heir. Nothing was secure without one.

Edric sighed. "No. Though perhaps it should be."

"You need an heir."

"It was my father's dying wish for me, Daufina. I *know* I need an heir." His blue-gray eyes settled on her, and she saw the heaviness in them. "Maybe if I had cared more for that than what is troubling me, I would already have a baby on the way. But that's not possible when you haven't been with your wife."

"At all?" Daufina asked with raised eyebrows. "Edric—"

"I know!" he snapped. "I should. It is my duty, and it must be done."

"Then, is it Cyrene? I thought you closed that matter when we arrived. I know her safety concerned you, but you stopped showing her favor. I thought—"

"Whatever you thought was mistaken. I stayed away to appease a wife who I do not love. Yet I am king, am I not? I should appease myself, should I not?" His voice grew continually louder as if he were convincing himself more than her. "I invited Cyrene to my rooms."

Daufina tried to rein in her surprise. Edric had sworn up and down that he never wanted a mistress...not one in competition for his heart. He had tried so hard to love Kaliana, but the woman made it impossible for anyone to do so.

"So," she said quietly, "if you invited her to be with you, why are you angry? Are you angry with yourself for deciding to go through with it?"

Edric laughed without humor. "She never came to me. She promised she would. I waited all night. I sent a maid to her chambers. She refused to even answer the door. It appears that even the King gets rejected."

"She is a fool to have done so."

"And do you know that it just makes me want her more?"

"Oh, Edric—"

"Your Highness!" a maid cried, scurrying into the study unannounced.

Her face set in stone, Daufina turned to face the woman. No one burst in on the King of Byern. Even if she was here for the Prince of Eleysia, she should announce a royal emissary.

"What do you want, girl?" Daufina asked coldly. "You just interrupted the King."

"My apologies," she sputtered. She sank into a deep curtsy. "I just…went into the Pearl Bay Chambers to bring Affiliate Cyrene her morning breakfast and found her *missing*! Her room was in disarray, and some of her things were gone!"

"What?" Edric and Daufina cried at the same time.

"Yes. I know I was sent…last night." Her cheeks colored. "I think…she must have been gone already! Do you think the killer somehow got into the castle?"

"Absolutely not!" Daufina said.

But one look at Edric's pale face said otherwise.

"Start a search immediately, Daufina. Look everywhere. Find any information you can."

"Edric, you're not seriously considering that something happened to her?" she asked softly.

"It all makes sense. She was the target, she was supposed to be with me last night, and now, she is missing. I think it is a very real possibility." He strode around the desk and reached for her. "We cannot let anything happen to her, Daufina."

Just then, a Royal Guard walked inside. "His Royal Highness, the Prince of Eleysia."

Edric cursed under his breath. "Take care of this for me. I have to deal with the trade negotiations, but I won't rest until she is found. Mark my words," he cried before storming from the room.

Daufina watched his retreating back as fear set in. If Cyrene was missing, potentially captured by this mysterious killer, then it meant none of them were truly safe, not even in the castle. And just as bad—in her mind at this point, even worse—Edric would not recover from this. She knew him too well. He would blame himself. He had already blamed himself. And she did not know what would happen to her King under such circumstances.

40

The

DESTINATION

CYRENE HASTENED HER STEPS TOWARD THE TUNNEL entrance and swallowed back the pain of leaving Edric behind. She knew that once she'd stepped out the door, she had lost him forever. And no matter what the Braj had said about the rightful Dremylon heir, her heart still ached at the thought. But there was no turning back. She couldn't stay here and wait for the Braj to come after her, hoping she would figure out her powers on her own. She had to take action. If that meant losing everything she knew...and loved, then so be it.

Taking the most direct route to the hallway where the entrance was, she waited for the corridor to empty and then darted through the door. She slammed it shut as quickly as she had entered and took a deep breath. She wrenched the still burning torch she and Maelia had left on a hook at the top of the stairs and followed them down to the bottom.

Rhea was waiting for her, as promised, on the last step, pacing impatiently. "Cyrene!" Rhea cried when she appeared.

"Sorry it took so long. I got held up."

"I'm just glad you're safe." Rhea tugged at her red braid. "I know you're not telling us something. You're so determined to go to Eleysia because something is happening to you, but I don't know what it is. I've been your best friend your entire life. I know you. So, what's going on?"

Cyrene sighed and nodded. She hated that they had to have this conversation now, but she didn't know when they would be alone again. "I haven't trusted anyone with this, Rhea, but I trust you."

"Of course you can trust me. We've known each other our entire lives." She sounded as confident as ever, but a crease formed in her brow, and her lips were pursed with concern.

"But, Rhea, you don't understand."

"And how can I if you don't even begin to explain?"

Cyrene tightly gripped her leather bag in her hand as she retrieved the book from within. *If I can't trust Rhea, who out there can I trust?*

She cracked it open to the first page, and when she looked down at the beautiful font, the words were clear. Her heart rapidly sped up when she saw that she could read them.

"I got this book from Elea the day of my Presenting. Do you see anything here?" She pointed to the iridescent font with its sharp edges and looping swirls.

"No," Rhea said, turning her head to look at the page. "It's blank."

"No, it's not. Words are there. I can see them. I'm the only one who can see them," she said, her voice remaining level.

"What do you mean?"

"I mean exactly what I said."

Rhea stared at the page like the words might suddenly appear for her. "I'm sorry. I don't see it. What does this have to do with the Braj and leaving for Eleysia?"

"It's the real reason I have to leave Byern." She swallowed, not ready to tell her friend but knowing she had to tell someone. "I have…abilities, Rhea."

"What kind of abilities?" She narrowed her eyes.

"It's going to sound mad, but remember when you first found out about Master Barca? How you thought Bursts were magic?"

"Yes," Rhea answered hesitantly. "But they're not."

"No, but I am. I have powers, Rhea," she whispered. "I just found out, and I need to learn what it all means…how to control it."

Rhea stared at her, dumbfounded. She was so logical, such a straightforward, book-smart type of person. She probably couldn't process this information. But it was out there now, and Cyrene couldn't take it back.

"Powers? Like magic told in stories?"

"Kind of. I don't know," Cyrene admitted. "I don't know what I can do or how to do it. I couldn't show you or anything. But if Braj are real…is this that far-fetched?"

"So, you think you have powers?"

"Rhea, I do have powers. I think…it's what the Presenting letter said. *What you seek lies where you cannot seek it. What you find cannot be found.* Rhea, I can't seek out magic because it was already there, hidden away inside of me. And it can't be found because I couldn't look for it. It just was. No one else could find it unless they already had it, and I already had it. I feel like maybe…I've begun to fulfill my Presenting letter," she said, "to fulfill the prophecy."

"By the Creator!" Rhea said, her hand going to her heart. "It actually…makes sense."

"I can't tell the others yet. I told them as much as I was comfortable with. Will you hold my secret while we travel?"

Rhea peered down at the dirty floor. Her face was a mask, but Cyrene instantly knew what her friend was thinking. She had known Rhea too long not to see it in her face. She really hoped she was wrong though.

"I can't," she finally said. She twisted her finger around her long braid.

"Rhea, come with me," Cyrene pleaded. "We don't have much more time to waste, but I need you with me."

She shook her head. "I can't. I'm not like you, Cyrene. I never wanted adventure. I never wanted to leave Byern. I love Albion now, but that's only because I was fortunate enough to have the best Receiver. Master Barca is a good man, and he treats me well. I've learned so much from him, and I enjoy the work. I thought I wanted to be an Affiliate. I thought I would be happy as an Affiliate, but I was wrong. I don't think anything could make me happier. So, I can't go. I know you'll do great things because you were born to, Cyrene. I think I was born to watch you from the sidelines."

A tear fell down Cyrene's cheek. She grasped her friend in a tight hug, ignoring her side. She hadn't wanted to let Rhea go that afternoon in the pouring rain when she had made Second Class, and she didn't want to now. It seemed so unfair that she would have to leave her best friend behind twice.

315

"You're going to do great things, Cyrene," Rhea said. She hiccupped and covered her mouth as she struggled to hold back tears. "Know that I'll always be here. I'll always be looking out. I'll always be your best friend. I love you."

"I love you, too," Cyrene gasped out.

"Just be safe, all right?" Rhea squeezed her hand.

"I'll do my best."

"Good-bye, Cyrene."

"Just until next time," she amended.

"Next time," Rhea agreed with a smile.

Cyrene wiped her eyes and then nodded. She placed the book back in her bag and then started out. She glanced back once at Rhea and gave her a faint smile before new tears fell.

After she had walked a distance away from the castle, she pulled out the small map Orden had sketched for her—a direct underground route to their checkpoint—and followed it as it was written. Her side kept troubling her, and she had to take frequent breaks. She didn't know how far she was going, but it felt like leagues and leagues underground with no light source other than the torch and no way to tell time.

When she took the final bend, she was anxious to be above ground. There, before her, was a door. She hooked the torch back up, rushed the door, and pulled on the handle. It wouldn't budge. She grunted in frustration as she tried to open it, but it seemed to be locked.

She ran her hands along the seam of the door. There was a hole at one point that looked like it fit a key, and she had to assume that it was locked. She kicked out at the door. She was so close. She just needed to be on the other side of that door. There were no alternative routes in the tunnels, and she felt completely trapped.

In an act of desperation, she placed her right hand on the wall near the hole and closed her eyes like the person in her dream of Serafina had done to open the door. That dream had allowed her to be able to read the book, so she might as well see if anything else in there had been useful.

Cyrene waited for a few seconds, and seconds turned into a few minutes. She concentrated so hard that sweat was bursting out on her forehead, and her cheeks were flushed. And then, when she thought she was about to give up, something clicked into place, and the door swung wide.

Her mouth fell open, and she stared down at the door in surprise. *By the Creator! How did I do that?*

She accepted it, albeit begrudgingly, that she had just done it. And it would take a while for her to understand *how* she had done it. It was her whole purpose in leaving. It was her whole purpose in going to Eleysia. It was her whole purpose in seeking out Matilde and Vera when they should have died two thousand years ago.

As she ascended the stairs, the early morning light greeted her in a small green field on the very edge of Albion borders. Ahlvie and Maelia were pacing a track into the grass between four horses. Orden was a distance off, looking out away from the city, standing next to a massive brown horse and a smaller packhorse with their bags and supplies loaded on it.

"I made it," Cyrene said.

Ahlvie and Maelia jumped and rushed over to her. Ahlvie sagged in relief, and Cyrene could see the worry line across Maelia's forehead.

"We thought you were done for," Maelia admitted.

"Such faith," she whispered, not wanting them to know how close she had been.

"We're glad you're safe," Ahlvie told her. "Where's Rhea?"

Cyrene pushed back tears and shook her head. "She's not coming."

"I see," Ahlvie said.

Maelia gave her a hug. "I'm sorry."

"Right then. We have a long road ahead of us," Orden interrupted, wearing his big brown hat again. "Let's be on our way."

Maelia gave her a wistful smile and then followed Ahlvie to their mounts. Cyrene followed, brushed her hand against Ceffy's nose, and smiled at her dear friend. She placed the contents of her leather bag into her saddlebag where it belonged, close to her. Her foot hooked into the stirrup, and she pulled herself into the saddle, adjusting to the seating.

Cyrene looked behind her at what she was leaving behind—her city, her Affiliate position, her best friend, and Edric. She said a silent good-bye for now and promised to see them all again one day.

Then, they set out, riding through the open field to the dirt road leading out of Albion to Aurum and beyond.

And she hoped she would find all her answers.

To Be Continued...

ACKNOWLEDGMENTS

As A BOOK SEVERAL YEARS IN THE MAKING, THE NUMBER OF people who have helped this become a reality are numerous. This all started as a random idea right after I graduated with my master's with a small moleskin of notes, a long list of potential names, and a hastily sketched map. The iterations have been numerous, and I'm proud of the final project. Mostly, I'm thankful for all the people who stuck it out with me to this point. You guys are awesome!

First, of course, I have to thank my family. They have all read *The Affiliate* in some form or draft and helped make it a better book— from Brittany sending me names in the middle of the night, Shea reading up to the procession five-plus times because I kept changing things, Anmar reading for the guy's perspective on the fantasy bend, to Mom and Dad always believing in me. And, of course my husband, Joel, who knew Cyrene's story would be out in the world one day and encouraged me not to change her feistiness. Plus, Riker and Lucy who stayed up with me on countless nights while I was revising.

This book wouldn't be possible without a few people who helped bring a few characters to life. So, thank you, Meera and Kiran Bhardwaj, for acting like twins and letting me watch you together for months. Thank you to Brian Alvarez and Haven for your unique personalities and epic debates about who is more important.

My betas, early readers, and emotional support team! I know you have been on a long journey with me for this book. Thank you for sticking it out with me! Jessica Carnes, Bridget Peoples, Rebecca Kimmerling, Katie Miller, Tammi Ahmed, Shannon Stephens, and Christine Estevez.

A big thank you to Bethany Hagen and Susan Dennard for the amazing blurbs for this book. I cherish them! Sarah Hansen at Okay Creations for the stunning artwork on the cover. You took my vision and made it a thousand times better than I could have ever imagined. Nicole Zoltack for exceptional content editing on this baby when it was in its infancy. Jovana Shirley at Unforeseen Editing for the most amazing editing and formatting imaginable. You cleaned this book right up. Christy Peckham, who proofread this book for me and hopefully caught all the little errors I missed after reading it a million times! InkSlinger, especially Nazarea Andrews and KP Simmon, for the promotional support and all the incredible things you do to help books find their homes! Special shout-out to Donna from Book Passion for Life for helping me in every way you could to make this release a success!

Since this book sprang up out of my personal love for fantasy and young adult fantasy, I thought I would thank the authors who inspire me to keep writing every day—Robert Jordan, Philippa Gregory, Sarah J. Maas, Eleanor Herman, Leigh Bardugo, Cassandra Clare, Alexandra Bracken, Marie Lu, and many, many more!

Most of all, I want to thank YOU! Thanks for giving this book a chance. It may not be your normal read, or it may be right up your alley. Either way, I appreciate you taking a chance on the book! And finally, my FictionPress loves! This book originated there, and many of you have been waiting a LONG time for its conclusion. Thanks for waiting it out, and I hope everyone enjoyed it! Look for the sequel, *The Bound*, out in 2016!

ABOUT THE AUTHOR

K.A. LINDE GREW UP AS A MILITARY BRAT, TRAVELING THE United States and even landing for a brief stint in Australia. She created fantastical stories based off of her love for Disney movies, fairy tales, and *Star Wars*. A former political campaign worker, K.A. is the *USA Today* bestselling author of the Avoiding Series. She now lives in Chapel Hill, North Carolina, with her husband and two super adorable puppies. In her spare time, she is an avid traveler, and she loves cruising, reading young adult novels, and bargain-hunting.

Additionally, K.A. has written thirteen adult novels and does not encourage anyone younger than eighteen to pick those up.

K.A. Linde loves to hear from her readers!

You can contact her at kalinde45@gmail.com or visit her online at one of the following sites: www.kalinde.com, www.facebook.com/authorkalinde, @authorkalinde

CPSIA information can be obtained
at www.ICGtesting.com
Printed in the USA
BVOW04s1634190317
478877BV00001B/122/P